Praise for *Arro...*

**Named one of the top 12 mystery novels of 2017
by *The Strand Magazine***

"The Victorian workingman's answer to the higher-class
Sherlock Holmes—a foul-mouthed, hard-drinking, shabby
detective with a seriously bad attitude toward his more famous
counterpart…. It's a terrific premise… Finlay has fun referencing
the Holmes canon, and he gives his hero a skill that the more famous
detective lacks."

—*The Seattle Times*

"Finlay debuts with a tale built on a wonderful premise: a downscale
Sherlock Holmes for the rest of us…. Finlay has a fine time recasting
the friendship between Holmes and Watson, as Arrowood and Barnett
repeatedly quarrel, swap obscenities and threats, and pummel each
other."

—*Kirkus Reviews*

"If you ever thought the Sherlock Holmes stories might benefit from
being steeped in gin, caked in grime and then left unwashed for
weeks…Mick Finlay's 1895-set detective debut is for you."

—*Crime Scene*

"Crackles with energy and wit."

—*The Times*

"A fantastic creation."

—*The Spectator*

"Richly inventive"

—*Daily Telegraph*

Also by Mick Finlay

Arrowood

Look for Mick Finlay's next novel,
available soon from MIRA Books.

THE
Murder Pit

MICK FINLAY

Finlay

mira

If you purchased this book without a cover you should be aware
that this book is stolen property. It was reported as "unsold and
destroyed" to the publisher, and neither the author nor the
publisher has received any payment for this "stripped book."

mira

Recycling programs
for this product may
not exist in your area.

ISBN-13: 978-0-7783-6930-1

The Murder Pit

Copyright © 2019 by Mick Finlay

All rights reserved. Except for use in any review, the reproduction or utilization of this work
in whole or in part in any form by any electronic, mechanical or other means, now known or
hereafter invented, including xerography, photocopying and recording, or in any information
storage or retrieval system, is forbidden without the written permission of the publisher,
MIRA Books, 22 Adelaide St. West, 40th Floor, Toronto, Ontario M5H 4E3, Canada.

This is a work of fiction. Names, characters, places and incidents are either the product
of the author's imagination or are used fictitiously, and any resemblance to actual persons,
living or dead, business establishments, events or locales is entirely coincidental.

® and TM are trademarks of Harlequin Enterprises Limited or its corporate affiliates.
Trademarks indicated with ® are registered in the United States Patent and Trademark Office,
the Canadian Intellectual Property Office and in other countries.

For questions and comments about the quality of this book, please contact us at
CustomerService@Harlequin.com.

BookClubbish.com

Printed in U.S.A.

To the good people of Haslemere Avenue and 33P.
Late '80s, early '90s.

Acknowledgments

Very many thanks to my friends Vincent Wells, Karen Johnston and Lizzie Enfield for their honest and helpful comments on early drafts of this book. Thanks also to my agent, the ever-supportive Jo Unwin, and to my editor, Sally Williamson, for her patience, good humor and guidance throughout.

Author Note

In the 1890s, the terms "idiot" and "imbecile" were used to refer to people we now describe as having learning, developmental or intellectual disabilities. Down syndrome was known as "Mongolism" and people with the condition were often called "Mongolian Idiots," "Mongoloids" or "Mongols." Although it's uncomfortable to hear these labels nowadays, the term "Down syndrome" only came into use in the 1960s.

Chapter One

South London, 1896

Horror sometimes arrives with a smile upon her face, and so it was with the case of Birdie Barclay. It was early New Year, the mud frozen in the streets, smuts drifting like black snow in the fog. Horses trudged past, gasping and shuddering, driven on to places they didn't want to go by sullen, red-faced men. Crossing sweepers stood by waiting for punters to drop them a coin, while old folk clutched walls and railings lest they should slip on the slick cobbles, sighing, muttering, hacking up big gobs of germs and firing them into the piles of horse dung as collected at every corner.

We hadn't had a case for five weeks, so the letter from Mr. Barclay inviting us to call that afternoon was welcome. He lived on Saville Place, a row of two-bedroom cottages under the train lines between the Lambeth Palace and Bethlem. When we reached the house we could hear a lady inside singing over a piano. I was about to knock when the guvnor touched my arm.

"Wait, Barnett," he whispered.

We stood on the doorstep listening, the fog bunched thick around us. It was a song you'd often hear in the pubs near closing time, but never had I heard it sang so very fine and sad, so full of loneliness: *"In the gloaming, oh my darling, when the lights are dim and low, and the quiet shadows falling, softly come and softly go."* As it built to the refrain, the guvnor shut his eyes and swayed with the chords, his face like a hog at stool. Then, when the last line came, he started singing himself, flat and out of time, drowning out the lady's mournful voice: *"When the winds are sobbing faintly, with a gentle unknown woe, will you think of me and love me, as you did once long ago?"*

I think it was the only line he knew, the line that spoke most direct to his own battered heart, and he ended in a choke and a tremble. I reached out to squeeze his fat arm. Finally, he opened his eyes and nodded for me to knock.

A broad, pink-faced fellow opened the door. The first thing you noticed was his Malmsey nose, round at the end and coated in fine fur like a gooseberry; beneath it the thick moustache was black though the hair around his bald scalp was white. He greeted us in a nervy voice and led us through to the front room, where a tall woman stood next to a pianoforte. She was Spanish or Portuguese or somesuch, dressed in black from head to toe.

"These are the detective agents, my dear," he said, wringing his hands in excitement. "Mr. Arrowood, Mr. Barnett, this is my wife, Mrs. Barclay."

On hearing our names a warm smile broke over her face, and I could see from the way the guvnor bowed and put his hand flat on his chest that he felt humbled by the lady: by her singing, her deep brown eyes, the kindness in her expression. She bade us sit on the couch.

The small parlour was packed out with furniture too big for it. The pianoforte was jammed between a writing desk and a glass-fronted cabinet. The couch touched the armchair. A gilded Neptune clock took up most of the mantel, its tick ringing out maddeningly loud.

"Now," said the guvnor, "how about you tell us your difficulty and we'll see what we can do to help?"

"It's our daughter, Birdie, sir," said Mr. Barclay. "She was married six months ago into a farming family, but since the wedding we've heard nothing from her. Nothing at all. No visits, no letters, not even this Christmas last. I've twice tried to call for her but they wouldn't even let me in the house! Said she's out visiting. Well, sir, it simply cannot be true."

"Surely young ladies visit?" asked the guvnor.

"She's not the type to visit, sir. If you knew her you'd understand that. We've been driven wild with worry, Mr. Arrowood. It's as if she's disappeared."

"Did you have a quarrel before the wedding? It can be a very upsetting occasion."

"She isn't like that," answered Mrs. Barclay. Against her husband's nerves she was a woman of great calm. Her long face was tan; her black hair fell loose down her back. Three small moles dripped from one eye down the side of her cheek. Noticing me watching, her humble smile returned. "Birdie never quarrels. She'll do what you say even if it hurts her, that's why we're so concerned. She'd never cut us off. We think they must be preventing her."

"Very worrying," said the guvnor, nodding his great potato head. His side-hair was tangled and stiff; his belly strained the buttons of his shabby astrakhan coat. He took out his notebook and pen. "Now, tell us about her husband. Leave nothing out."

"Walter Ockwell's his name," said Mr. Barclay. His hands flitched as if it irked him to speak of his son-in-law. "The family own a pig farm outside Catford. We don't trust the man. He's odd, and not in the usual farmer way either. I can't describe it any better. Doesn't meet your eye. We didn't know it before the wedding but he's had a spell in prison for clubbing a man half to death in a fight. The parson told me when I was last there. Hit him so hard on the side of the head the eye just exploded. Shattered the cavity, you see. The eye was hanging down his cheek on a bit of string." Mr. Barclay shuddered. "Well, sir! That parson might have told us before the wedding, don't you think? And if that wasn't enough, it turns out he's been married before. The poor woman passed over some two years past."

The guvnor stopped writing and gave me a look.

"How did she die?" he asked.

"A wagon fell onto her, that's what the parson says. We went to the police, but they were no help. Sergeant Root told us Birdie'd likely see us when she was good and ready. That's why we've come to you, sir. It could be he's hurt her and they don't want us to know."

The guvnor's face was grim. Gone was the warm smile.

"And you haven't heard from her even once?"

"It's as if she's disappeared. She might be dead for all we know."

"Who else lives on the farm, sir?"

"There are five of them. The mother's bed-bound. Rosanna's the sister, she's not married, and Godwin the brother, and his wife Polly. It was the sister wouldn't let me in both times. I asked for Walter but he was away in the north somewhere looking at pigs. There was no welcome there for me, I can tell you. I demanded she let me in but she out and out refused. What could I do? I told her to ask Birdie to visit us on a matter of urgency but I don't know if she even got the message. Same with our letters. Do you see, sirs? Our daughter's become a ghost!"

"How did she meet her husband, if I may ask?" asked the guvnor.

"We had an introduction from an associate at my firm. We wanted a better match but her mind was set. And also—" Here he glanced at his wife. "We weren't sure another man would have her."

"Dunbar!" she cried.

"The agents must know everything, dear." He turned back to us, the pressure gone from his voice. "Birdie suffered some damage coming into this world and never quite developed fully. She needs a lot of guidance. The doctor called it *amentia*. Weak-minded, in other words. Walter's not too far off either, I'd say. We both thought that, didn't we, dear?"

"She's mentally defective?" asked the guvnor, writing in his pad.

"She's only mild," said Mrs. Barclay. "She understands perfectly well though she's a bit slow with her talking. You wouldn't know from looking at her and she's a good worker: they've no cause for complaint there. She'll do just what she's told."

"And what would you like us to do?"

"We want you to bring her back home," replied Mr. Barclay, stepping over to his wife but then changing his mind and retreating to the fire.

"What if she doesn't want to be brought, sir? What then?"

"She doesn't know her own mind, Mr. Arrowood," said Mr. Barclay. "She'll believe anyone, do whatever they say. If they've turned her against us, we need to get her away from

13

them. If we can get her back here we've a doctor who'll swear that the marriage's invalid due to her being mentally unsound. We can have it annulled."

"You want us to kidnap her, Mr. Barclay?" asked the guvnor in his sweetest voice.

"It's not kidnapping if it's for the parents."

"I'm afraid it is, sir."

"At least find out if she's safe," said Mrs. Barclay, her voice a-quaver. She dabbed the corners of her eyes with a handkerchief. "That's she not mistreated."

The guvnor nodded and patted her hand. "We can do that, madam."

He tapped me on the knee.

"The price is twenty shillings a day plus expenses," I said. "Two days in advance for a case as this."

As I spoke, the guvnor hauled himself to his feet and stepped over to inspect a picture of a sailing ship hanging by the door. Though he was tight with his money and often short of it, Arrowood never liked asking for payment. He had a high opinion of himself, and was ashamed to be the sort of gentleman who needed compensation for his services.

"If it only takes a day we'll repay you what we haven't used," I said as Mr. Barclay pulled a purse from his waistcoat and counted the coins. "We're honest. No one'll tell you any different."

When it was done, the guvnor turned away from the picture.

"How long have you lived here, madam?"

"How long?" asked Mrs. Barclay, glancing at her husband.

"Oh, a few years," he said, leaning his elbow on the high mantelpiece then jerking it off again as if he'd landed it on a hot plate. "Perhaps five."

"Five years," the guvnor said with a nod.

"Yes, it's a respectable area. Kipling's brother lived on this street, you know."

"Well, well, how wonderful," muttered the guvnor. "May I ask what your profession is, sir?"

"I'm senior clerk with an insurance agent, sir."

"Tasker and Sons," said his wife. "Dunbar's been with them twenty-two years. And I'm a singing instructor."

"You have a delightful voice, madam," said the guvnor. "We heard you earlier."

"She was taught by Mrs. Welden. My wife was one of her best. She's sung with Irene Adler at the Oxford: Lord Ulverston paid her a special compliment."

"That was a few years ago," murmured Mrs. Barclay, dropping her eyes. She went to the little writing desk and opened it, pulling out a bright blue peacock's feather. "When you see Birdie, give her this. Tell her I love her and miss her."

"And tell her I'll buy her a new dress to match it when she comes back," added her husband.

The guvnor nodded. "We'll do our best to help you. You did the right thing calling us."

Before leaving, they gave us a photograph of Birdie and directions to the farm. As we walked down Saville Place, a boy with two scarves wrapped around his head came towards us out of the fog.

"Hey, lad," asked the guvnor, pointing back at the little house. "D'you know where they've gone, the people who lived there before the Barclays?"

"Mr. Avery's gone to Bedford, sir," replied the boy, his breath coming out white from his mouth, his hands clasped under his armpits for warmth. "You want the address? My mum'll have it."

"No, thank you. And when did the Barclays move in?"

"Maybe two month past, sir. Maybe three."

As we turned into the Lambeth Road, I asked him how he knew.

"All that furniture was recently bought," he replied. He reached inside his waistcoat, pulled out a punnet of chocolate stars and offered me one. They were warm and melting from his having stored them so close to the heat of his chest fat. He took a couple and threw them in his mouth. "Not a mark on any of it. When I asked Mrs. Barclay how long they'd been there she didn't seem to know what to say. I thought that very queer. And did you notice the outlines of all those missing pictures where the wallpaper had been protected from the soot? They'd have had a fire in that room for the last few months, so those pictures weren't long removed. The only one they had was that great ship. I had a look at the wall underneath and there was no picture trace at all, Barnett. It must have been put up recently."

"A bit of a guess then, sir."

He laughed.

"It's always a guess, Barnett. Until confirmed. Anyway, we must watch out for those two. They're hiding something."

I smiled to myself as we walked. Though it would irk him to hear me say it, he was sometimes more like Sherlock Holmes than he realized. He put the last chocolate star in his mouth and dropped the empty punnet on the street.

"What d'you think of the case?" I asked.

"It could be nothing, but if I were the parent I'd be worried. A weak-minded young woman being prevented seeing her family. A violent husband." He licked his fingers and wiped them on his britches. "Poor Birdie might be in a lot of trouble. The problem is, I'm not sure what we can do about it."

Chapter Two

Next morning we took the train from London Bridge. It rattled slow as an ox above the sooty terraces and warehouses of Bermondsey, then out through Deptford, New Cross and Lewisham. The further we got, the more the fog thinned until, just before Ladywell, it wasn't there no more.

The guvnor put down his paper, opened the document case he'd brought, and pulled out the Barclays' photograph. It was a picture of five women in summer bonnets standing in a park. Birdie was the shortest of them by some way. She stood open-mouthed between her mother and a young woman whose hand she held. She wore a drab cotton dress, her head tilting to the side as she looked at the young lady next to her. Birdie seemed lost in a pleasant dream.

"I'm not familiar with the feeble-minded, Barnett," he said. He wheezed a little as he talked, his side whiskers spurling from his cheeks like woollen clouds. "I'm not sure I'll know if she's being coerced. Are they harder to read, d'you think?"

"There was one lived below when I was growing up," I told him. "He used to get right cross with things. Don't think he ever left his old ma."

"Little Albert's the only one I know," he said, staring at the photograph. "I must say I've never felt I understood quite what's going on in his head. Isabel had a soft spot for him."

"Did you hear from her over Christmas?"

The guvnor's wife, Isabel, had left him a year or so ago and now lived with a lawyer in Cambridge. Recently she'd asked him to petition for a divorce, using her infidelity as grounds. He hadn't done it.

"She sent a card," he answered with a wave. "I think she's beginning to see through that little swindler."

"What did she say?"

"She asked when the building work would be finished."

I nodded slowly, holding his gaze.

"I'm reading between the lines, Barnett!" he said, a little irritation in his voice. "If she's wondering when our rooms are going to be finished it means she's thinking about coming back to London. It was always him pushing her into it anyway."

"Don't get your hopes up, sir," I said. "Remember what happened last time."

He fell silent. The train stopped between stations and we waited.

"What did you bring that briefcase for?" I asked him.

"I'm going to try something. But I forgot to ask about your Christmas, Barnett. Did you enjoy it?"

I nodded. I'd spent it alone getting hammered in a pub on Bankside where nobody knew me. I couldn't tell him that, just as I couldn't tell him why. It had been more than six months, and still I couldn't tell him.

"My sister cooked a bird," he said. "Lewis doesn't celebrate, of course, although he did eat more than his share. Ettie was off delivering sugar mice to the street children for half the day. Then Lewis was abed with cramps. What a glutton he is, and don't ask me about my sister. Lord, how that woman can eat. And she's the cheek to urge me to take purgatives. Ah, that reminds me."

He reached inside his coat and held out a knitted thing to me.

"It's a Christmas gift, Barnett. A muffler. That thing you're wearing's in tatters."

He'd never given me a gift before, and I was touched. I opened it out, a red and grey scarf of thick wool. I wrapped it around my neck.

"Thank you, sir."

"Remember that next Christmas." He patted me on the knee and picked up his newspaper again. The train started to move.

"More on the Swaffam Prior murder," he said. "They're calling for the Police Inspector's dismissal. Look here, a whole column on the poor chap. Damned editor doesn't understand the nature of evidence. God forbid they ever get hold of one of our cases. And this campaign! The Sheriff of Ely, the Bishop. All sorts of do-gooders. How can they know? I mean *really*. They assume a fourteen-year-old boy can't remove an old woman's head. Tripe! A fourteen-year-old can do anything a man can do."

He turned the page.

"Oh, Lord," he groaned. "What's happened to this paper? That charlatan's never out of it."

"Sherlock Holmes again, sir?"

"He's been asked to investigate the disappearance of some young Lord from his school. Son of the blooming Duke of Hodernesse. Well, he'll be right at home there." He read on a bit, his purple lips hanging open among the tangle of his whiskers. "What? No! Oh, Lord. Oh, no, no." He was blinking convulsively, confusion writ upon his brow. "There's a six-thousand-pound reward, Barnett. Six thousand pounds! I could solve five hundred cases and not earn half that amount!"

"They're an important family, sir," I said. "Isn't the Duke a Knight of the Garter?"

He snorted. "Holmes used to be more discreet."

"You don't know it was Holmes told the press."

"You're right. It was no doubt Watson, trying to sell a few more books."

There were no cabs at Catford Bridge station so we walked down past a row of almshouses towards the green. It was a frosty day, the sky low and dark over the buildings. Though it wasn't bright, it was some relief to be out of the murky air of the city. I felt my steps grow lighter, my head clear.

Catford was an old farming village being eaten by London. There was building work going on everywhere: a tramway to Greenwich was being laid; bricklayers were putting up the walls of a bank next to the pump; foundations were being dug out for a grand new pub. Off the main street, past the small houses near the station, big villas for merchants and city workers were rising. Poorer areas were hidden here and there, in the shadows of the tram depot and the forge, where the families of farm workers lived in rickety sheds and damp basements, crammed into wretched houses with boarded windows and broken gutters.

The Plough and Harrow was just the sort of place you found outside town—a stone floor that could have done with a broom for the mud, walls panelled in dark wood, a half-door that served as a counter. A glum grandma sat with a blank-faced younger fellow on the benches at one side of the fire, while three old blokes with veined cheeks and pipes in their mouths played dominoes on the other. An ancient dog with matted hair chewed a stick by their feet.

"Any cabs around here, madam?" the guvnor asked the landlady after we'd got a couple of pints.

"The lad may take you in the cart if it's local," she answered. She wore a cowboy hat like you see in the Buffalo Bill shows.

"The Ockwell farm," said the guvnor. "D'you know the family, madam?"

"Godwin's in here often enough. Why you asking?"

"We've some business with them, that's all," answered the guvnor, taking a swig of his porter. He smiled at the lady. "I do like that hat."

"Why thank you, pardner." Her face softened; she ran her finger along the edge of the brim. "American fellow gave it me."

"Decent people, the Ockwells," growled one of the old men by the fire. "Family been here two hundred year at least, maybe more."

"They be straight with you long as you be straight with them," said another. He lifted his foot and shoved the old dog away from their table. "Ain't nobody's fools, if that's what you're thinking."

The door opened and two builders, both with wild, grizzled beards, walked in. One was a big, bald fellow wearing a muddy moleskin suit with two jackets, a peaked cap topped with a knob of wool. The other was just as tall but thin, a red cloth wound around his neck, his corduroy jacket covered in rips and poorly made repairs. A shock of grizzled hair sprouted from his cap and ran into the tangle of his beard.

"Morning, Skulky, morning, Edgar," said the landlady, setting out two tankards for them. Without a word, they began to drink.

"The brothers are up Ockwell farm at the minute, fixing their well," she said to us. "Ain't you, lads?"

"That's their concern, is it?" asked the thin bloke.

"These gentlemen was just asking about the farm, Skulky," she said. "Got some business with them."

"From London, are they?" he asked.

"South London," I said. "You know the family, do you?"

"Perhaps you could tell him this ain't London, Bell," said the bald one, scratching his beard. "Perhaps you could tell them folk respect each other's privacy down here."

The builders finished their pints and left.

Chapter Three

Five minutes later, a boy of nine or ten came in and led us out to an ancient cart. He drove us down along the green, turning off the main road onto a narrow dirt lane where the houses gave way to fields. We lurched and rocked down a hill into a dip then began to climb again. At the top we joined another lane more pitted and uneven than the last. On either side were fields of frozen mud and frosted grass. Little huts were scattered here and there, and pigs stood around everywhere like fools. A cold wind raced across the brow of the hill.

"Up there, sir," said the boy.

Ahead we could see the farm buildings. Two barns, a stables, some tumbledown animal sheds with rusty corrugated iron, and on the other side of them a big house. Everything looked like it needed fixing: slates were missing from the roofs, doors sat crooked, weeds grew from the guttering. A couple of old ploughs lay broken and mouldering outside the gate. Nothing about that farm looked right. And just as I took it all in, the dogs began to bark.

They guarded the main gate, straining at their ropes in a wild fury. One was a white bull terrier, all muscle and teeth, the other the biggest bull mastiff I ever saw. Its short coat was tan, its snout black. Instead of trying to get past them, the boy drove the cart around the back of a barn and in a side entrance right next to the house. When the dogs saw us appear again, they hurtled back across the yard but were brought up just short of the wagon by their ropes. It didn't improve their temper none.

"Mr. Godwin fights them," said the boy. "Best in Surrey, they reckon."

Just then, a couple of filthy men came through the main gate and crossed to one of the huts on the other side of the yard. Both wore coarse old clothes, smocks bulked out with what looked like sacks padded underneath them. One stared at us, his muddy face thin and severe. The other, a Mongol, waved with a great, wide smile. This one had just the crown of a bowler hat upon his head, the rim missing. I waved back. The mastiff sniffed the air, turned away from us, and tore off towards the workers. The Mongolian let out a cry, a look of horror on his face, while the thin bloke grabbed his sleeve, pulling him into the shed before the dog reached them.

We climbed down from the cart, the guvnor keeping his eye on the bull terrier, who snarled and strained at its rope just ten foot from us. The yard, which would have been nothing but thick mud on a warmer day, was frozen solid, rutted and pitted and hard to walk on. A pile of dung the size of a brougham lay up against one of the stock sheds. The farmhouse itself had seven windows upstairs, six below, with a green-tiled dairy at the far end. Everything was gone to seed: the walls of the house were spattered with mud up to the eaves; the chimneys were cracked and in need of repointing; the thatch was rotted, bare in places, ragged.

The guvnor knocked hard on the door. Nobody answered, but after we'd knocked a few more times one of the sheds wrenched open and a man stepped out. He wore a patched canvas apron that went down to his boots. Mixed with the mud that covered it were bloody smears of purple and crimson, stuck with bits of yellow fat. Behind him in the shed, a row of white pigs hung upside down from a beam, twitching and bewildered, the odd, defeated grunt falling from their lips.

The man's face was wet with sweat. His blond hair was thinning and combed tight over his forehead, across which was a red line where his cap would have sat. His eyebrows and eyelashes were also blond, giving him a half-born look. He walked towards us, stopping to pet the dogs on his way. They went quiet at his touch.

"Morning," he said when he reached us. He looked at us in a strange, innocent way.

"We've come on official business to see Birdie Ockwell, sir," said the guvnor, his eyes fixed on the butcher's apron. "Are you her husband?"

The man stepped in the house and shut the door.

The guvnor was about to knock again when I stopped him. "Wait a bit, sir."

He pressed his ear to the door and listened. After a few minutes, it opened again. She was a small, pinched woman, her eyes keen and bright, her mouth down-turned. A silver cross hung from her neck.

"Yes?" she asked, taking us in with a quick flick of her eyes.

"I'm Mr. Arrowood," replied the guvnor. "This is my assistant, Mr. Barnett. We're here to see Birdie Ockwell."

"I'm her sister-in-law," said the woman sharply, her accent not as poor as her clothes. "I look after Birdie. You may talk to me about anything that concerns her. What matter is it?"

"It's a legal matter concerning her family, Miss Ockwell," answered the guvnor, lifting his document case for her to notice. "Something I believe she'll be pleased to hear."

She looked at the case for a moment, then showed us through to the parlour. It was five times bigger than the Barclays', the furniture grand and solid, expensive in its time but now aged. The long sofa and chairs were frayed and split at the padding, the oak chest scratched and chipped. The big Persian rug was faded, eaten bare in places by moths. By the window stood the newly born man, his fingers fiddling with his bloody apron.

"Lawyers, Walter," she announced. "Bringing some good news for Birdie." She turned to us. "This is her husband, Mr. Arrowood. You can tell him, I suppose?"

She crossed the room, sat in a low chair under a lamp, and began to sew.

"What's it about?" asked Walter. He had the same accent as his sister, but his voice was slow and over-loud. "Someone left her some money, did they?"

"We really must speak directly to your wife, Mr. Ockwell," said the guvnor. His tone had changed. At the door he was gentle and friendly, but now, in the house, his voice was hard as a judge handing out sentence. "Please summon her immediately."

"She's not here," said Walter.

"I'd appreciate it if you'd be more specific," said the guvnor. "I do have other things to do today. Where exactly is she?"

"Visiting her parents, isn't she, Rosanna?" said Walter, looking back at his sister.

"Oh, dear, dear." The guvnor tutted and shook his head. "We've come such a long way. We'll have to go directly to the Barclays' house, I suppose." He picked up his briefcase and turned to me. "Come, Mr. Barnett. Saville Place, isn't it?"

"Yes, sir."

"My, but this has been a waste of time."

He marched towards the door with me behind him.

"Wait, Mr. Arrowood," said Miss Ockwell, getting up from her chair. She smiled, straightening her skirt. "It isn't her parents she's visiting but Polly's. Our brother Godwin's wife. Walter has a habit of only half-listening. Due to spending so much time with the pigs, so we like to tease him. The old woman's poorly so it wouldn't be right for you to visit Birdie there, but if you just tell us what it's about we'll make sure she knows."

"Please, Miss Ockwell. I'm a busy man and I've little patience for repeating myself. When will she be back?"

"Tomorrow."

"Then she must come to London to see me. Send me a note with a time, either tomorrow or the day after. No later. We need to conclude the affair."

"Of course, sir," said Miss Ockwell.

The guvnor gave her the address of Willows' coffeehouse on Blackfriars Road, the place where we usually arranged our meetings.

She walked us to the hallway.

"We'll tell her when she returns," she said as she opened the door. "It's about a will, did you say?"

"As soon as possible, Miss Ockwell," replied the guvnor, jamming his hat on his head. "Good day."

Outside, the lad was shivering. The dogs were over the

other side of the yard with Edgar, one of the builders who'd welcomed us in the pub. He was feeding them something out of an old rag, stroking them as they ate. He stood up when he saw us and muttered to his brother, who was hammering at something inside the wide doors of one of the stock sheds. Skulky stopped, his red cloth tied tight over his mouth, the mallet clenched in his hand. The two of them watched us as the lad drove out the side of the yard.

We rolled along behind a long barn, then onto the rutted drive and past the main gate. When we were out of sight of the builders, the guvnor asked the lad to stop. He turned to look back at the ragged farmhouse, his face hard, his eyes screwed up against the wind. He shook his head. Alone on the top of the hill, under the heavy grey sky, that wretched farm looked like the sort of place you could arrive at and never leave.

"Look," he murmured.

One of the leaded upper windows was opening. We couldn't make out anything behind the thick, black glass, but a hand appeared, throwing something light into the breeze. The window closed. It was a long way off, but we could tell what it was by the way it rose and danced in the air, drifting and twisting before disappearing behind the barn.

It was a feather.

The guvnor turned to me and nodded.

"She's in there," he said.

Chapter Four

When we went for coffee the next afternoon, Ma Willows handed us a wire. It was from Rosanna Ockwell, saying that Birdie was back and that they'd call on us the next day at four. The guvnor clapped me on the back, collected the newspapers from the counter, and sat heavily on a bench by the window.

"Some of that seed cake, Barnett!" he called over, flicking through the *Pall Mall Gazette*. "Big slice, Rena, if you don't mind," he added.

Rena Willows rolled her eyes at me. Her coffee shop wasn't the finest place, but we'd done a lot of our business there over the years and Rena never interfered. I wondered sometimes if she had a fancy for the guvnor, unlikely as that seemed with his head like a huge turnip and that belly as stretched like a great pudding right down between his legs when he sat.

He ate the cake down quick, as if he hadn't eaten for days

though I knew from my own eyes that he'd wolfed a great plate of oysters not two hours before. He blew on his mug of coffee and wiped the crumbs from the newspaper.

"D'you reckon they'll bring Birdie?" I asked him.

"They're living on their uppers by the look of that farm. If they think there's an inheritance, they'll bring her."

"Why did you act so short with them yesterday?"

"They didn't strike me as people who'd be affected by kindness, Barnett. People like that are impressed by authority. When they decided I was a lawyer, it seemed a good idea to try and confirm their expectations, and better to do that by my manner rather than by telling them falsities. Birdie was in that house, I knew it as soon as Walter told us she was at her parents'. It couldn't have been a mistake: she hasn't seen her parents since the wedding and he'd certainly know that. The man just doesn't think quickly enough to lie well." He gurgled as he sipped his coffee, then without warning sneezed over my hand. "But why won't they let us talk to her? That's the question."

"Maybe Walter's hurt her and they don't want anyone to see it," I said, wiping myself off on my britches.

"Well, with luck we'll have a look at her tomorrow. We must get the Barclays here at the same time; we may just close the case. Not even Holmes could have done it faster. I had a note from Crapes this morning by the way: he might have some work for us. Just as well, as we'll not be earning much from this one."

Crapes was a lawyer who sometimes put work our way. It usually meant keeping a watch on a husband or wife for a few days and trying to catch them in an affair. We didn't much like those cases: what the guvnor really wanted was something as would earn him a reputation, as would get his name in the papers like that other great detective in the city.

He turned back to the paper spread out on the table before us.

"Did you hear about this lunacy case in Clapham?" he asked after a while. "The woman didn't believe in marriage. She wanted to live with her lover, so the family had her committed to the Priory. They found a doctor to diagnose her with monomania." He looked up at me. "Caused by—listen, Barnett, I'm talking to you—caused by attending political meetings while menstruating. Have you ever heard of such a thing?"

I shook my head.

"No, because the fool doctor's just made the diagnosis up," he said, turning the page violently. Immediately his brow dropped and a groan came from his throat. I looked down to see what irked him:

LORD SALTIRE FOUND SAFE. SHERLOCK HOLMES SOLVES MYSTERY. "BEST DETECTIVE THE WORLD HAS EVER KNOWN," SAYS DUKE OF HOLDERNESSE.

The whole column was given to the story. The guvnor breathed heavy as he read it, shaking his head in despair.

"What's he done now?" I asked.

"Earned himself six thousand pounds, Barnett," he said, flinging the paper across the coffee shop. His lip quivered like he was weeping inside. His voice dropped to a whisper.

"For two days' work."

We were back at Willows' the next afternoon. It was already getting dark, and a cold rain had been falling all day. The Barclays were inside, wrapped in their coats and hats like they were sat on an omnibus. Mr. Barclay was nervy, his pink face pinker from being out in the freezing wind, while Mrs. Barclay sat calm and noble, her chin high, looking over the other punters. The guvnor, afraid that Birdie might do a runner when she saw her parents, moved them to a little table at the back of shop, behind a bunch of cabbies having a break from the cruel streets.

"This is your chance to see how she is," he said. "Be gentle and don't do anything that might anger Walter. Don't accuse him. And don't make your daughter feel guilty."

"Of course not," said Mr. Barclay. His eyes darted here and there; his leg jiggled, making the table shudder.

"Barnett, go and wait outside. Let them enter first. If they turn back when they see Mr. and Mrs. Barclay you must block the door until I've a chance to persuade them." He turned back to our employers. "Then it'll be up to you."

I went and stood on the street, my hands jammed in my pockets against the cold, my cap collecting the fine rain. Three empty hansoms were parked by the kerb, their melancholy horses standing silently. Two young girls out on the monkey wandered past, their hands out to everyone they passed. On the other side, a crumpet man marched along with a tray on his head, clanging his bell and wailing, but he surely knew that nobody eats crumpets in the rain.

It wasn't long before I saw Rosanna Ockwell striding down Blackfriars Road towards me. She was wrapped in a thick brown coat, a scarf, a plain black bonnet tied under her chin.

"Mr. Barnett," she said with a brisk nod. "He's inside, is he?"

"He is." I opened the door for her.

She stepped into the shop, looking around the busy tables until her eyes fell on the Barclays.

"What's this?" she asked sharply, turning back to me. "Why are they here?"

"It concerns them, ma'am," I answered, blocking the door.

She glared at me, anger in her keen eyes. There was something uncanny about those eyes: when she laid them on you it was as if she could see your every weakness, every bad thing you'd done.

"Is Birdie with you, Miss Ockwell?" asked the guvnor, rising from his seat.

"Around the corner," she replied, turning to him. Her face was quite white except the few strong hairs about her lip. "She won't come now, though. Not with these two here."

"But why not?"

"She doesn't want anything to do with them, that's why. They never treated her right. Never wanted her."

"It's a lie!" cried Mr. Barclay, leaping from the table. "It's your family that's put her up to it! You fetch her here, or there'll be trouble, I warn you!"

The cabbies had gone quiet, turning on their benches to watch the show. Rena stopped her work and crossed her arms over her great belly.

"Pray, have a seat, Miss Ockwell," said the guvnor in his softest voice. "Let's talk this out."

"She wants rid of them."

"She does not!" shrieked Mr. Barclay, slapping his hand down hard on the table. "You're a damned liar!"

"Be quiet, Mr. Barclay!" barked the guvnor.

"Birdie's a young lady that needs someone to stand for her and I'm happy to do it, Mr. Arrowood," said Rosanna. She spoke clear and firm. "I promised Birdie to keep them away and that's what I'll do."

"Oh, dear, dear," said the guvnor. "But there's some nego-
tiation. Details and so on."

"I won't allow them to talk to her. They only upset the
poor girl."

Mr. Barclay jumped to his feet again.

"Who the blazes d'you think you are telling us we can't
speak to our own daughter?" he cried. "It's you that's poi-
soned her to us, madam. You and your blasted brother. Take
us to her now or there'll be trouble!"

"Sit down, sir!" said the guvnor. He turned back to Miss
Ockwell, took her arm gently, and led her towards the counter so as the Barclays couldn't hear.

"Don't fight with them," he said, his voice low. "We'll
never get this business done that way, and we do need her,
Miss Ockwell. How about you go and get her, eh? I'll control Mr. Barclay."

As he spoke, Mrs. Barclay rose from the table and crossed
the room. She pushed past me, opened the door to the street,
and stood holding it for Miss Ockwell, her long face with its
three teardrop moles sombre beneath her neat hat.

"What are you doing?" asked Mr. Barclay. "We haven't
finished!"

"We'll wait for you here, madam," said the guvnor to Miss
Ockwell.

Miss Ockwell turned to leave, but as she reached the door,
Mrs. Barclay, quite a foot taller, stepped in her way. For a moment there was confusion as Miss Ockwell tried to get past,
first this way, then that. Then, just as suddenly, it was over
and she'd left the shop.

"What the blazes did you do that for, Martha?" asked her
husband.

"You were making it worse, Dunbar."

"Get after her, Barnett," said the guvnor. "Make sure they come back."

I was already out the door as he said it. Up ahead I could see the short figure of Rosanna Ockwell, marching quick towards St. George's Circus. I ran after her through the crowds. At the junction she turned down Charlotte Street. I reached the crossroads just in time to see her going into the Pear Tree Tavern, a big place near the corner.

I waited outside for a few minutes in the wet, but it wasn't a pub I knew and I started to worry there was another way out round the back. Just as I was crossing to go inside, a hansom came out one of the side alleys, pausing to let a coster's cart loaded with turnips pass on the road. The street there wasn't too well-lit, and it was only when the cab began to move off that I saw the three figures inside. It was Rosanna and Walter, both staring ahead in silence. A woman sat on the far side of the cabin. Her face was turned to the other window, but I knew it had to be Birdie.

I guessed they must be going to London Bridge station, so I hopped into a passing hansom. When we arrived, I raced up the stairs and saw them ahead making their way to the platform. Walter towered over the two women; though Rosanna could only have been five two or so, Birdie was even shorter.

The train was waiting, its steam up.

"Oi!" I shouted, running over to them.

They turned. Birdie's mouth hung open in her thin face; her old coat and drooping felt hat were made for a thicker woman. In real life she did look like a birdie, like a finch with a tiny, hooked beak and round, innocent eyes.

"You chased us?" demanded Miss Ockwell.

"You said you were coming back, ma'am," I said.

"She didn't want to, did you, Birdie?"

Birdie looked at me curiously, her eyes deep and brown like her mother. One of her hands was bandaged round and round in a stained rag. In the other she held a grey pigeon feather. She said nothing.

"I'm Norman, ma'am," I said to her. "I know your mother and father."

"Hello, Norman," she said, her voice low. Her mother's gentle smile appeared on her face, and I warmed to her there and then.

"I like that feather," I said.

She held it up to show me, her smile lightening up the gloomy station. I smiled back.

"Your parents really miss you, Birdie," I said. "They're only round the corner. Would you like to come see them?"

"She doesn't have to if she doesn't want," said Walter, his voice flat. He wore a proper collar and tie, a dark suit, a bowler hat over his thin, blond hair. He seemed out of place in the city.

"Maybe just for a minute, eh, Birdie?" I asked. "Come and say hello."

Birdie said nothing; still she smiled, but her eyes fell to the floor.

Ahead of us the conductor cried, "All aboard!" and gave his whistle a toot.

"Come now," said Rosanna, gripping her sister-in-law's arm and marching her towards the train. She must have been pinching real tight as Birdie let out a little gasp.

"You can get the next one, Birdie," I said, following along. "Come on, they're waiting for you."

"He can't tell you what to do, girl," said Walter. "He doesn't own you."

Just as they reached the train, Birdie's boot caught on a

missing cobble. She fell, crying out as her head struck the wet flagstone, but straight away she was up onto her hands and knees and reaching out for her hat. It seemed to me that the little woman was used to falling.

"Get up!" ordered Rosanna, taking Birdie's arm and yanking her hard to her feet. Birdie gasped again.

"You're hurting her," I said.

"I'm not hurting her, I'm helping her."

Birdie's smile was gone, her eyes full of tears. It was only then, with her hat off, that I saw the scar at the back of her head where her hair should be. It was about the size of an egg, a shocking bright red of sore, livid flesh, the hair above and below gummed with yellow pus. It seemed as a whole patch of her scalp had been torn off.

"What happened to your hair, Birdie?" I asked as clouds of steam rose around our feet.

"Got it caught in the mangle," said Rosanna, pulling the hat from Birdie's hand and fitting it on her head so it covered the scar. "Didn't tie it up right, did you, silly girl?"

Birdie looked at me. Her eyes flicked real quick at Rosanna, then back at me.

"It hurt, Norman," she said, her voice so soft and low.

"Who did that to you?" I asked.

"I didn't do it," said Birdie.

"It was the mangle," said Rosanna. "Now, come. Get on the train."

"Your mama misses you, you know," I said as a couple of men in black overcoats pushed past us to the carriage door. "Why not just come and say hello? Just real quick."

Birdie was opening her mouth to speak when Walter seemed to explode with rage. He smashed his fist hard against the panel of the train, a wild look in his eye.

"Stop talking about her mama!" he bellowed. "She doesn't want to hear about them!"

He stepped forward and took hold of my coat, but he was slow and before he'd got a proper grip I swung my arm, knocking his hands away. For a moment he looked surprised, then the fury returned and he started towards me again.

"Calm down, Walter," ordered his sister, getting hold of his arm and pulling him back. "Get on the train."

She pushed him to the door. He did as she told him, like her touch had made him go soft. As he climbed into the carriage, his too-short britches rode up his legs, showing his dirty grey drawers tied at the ankles.

"She doesn't want to see them, Mr. Barnett," said Miss Ockwell, now guiding Birdie aboard the train as well. "You've given her the chance. She'd have said if she did. Ask Mr. Arrowood to send the documents and any questions to our lawyer, Mr. Outhwaite, forty-two Rushey Green. We'll see she signs."

She climbed into the carriage and slammed the heavy door. I watched them through the window as they took their seats. The train wasn't fitted with lights, but I could see Birdie sat between them on the bench, her hands clasped on her lap. Her mouth hung open, her eyes looking down on her knees. She seemed so alone. Walter sat by the window nearest me, his elbow rested on the ledge, his eyes shadowed by the rim of his bowler.

The conductor gave two blasts on his whistle. With a great hiss of steam and a clanking of the wheels, the train moved off. At the last moment before they were gone, Birdie looked up at me again. Now she didn't smile: instead her brow furrowed and her lips tightened. It was the saddest look I'd ever seen.

Chapter Five

As we walked along Blackfriars Road, the guvnor was silent. He tapped his walking stick against the kerb, humming Mrs. Barclay's sad song to himself. I kept quiet, knowing he was pondering our next step.

"Tell me again what happened at the station," he said at last, shaking his head as if to loosen a tangle of thoughts inside. "Exactly. Every detail."

As I went through it, he asked me about their faces and how they stood, how they looked at each other, how they spoke. I knew he'd ask, and on my way back to meet him I'd gone over the details in my mind, describing it to myself lest I'd forget. The guvnor saw people clearer than me, clearer than most people. It was why he was a good detective. He was always trying to improve himself, always reading books on the psychology of the mind and buying pamphlets and papers to follow the big cases as were going on. Lately he'd been into a book by Mr. Carpenter about unconscious cerebration, as he was fond of explaining to us, but his favourite for the last couple of years was a book on emotions by Mr. Darwin. He'd studied all the pictures in there, learning all the different ways emotion is displayed in the body.

"It's clear they control her," he said when I'd finished. "But more important is why she didn't answer your questions when she had a chance. Perhaps she didn't want to disagree with either of you. That would fit with what the Barclays told us about her being meek." He ran the tip of his walking stick along the railings next to the pavement. "Or she might be unsure of her own mind. It's likely she's not used to making decisions for herself."

"I wasn't sure she understood what I was asking."

"Her parents said she understands everything. It's talking she's not clever with."

He paused as we reached a pea soup man, his belly gurgling. Then he shook his head and walked on.

"And Walter said, '*He can't tell you what to do,*' did he? That's interesting. He could have said, '*Ignore him, Birdie.*' He could have told you to leave her alone. But he chose to say it this way. It suggests he's concerned about who has the power to tell who what to do. The Barclays say he's rather slow. Did he strike you that way?"

"Hard to say, sir. His voice is flat and he seems a bit clumsy. Looked like his sister had charge of him."

"I thought the same when we were at the farm. I wonder if he's concerned about people telling *him* what to do. And he said, '*He doesn't own you.*' Is that how he sees marriage, I wonder?"

We stepped onto the street to avoid a bent old woman carrying two great sack bundles over her shoulders. A bit of carpet was tied over her head; her filthy overcoat trailed along the greasy street. Behind her wandered a bloke sucking on the bones of a pig's trotter.

"Keep up!" she croaked.

He darted after her, his black suit shining with filth under the gas lamps.

"Walter's temper worries me, Barnett. Was he really going to assault you?"

"Looked like it."

"I don't like the sound of that scar either. Did Birdie confirm it was the mangle?"

"She said, '*I didn't do it.*' I don't know if she meant she didn't tie her hair up or that it wasn't her fault."

A boy turned into the street ahead of us, a tray of muffins hanging around his neck. His cap was torn and too big for him; his smock was stained.

"Lovely muffins!" he cried at the streams of tired folk trudging along with their carts and sacks.

"Hello, lad," said the guvnor, a great smile lighting his face.

"Mr. Arrowood!" cried the boy.

It was Neddy, the lad we used now and then when someone needed watching or messages needed taking. He was eleven or so, maybe twelve or ten, and always up for earning a bit of money: his ma liked a drink too much to bring in food regular so it was down to him to feed his two little sisters. Neddy lived on Coin Street, same as the guvnor, but we hadn't seen much of him that winter. There'd been an arson attack on the guvnor's building six month before, and him and his sister Ettie had been staying with his oldest friend Lewis as they waited for the builders to repair their rooms.

"Oh, but it's good to see you, my dear," said the guvnor, giving the lad's shoulders a squeeze. "And how's your family?"

"Always hungry, sir. The more I get the more they want, far as I can see. The little one got right chesty over Christmas. Had to get the doctor in for her."

"Is she better?"

"Still cries a lot, sir."

The guvnor peered through his eyeglasses at the boy's face. We were just between the light from two street lamps.

"When's the last time you had a wash?"

"This morning," said Neddy, wrinkling his nose.

"Ha!" laughed the guvnor. "Here, give us a couple of muffins, you little imp."

He took the muffins from Neddy and handed over a coin. Then he fished in his waistcoat and pulled out a shilling. "Take that in case you need to get the doctor in again."

"Thank you, sir."

"Should have some work for you soon, my boy," he said, handing one of the muffins to me.

"It's rock hard," I said. "How old are these?"

"Old enough, Mr. Barnett," said Neddy with a smile. One of his front tooths was missing from the Fenian case; his hair fell into his eyes.

The guvnor laughed. He loved that little lad.

"Mine's still warm," he said, taking a bite. "You took the wrong one, Barnett. Anyway, we'll let you know about that work, Neddy."

"Any time, Mr. Arrowood. You let me know."

We watched him dart after a couple of other punters.

"So Birdie looked in low spirits in the train?" he asked, shoving the last piece of warm muffin in his gob.

"That's what it looked like to me. And I felt she wanted to

show me too. But I couldn't swear by it. It was dark, and she only looked up quick."

"We can all recognize grief," he said. "Mr. Darwin says it's universal: raised inner eyebrows, furrowed forehead, lowered mouth corners. The Hindoos, the Malays, the ancient Greeks—all the same. If we couldn't recognize sadness in others we couldn't sympathize. And what would society be without sympathy, Barnett?"

"Like London sometimes, sir."

We reached St. George's Circus, where I was going to take a different road back to my rooms in The Borough.

"Now, what of Mrs. Barclay?" he asked me, stopping by the church stairs. He uncapped his pipe and pushed down the tobacco with his thumb. "What restraint, though? Surely the greatest insult to a mother is to tell her she's done wrong by her daughter?" The guvnor was getting worked up now, his brow arched in excitement. "And then she passes that note."

"Who passes a note?"

"Why, Mrs. Barclay. You didn't see?"

He laughed at my surprise.

"It was when they bumped: she slipped it into Miss Ockwell's hand in the confusion. You didn't see?"

"I said I didn't see."

"I thought it best not to ask her about it at the time. If she was hiding it from Mr. Barclay, the chances are she'd deny it." He lit his pipe, his eyes a-twinkle under the gaslight. "Meet me at London Bridge station tomorrow at half past midday, my friend. We're going back to Catford. We're going to help poor Birdie with whatever trouble she's in."

I watched him as he walked off towards the Elephant and Castle, his great behind juddering like a shire horse. I smiled to myself. The guvnor had finally got interested.

Chapter Six

Arrowood was in a cheery temper the next day when I met him at the station. I could tell he'd been up to something but he wouldn't say what; he just tapped his finger on his hooter with a wink. I wondered if maybe he'd been seeing a woman. I hoped so. I was sure Isabel wasn't coming back, and him holding out for her so long only caused him frustration. He never once blamed her for leaving him: he knew he'd driven her away, but now the hope she'd come back kept him going and drove him mad at the same time. He was sure the lawyer she'd taken up with in Cambridge was pushing her into it. The lawyer was younger than him, more reliable, more comfortable. The lawyer gnawed at him as bad as Sherlock Holmes himself, eating him from the inside, giving him acid in his gullet and cramps in his belly. The man was a bleeding macer, a bug hunter, a pissening hound, and the very thought of him brought on the guvnor's gout, made him itch his arse furiously when he sweated, caused him murderous headaches after a night in the Hog.

There were no cabs at Catford Bridge and the lad at the pub was out so we had to walk to the farm. Nobody passed us on the lane, and we had to stop regular for the guvnor to catch his breath and curse his shoes. The dogs started barking before we reached the gate, but we went the way the lad had taken us, round the back of the barn and coming into the farmyard at the far side. Still they ran at us, barking and snarling, wild and angry. The guvnor flinched as the ropes brought them up just short, his hand on my sleeve, taking care to stay behind me as we approached the house.

A man answered the door. He had a jaw like a bootscraper, his face lined and weather-beaten, his head bald under his brown cap. One arm hung limp by his side, the hand cupped in his pocket. It had to be Godwin Ockwell.

"Afternoon," he said, his eyes moving from the guvnor to me and back. He spoke like a drunk, with only one side of his face moving. The dogs kept up their noise behind us.

"I'm Mr. Arrowood, this is Mr. Barnett. We've some official business with Birdie Ockwell."

"I know who you are, Mr. Arrowood, but Birdie won't see you. I think my sister told you that already."

A crashing sound came from inside the house, then, buried beneath all the barking, a woman shouted.

"Dogs!" cried the man. They stopped for a moment, then started up again. The man picked up a stone from a pile as lay by the door and hurled it at them. They jumped back, whining.

"We've come all the way from London," said the guvnor. "It really is most important we talk to her."

"You're to do it through Mr. Outhwaite." Though his words were slurred he spoke correct, like his brother and sister.

"We cannot do that, sir," said the guvnor, trying on his kindest smile. "We've no choice but to return until we see her."

"You don't want to become a nuisance, old chap."

The guvnor thought for a moment, then said, "I'm going to be honest with you, Mr. Ockwell. We aren't lawyers. Birdie's parents sent us. They're worried she hasn't answered their letters. They wanted us to talk to her, to make sure she's content. All we need is five minutes with her and then we'll never come again."

"So there's no inheritance?" asked Godwin Ockwell, lifting his hand to wipe away some spit from the droopy side of his mouth.

"I'm afraid not. I said we were on legal business, that was all. Miss Ockwell assumed we were lawyers. I'm afraid I didn't correct her."

"Three rail fares that cost us."

The guvnor fished in his purse and pulled out a shilling and a sixpence. "I'm sorry for the trouble, sir."

Godwin took the coins. "Now bugger off, and don't come back or you'll taste my shot."

"Just five minutes, Mr. Ockwell. Please."

"Tell her parents she's happy as a lark," said Godwin, and slammed shut the door.

The guvnor cursed. He looked up at the windows then around the yard, at the wretched buildings and farm rubbish strewn all over the place. At the corner of the house he spied a rusty iron rod. He hurried over to collect it, then, making sure he was out of range of the dogs, began hammering on a milk urn as stood by the door.

"Birdie!" he cried with each blow. "Birdie! Birdie!"

The hounds became frantic, tearing and pulling at their ropes.

"Come along, Barnett!"

I took up a stone and started beating an old tin bath as was half-filled with water, shouting Birdie's name along with the guvnor.

We'd been whacking away for a minute or two, when suddenly the guvnor stopped.

"Up there," he whispered, stepping away from the house so he could see better.

In a window above the parlour was a ghostly face. It was the same window the feather was thrown from the first time we visited.

"Is that you, Birdie?" called the guvnor gently.

The face moved towards the glass.

It was her. The glass was grimy and uneven, but it was her all right. She gave a quick smile, then looked behind her into the room. We could see her head, her hair covered in a dark scarf, her shoulders. Her mouth hung open. She raised her bandaged hand as if to wave, but held it there like she wanted us to see it.

"Open the window!" called the guvnor.

She bent her head below the ledge and came up again, fiddling with something on her lap. Then she pressed the open page of a magazine to the glass, showing us a picture.

"What is it, Barnett?" asked the guvnor.

"I think it's the Royal Pavilion. In Brighton."

"Open the window, Birdie!" called the guvnor once more. "Talk to us!"

As he spoke, the front door opened. It was Godwin again.

"I warned you, Arrowood," he said softly. In his good hand was a shotgun.

He raised the gun at us, the butt planted on his belly. He was panting, his face red: there was something unhinged in his eyes as told me he'd lost control of himself.

I stepped back, pulling Arrowood with me.

There was a roar and smoke was all around us. It caught in my throat, making me choke; my ears were ringing. As I tried to get hold of my senses, Godwin quickly turned the rifle around and lashed out at me with the butt.

It cracked me in the side of the head, sending me staggering towards the raging dogs. I just caught myself in time, jumping back out of their reach while Godwin swung out at me again with the shotgun. This time he missed.

"The next shot's in your shoulder, Arrowood," he hissed, his eyes burning. He thrust the rifle barrel in the guvnor's chest. His finger was on the trigger; his shoulders jerked compulsively. "Leave us alone!" he bellowed.

The boss was pale.

"C-calm, sir," he stammered, pulling me back by my arm. "W-we're l-leaving."

We quickly backed away, along the side of the house, past the barn. Ockwell watched us all the way, his shotgun following our movement. When we'd turned the corner and were out of sight, we ran.

We only slowed when we reached the lane. The guvnor was short of breath, his steps quick, his ankles weak. He looked back at the farm buildings again, then stepped up on a fence to see the fields running along the road. Behind us, in the stock sheds, a ruckus of pig squealing started up. We walked on, down the hill.

"What now?" I asked as we reached the bottom and started back up the other side.

He clutched my arm as we climbed the slope. He was puffing hard. "I think we'll pay the parson a visit. They usually know everybody's business. Perhaps he can talk to Birdie."

We'd just got to the brow when we heard the sound of a horse and cart behind. It was Godwin, whipping his horse, hurtling up the hill towards us.

"Christ," I said.

The horse was galloping, its head tossing, its eyes bulging. The lane was banked high on either side with hedgerow: there was no way off, nowhere to hide.

"Has he got his gun?" asked the guvnor, moving behind me.

"I can't see. It's not in his hands."

In moments the horse and cart reached the brow and came flying towards us. We pressed ourselves against the wet thorns of the bank, trying to get out of the way. Godwin clutched the reins tight, a scarf wrapped round his mouth, a cap low over his eyes. He stared straight ahead like we weren't there, a grimace on his face, his long jaw jutting forward like a trolley bus. The cart passed inches from our feet.

And then he was ahead, charging towards town and disappearing around the corner.

Chapter Seven

***

It was almost dark when we reached the village. As we passed the pub, we spied a fellow leaning against a woman in the dark of the side alley. Night was falling and we couldn't make them out too clear, but we heard him murmur something in her ear and she laughed in a loose, half-cut way. The guvnor stopped to have a better look. There was a shuffling as the bloke pulled her skirt up over her knees, then he started to thrust up against her. She let out a squeal, holding her bonnet to her head with one hand and gripping his shoulder with the other. He grunted; his cap jerked to the floor. His limp arm hung by his side.

I pulled the guvnor away.

"Well, well," he said when we were further down the road. "Clubbing you must have excited him. I hazard that wasn't his wife he was wooing."

We walked along the side of the green, the grass silver with frost in the fading light. A gravedigger was working alone on the far side of the churchyard, swinging a pick at the frozen turf. The old bloke looked over as we walked up the path to the parsonage, tipping his cap and taking a moment to rest.

The parson opened the door with a great smile.

"How nice of you to call," he said when the guvnor had introduced us. His voice was quite hoarse. "I'm Sprice-Hogg, parson here at St. Laurence's. I think I saw you the other day at the station."

He invited us into the parlour, where a warm fire was smoking.

"Now, before we talk let me have some tea brought," he said. "And a little mutton, perhaps? I was about to eat."

"Please don't go to any trouble," said the guvnor.

"No trouble at all," said the parson with a smile. "*Do not neglect to show hospitality to strangers, for by this some have entertained angels without knowing it. From Hebrews.*"

"Ah!" said the guvnor. "A favourite quote of my father's, Reverend."

He left us warming our hands. The room was big and gloomy, and there wasn't enough furniture to fill it. A small writing desk, a sofa, and a high-backed chair were on one side. An old dining table was at the other. On the mantel stood a picture of Jesus Christ knocking at the door of a poor English cottage.

The parson returned with a tray of food. The maid followed, carrying a teapot and cups. She was a solid young woman, very broad in the shoulders and thin in the ankles, with just a little curve to her back that wasn't going to get any better as she got older.

The meat was fatty and a little past its best, but I was feeling weak from the cold and it was good to get it down. As we ate, the parson talked about the renovation of his church, the organ fund, the history of his bell. His face held a kindly look, and on his nose were little round spectacles. His thick, white hair was golden in the gaslight, the edge of his moustache wet from the teacup.

"That was very tasty," said the guvnor, wiping his mouth on his sleeve. He sipped his tea and held down a burp. "Are you married, Reverend?"

"Oh, no, no," laughed the parson, picking up a decanter of port from the desk and pouring out three glasses. "The parish keeps me occupied."

"It seems a prosperous place," said the guvnor.

"We've become a London suburb. The newcomers are building the big houses, but we have an older community and some areas of quite poor housing. Agricultural wages are so very low these days, I'm afraid. The farmers always complain they can't find workers."

"Perhaps they should pay more, Reverend," I said.

"Many farms are in debt, Mr. Barnett," answered the parson, finishing his port quick and pouring each of us another glass. "So, tell me. What brings you to Catford?"

"We're private investigative agents," explained the guvnor.

"Good heavens! Are you investigating a case here?"

The guvnor told him about the Barclays' worries and the difficulties we'd had trying to speak to Birdie.

"We saw her in the upper window today," he said, taking out his notebook and pencil. "She pressed a picture of Brighton Pavilion to the window. D'you have any idea what that might mean, Reverend?"

The parson shook his head. "I'm afraid I've no idea. But

the Ockwells are a good family. I can't imagine they're preventing her seeing her parents."

"You told the Barclays that Walter had a violent history,"
I said.

"Yes. A bad story, that was. He'd been to market at Lewisham to sell some pigs and somehow lost the money. He hasn't
a full share of good sense at the best of times but he'd taken
too much brandy and got himself into a rage. Set about one
of the local men with a stick. The chap lost an eye. He was
quite wild, they say: a few fellows had to hold him down until
the police came. The constables found the money in Walter's
wagon. He was in prison for two months for that. It's was all
over the papers."

"How did his first wife die?"

"She was walking up a hill behind a loaded wagon. The
axle broke and the whole lot fell on her, broke her spine. She
died a few days after. It's a rather common story on the farms,
I'm afraid. Even a child knows that's something you should
never do."

"Was Walter with her when it happened?"

"Yes, but there was no suggestion he was responsible, except for not maintaining the wagon, of course." He poured
us more port.

"D'you think he's a danger, Reverend?"

"Not usually," answered the parson, standing to get his
pipe from the writing desk. "But he can have quite a temper
when he thinks someone's making fun of him or if he's taken
a drink. He's a strong fellow. The Ockwells had been having some financial troubles and losing that pig money would
have been hard for them. The farm's been in decline since
old Mr. Ockwell died. They only moved from arable to pigs
in the first place because of the grain imports. Nobody ex-

pected meat would be next. Free trade and all that, Mr. Arrowood. Quite a disaster. Godwin took out a loan to buy a patent for a movable steam engine a few years ago. Thought he'd lease it out but the damn thing turned out to be quite useless. That's when he was attacked with apoplexy—you noticed his speech?"

The guvnor nodded as he scribbled away in his notebook.

"I don't know how they keep going, frankly. They've been lucky to keep their workers."

"Who knows them best around here?" asked the guvnor.

"The family have always kept to themselves. They were packed off to boarding school when they were young, so they didn't really get to know the local children."

"And Birdie? D'you think she's happy?"

"She's so quiet. It's hard to get a word out of her at church."

"Does she attend regularly?"

"She didn't attend at all for the first few months. Then she came regularly for a few weeks, but she seems to have stopped again. Rosanna always attends. She's extremely pious, always has been, and she's had her own disappointments, of course. Her fiancé died a month before her wedding. This was when her father was alive. Then she was all set to go to university to study medicine when Godwin got them into further debt." He shook his head. "She's borne it all with such strength."

There was silence as the guvnor wrote it all down. Finally he looked up. "And Godwin's wife?"

"Ah. The beautiful Polly Gotsaul. She used to attend every week, but she hasn't been for more than a year. A nervous disorder of some kind, I'm told. Makes it difficult for her to leave the house." He sighed. "I used to so enjoy looking on her heavenly face from the pulpit."

"Do either of them come down here to the shops?" I asked.

"Rosanna does the shopping."

The maid pushed open the door, a tray in her hands. The draught from the hallway came in quite strong, blowing an envelope off the mantel and directly into the coal fire.

"Sarah!" cried the parson, leaping from his chair and hurrying over to the grate. Quick as a mouse he took hold of the tongs and fished the letter out, blowing down the flames. "You've done it again, you careless girl! How many times must I tell you not to put my letters there?"

"Sorry, sir," she said, her head bowed. The tray trembled in her red hands, rattling the knives.

"Well, get on with it," he growled.

She passed us each a plate of fruit cake. The parson poured more port, while she poured him a mug of milk from a jug.

"Do you know Birdie Ockwell, Sarah?" asked the guvnor, his mouth full.

"No, sir," she said. "I seen her in church but only that. My sister works up there in the dairy, sir."

"And what does she say about Birdie?"

"Don't know as she does, sir. She's sick with the diphtheria. Hasn't been there for two week at least."

"Could we talk to her, Sarah, d'you think?"

"She ain't well, sir. Ain't really with us." She bit her lip. "Won't be long, so says the doctor."

"Ah," said the guvnor. "I'm so sorry."

Sarah's eyes filled with tears. She covered her face with her hands and turned away.

"Watch the door!" the parson barked after her. He drained another glass of port, then took a big swallow of milk. He cleared his throat. "I've told her about the draught a hundred times. Some of them just won't learn anything."

We sat in silence for a few moments, staring into the fire.

"So, private agents," he said at last, recovering his cheer. "How exciting! Did you read how Holmes rescued the young Lord Saltire? What a genius! I suppose you study his methods, do you?"

The guvnor took another drink before answering.

"Holmes is a deductive agent," he said at last. "He relies on clues and documents: footprints, marks on the wall, shipping tables and so on. The Saltire case was solved by examing bicycle tyre tracks." He stopped as if remembering something. His eyes narrowed, his voice dropped. "Tell me, Reverend, are you familiar with the case of the naval treaty?"

"Yes, quite astonishing. If not for Holmes we'd be at war this very day."

"That's certainly a popular opinion, sir, but there's an interesting detail in that story. Easily missed. Holmes admits that he's helped the police on fifty-three cases, and only claimed the credit for four. That means Watson hasn't written the other forty-nine. It seems rather a lot of cases to keep hidden away given his great appetite for publicity, don't you think? I can't help wondering about all those cases. Could it be that on those occasions his method failed him?"

"Failed him? How?"

"Holmes works by physical clues and his famous logic, but I've found in my work that many cases do not have clues. Instead, they have people, and people are not logical. Emotions are not logical. To solve those cases you need to get inside the person. You must understand their pain, their confusion, their desire for recognition. You must try to see how they see the world, and I'll give you ten to one they don't see it as you do. I've nothing against Holmes, Reverend, it's just that he believes emotions are antagonistic to clear reasoning. I work differently. I'm an emotional detective. I try and solve my cases by understanding people."

"Bravo, Mr. Arrowood!" exclaimed the parson, tossing the remainder of the port down his throat. "I've some knowledge of the criminal mind in my work as a magistrate too, you know. My experience has taught me that we don't talk enough about Hell to the criminal classes. About the woe unutterable, unimaginable, interminable. If we did, perhaps there'd be less crime in this world, don't you think?"

Arrowood peered at him over his eyeglasses, his open lips wet with port. He seemed to have gone blank.

"Ah, but I'm on my hobbyhorse again," said the parson. "Please, tell me all about your work."

For the next half hour the guvnor told him stories of our cases, while the parson fed us port and drank just as much himself, always following it with a clutch of his chest, a clear of this throat, a drink of milk. He seemed thrilled by it all, gasping with surprise, choking with delight. He asked question after question. The guvnor was happier than I'd seen him for a long time.

"You're a fascinating man, Mr. Arrowood," said the parson, walking us through to the front door where two cricket bats danced in the corner. "I've had a delightful evening."

"William," said the guvnor. "Call me William."

"Good Lord! And I'm also William. Call me Bill!"

They looked at each other with such affection it seemed they might break into a mazurka.

"May I ask you a favour, Bill?" said the guvnor. "Would you have a word with Birdie about this business? Perhaps drop by at the farm?"

"Of course I will, William, although I'm sure the Barclays are mistaken. Miss Rosanna would never allow Walter to prevent Birdie seeing her parents. Now, you must call in next time you're in Catford. Here, wait. Let me lend you a book I authored on the bells of Kent and Surrey." He pulled a blue volume from a small pile by the front door. "Have you read it?"

"No, I haven't, Bill," said the guvnor as he inspected the cover. "I must have missed it somehow."

"I'd like to know what you think of it. Come for tea the next time you're here. Any day at all. It's been such a delight. Promise me. I'll be offended if you don't."

"What an excellent evening," said the guvnor as we walked along the new tramlines towards the station. "He'll be an ally, I think. And we might need one in this place."

The moon was clear in the frozen sky, the trees and buildings picked out in silver and grey. Nobody was about but for three men up ahead, pulling a tarp over a wagon stood outside one of the building sites. When they noticed us, they quickly tied off the ropes, whispering to each other as they worked. There was something in the way they moved that wasn't right—I'd seen it too many times before.

"Maybe trouble, sir," I whispered, gripping the cosh in my pocket.

"Keep walking," he murmured, increasing his stride.

They stood by the wagon, watching us get near. Though their caps were pulled low over their faces, I recognized the two overgrown builders from their grizzled beards. It was Skulky and Edgar. The other fellow, shorter but thickset, wore a scarf under his bowler and over his ears. He had his arms behind his back; the outline of a cudgel jutted from the tails of his coat.

"Evening, lads," I said.

They didn't reply. As we passed, the short fellow pulled

the stick from behind his back. I turned quick, the cosh in my hand.

"Leave it, Weavil," growled Edgar.

The short bloke stepped back behind the cart.

We walked on quickly, the men's eyes on our backs all the way.

"D'you think they meant to rob us?" I asked when we were sure they hadn't followed.

"I hope that's all it was," he said, glancing back.

We hurried towards the station, the guvnor lurching and stumbling from the port. In his gloved hands was clasped the parson's book on the bells of Kent and Surrey.

Chapter Eight

The guvnor was abed when I got to Lewis's house in the Elephant and Castle next morning. His sister Ettie went to rouse him while I waited in the parlour. There were no lamps lit and the fire was cold. Crates of the guvnor's books and crockery were piled here and there between the stained and threadbare furniture; a bunch of old swords from Lewis's shop was stacked against the wall.

When the guvnor came down, his eyes were barely open. A great stink of fish and stale grog filled the room, and from his face the colour of pork fat and the sweat that speckled it I could see he'd gone to the Hog on the way home last night. I should have known he'd stop there to poison himself with cheap gin after getting such a start on with the parson. Ettie, wearing a tight frown, folded her arms over her thick jacket as she sat. He opened his mouth, to ask for tea no doubt, but seeing her eyes fire up he shut it again and looked at me. His hands shook as he reached for the laudanum on the side table.

"We need to get another payment, sir," I said.

He nodded and took a sip. He burped.

"William, please control yourself," whispered Ettie.

He nodded again, took another sip, shut his eyes. I bit my lip, trying to prevent the smile as was forcing itself on me. I'd often seen him like this after a night in the Hog, where most times he'd end up in the arms of Betts, the woman who worked the punters there in the back room. Betts had offered him comfort since Isabel left. Though he suffered for it next day, I knew it to be a good thing for him. He was a man as sometimes needed to hurt himself a little to stay balanced.

"Are you off to the mission today, Ettie?" I asked, giving the guvnor time to settle himself.

She nodded, pushing a finger under her scarf to give her neck a bit of a scratch. Ettie spent half the week working for a mission as visited the slums and provided refuge to young women who'd been forced to work the streets by their menfolk. They had a campaign against the three most notorious slum landlords too, the ones who supplied only a couple of privvies for three hundred or more people and were happy to let open sewers run through the middle of their courts. Thomas Orme Smith, Samuel Chance and Dr. Bruce Kennard were they, with Orme Smith owning the worst slum of all, a dark and diseased warren named Cutlers Court. The mission sent letters to the papers and held vigils outside their houses, embarrassing them before their neighbours. It caused a lot of bad feeling, and there were many in London hated that mission and the women associated with it.

"We've two new girls in," she said, sitting forward. As the guvnor reached for the laudanum again, she snatched it from the table. "Last night we had bricks through the refuge windows again. Some people in this city are unforgivable, Norman. As if those women haven't had it hard enough already."

Her eyes were bitter and it made me sorry. It was my city, from my first breath through all the good and bad things that ever happened to me. London was part of me, and I felt shame for what it could do to people.

She breathed in deep and made herself smile.

"You know I've known you for over six months and never met your wife, Norman? We thought you might visit over Christmas."

"She's been away," I said, feeling my voice change.

"Where?"

"It's been..." I started to say, but then a terrible weariness came over me and I couldn't go on. I'd lived with the secret for so long it felt like the truth was frozen inside.

I shook my head, realizing that it wouldn't be my decision in the end. Ettie was looking at me like she could see something of my thoughts. I turned my eyes back to the cold, grey ash in the hearth. The wind rattled the windows.

"Did you manage to see Birdie yesterday?" she asked after a while.

As I told her what had happened, the guvnor's shakes began to ease and the colour came back to his face. He drank from a jug of water at his side. Again and again his cheeks inflated with a parade of silent burps.

"It doesn't sound as if you know any more than the Barclays told you," she said when I'd finished.

"Of course we do," growled the guvnor. "Every step takes us nearer. That's how these cases work."

"Does that apply to our builders, William?" asked Ettie,

suddenly vexed. "Are we nearer getting our rooms back each day they do no work?"

"They've promised they'll be back this time."

"We can't impose on Lewis much longer. Please, William. It's not fair."

"I'm doing my best!"

"They're playing you for a fool. Why don't you take Norman to see them?"

"No, Ettie!" cried the guvnor.

"Will you talk to them, Norman?"

"If you want," I said, my voice hollow.

She heard my tone and her face fell.

"I didn't mean—"

"I'm happy to do it, Ettie."

I looked away. Whenever I started to feel easy, one of them'd remind me how they really saw me. I was his rough. What else could I be with these worn-out boots, this voice thick with the Bermondsey slums? Though I only lived in that foul court for six years, it seemed I'd never escape it.

"Norman, I'm sorry," she said, her face as serious as I'd ever seen it. "I shouldn't have asked."

"It's fine," I said. "Really."

She looked at me for a while, not knowing how to fix it, then went off to make some tea. The guvnor rested his head on the antimacassar and shut his eyes, working at healing himself.

Soon Ettie came back with the tray. I took a biscuit: the guvnor took four.

"She's asking for our help," he said when he'd refreshed himself. His face was sombre. "I'm sure of it. It kept me awake last night, seeing her up there, that picture, wondering what it means."

"But she didn't actually speak?" asked Ettie.

"No, but I felt her sadness so clearly. Her fear. Norman felt the same when he saw her on the train. Sometimes all we have to work with are our feelings."

"Our feelings can lead us in the wrong direction, William, as well you know."

"Remember that book I was reading on crowd behaviour?" He peered down at the pile of books by his chair and pulled out a green volume to show us. "Le Bon writes that emotions are contagious. I can't say I properly understand how it works, and I'm not sure he does either, but there's no doubt that emotions can be transmitted from one heart to another if we attend with care. Music can do it, can't it?"

"I suppose," said Ettie slowly.

A screaming started up in the road just outside the house, a child. The guvnor flinched, clutching his head. Then a woman's scolding voice, then a man's gruff roar joined in. They fought on and on as Lewis's three clocks, each out of time with the others, ticked on the mantel.

"We need to get to her, damn it!" he cried suddenly, his fist banging down on the side table. "She couldn't be more vulnerable! And that scar on her head might just be the start of a terrible journey. We have to think of something, Norman."

"Why don't I go up there and try?" asked Ettie. "They might react differently to a woman."

"No, Sister."

"But why not? The Ockwells aren't going to let you in, that much is clear. The Barclays have tried the police and they won't help. You've no other way to get to her."

"This is our work, Ettie. Walter has a history of violence. I don't want you up there on your own. Anyway, why would you have more success than us?"

"Women can sometimes do things that men cannot," she

said, her chest rising in indignation. "What other choice have you, William? She's asking for help. You said it yourself."

He gazed vacantly at his sister across the room, pondering. His stomach groaned like a lonely cow. Finally he turned to me.

"Remember those two labourers we saw the other day in the farmyard? The ones chased by the dog? Let's see if we can find them in the fields. They might be able to tell us something. But first run down to the shop and get us a kidney pudding, will you, Barnett? And a dozen oysters."

Chapter Nine

We happened to find a butcher's cart on its way to the Ock-well farm as we set out from the station that afternoon. He dropped us in the dip before the lane rose to the farm entrance, out of sight of the house, and there we pushed through a hedgerow. The field to our right was full of pigs, their heads bent, guzzling a scatter of turnips on the ground. The ground was frozen hard.

We followed a path between a small woodland and a paddock, where a couple of sulky horses stood, their bodies wrapped in coal sacks. They glanced at us with a hungry look in their eyes but didn't come over. That suited me fine: I never believed a horse was a man's friend like some folk said. A London horse is a slave, that's what I always thought, and if you looked deep enough into their eyes you could see how they'd like nothing more than to give you a good kick up the arse.

Now we could see the barns up the hill. We moved on to the fields on the other side, making a wide circuit around the edge of the farm. There was nobody about. A dozen scrawny cows; some winter cabbages; another pig field of hard mud and low huts. The guvnor was limping, puffing, sneezing, unhappy with so much walking. After another ten minutes we found ourselves on a small path through a copse, a field on one side, a stream on the other. The water was black and half-frozen over, the trees above bare but for a handful of rooks crying out. Soon we could see the lane ahead.

"Damn these shoes," complained the guvnor, wheezing proper now. His boots had got burned in the fire at his rooms, and, being a bit tight with his money over certain things, for the last few months he'd been loaning a pair of Lewis's shoes that didn't fit him too good. "I was hoping Ettie would get me a pair for Christmas. She gave me another bible."

I broke a couple of pieces of toffee from the slab in my pocket and handed him one. His scarf was wrapped around his chin, his bowler pulled so low all I could see were his puffy eyes and running nose. For a few minutes we worked on the toffees.

"Monogrammed," he said at last. "Just like the last one."

"Is Petleigh still visiting her?" I asked.

"He came before New Year with a plum cake. I've never met anyone who plays cards so badly. He's even worse than you."

Isaiah Petleigh was an inspector with Southwark Police. He'd helped us with a few cases over the years and caused us problems on a few others. A few months back the inspector had taken an interest in Ettie and started calling upon her.

"What does she think of him?"

"I don't know, Barnett. Ettie's Ettie. She gets on."

"You lost, masters?" came a voice.

It was an old woman, sat on a fallen tree behind a big mound of ivy. Her hands were wrapped in rags and layers of old skirts covered her legs. She wore a most fantastical coat, like a stuffed blanket, red and gold and purple and tied round the middle with a rope.

"Don't get many gents walking through, is all," she croaked, her eyes shining bright from her sooty face. Further back in the copse, next to a narrow track, was a wooden caravan, its doors open, black pots hanging from roof hooks and a tin chimney poking out the top. A nag in a ragged coat stood chewing a pile of straw. "You the new land agent?"

"No, madam. I'm Mr. Arrowood. This is Mr. Barnett."

"Mrs. Gillie," said the crone.

"D'you know the people who own the farm over there, Mrs. Gillie? The Ockwells?"

"Been stopping here all my life, sir. Knew old Mr. and Mrs. Ockwell since way back. He'd be turning in his grave if he saw the place now. She can't be too happy neither, in her bed knowing all what's going on. Richest farm round here, it was. Place's a ruin these days. Fields ain't draining proper; fences held together with string. Them pigs ain't happy neither."

"How d'you know the pigs aren't happy?" asked the guvnor.

"Spend too long lying down. A happy pig snorts merry, like. A merry snort. Like you, I shouldn't wonder, like you when you've had a skinful."

"I never snort, madam."

The old tinker laughed, showing us the most awful mouth I'd ever seen. There was only one tooth you could see in there, growing up from the bottom and separating halfway up, where the two parts twisted, one behind the other, like two burnt black twigs.

"D'you see much of the family, mum?" I asked her.

"Don't have nothing to do with them, not since the old master died." She nodded back towards the village and sighed. "My Mr. Gillie was beaten on the road over there a few year back. Old Mr. and Mrs. Ockwell took him into their house. Poor old bugger didn't last the week."

"I'm very sorry to hear it," said the guvnor.

"What's your business with them?"

"We're private investigative agents, working on a case."

The old woman looked at us for a time, her jaw moving like she had a bit of pork rind in her mouth she was working on. A frozen cat padded out from behind the caravan and rubbed its back against her legs. Below her skirts she wore a pair of old soldier's boots, cracked and worn and bound round with leather cords.

"Somebody should investigate them children," she said at last. "Heard three of them joined the angels, yet only one was buried."

"Which children, Mrs. Gillie?" asked the guvnor.

She hung a kettle over the fire and threw on a few sticks, getting a bit of a blaze going. As she straightened up, her hand clasped on her back, her face screwed up in pain. She was taller than you'd think from her little head, six foot at least.

"You want to buy some wooden flowers, sirs?" she asked.

"No," said the guvnor. "Whose children are you talking about?"

She plodded over to the caravan, where a red box was fixed to the side. The flower she pulled out was painted blue and yellow and orange. She held it careful, like it'd snap at the smallest pressure. "Pretty, eh? Look nice in your house, I suppose. Only a shilling and cheap at the price."

"A shilling?" said the guvnor. "It's worth no more than a penny."

"Price is a shilling."

The guvnor grunted and fished a coin from his purse. She gave him the flower. "Be careful with that, your Lordship. It's very fine."

"How did the children die, Mrs. Gillie?" I asked.

She drew another wooden flower from the red box.

"You like this one, Mr. Barnett? A penny to you."

"A penny!" cried the guvnor. "But I paid a shilling!"

She tutted and shook her head. Then she laughed.

It was only when I paid up and took the flower she answered the question.

"Couldn't say how they died, sir, but I'll tell you something else. Only but one was baptized and only but one's buried down in the churchyard."

"Whose children were they?" asked the guvnor again.

"I've said enough. Last thing an old tinker needs is trouble from a landowner, specially with me down here on my own."

"Where did you hear about this?" asked the guvnor.

"You could say a little fairy told me."

She wandered over to the old nag and gave it a kiss on the nose. A great, wracking cough took over her body, and she had to grip the horse's neck to keep herself upright. Her thin, sooty face turned pink and tears fell from her eyes as she choked and hacked. The guvnor held her shoulders, then, when she'd finished, hugged her to his chest. After her breathing steadied, she pushed him away.

"Kettle's boiled." She spat on the floor then ground it into the mud with her boot. "Set yourselves down while I make some tea."

We watched her as she poured the hot water into an old can.

"Ain't married, are you, sirs?" she asked as she held out a wooden mug for the guvnor. It was roughly carved, its outside singed and stained black, its handle broke off.

"I certainly am," answered the guvnor, sneezing into his belcher.

"Are you? Got a sense you weren't."

"A sense?" asked the guvnor, his smile a little unsure. "What sense?"

"A desperate sense, if you like." She handed me a slimy glass jar, then pulled a few broken biscuits from her pocket and gave us each a piece. "You as well, Mr. Barnett."

"Well, we are desperate, Mrs. Gillie," said the guvnor. "We're investigating a case concerning Walter Ockwell's wife, Birdie. We're sure she's in some kind of trouble but we can't get in to see her. The police refuse to help."

"Sergeant Root won't do nothing against the family. It was the same when my old man was beaten over there on the road."

"You think that had something to do with the Ockwells?" I asked.

"Ain't many use this road. Goes to the farm and then on a ways, but folk ain't got much cause to come here. Only the Ockwells really. Most times it's empty. Happened the day of Spring Fair. A lot of drinking goes on with the young lads at Spring Fair. Always does. Then they wander home."

"Are you saying it was the Ockwell boys?" asked the guvnor.

"All I can say is old Mr. and Mrs. Ockwell took Mr. Gillie in and tended to him good when it happened, right up until he passed to the angels. Paid for a doctor and all. Why they did it, I couldn't tell you. Could have been good Christian charity, could have been something else."

"But you suspect?"

"All I know is nobody was never even questioned. Sergeant Root wouldn't investigate. Said it was a tinker feud." She shook her head. "My old man never had a feud with nobody. Never in his life."

"That's terrible, Mrs. Gillie," said the guvnor. "But why d'you stay here with all that's happened? Aren't you afraid?"

She looked up into the tangle of bare branches. "I like to be near him. He ain't left yet, see."

We sat for a while drinking tea and listening to the crows move in the trees above. Her cat sat by the fire, licking its paws.

"Can you tell us anything else about those dead children, Mrs. Gillie?" asked the guvnor, his voice soft and kind.

"No chance, mister, not with me so old out here on my own all winter and my Tilly lame. I helped you enough already. But I tell you that farm's a sorrowful, hateful place. Sometimes I hear those pigs screaming so bad I want to tear off my ears."

She pushed a bit of biscuit in her mouth and softened it with a drink, wincing as the hot tea hit her devilish black tooth.

"I've never seen a coat like that, Mrs. Gillie," said the guvnor after a minute or so.

"Best coat I ever had. Bought it in Newmarket when autumn turned and wore it ever since. I'll be buried in it too, if undertakers don't filch it off my carcass." Her voice fell. "Listen, my lover. I left a note in the caravan if I happen to be alone when I go, and that may be any day now at this awful age I am. About the horse and the caravan and whatnot. A will. Willoughby knows up there on the farm, but you seem an honest man, Mr. Arrowood, so if I croak when you're still around, sir, just remember. In the black jar. I'd be obliged. I aim to still be breathing come spring when my sons come for me, but at my age I got to think about it."

The guvnor nodded. "Of course, Mrs. Gillie, though I'm sure it won't be necessary. Tell me, have you heard anything about Birdie, ma'am? About how she's treated?"

She shook her head.

"Who could we talk to?"

"You could try Willoughby, I suppose," she said. "Willoughby Krott, one of their workers. Maybe he can tell you. Wears a bowler with no brim."

"How many workers do they have up there?"

"Just Willoughby and Digger, but he don't talk. And there was Tracey used to work there up till a few month ago."

"Where can we find this Tracey?" he asked.

"You won't find him. He's gone. I hope he's somewhere better, is all. Ockwells work them too hard, they do. Work them to death up there."

"Does Willoughby live on the farm?"

"In the barn. The two of them come see me. I give them a bit of soup when I can. Always hungry, those lads."

"Can you ask him to meet us?"

She looked hard at the guvnor, then picked up her cat and gave it a good old stroke.

"Please, Mrs. Gillie. We must find out if Birdie's safe, and we've nobody else to talk to. Godwin threatened to shoot us if he saw us on the farm again."

She shut her eyes and finished her tea.

"Come at noon tomorrow," she said at last. "I'll do my best. Only promise me you won't ask Willoughby where he come from before the farm. He don't like it and I won't see him upset."

"Why's that?" I asked.

"His people put him away in Caterham asylum. Gets quite beside hisself just to think about it." She tapped her chest, her bright eyes a little moist. "You treat him good. Got a special place for him in here, see."

The guvnor nodded and got up from his stool. "Thank you, Mrs. Gillie."

"And you'll look into those three dead children? Promise me that, lover."

"I promise," said the guvnor solemnly.

As we started off down the path, she said, "You ain't really married, are you, Mr. Arrowood?"

"Yes, I am."

"Where's she staying then? Not with you, I don't think."

The guvnor turned. His voice was low.

"She's staying with friends a little while. Good bye, madam."

"Best get a move on, sir," I said, taking his arm and pulling him on, fearing what was going to come next.

"And where's your wife, then, Mr. Barnett?" called Mrs. Gillie after us.

That old tinker must have had some magic about her, for I found myself stopped still, my feet stuck to the ground. Big as I was, I felt a hot tear under my eye. I shook my head, knowing the time had come.

"She's dead," I said, my throat clamping up.

"Ah, sorry, darling."

The guvnor was stood there on the path, staring at me, his mouth hanging open.

I turned to walk away.

"Norman," he said, taking my arm.

I nodded, pulling away from him, walking on. He took my arm again to stop me. "When did this happen?"

"Summer."

"Summer? The Cream case?"

"Before that. She went up to Derby to see her sister. Just went for a visit, to see the nippers. She had some presents for them."

My throat clenched up. I coughed, feeling my ears ringing. He rubbed my back. A gust of icy wind raced through the copse.

"She loved those children, didn't she?" he said at last.

I nodded, staring at the wet, grey leaves on the floor.

"Caught the fever and that was it. Took her in two days."

"Oh, Norman."

"Never came back. I didn't even know she was sick."

He breathed heavy.

"And that was it." I took a deep breath to steady my shaking body. When I spoke again my voice was broken. "I never saw her again. Never even said goodbye."

"You should have told me," he said after some time.

"I…couldn't."

I couldn't. I didn't want his comfort. I didn't want him or Ettie to make it easier. I wanted to suffer. I needed to suffer. I shook my head, and finally, standing there in the damp, cold trees, the rest of it came out too, our room, the silhouettes on the wall, the blankets like sheets of ice, and all her things around me damp and spidery. I told him about her smell, her sense that sometimes I was sure was watching me as I shivered in the dust and the draughts and then I wasn't sure, and then I was, and how I woke one morning to find my torn sock darned as I'd slept. I told him how I couldn't bring myself to talk to anyone but her brother Sidney, how I couldn't hardly even say it out loud to myself because when I did it was like losing another piece of her. It all came out in a rush and a tumble, all those months it was buried inside me, like a hot dam busting. And when it was all gone, I fell silent and empty. Then, in the freezing dusk, the crows began to caw in the trees all around us, the noise getting louder and louder, like they were jabbing me, clawing me, biting me. I turned and hurried out of that copse, feeling his hand upon my back and all my thoughts drowning in the evil mess of the screaming crows.

"I'm so sorry, Norman," he said as we climbed the hill back to the village. "We thought she'd left you. Oh my poor, dear friend. I knew there was something changed about you. I just never thought it was this."

Darkness was falling, and the cold had crept into my blood. I couldn't stop my hands from shaking.

Chapter Ten

As we gained the almshouses, a young copper of eighteen or so came up to us. He wore a dented helmet and a badly shaped overcoat, long in the sleeve and frayed, like he'd been given it from an older copper who'd worn it all his life.

"Excuse me, sirs," he said, his voice unsure. "Sergeant Root says you're to come to the station for a word."

Without waiting for an answer, he turned and marched up the road, hoping no doubt we'd follow without him having to speak again. I was glad of it: I needed something to move us on from the silence of the walk back to town.

It was a bare room, unswept, unpainted, cold enough to freeze the nose off a brass monkey. Mould speckled the ceiling; damp rose from the floorboards. Sergeant Root was sat at a desk reading a paper. He had a long, droopy face, his neck hidden by a double chin. His moustache was thick, his eyes melancholy.

"The agents, Sarge," said the lad.

"Right," whispered Root.

The guvnor offered his hand. "I'm Mr. Arrowood, Sergeant. This is my assistant, Mr. Barnett."

The copper nodded, his eyes losing what little light they had in them. He looked the guvnor up and down, at his shoes starting to split at the knuckle, at the blue astrakhan coat rubbed bare around the buttons, at the nose blooming like cockscomb. He turned to the boy. "Here's a lesson for you, lad. These fellows get paid to watch folk. Spying through windows. Hiding behind trees. Cause a lot of trouble for decent families, they do."

"Yes, sir."

The guvnor started to protest but Root held up his hand.

"I've had complaints about you, Arrowood, poking your nose into the Ockwells' private affairs. I know what Mr. Barclay's been saying about them, but it ain't true. They're a good family. Been running that farm for generations. It's no crime if a married woman doesn't want to see her parents. Never has been, never will be. Now, I don't want you upsetting folk here on my patch. D'you understand?"

"But she's in trouble, Sergeant," said the guvnor. "The Ockwells refuse to let us talk to her. Yesterday Walter chased us off with a shotgun. He assaulted Mr. Barnett."

"Way I heard it you refused to leave his property."

"Birdie was in the upper window," said the guvnor. "She was trying to signal to us."

"Was she now. What did she say?"

"She didn't speak. No doubt she was afraid of being overheard. She held a picture of Brighton Pavilion to the glass."

The sergeant raised his eyes at the young copper who dropped his head, hiding his smirk.

"I'm certain they're keeping her prisoner, Sergeant," said the guvnor. "She was asking for help."

"Asking for help, was she? Listen, Arrowood, in my experience a person never shows a picture of Brighton Pavilion when she needs help. Not in my experience. You know she's weak-minded, I suppose?"

"She has a scar on her head where the hair's been torn out." The guvnor's voice was rising. I could see he was getting up steam, so I took his arm to remind him to keep civil. "You know Walter's a violent man. You must at least make sure she's safe. It's your duty."

"Don't tell me what I must do!" barked the copper, suddenly losing his patience. "Get out! And if I hear you've been bothering anyone again I'll haul you in for creating a nuisance."

"We've heard of three dead children on the farm," said the guvnor, wrenching out of my grip. "D'you know about that?"

"Three dead children? What are you talking about?"

"Mrs. Gillie said there'd been three dead children at the farm over the last few years yet only one buried."

"Mrs. Gillie," said the sergeant, shaking his head that had no join with its neck. "You listen to me, Arrowood. She's a mad old fox, that woman. Sits in those woods doing all knows what, spells and whatnot. Middle of the night, all on her own. Ain't nobody hasn't suffered something on account of that old devil. She's just making trouble as she always does. Take my word on it, if there'd been dead children I'd know about it."

"But you have to investigate!" demanded the guvnor.

"Make sure they leave, PC Young," said the sergeant, stepping into the back room and shutting the door.

★ ★ ★

Later that evening we paid a visit to the Barclays to tell them what had happened on the farm.

"We think she was trying to communicate," said the guvnor. "Does the picture mean anything to you?"

The Barclays looked at each other.

"We did take her to Brighton once," said Mr. Barclay. "Yes, we did. She must have been saying she wants to come home to us."

"She used to keep magazines," said his wife. "She carries things she's attached to. Feathers as well. She was always picking them up from the street."

The guvnor put on his thinking face and stared at the unlit fire.

"Feathers," he muttered. "So I was right. She was trying to attract our attention that time as well."

"What'll you do now?" asked Mr. Barclay.

The guvnor sighed. "We hope to talk to some of the labourers tomorrow, see what they know. But since the family won't allow us to see her and Birdie never leaves the house alone, we really do need the police to help. Root won't budge, so we need someone higher. D'you know anyone of position who could exert some influence?"

"I'm afraid we're not well connected, Mr. Arrowood."

"What about Kipling's brother?"

"He moved away before we arrived. We never met him."

"Your employer, then. He's a wealthy man, I suppose. He must know someone."

"I could try," answered Mr. Barclay with a shudder.

When I asked for another payment, Mr. Barclay gave it with no objection. We promised to report back to them in two days' time.

★ ★ ★

When we reached the camp next morning there was no sign of Mrs. Gillie. The caravan door stood open, the old horse watching us from its tether. It was wrapped in piles of sack, yet still it shivered and snorted and moved from leg to leg. A bucket with the mugs we drank from the day before was on its side by the fire.

The guvnor called out for the old woman, his voice rising through the bare trees. He called again. He pulled his watch from his waistcoat.

"Quarter to noon," he said. "Perhaps she's relieving herself."

"D'you think she's got second sight?" I asked. "I mean, what she said about our wives?"

"I don't know. But she's alone; she lost her husband. She might have just recognized the same in us somehow."

I went over to feel the fire.

"Stone cold. Hasn't been lit yet today."

He climbed the wooden stairs of the caravan and peered inside the doorway.

"Mrs. Gillie? Are you there?"

He stepped in. A moment later he turned back to me.

"Have a look around the trees, Barnett. She might have had a fall."

It wasn't a big copse. Perhaps a hundred yards over to the lane, and two hundred wide from the Ockwells' field to the neighbour's. I wandered around, calling her name. The trees were bare, the ground crisp with frozen leaf: not many places she could be hiding. I ducked under some rhododendron, where I found Mrs. Gillie's privy hole. I checked behind a couple of fallen trees overgrown with ivy and poked around a bramble thicket by the neighbour's field. Mrs. Gillie was nowhere to be found.

"Look at this," said the guvnor when I got back. I followed him up into the caravan. It was dark inside. The shutters on the window were closed; the door, shaded by a hood, let in little light. He pulled the blanket from the bed and held it up. Underneath was her striped coat.

The guvnor groaned as he lowered himself to his knee. He reached under the bed and drew out her soldier's boots.

"Gone out without her coat and boots," he said with a shake of his head. "On the coldest day of the year."

I lit the tallow candle on her table and we looked around the little wooden room. The guvnor was twitching, the way he does when he's worried. He wrung his hands and cleared his throat; he stepped from one foot to the other.

We went back outside, where he called out again. The crows cawed in the trees above.

"Barnett, look!"

He was pointing with his walking stick at the red box she kept her wooden flowers in. It was on its side in the leaves below the caravan, its lid hanging open. Two flowers, broken in pieces and dirty with mud, lay upon the floor.

"Something's happened to her," he said quietly.

Just then we heard someone walking through the leaves on the other side of the stream.

"Thank the Lord," he exclaimed, clapping me on the arm. "She's back."

But it wasn't Mrs. Gillie who came through the trees. It was the two fellows we'd seen before up at the farm. They were dressed miserably, in greasy old smocks, patched and stitched so you almost couldn't see what colour they were. Whatever they wore on their feet was wrapped round with rags thick with mud. The tall one wore an ancient felt hat that hadn't any shape; the short one, the wide-faced Mongol, wore the same battered brown bowler with its rim torn off as before. His smile was full and warm.

"Good day, sirs," he said, his voice all nose and little lung.

"Good day," said the guvnor and me almost together.

The fellow walked straight over to the nag and stroked its neck. "Hello, Tilly, how's your leg?" he asked, gentle as a child. The horse snorted, throwing its head back. "Oh, you hungry, girl? That it?"

The tall fellow stood watching as the Mongol felt under the axle of the caravan and pulled out a nosebag. He hooked it over the horse's head, then rested the side of his face on the horse's flank as it ate.

"That's better, Till," he murmured, running his hand up and down its belly. "That's what you wanted."

"My name's Arrowood," said the guvnor to the tall bloke. "This is Barnett."

The bloke didn't reply. His weather-worn face was run through with thin blue veins, his head shaved like he had nits. There was an anger in his eyes I'd seen before in drinkers spoiling for a brawl, made harder with his sharp nose and upturned eyes. His wiry beard was more dried mud than hair.

"Digger don't talk," said the Mongol, coming over to us. "I'm Willoughby, sir."

"I'm most pleased to meet you, Willoughby," said the guvnor. "And you, Digger. Is Mrs. Gillie here?"

"Back soon, I reckon." Willoughby's thick tongue curled out between the black stumps that were his teeth. Then, for no reason that I could see, he added, "I'm happy."

"That's good to hear, my friend. And you both work at Ockwell's farm, do you?"

"Best workers, we are. Got three horses. Count Lavender, he's the big white shire. You got a horse, sir?"

"I'm afraid not."

"Mrs. Gillie's my friend, she is. She leave soup?" he asked, patting his belly. "Got pinchy in here."

"No, Willoughby. The fire's out."

Digger made an angry noise with his throat.

"No soup?" said Willoughby, stooping to check the pot.

"I don't think so, son," said the guvnor.

Willoughby looked quick over his shoulder, across the stream to the field they'd come from. "Got to hurry. Get back to work."

"D'you know Mrs. Birdie, Willoughby?"

"She's my friend, she is. I like Mrs. Birdie."

"We like her too, Willoughby. How is she, d'you think?"

"Happy, sir."

"I see." The guvnor reached into my coat pocket, pulled out the block of toffee, and broke off two pieces. He gave them to the men.

"Thank you, sir!" said Willoughby. His eyes shone in delight, his mouth wide like he was laughing. But instead of eating it, both men put the toffee in their pockets.

"D'you think Mrs. Birdie's in any trouble?" asked the guvnor in his gentle voice.

"She's happy. Pretty lady. And Dad is."

"D'you know why she won't see her parents? They're worried."

Willoughby shook his head. "Won't see her parents, no."

"But why? D'you know why she won't?"

"Not allowed in the house. Me and Digger. Miss Rosanna say."

"You're not allowed in the house?"

"Not allowed. Get mud all over, see. Mud and stink. You ain't got a horse, sir?"

"No, Willoughby."

"We got three horses. I look after them, I do. You my friend, Mr. Arrowood?"

"Yes, my dear. Listen, can you bring Mrs. Birdie to meet us? It's very important we talk to her. We'd give you a shilling if you'd do it."

Willoughby shook his head. "Not allowed. She only come out for washing."

"Then how do you know she's happy?"

"She's happy, sir," answered Willoughby. This time he was a little quieter, a little less smiley. He looked at me. "You my friend, Mr. Barnett?"

"'Course I am, mate," I said.

"D'you know her, Digger?" asked the guvnor.

Digger looked up, the anger returning to his sharp face.

"He don't speak," said Willoughby.

"Does he understand?"

"Understands. Don't speak is all, sir."

"Well, it's good to meet you both. So very good." The guvnor grasped Willoughby's arm and squeezed it. When he made for Digger's, the bloke stepped away.

"Tell me, Willoughby, what do you do on the farm? What work?"

"Yeah, work. We do."

"But what work? What d'you do?"

"Do horses, feed the pigs, clear the dung. Berkshires, they are, sir. Few Large Whites. Sowing, but that's not much. Turnip, potato. Do the, spread the dung too. Helps them grow, sir." Here he had to catch his breath. He couldn't seem to talk for long before starting to pant. "Best workers. That's Digger and me. And Tracey Childs. He's gone now. Three best workers. Three brothers. Look after each other."

"D'you like working for the Ockwells?" asked the guvnor.

"Happy," said Willoughby. "Going back to my brother's soon. Go live there. Dad do it."

"Your father? That's good."

"No. Dad, he do it."

"Not your father?"

"Mr. Godwin, he's my dad. We're family now."

"Mr. Godwin's your father?" asked the guvnor, his head tilted in confusion.

"He died, he did. Mr. Godwin's my dad now. Dad, I call him."

"Ah, I see. You mean you just call him Dad."

"Call him."

"Did you grow up here in the village, Willoughby?"

"Kennington, with John. My father died. And ma."

"And what about Digger? Where's he from?"

"He don't talk."

"D'you like working here, Digger?" asked the guvnor. "You can nod or shake your head."

Digger held the guvnor's eye for a moment. His breath caught, like he was nervy. He looked away.

"We're best workers," said Willoughby, his smile broad again. "Dad say it. Best he's had. We're family now. And Mr. Walter, and Miss Rosanna. They love us. Like family. D'you know my brother, Mr. Arrowood? John. D'you know him?"

"I'm afraid I've never met your brother."

"I go live with him. Dad say. Dad knows John."

The fellow nodded. His tongue came out of his mouth and passed over his cracked lips.

"Willoughby, I want you to think hard now. Is there any reason Birdie's not happy? Any reason at all?"

"Happy," he said, but he didn't sound sure.

"Do they hurt her?"

"Hurt her."

"They do?"

Willoughby fell silent. He looked up at the crows, his mouth opening and closing.

"I'm happy," he said at last.

The guvnor looked at me and frowned. "Tell me, do they have any children up there?"

Willoughby shook his head and looked over at the field again.

"Got to go, sir. Get back to work."

Digger had already turned and was crossing the stream. Willoughby followed.

"D'you know where Mrs. Gillie is, Willoughby?"

"Seen her last night. Over larch field."

"Well, bye bye, lads," said the guvnor. "We'll call on you again."

"I hope so," said Willoughby. "I'll dream of that."

"What a pleasant boy," said the guvnor as they disappeared through the trees.

"Reckon he's a man, sir," I replied. "Twenty-five year at least."

"Well, I like him." He sighed, patted his belly, and looked around the camp. It was only then I spotted the crows, three of them, standing by a bush on the other side of the stream. They were pecking away at something hidden in the leaves. A bad feeling came over me. As I approached, the birds hopped away, watching me with their dead, black eyes. One had a string of flesh hanging out of its mouth. It was only when I stepped over the fallen tree I saw what they'd been picking at: it was Mrs. Gillie's cat, its innards pulled and scraped from its shell.

"Look, William," I said, pointing.

Its skull was beaten to a pulp.

Chapter Eleven

The same young fellow was behind the desk of the police station when we arrived. He went into the back room to fetch Sergeant Root, who listened to the guvnor's story with a frown, his dirty fingers tap-tapping on the desk.

"She's joined another camp," he said when the guvnor finished, his eyelids drooping like he was bored. "They don't stay in one place long."

"She's left her horse, her coat, her boots," answered the guvnor. "Her caravan door was wide open, Sergeant."

"They're easy like that. I appreciate you letting us know, sir."

Root turned back to the room.

"Sergeant!" said the guvnor sharply. "You must at least go down and have a look. She's an old woman, for pity's sake!"

"Tinkers disappear, that's what they do. And usually after

they've emptied a house of its silverware. You know they've been thieving from the building sites, I suppose?"

"There's been trouble, I tell you," said the guvnor. "The flowers she sells are scattered on the ground. And how d'you explain the cat? No animal could have done that."

"Killing a cat ain't a crime, Arrowood, just as not wanting to see your parents ain't neither."

The young copper nodded at this. His neck was pale and long out of his frayed uniform jacket. Root pulled out his watch.

"Half one, Thomas," he said to the lad. "I'm off for dinner. You hold the fort."

He took a thick, black overcoat from the peg and wrapped himself in it.

"Please, Sergeant," said the guvnor. Though he seemed to be asking a favour, his voice had a hard edge to it. "Have a look. That's all we ask."

The copper buttoned his coat, then pulled his gloves from his pocket. He took his helmet from another hook and jammed it on his head. Finally, he replied:

"Mr. Arrowood. I'm grateful you bringing this to me, but it's honest folk as pay our wages, not the likes of them. If she's had trouble it's from her own kind. They don't want to be like the rest of us. Don't want to be in with us." He opened the door and stepped out. "Her and her lot been staying round here when it suits them ever since I can remember. They've their own justice. Don't appreciate the police poking around their affairs."

"She might be in danger!" exclaimed the guvnor, making a grab for his arm.

"Get off me!" barked the copper, his face and neck come

over quite red. He prised the guvnor's fingers from his arm, stepped out into the cold street, and banged shut the door.

"Damn!" cursed the guvnor. He looked at the lad. "I don't suppose you'd come and have a look, son?"

"Wouldn't know what to look for, sir," said the boy. "I only started here last week. Just been stood here, really."

We had a sandwich in the pub, then called on Sprice-Hogg. The parson was on his way out. His overcoat was missing two buttons; his curly white hair fell from his broad-brimmed hat.

"We enjoyed ourselves the other night, didn't we, gentlemen?" he asked, his smile like a basket of chips.

"That we did, Bill," replied the guvnor.

"I visited Birdie yesterday. She really does want nothing to do with her parents. It seems they wanted rid of the poor girl."

"And she told you that, did she?"

"Rosanna told me, but Birdie was there. She wanted Rosanna and Walter with her. She lacks confidence in her speaking."

"Did Birdie tell you she wanted them with her, Bill?"

"Well, it was Walter went to fetch her. I believe she asked him."

The guvnor frowned for a very brief moment. "But we don't know if she really did want them there?"

"Ah, I see. You think like a detective. I'm afraid I don't, but I can't imagine they prevented her seeing me alone. I've known them for years. They wouldn't do that."

"Thank you, Bill," said the guvnor with a sigh. "Listen, we wanted to catch Godwin away from the farm. D'you know if he goes to the pub very often?"

"He'll be there tonight, I'm sure. A bit too fond of a drink, that man."

Sprice-Hogg had an appointment, but he suggested we wait in the parsonage until evening, and soon we were sat in his parlour warming our feet by the coals. Sarah brought us tea and the papers, and we spent a few hours in comfort.

"Idiots!" declared the guvnor, waking me from a doze.

"Sir?" I asked, my mind fugged from sleep. He was reading the *Illustrated Police News.*

"A whole page on the damn Swaffham Prior case. They've found another fool to blame. Some bombazine. Good Christ, the paper's all but tried and convicted him. And there were more speeches in Parliament defending the boys."

He turned the page furiously.

"Another article on criminal anthropology," he murmured. He studied it for a few moments. "D'you believe Lombroso's scheme? That you can identify a criminal from his face?"

"Maybe. I don't know."

"They've some pictures here." He studied the paper, then peered at me through his eyeglasses. Then he examined the paper again. "Well, look at you," he said at last. "Oh, dear, dear, Barnett. I believe you're one of these types. Bulging forehead; long lobes; eyes far apart. Dear, dear. It appears you're a degenerate, my friend."

"I haven't got a bulging forehead."

"It bulges, Barnett. Don't be vexed with me for saying it."

"My eyes are no more apart than yours."

He concentrated on lighting his pipe, but I could see he was trying to stop himself grinning. When it had a blaze, he said, "I didn't say I agree with Lombroso. You just match one of his types."

I said nothing. Truth was I sometimes suspected I was a degenerate. He didn't know some of the things I'd done back when I lived with my ma in one of the worst courts in Bermondsey. Down there you had to be a degenerate to get by, and I'd done a few things I wasn't proud of, things he'd never had to do coming from the background he did. It started when I was eleven, the very week we moved out of the spike to that dismal room with the wet floor in the most run-down building in the court. We could only get the room on account of me getting a job in the vinegar factory, but that very first Saturday three older lads jumped me on my way home and nicked my wages. The same happened the next Saturday, and the Saturday after, and soon ma and me were four weeks behind on the rent and run out of tick in the shop. That's how I went out late one night, when my ma was asleep, looking for them. I didn't know what I'd do until I found the youngest passed out from gin by the outhouse. Then I knew: I went back to the room where there was a can of paraffin, almost empty. A box of matches. I set him alight and watched him burn until he woke, screaming and twisting. That was the start of it all, of all the things I've tried to forget.

"What are you going to do, Norman?" he asked, bringing me back from my thoughts. "Now that Mrs. Barnett...well, now you're on your own?"

"Just keep on, William. What else?"

"I mean, are you going to stay in that room? Isn't it lonely?"

"For now," I said, hearing my voice lose its strength. "But we'll see. I just don't know."

He watched me for some time, then we fell back to reading our papers. My eyes scanned the words but now my head was so full of memories I couldn't take in any of the meaning. Soon the guvnor's paper fell on the floor. He was asleep, his chin fallen on his chest, snoring like a fattened Berkshire. I took the pipe from his mouth, put it on the mantel, and left the house.

★ ★ ★

The Ockwell graves were in a corner behind the church. I found the baby's marker quickly. The small stone was still fresh, a simple crucifix above the name: *Abigail Ockwell, 12 November–13 November, 1893. Beloved daughter.* There were no other recent graves, no other little Ockwells by her side. Her grandfather was buried there, 1891, his stone bigger than the child's, almost up to my waist, a space on it for his wife still clinging on to life from her sickbed. At the bottom of the stone, a fourth child: Henry Ockwell, died aged four, 1863. Around these two graves the grass was clipped short, but further back it grew longer. Here were the ancestors, the great- and great-great-grandparents, great uncles and aunts, the dates stretching back to the 1600s.

It was half three or so when I reached Mrs. Gillie's camp. The trees all around were still, even the shining black crows above were silent. There was old Tilly, packed in sacking, looking at me like I'd come to rescue her. There the remains of the fire, the kettle. There was little left of the cat but bone and bloody fur. I opened the caravan door and went in: her coat and boots were just as we left them. The red box that had been on the floor outside was now inside, the broken flowers gone. Someone had been here and tidied them away.

I walked around the copse again, checking under the rhododendron and holly, kicking through piles of dead leaves. I climbed over the fence into the fields and searched the ditches and hedges and paths all around.

She wasn't there.

In the cold twilight, I led the horse over to the stream, where I broke up the ice for her to drink. Then I tied the horse again and filled her nosebag. She looked at me like she wanted an explanation.

"No idea, mum," I said. She snorted and pushed her muzzle into my shoulder.

When I got back to the parsonage, night had fallen. Sprice-Hogg was back, and he and the guvnor sat in the parlour drinking port, a bowl of boiled eggs between them upon the couch, their stockinged feet stretched out to the fire.

"They've cleared away the evidence," said the guvnor when I'd told them about the red box. He rose, brushed the bits of eggshells from his crotch, and began to pace the painted floorboards. "But where is she, damn it! She could be lying injured somewhere. And it's our fault."

"Your fault?" asked Sprice-Hogg.

"People who've helped us with information have been hurt before," said the guvnor. His eyes fluttered. "She had a premonition. Why else would she talk about her own death the way she did? She must have worried we'd tell someone and we did. We told Root what she'd said."

"We don't know it had anything to do with her talking to us, sir," I said. "It could have been thieves, or someone come looking for her sons."

"It was right after she told us about her husband and the children!" barked the guvnor. "Someone doesn't want us investigating. Why else would they clear away the evidence of a struggle? Tell me, Bill, d'you know anything about three children dying at the farm in the last few years? Mrs. Gillie mentioned it. Only one was buried."

The parson shook his head. "Polly's poor child died about three years ago, God rest her soul, but there haven't been any other children up there for years. William, really, I wouldn't take what Mrs. Gillie says too seriously. A little too fond of the gin, that one."

"D'you really think Root let it out?" I asked.

"He'd only have to mention it in the pub," answered the guvnor. "Either that or we were being watched."

"I'll go down to her caravan in the morning," said Sprice-Hogg. "I'm sure she'll be back by then. If not, I'll try and persuade Sergeant Root to organize a search party."

"Thank you, Bill, that would help. One more question: d'you ever see the farm labourers?"

The parson shook his head. "They've never been to church, I'm afraid, and I don't think I've seen them in town either. They keep to themselves."

Sarah pushed open the door and began to lay the table for soup.

"How's your sister, Sarah?" asked the guvnor.

She shook her head. "Not long now, sir," she said, so low it was hard to make out. It must have distracted her, for as she lifted the soup tureen from the tray she stumbled. Sprice-Hogg let out a shriek as it fell on its side on the table, its lid off, the soup pouring out over the napkins and cutlery.

"Useless heifer!" he barked, raising his arm as if to strike her. Sarah flinched, covering her face, but he checked his hand, lowering it slowly to the table.

"I'm sorry, sir," she said, again and again, trying to mop it up with her pinafore. She began to cry.

"You are a singularly stupid girl," muttered the parson, sitting watching her from his chair. "Don't think I've forgotten about that blue streak last week either."

"It wasn't her fault, Bill," said the guvnor, kneeling to clear the floor with a napkin. "Her skirt snagged on a nail."

The parson glared at her; she kept her eyes down, sniffing, scraping the thick soup from the table onto the tray. Finally, she turned and hurried from the room.

"Have a seat, gentlemen," said Sprice-Hogg, the irritation still in his voice. "At least there's enough for half a bowl each."

When we'd eaten, the parson brought over the decanter of port. After two more glasses, the guvnor shook his head.

"We've work to do this evening, my friend."

The parson's face fell.

"Please, indulge me, William. It's an excellent barrel. And I'm eager to hear if you enjoyed my book."

"I haven't had a chance to read it yet, though I'm looking forward to it very much. But now we must go and see if we can find Godwin. I'm hoping he'll be more approachable with a few drinks in him."

"Just one more? For friendship sake?"

"We cannot."

"Of course," agreed the parson, putting the stopper back on the decanter. He looked at the ruby liquid as the flame from the lamp played on it and sighed. "We did enjoy ourselves the other night, didn't we?"

Chapter Twelve

The pub fell silent as we came through the door. It was packed out: the three old blokes who never seemed to leave were there, the fellow with the wizened grandmother, Skulky, Edgar, and twelve or thirteen others, all of them red-faced in the close heat of the fire. Under one of the tables slept a baby in a wooden box, a bottle of Dalby's Calmative in her hand; a girl of four or five smoked her ma's pipe by the fire. Even Root was standing at the counter, his eyes half-closed.

Godwin sat in the corner next to the lady he was having a shunt at before. He was the only one in that baking hot pub with his jacket on and was suffering from it: his brow was damp, his neck out in blotches. He scowled at us as we found a couple of empty seats by the door.

"Thought you said you chased these two off, Godwin!" cried the coalman, a great Welsh bloke with a glass eye that shone out of the grime of his ruined face.

"What'd you do, wave your flipper at them?" called one of the old blokes from across the room. A great peal of laughter arose.

Godwin looked away, taking a long draw of his tankard. He whispered to the woman, who nodded and patted his knee.

I got us some drinks. The landlady was half-cut: she moved about like she had two wooden legs and now and then let out a growling burp into the great hubbub of the drinkers. The old dog staggered over to me very slow, his legs shaking, his eye gunked like a smashed-up egg. I pushed him away towards the little girl, who made a grab for his fur.

We sat there in the noise, watching them all drink and shout, spending their wages, baked by the blazing fire and the heat of their chat.

"My Lord, this is a drunken pub," said the guvnor at last. I could tell he was uneasy by Skulky and Edgar being there, so sure was he that they'd been about to rob us the other night. They stood by the skittles table in their checked shirts and waistcoats. Their beards were wilder and bushier than any other, and it seemed to give them a level above the other men. Next to them was a short bloke in a moleskin jacket and a battered bowler: Weavil, I guessed. They were watching us, whispering.

Root staggered past, his helmet crooked, and fell out the door.

As I supped my porter, a cockle shell hit me in the brow and fell onto the floor; a laugh went up from the other side of the room where three butchers sat with a couple of women in aprons.

The guvnor went to the counter and ordered drinks for Godwin and his lover. He paid and came back to sit with me, while the landlady squeezed out from the counter and thumped a tankard and a mug on Godwin's table. She pointed at us and burbled something to him.

"I'll buy my own drinks, Arrowood," called Godwin across the room, pouring the beer into an ash bucket on the floor. His lady didn't want him to take the gin, but he got it off her and did the same. It was clear he'd had a few already.

Some of the punters turned to watch.

"I'm sorry if I've offended you, Mr. Ockwell," said the guvnor. "I haven't come to cause any trouble."

"You're a bloody nuisance, you two," snarled Godwin. "You sent the parson to examine us. You accused us to the police. You've been asking questions in here. You found nothing against us and now here you are again dogging me. So how about you just finish your drinks and leave? There's no one wants you in here."

"I wanted to apologize, that's all, sir," said the guvnor. "Let me buy you and your friend a meal, how about that?"

"Leave!" cried Godwin, slamming his fist on the table. Everyone there, even the baby, was watching him now. "Go on. Hook it!"

We didn't move. He glared at us for a moment, then hunched in towards the lady and they started to talk again. As they did, he glanced over at the other punters. His cap came off, his hand travelled over his bald head, the cap went back on again.

Soon the old men went back to their dominoes. The grandma and her bloke turned back to the fire and stared at the flames, their heads drooping. The coalman said something to the butchers. They laughed. The talk got louder, the men vying with each other to be heard. The two women in aprons, their arms around each other, looked on with broad smiles.

We watched it all for a while longer, the guvnor chewing his lip, thinking hard. Finally, he leant over.

"Look at him," he whispered. "How he hides that lazy arm in his jacket. The two of them sit on their own while all the rest are enjoying each other's company. See how he keeps looking over at them?"

He gazed across at Godwin again and thought on it. The lady had her hand on the farmer's knee as she talked. Godwin nodded and drank steadily, a sour look on his face.

"Doesn't he seem alone, Barnett?"

"He does, sir."

He leant closer to me and whispered: "I want you to try and make love to his lady-friend. Go and talk sweet to her. Provoke him."

"How's that going to help?"

Another cockle shell come through the air, bouncing off the guvnor's mug. He ignored it.

"He's feeling humiliated. We've diminished him in front of all these people by not leaving when he told us. The only way he'll talk is if we give him a chance to get back his pride. Act as if you're cowed by him, then skulk back over here. Let him dominate you; put on a show of it."

"Could make things worse, sir."

"Just do it, Barnett."

I drank my pint down in one go. As I did, Godwin got up and went to the counter with his tankard. I was straight over to his table, sliding up the bench next to the lady. She looked at me, her movements lazy. She was stewed, like everyone else in there.

"Hello, sugar," I said.

She nodded and took a swallow of gin. The green scarf

round her neck had fallen, showing the skin as rough and sooty. She smelled of pineapple.

"Fancy getting a bit of fresh air?" I said, putting my hand on hers. "Away from this lot?"

"Leave off, will you?" she said with a giggle. Her lips were painted a funny orange colour; a patch of red was on each cheek.

"What's your name?"

"Lisa," she said, soft enough so Godwin wouldn't hear.

"You ever been up to the city, Lisa?"

"A lady ain't safe up there, mate. Not till they catch old Jack."

I put my arm around her shoulder and whispered in her ear, "I'd keep you safe, Lisa. You can take your davy on it."

"Oh yeah? Don't think my fella'd like that."

I leant in and gave her a kiss on the cheek.

"Here!" she cried, pulling my arm off her shoulder and sliding away from me. I looked up to see Godwin standing over the table, a pint in one hand, the other hid inside his jacket.

"Get out of it," he hissed.

"We're just talking, mate."

"Yeah? Well you can go fuck yourself, *mate*. I said get out of it! Now!"

"All right." I stood up, holding my hands in the air and trying to look scared. "Steady on, mate. No harm done."

"Hook it!" he barked, getting braver the more afraid I acted.

As I tried to get past I nudged his arm, making some of his pint spill over his hand.

"Watch it," growled Edgar, getting up from his stool.

Godwin put the tankard down, slipped his good hand inside his overcoat, and brought out a truncheon, its tip black with lead.

"Hold on, mate," I said, backing away. "No need for—"

He belted me hard on my hand before I could finish. I cursed, the temper rising in me, and was about to swing at him when he took another shot, this time at my knee. I collapsed on the floor in the ash and the spilt beer, the pain running like a wave through my body. And just as my head hit the ground he landed his boot in my belly. A cheer rang out, drowning the groan as was forced out of me. I heaved; I couldn't catch my breath.

"Oi!" cried the landlady. "That's enough, Godwin Ockwell. You sit down."

"Give him another!" barked Skulky.

The old fellows playing dominoes cackled.

I was gasping and choking, bent in two on the stinking floor, clutching my belly as the good folk of Catford laughed. Godwin's dirty boots were no more than a foot from my face, and I feared I'd get one straight in the teeth next. I twisted away from him, trying to get up, wanting to wrench his dirty neck.

"What in damnation were you doing, Barnett!" cried the guvnor, only now stepping over to us. I tried to get to my feet, but my knee wasn't having any of it. And as I hunched there on all fours like a dog, the guvnor struck me hard on the back with his stick.

"That'll teach you, you damn fool!"

He turned to Ockwell and took his arm. "I'm so very sorry about that, Mr. Ockwell. And madam, I must apologize for my brute of an assistant. I'll dock him a day's pay for this, count on it. But you taught him a lesson there, sir. You certainly did."

"You did that, Godwin," said Skulky, raising his mug to him. "You got him there, matey."

I bit back my fury. There were noises of congratulation

around the pub. Godwin smiled and raised his tankard, taking a toast from the crowd. When the guvnor handed him his cap from the floor, he bent and gave Lisa a big kiss, right on her painted lips. She laughed as he pulled away. Then he stood up again, tall and magnificent, enjoying the appreciation of all those folk who liked nothing more than to see a stranger get walloped.

He gave a little bow.

Chapter Thirteen

I staggered over to my seat, angry as hell. My eyes were bleary, my knee throbbing like it was split open. I sat with my arms resting on my legs, trying to steady my breath and push back the nausea. Another cockle shell hit my head and fell by my feet. Another round of laughter from over by the fire.

"As an apology, sir, direct from Pall Mall," said the guvnor, handing Godwin a cigar. He struck a match and lit it up. "My man's disgustingly drunk. You're an honourable gent, I can see that. Don't like to see a lady put upon and neither do I. You must let me buy you a drink for your trouble."

"I don't suppose it'd do any harm," said Godwin, still flushed with his triumph. "Brandy for me, gin for Lisa here."

"Madam landlady," said the guvnor, turning to the counter. "Brandy and gin for Mr. Ockwell and the lady. And brandy for me."

Without waiting to be invited, the guvnor pulled over a stool. I listened as he complimented Godwin on his thrashing skills, the lady on her grace. He admired the truncheon, feeling the weight of its lead tip. They drank. The air filled with the smell of their good cigars.

The little girl came over and stood by me, a sweet, filthy thing no more than three foot high in a dress made from a blanket. She put her hand on my knee.

"What in damnation were you doing, mister?" she asked.

I pulled away, grunting with pain.

She put her hand on my other leg. "He beat you, mister, didn't he? Ma says you ain't no good at fighting."

She twisted to and fro, her little hand on my knee. I pulled out a penny.

"I'll give you this if you let me be, darling."

She made a grab for the coin then skipped over to show her ma.

When I felt up to it, I limped outside to the pisser. It wasn't anything more than a brick ledge in front of a hole with a bitter smell coming out of it. I'd just let loose when I heard the door open and footsteps come up quick behind me. It was Skulky and Edgar, staggering and stinking, and before I even had time to shove the old man back in my britches they took my arms and wrenched them up my back. I struggled but it was no use: they had me held tight, and with each jerk my shoulder cried with pain.

They shoved me to my knees on the wet floor, my forehead against Skulky's dirty gaiters.

"Fuck off," I growled.

"Ain't so big now, are you, mate?" asked Skulky, twisting my arm hard. I gasped. "Think you can come down here from

London lording it over us, do you? Think just 'cos you're big you can push your weight around?"

"Bloody yokels."

Edgar's boot landed hard in my side, so hard I jumped an inch off the floor, and just as I was landing Skulky took my hair and smashed my head against the wall. Then, without a word, they let go of me and went back to the pub.

I got to my feet, my body wracked with great shivers. For some time I leant against the mouldy wall, trying to steady myself. Slowly the shivers calmed, but now I had more pains than I wanted to think about. I went back into the pub and ordered a big mug of hot brandy.

"You all right, mister?" asked the landlady, taking a lug of something from a wooden jug.

"Been better, I reckon."

"Got a bit of blood on you. Here, have a drink of this. It'll put the pain to sleep."

It was a vial of chlorodyne. I took a good swallow, then a couple more and passed it back. Edgar and Skulky were playing skittles, laughing, drinking. I really wanted to get the guvnor out of that pub before anything else happened but I knew he wouldn't come: he was in the middle of something. He was working on Godwin.

I turned to the table and held out my hand to the bloke.

"No hard feelings, mate," I said. "You taught me a lesson there, I reckon."

Godwin looked at my hand for just long enough to rile me up more, then took it. I thought about making a grab for his weakend arm and twisting it right off his shoulder.

"More drinks, Barnett," said the guvnor, handing me a shilling. "And oysters!"

When I was back with the drinks, he was saying: "You and

your family don't deserve all this trouble, I can see that now, sir, so I've decided to tell the Barclays I can't continue with their case. I hope you'll pass on my apologies."

Godwin's shoulders fell; a smile almost came to his broad chin. He wiped his hands on his corduroy britches. "Glad to hear it, Mr. Arrowood. You're an honest man."

Someone started to play an accordion over by the fire. The women began to sing. The guvnor tossed an oyster into his wet gob and pushed the bowl over.

"I knew you'd understand, sir," he said, his voice rising over the song. "In this line of work there's always a risk of upsetting good people like your family. You never know if a case is genuine until you investigate, that's the trouble. It's an aspect of my job I'll never get used to. I haven't always been a private agent, you know. I used to be a man of commerce, but…well, I had a little poor fortune and here I am. Yes, a little…poor…"

The guvnor fixed his eyes on Godwin, a queer smile on his face. He shuddered. He sighed. Godwin watched him, waiting for the end of the sentence. It never came.

"What happened?" asked Godwin at last.

"It's of no matter. I took a risk on a business venture but was played false by a man I trusted. I've no regrets. Business is about risk. Life is about risk."

Godwin nodded. He took an oyster with his strong hand, the weak one lying cupped upon his knee, hidden by the table.

"I'm not ashamed to admit it," the guvnor went on, his face serious. "The country's built on the backs of the thousands of men and women prepared to fail in pursuit of something better. Prepared to suffer the criticism, even the despair of their family. That's my philosophy, sir, and you can hang me if you like. Without the risk-takers where would we be? Back in the dark ages, that's where."

"He's a risk-taker, is Godwin," said Lisa. Her eyes were shiny with gin, her chin with oyster juice.

"Are you, sir?" asked the guvnor. "I had a feeling."

"And I've suffered for it in just the way you say," said Godwin. "Had a patent for a farming machine, a good one too."

"I knew it! A fellow adventurer!"

"He's an adventurer and all," said Lisa with a burp.

"Would've made a lot of money but for some northern machine that came along at the last minute," Godwin went on. "If it wasn't for that we'd be in clover."

"I'm sorry to hear it," murmured the guvnor, shaking his head. "You cannot control Providence, that's the truth, my friend."

The chlorodyne was taking its effect: my stomach was settled, the pain in my knee fading. My left hand was starting to swell, but I was getting numb. I didn't feel half bad. I looked around the pub: Skulky and Weavil were sat next to each other, staring at me, their moustaches wet with beer and a look of pickled hate in their eyes. It seemed like there was more to come from them tonight, but I just couldn't seem to care at that moment.

"You have another plan, I'll wager," said the guvnor.

"Soft fruits," said Godwin.

"Soft fruits!" cried the guvnor. "Brilliant!"

"Strawberries, raspberries." Godwin raised his lazy arm in a sweep, his slur getting worse with each sip. "That's the way forward. Convert it all over. Glass houses for tomatoes. Bottling plant. That'll get the old place back to profit."

Lisa jumped up and pushed her way past the counter to the outhouse.

"And you'll make a success of it, I'm sure," declared the guvnor. He leant in. "Is your wife well? She seems a little unsteady on her feet."

"She's not my wife," answered Godwin, giving us the wink.

"Oh my!" laughed the guvnor, patting him on the hand. "Lord, but you're a lucky man, Mr. Ockwell. I must say, a very lucky man. She's a beauty."

"She does right by me." Godwin swallowed the last oyster and finished his drink. The guvnor nudged me; I got up and ordered more. The song ended. The accordion player began to play 'My Dear Old Dutch.' The punters cheered.

"Your wife accepts it?" asked the guvnor.

"My wife?" said Godwin with a sneer. He paused to wipe a bit of drool from the weak side of his mouth. "That woman's no good to me. No use to any man, crying at the least little thing."

"Emotional?" asked the guvnor. "Dear, dear."

"She wasn't so bad at the start, I'll give her that. Ever since the little one died she won't let me near."

"I'm sorry," said the guvnor in his kindest voice. "You lost a child?"

"A day old. Couldn't breathe proper from the moment she was born."

"Ah. That's awful, my friend."

"Yes." Godwin's head drooped on his chest, his eyes brimming over with brandy and sorrow. He scratched his armpit suddenly. He wiped his nose, put the tankard to his lips, and swallowed half of it in one draught. Then he took a big lug of the brandy.

A cockle shell hit my ear, then another. The song got louder.

"It was the doctor advised me to take a lover," said Godwin, his voice hushed. "For my health. When the seed goes bad inside, that's when the problems start."

"Is that what happened to your arm?" asked the guvnor. "The bad seed?"

"Apoplexy." He took his weak hand and held it on his belly. "It just came on one night out of nowhere. My leg lost its power, just like that. The voice went too—that's why I sound as I've taken a few drinks."

"My uncle had the same," said the guvnor. "He wore an electric girdle."

"Nothing helps. I've tried everything."

The door opened and Lisa came back, clutching onto the wall as she walked.

"You ill, Lisa?" asked Godwin.

"I'm righteous," she said, lowering herself to the bench. Her eyes were blurred like she'd been crying, and there was a bit of sick in her long curls. She took another sip of her gin. "Lord, look at all those buttons missing from your waistcoat," she said, running her finger down Godwin's front.

"Providence hasn't favoured you, Mr. Ockwell," declared the guvnor.

"You're right, there, Mr. Arrowood. And now we hear our dairy girl's got the fever and doesn't look like recovering. You try and find a girl wants to work for farm wages so near to London."

"Can I ask you one last question about the case, my friend?" asked the guvnor. "Just to help me understand. Why won't Birdie talk to her parents?"

"They're climbers, those two," said Godwin. As he spoke, he picked up an oyster shell and started scraping the grime from the edge of the table with it. "Trying to be more respectable than they are. Birdie was an embarrassment. They were desperate to get rid of her and she knew it. That's why she won't have anything to do with them now."

"But why would they hire us?"

"I suppose there's something they aren't telling you. They can't be trusted, Mr. Arrowood. They misled us about her. We thought she was just quiet, but she's slower than Walter. We thought she'd be able to take charge of him." He shook his head. "We've grown to love our sweet Birdie since she arrived, even with her weaknesses, but she couldn't take charge of a spoon."

"Listen, my friend, could I ask you a favour? We're not wealthy men and the Barclays won't pay us until we've spoken to Birdie. All we need is five minutes with her. Please, sir. Just to hear it from her own mouth."

"I'd allow it if I could, but we've given our word we'd protect her from her parents and she thinks you've come to take her away. She sees us as sanctuary. I like you, Mr. Arrowood, but I just cannot break my word to her."

Lisa made a grab for Godwin's arm. "I got to go," she mumbled, getting up, stumbling as she got out from behind the table.

"You sick?" he asked.

She nodded, her eyes shut. "I got to go. Help me, darling."

Godwin drained his mug and stood, shaking his head. He picked up her coat, her scarf. He pulled on his gloves, swaying as he did.

"Well, goodnight, gentlemen. Glad we sorted this out."

And with that he helped Lisa out of the pub.

As we stood to leave, a queer calm fell over the place. Sensing trouble, I hurried the guvnor on with his coat, then found my own. When I looked up again, Edgar was stepping forward, laying his arm across Arrowood's shoulders. His cap was far back on his shiny, wet head, his eyes hard.

"You like poking around in people's business, do you, matey?" he growled. His battered face was flushed, drops of sweat glistering in his bushy beard.

"No, my friend," said the guvnor, trying to step away. "We've made our peace with Mr. Ockwell. All's well now."

Edgar held him fast.

One of the butchers called "Out!", then the coalman, then another bloke, and soon they all began to chant, banging their fists on the tables and benches. "Out! Out! Out! Out!"

"Think you can come down from London and study us like we was beasts?" Edgar barked over the noise.

"You sit down and leave him alone, Edgar Winter!" called the landlady.

The guvnor tried to pull free, but Skulky stood right behind him. Weavil came up on his other side. He was doing his best to be calm, but I could see his fear plain as day. All around the chanting was getting louder, filling the pub like a spiteful engine.

"Out! Out! Out!"

Edgar gave him a shove. He fell back onto Skulky, who gave him a shove back to his brother.

"Like we was beasts," hissed Edgar, pushing him back at Skulky again.

I grabbed the guvnor's danders and pulled hard, sending him flying towards the door. Before the blokes could react, I had us both out onto the street.

It was real dark out there, darker than it ever was back in town, and we hobbled and stumbled along past the tramlines, all the time turning back to see if they were coming after us. Only when we reached the almshouses did we slow to a walk.

A fox darted out of a bush and the guvnor started, clutching my arm. He was feared all right.

We got the last train home, and as we rolled towards London in the dark, cold night, I thought about old Tilly out there in the trees. I hoped she wasn't alone. I hoped she wasn't as alone as I'd be when I got home tonight in that room as was colder and darker than ever it was when Mrs. B was alive. Seemed like I had more in common with that old nag than with anyone else in that hateful suburb.

I looked at the guvnor, deep in thought, and felt a sudden rage. In a flash I'd snatched the walking stick from his hand and jabbed the end hard in his stomach. He gasped, his hand scrabbling to pull it away, but I only pushed harder, pinning him back against the seat like a beetle to a card, burying the tip right in the folds of cloth and belly fat, swollen from porter and oysters and puddings.

"Barnett!" he cried, his eyes watering. "Stop!"

"Don't you ever hit me again," I said.

I held him there for a minute or so, staring him in the face as he struggled to free himself. Then I pulled the stick away and snapped it over my knee.

Chapter Fourteen

The fog was thick when we arrived at Saville Place next morning. People in their Sunday best came and went like phantoms, swallowed by the freezing brown cloud. The guvnor held my arm as we plodded down towards the Barclays' house, afraid he'd slip on the icy cobbles. I wasn't too steady myself—my knee'd swelled up overnight and wasn't bending like it should. I had a pain in my head, a great bruise below my ribs from Skulky's boot, and if that wasn't enough my wretched hand was almost out of action.

As we neared the house, we could hear the chords of the piano inside, and then Mrs. Barclay singing. It was 'My Dear Old Dutch,' the same jaunty little song we'd heard in the pub the night before, but the way she sang it was sad, sad as a song of fishermen lost on the sea. Ignoring the guvnor's tug on my sleeve, I rapped on the door.

"You've a beautiful voice, madam, if I may say," he told her as she led us into the parlour.

"Singing's everything to me." Her fingers rose to touch the three moles below her eye; she smiled modestly. "My heart. My world."

"I also enjoy singing," confessed the guvnor. "I take lessons."

I looked at him in surprise.

"Then we must sing together one day, Mr. Arrowood," she said, her eyes a-twinkle.

"I'd enjoy that very much, Mrs. Barclay. Very much indeed."

The fire was unlit, and it was no warmer inside than out: she wore layers of black woollen shawls beneath her apron.

"I'm afraid my husband's helping at church today," she told us. The parlour was more roomy without him there: even the furniture seemed to have a bit more space that day. "But Mr. Tasker says he cannot help. I thought the family would feel some duty, but no. Twenty-two years service counts for nothing."

"We must think of something else, then. Now, Mrs. Barclay, last night we were able to talk to Godwin."

"What did he say?"

He breathed in deep and shook his head to warn her she wouldn't like it. "He said you were quite desperate to get rid of Birdie, that you hid the nature of her condition from them, and that you found her an embarrassment."

"That's a lie, sir." She spoke softly, with a grace her husband didn't come near. "I own it was sometimes hard to raise her, but we always saw her as a blessing, and I've been broken-hearted for missing her. Birdie wanted marriage more than anything. She knew her deficiencies, but she thought being a wife meant she was a normal lady. She took a fancy to a baker before Walter, and the curate before that. We hid nothing from them. They'd met her. They knew about her. Anyway, Walter himself has a bit of a weak mind."

"But it doesn't make sense, madam."

"What doesn't make sense?"

"What reason would they have to keep Birdie from you?"

"I don't know!" she snapped. In that moment, her face was transformed. Her brow fell low, her eyes came over black as pitch, and I felt a sense of unease that I couldn't fathom. "You've made no progress at all, have you? If it was Sherlock Holmes he'd have brought her back by now."

"Sherlock Holmes wouldn't take your case," answered the guvnor. "If you were missing a prize-winning racehorse, perhaps. If you'd lost a naval treaty, I'm sure. But not a case like yours, and certainly not for twenty shillings a day. You've read of the Saltire case, I presume? Well did you know he dropped two other cases when that came along? And why? I'll tell you why. Because there was a six-thousand-pound reward to recover that little aristocrat."

"That's unfair! Sherlock Holmes is always ready to help a woman in distress."

"He's what?"

"Always ready to help women in distress."

"You're playing with me, Mrs. Barclay."

"He's forever helping women, sir, and taking no payment for it. There are few agents a woman can approach who'll take her case seriously, but Holmes is one. You remember the Milverton case? And Miss Morstan?"

"I'm afraid women are never entirely to be trusted, Mrs. Barclay," said the guvnor, shaking his head.

"I beg your pardon?"

"Women are never entirely to be trusted, I'm sure you agree."

"Are you trying to insult me?"

"Not my words, madam. Sherlock Holmes, and in the very case you've just mentioned." The guvnor sat back on the little sofa, spreading his hands wide. "Of course, anybody might say something out of character. Perhaps he had a little fit? Perhaps he was trying to provoke. It might be better to examine his actions, then. In *The Case of Identity* for example—d'you know it?"

"I read it a few years back."

"Miss Sutherland comes to Holmes to help find her fiancé, a Mr. Hosmer Angel, if you remember. Angel made her pledge she'd wait for him if anything happened, then just before their wedding he disappeared and never came back."

"Yes. Holmes discovers it was her stepfather in disguise."

"Mr. Windibank, yes. He wanted to make sure she didn't get married else she'd leave home and he'd lose the inheritance she was due."

"But that proves my argument," she said. "Sherlock Holmes solved the case very quick."

"Precisely!" barked the guvnor, nodding his head. He took out his red belcher and blew his nose loudly into it.

"Yes, precisely," she agreed, placing her hands on her lap modestly.

"Precisely!"

"Yes," she said, a little confusion showing in her Spanish face.

"Precisely *the opposite*!" the guvnor cried. His chest was heaving; white spit appeared in the corners of his mouth; he glared at her with his bulging, raddled eyes. "You've forgotten the ending, Mrs. Barclay. He discovers the truth yet decides not to tell Miss Sutherland! He leaves her to wile away her days in her parents' house, waiting for a fiancé who doesn't exist. How cruel! How abominable! And why?" His fist, closed over his filthy belcher, was waving in the air, his face like a blood sausage. "Why does he utterly betray her? Because he says Miss Sutherland will never believe him. And why does he think this? Because she's a woman, Mrs. Barclay. Because, and I quote him, because *'There is danger for him who taketh the tiger cub, and danger also for whoso snatches a delusion from a woman'*!"

He finished by leaning over to her and flicking his belcher at her knee. Mrs. Barclay's brow furrowed in confusion. The guvnor adjusted himself on the sofa.

"You've quite a memory for his cases," she said, edging out of reach of another attack of the belcher. "I not so."

"I'm sorry for my emotions, madam. It irks me to remember how he treated that poor young woman." He removed his spectacles and cleaned them, then stuffed his damned belcher in his pocket. "There's something else I must ask you. In the coffee shop you passed a note to Miss Ockwell."

Here he left a silence.

"Yes," she said at last. "My husband has a habit of making things more difficult. I prepared a note in case things went wrong. It only asked if she'd meet me, alone. Women can sometimes do things that men cannot."

The guvnor grunted. "You sound like my sister, Mrs. Barclay. Tell me, how did you know Miss Ockwell would be there?"

"She rules the family."

He pushed himself to his feet and put on his bowler. He collected his stick. Mrs. Barclay also rose.

"Why did you deceive us about how long you've lived here?" he asked as he buttoned his coat.

She frowned.

"That was my husband's idea," she said. "He was promoted a few months before, that's how we've been able to afford our own house. He thought if we told you, you'd raise your fees."

He blinked.

"You think we're swindlers, Mrs. Barclay?"

"Not I, sir. My husband's suspicious of everyone."

He sighed, his eyes shining with disappointment.

"Where did you live before?" he asked.

Her eyes travelled quick to the door then swept the mantel, as if she couldn't decide if she should tell us.

"Paces Walk," she said at last.

He nodded, then pointed at the wall. "What's happened to your nice painting of the ship? I was hoping to see it again."

"Mr. Barclay's moved it upstairs. He's always fiddling with things."

She led us through to the front door, pausing as she put her hand on the latch. "You will keep trying, won't you?" she asked. She looked at me for the first time since we entered the house, and there was something proud and suffering in her noble Spanish face as made me want to help her even more.

"We will, ma'am," I answered.

Finally, when we stepped back into the street, she gave us her smile, then quickly shut the door. As we made our way back down the icy cobbles of Saville Place, I felt uncommonly sad to think of her alone in that cold house in the thick London fog.

Chapter Fifteen

My wounds were bothering me, so I went off to find an apothecary while the guvnor returned home. When I'd got myself dosed up with Black Drop, I walked down past Bethlem to the Elephant and Castle. As I approached Lewis's, a girl of fifteen or sixteen stepped out of the house. She wore an old, worn coat, clean and well-patched. Her hair was tucked up neat under her bonnet, and her face was pockmarked all over. She glanced at me as she passed on the paving, her eyes red from tears.

Ettie and the guvnor were in the parlour.

"That was Ida Gillie who just left," he said. "Mrs. Gillie's granddaughter."

"She goes down to Catford every fourth Sunday to visit," added Ettie from her chair. "She's in service in Newmarket. She went this morning but Mrs. Gillie wasn't there. Ida says she's never missed a visit before."

"She found the coat and boots in the caravan. Mrs. Gillie doesn't have another pair."

He looked at me in silence, breathing heavy. We both knew for sure now that something had happened to the old woman. Two times before good people had been killed for helping us. We swore we'd never let it happen again.

"She tried Root but had the same answer as us," said the guvnor. "Sprice-Hogg told her we were looking into it, so she came to ask our help."

"What about Mrs. Gillie's sons?" I asked.

"All dead. Ida's her only kin."

"But she said her boys were coming in spring."

He nodded. "There's only little Ida. I promised we'd help."

"Of course."

He sat heavily on his chair by the fire, a great misery on his swollen, rutted face. He opened his mouth to speak, then shook his head and shut it again.

"I'll go down this afternoon," I said.

We sat there for many minutes in silence. The guvnor was suffering, I could see it, he was turning himself inside out with guilt. He knew he'd made a mistake in telling the copper we'd been talking to her. I knew it soon as he did it, but Root had riled him up. Though understanding emotions in others was a great strength of his, he hadn't a lot of control of his own when it came to the Old Bill, and even less when they started up shouting at him. That was supposed to be one of my jobs.

Finally, he got up and waddled off to the outhouse.

"Did you find out anything about the three children?" asked Ettie. I sat at one end of the sofa, she at the other.

"The parson said there was only one."

She nodded. "There's a woman at Cutlers Court, no more

than three and twenty years. She's had six children and all but one dead before their first birthday. She just carries on."

Her eyes tightened as she looked at me, and it felt like that story touched something in her own life, something I'd maybe never know. I had an urge to take her hand and give her a little comfort. I think she saw it in my face, as her eyes fell to her lap. It was some moments before she spoke again.

"What happened to your hand, Norman?" she asked.

"It's nothing. Godwin decided to clump me last night."

"Let me see it."

She knelt by the fire and took my hand, peering at it in the light of the oil lamp. Though her fingers were cold, being touched by her seemed the first real warmth I'd felt in a while.

"Move your fingers."

I did as she asked.

"That bone might be fractured. Is it sore?"

"It's only a bruise."

"I'm going to bandage it."

Ettie fetched a cloth from the kitchen and started to wrap my hand. She knew what she was doing: she worked as a nurse before coming to live with the guvnor six month before. I looked down on the top of her head as she bound me, at the spin of chestnut hair on her crown and the blue-white skin beneath. A smell of lavender soap rose from her warm head. She began to hum. Then, like she was in a dream, she stopped wrapping and with her sharp fingernail started picking out the muck as had collected under the nail of my thumb. I watched her do it, a bit shamefaced to be cleaned that way. Mrs. B had never done something like that to me, never cleaned me once and I didn't know what to think. I wondered if maybe it was something the nurses did overseas. She moved on to my finger, her sharp nail stabbing me as she tried to scoop out the dirt, our nails clicking with each bit she cleared. I didn't like the feeling at all but I didn't want to stop her somehow. Then she seemed to notice what she was doing and gave a little shiver. She fastened the bandage, rose and sat on the couch, a little further from the arm where she usually sat, a little nearer me. She noticed my grime under her own fingernail now, and as she began to pick it out and flick it on the carpet, I told her what had been happening. The guvnor came back into the parlour while I spoke, a newspaper under his arm.

"I only promised Godwin to give up the case because I thought I could win five minutes with Birdie," he said, falling onto his chair and scratching his gnarly head furiously. "I used all the tricks I could think of. We won his trust but we didn't get the meeting, damn it. How's he going to react when he finds out we're still on the case?"

"Is it possible the Ockwells are telling the truth?" asked Ettie.

"Birdie's unhappy. That we know. The two times we visited she tried to attract our attention, first with a feather, and then with that picture. I just don't know what she meant to say."

"Mrs. Barclay did try to make peace with Rosanna," said Ettie. "That must mean something."

"It speaks of good intentions. She has a very fine voice. We're going to sing together."

"You don't sing, William."

"I enjoy singing, you know that. I'm taking lessons."

"What?" she laughed. "No, you aren't!"

"I had one only yesterday."

"Lord save us!" She looked at me, her grey eyes shining with mischief. I tried to keep my smile hidden.

"My instructor says I show great promise," he said stiffly. "He says my tenor's like the boom of a wave on a hull."

"A wave on a hull? That cannot be good."

He began to unlace his shoes. "You know nothing about singing, Ettie."

"I'm sure you're right," she replied. She gazed into the fire, a look of contentment upon her face. She was so close beside me on the couch I could just feel her heat. One of the clocks chimed.

"What news from the builders?" she asked.

"Oh, Ettie, please don't go on so. I'll see them on Monday."

I knew she wanted to say more, but she stopped herself.

"Agh!" cried the guvnor as he freed his feet from Lewis's shoes. "These damn things are hell for my gout. Sprice-Hogg gave me some Blair's pills to try, did I say? They don't seem to do anything."

"What are you going to do now you've told Godwin you're not going to be investigating anymore?" asked Ettie.

"I'm trying to decide. But we have two cases now, and Mrs. Gillie's might be the most serious."

"Let me try and speak to Birdie. They don't know me."

"No, Ettie. This is no job for a woman."

"Well it's clearly no job for a man, is it!" she exclaimed, her back straightening in the stiff chair. "I was in the war in Afghanistan, unless you'd forgotten. And don't the police use women investigators?"

"The family are suspicious. They know they're being watched."

"I could at least try, William. What harm could it do?"

The guvnor rose and paced before the fire. He pulled out his belcher and rubbed his spectacles. He lit his pipe. He went to the window. Ettie's eyes followed him as he moved back and forth, muttering to himself. As he pondered, Lewis returned home and poked his head through the door. His face was pale and acned, his long, black overcoat buttoned to his knees. He wished us good day, then disappeared up the stairs for his afternoon nap.

The guvnor paced and puffed some more.

"The Ockwells are looking for a new dairymaid," he said at last. "Their woman's ill. But it might be dangerous, Ettie. If they're really keeping Birdie, that is. I just don't know. You could knock at the farm asking for work, I suppose. Say you're destitute. Have some hard luck story."

"I could!" Ettie exclaimed, clapping. "That would get me inside."

She was thrilled: I'd never seen such a smile on her face.

"But not with that voice, Ettie," I said. "Can you do something more common?"

"Can you do something more common?" she repeated, trying on a Cockney accent.

The guvnor and I both laughed. It sounded more like the jabber of a Battersea Park duck than a person. Ettie coloured up, but soon she was laughing too.

"Not very good?" she asked at last.

"Just awful," I said. "Here. Listen to me when I say it."

I did it again in my own dear Bermondsey tongue. She tried again, but it was worse. Again and again we tried. She never got close.

"You're too refined," I said. "You'll never get it."

"They won't believe you," said the guvnor.

"If only I could speak like you, Norman. You've got two voices. How do you manage it?"

"I learnt to switch when I worked in the law courts. Took me a few years, though, and I don't pretend you can't hear the Bermondsey in me still."

"What if she's mute?" suggested the guvnor, his elbow

upon the mantel. "Like that chap Digger? He seems to get on without talking."

"Yes!" cried Ettie. "I'll be mute."

"They might prefer a mute worker," said the guvnor. "Easier, I should think. Sometimes I wish old Norman was mute."

"William!" cried Ettie.

He laughed.

"You can take Neddy," he went on. "That'll make the story better. You're destitute with a child, starving hungry, nowhere to go. They'll know they can get you cheap. He can do the talking for you."

"But won't it be dangerous for the boy?"

The guvnor thought about it.

"Just keep out of Walter's way. Work there for a day or two, that's all you'll need. Just enough to see if Birdie's happy, how Walter treats her. Look for any evidence of violence. Even better if they'll take on Neddy for a few pennies. You can find digs in the village."

"I'll buy some old clothes this afternoon," said Ettie eagerly. "I'll go to Petticoat Lane."

"Make sure they're dirty," I said.

"And don't go poking about the house," said the guvnor. "Stick to your duties and keep that tongue of yours under control. Make sure you don't talk to Birdie unless you're sure she needs help."

"I shan't."

"What about the mission? Aren't you expected there?"

"Our mission is to rescue young women. The mission's everywhere."

"You must be careful, Ettie. This isn't a game. Stay out of Walter's way. He's got a short fuse and a violent nature. It might be a coincidence that Mrs. Gillie's disappeared after giving us information, but I fear it isn't."

"If there's a hint of danger I'll get out," she said.

"Are you sure about this, Ettie?" I asked.

"I can't see how else you're going to get to the bottom of it all. If she's really being kept there, the Lord would want me to do it."

I don't think I'd ever seen her so excited. Her neck rose high above her lace collar; her cheeks were rosy; her eyes sparkled. She looked at me with great confidence, tucking a few stray hairs into her chestnut bun. I'd noticed a couple of greys there lately, and it seemed to me they suited her well. She was a fine woman, all right.

I buttoned my coat to leave. "I'd better get off and check on the camp."

Ettie spoke swiftly, as if it pained her: "William told me about your wife, Norman."

"Ah," I said.

"I'm so sorry." She took my good hand and squeezed it. I clung on, my eyes cast down, something inside me preventing me letting go. "I wish I'd met her," she said.

The fire hissed. The three clocks upon the mantel ticked.

"I'm sorry for not telling you," I said when I'd collected myself.

"Don't apologize, Norman. I knew there was something wrong last summer. I just thought you didn't want me to ask."

Those words, and the feeling that she'd seen into me so true, made the tears rise up in me again. I shook my head and fought them back down. So stupid. It had been this way for months and still this idiot sadness came back from nowhere. At last I released her hand. She pulled me to her, her blouse against my winter coat, and gave me a quick, strong hug. I sniffed, wiping my nose, and turned to the door.

"I'll wait here you," said the guvnor. "Are you at a meeting tonight, Ettie?"

"Isaiah's calling. Didn't you remember? You must be here."

"Not again!" he groaned. "He was only here at Christmas."

"Well, he's coming again," she said sharply.

I slipped out to the corridor and let myself out.

Chapter Sixteen

It was raining by the time I got to the copse. The dark leaves on the ground were wet, the ash in the fire a milky paste. All else was just as we'd left it the day before. I fed Tilly the last of the oats and had a look in the caravan. It was cold and dark: a steady drip fell from the roof onto the thick rug. I found Mrs. Gillie's will in the black jar and read it in case there was a message for us. There wasn't: she'd left her horse to Willoughby, the rest of her possessions to Ida. I searched the trees again, remembering her wrinkled face, how she teased the guvnor, that awful black tooth.

I untethered the horse and we plodded up to the village, our breath in the wet air, past the almshouses, the pub, the building sites. I tied her to the parsonage gate and called on Sprice-Hogg. He told me he'd had no luck persuading Root to investigate, but he agreed to find old Tilly a home till we knew what had happened to Mrs. Gillie. I left her in the garden and the rain, cold and alone, a miserable look on her long face.

When I told the guvnor that Root still wouldn't investigate, he shook his head.

"They need to do a proper search of the area and check if anyone's seen her. It's too much for us. Petleigh'll be along later. I'll see if he can try and persuade them."

We were silent for some time. He stared into the fire, his brow lined with worry.

"Will you stay for supper?" he asked at last, his voice low and colourless. "You know how our favourite inspector likes you."

"I've got something on."

"At least have a cup of tea," said Lewis from his favourite chair by the fire. "There's a new charwoman in the back. She'll get you one."

"Mary Ann's ill again?" I asked.

"Who knows?" he muttered.

Mary Ann had been irregular since Lewis offered to marry her before Christmas, something the guvnor'd persuaded him was a good idea. Ettie warned him against it, and I wasn't too surprised when she turned him down. Lewis lost an arm when he was younger and tried to make up for it by neglecting just about everything else about his body. There wasn't even a looking-glass in his house. His stringy hair fell a long ways over his collar, his clothes didn't see a mangle as much as they rightly should, and, though he loved to eat more than anything else in the world, his hand was always dark with oil and grease. Mary Ann, who was none too particular herself, might have seen past this, but Lewis was a Jew, and Mary Ann was a bigot.

I went through to the kitchen, where a woman was on her knees on the floor adding coal to the range. She was a poorer sort than Mary Ann, with old black boots tied with rough string, a skirt too short for the yellowed petticoats, a couple of thick, threadbare coats held shut with a bit of old cord. Even through the smell of coal there was a bitter odour coming off her. Little Neddy sat upon a stool by the back door, playing with the bellows.

"Hello, Mr. Barnett," he cried. He held a bit of fruit cake in his hand.

"Hello, mate. I hear you're doing a little job for us."

"Yes, sir." His face was serious. Neddy loved to work for the guvnor—he never knew his old man, and Arrowood was as close to an uncle as the boy had. "Got to pretend Miss Arrowood's me ma."

The woman stood and turned to me.

"Ettie!" I cried in surprise.

She grinned.

"How do you like me, Norman?"

"You stink a bit, but otherwise I like you very well."

"My little lady's maid dressed me."

"I ain't a lady's maid," protested Neddy, his mouth full of cake. He picked the last of the crumbs from the green waistcoat he wore over his filthy shirt. As long as he kept growing, that waistcoat wouldn't fit him too bad in a few years, I reckoned.

Ettie's hair was cut uneven across her brow and held upon her head with old wooden hair-combs that didn't manage to keep it all in. Her neck was grimy, her hands dirty black. She held them up for me.

"He rubbed them in mud and coal dust. What do you think? Will I fool them?"

"That and more," I said. "You really will have to keep your mouth shut, though. Your teeth are too good."

"You wouldn't believe what they sell on those carts. I saw an old man buying a dirty coat sleeve. There was one cart piled with the most digusting old bloomers. They looked like they'd never been washed."

I smiled as she told me. I would believe. Most of the clothes I'd ever had up until I started working at the law courts were bought from those carts.

"We found Neddy that waistcoat."

He hopped off the stool and paraded up and down the room, his thumbs latched in the shoulder holes, his little arse swinging like a toffer. Ettie and me stood watching him as the kettle boiled, laughing.

I took the tea tray through and served up.

"How much you going to pay me, Mr. Arrowood?" asked Neddy.

"How does five shillings sound, lad?"

"Sounds good, sir," said the boy, having a look through the basket of swords in the corner. He scratched his head again.

"You got nits, lad?" I asked.

"No."

"You've always got nits, my dear," said the guvnor. "You came out of your mother with nits."

"I didn't!" protested the lad. "Got scratchy hair, is all."

"Six shillings would sound better," said Ettie.

"We agreed five," snapped the guvnor.

"Give him six, you miser."

"We said five. Now please be quiet, Sister."

"Six does sound better," said Lewis.

The guvnor gave him a vexed look. "Oh, all right," he grumbled at last. "Though we did agree to five."

"Thank you, sir," said the boy, his brown eyes shining in delight.

"When Ettie's back safe we need to talk to Willoughby again, Norman."

"Why?" I asked. "He couldn't tell us anything about Birdie."

"We were strangers. He might give us more a second time if we can just understand him better. I visited Jobbs this afternoon." He took out his notebook and opened it under the lamp. Jobbs, an old friend from his newspaper days, now had a position with the Royal Society. Whenever there was something the guvnor wanted to find out about the mind or some other scientific business, Jobbs would let him in to use the library.

"We found a report on Mongolian idiocy by Langdon Down, the fellow who used to run Earlswood Asylum. Says the condition's a racial degeneration to the Mongolian family. Born to Caucasian parents but with the ethnic features of Mongolians." He peered down at his notes. "Flat, broad face. Oblique eyes. Lips thick and large. Tongue long and thick, roughened. Small nose. Skin with yellowish tinge." He looked up to make sure we were listening. "Some ten per cent of congenital idiots are Mongols."

"The Mongolians once had an empire," said Ettie. "They can't be idiots."

"He lists other types of idiots: white negroes, some of the Malay type, American Indians."

"Are you saying that an American Indian can be born to English parents?"

"Down says it not I, Ettie."

"Ridiculous."

"I don't trust these race scientists," said Lewis, scratching his stump furiously. "Some of them say my people are inferior."

"How does a person degenerate to another race?" I asked.

"Tuberculosis in the parents is one cause," answered the guvnor.

"But how?" demanded Ettie. "Is he saying we have other races inside us?"

"I don't know, Ettie!" cried the guvnor, his face quite boiling over. "Ask Langdon Down. I'm just telling you what he's written. Anyway, the important thing is to understand Willoughby." The guvnor turned the page of his notebook. "Now, Down gives us some psychological characteristics of the Mongolian type: skilled at imitation; humorous with a sense of the absurd; more capable in the warmth than the cold. That's because of bad circulation—affects their mental capabilities."

"Me also," said Lewis.

"And me," said Neddy, who'd been listening in real careful.

"Wasn't there a scandal with Down a few years ago?" asked Lewis.

"That's right," said the guvnor. "Jobbs covered it when he started at the paper. The fellow was forced to resign from his position at Earlswood. It seems he was taking some of the private patients from their waiting list and lodging them in the attendants' cottages. Charging a pretty fee for it."

"There's money to be made from lunacy," said Lewis. "It's never out of the papers."

Ettie picked up the sock she was darning.

"No so thick this time, Ettie," said the guvnor. "That last one gave me a blister."

She threw the sock at him. "Do it yourself, then."

He collected it from the floor and, without a word, put it upon the table next to her. Then he went to one of the crates as held his possessions and retrieved a book.

"It made me wonder if Digger's also feeble-minded. Listen to this from Maudsley." He found his place halfway through.

"High level idiots. *'Pleased with toys and trifles.'* The toffee, Barnett? He grabbed for that, didn't he? *'Manifest an animal-like loving for those who feed them. Occasionally paralysis and arrested growth on one side of the body.'* Well, possibly. Hard to tell. *'Usually associated with epileptic attacks.'* Could be, could be. *'Short and flabby fingers.'* Did he have flabby fingers, Norman?"

"I didn't see."

He frowned and tutted, peering at me over his eyeglasses.

"Try to be more observant, please, Norman. I keep telling you how important it is."

"I couldn't see for the brown canvas gloves he wore, sir."

Ettie and Lewis laughed.

The guvnor ignored me and read on:

"*'Badly planted ears.'*" He nodded. "Yes. His ears were quite ridiculous. *'Deformed heads.'* Difficult. He was wearing that hat. *'Puffy skin with abnormal dryness.'* Well, he was certainly flaky. *'Unequal length of arms and legs.'* I'd be willing to wager one side was shorter than the other from the queer way he walked." He shut his book and looked up. "Both of them are feeble-minded."

"They are?" asked Lewis. "How exact must the match to that list be?"

None of us knew the answer to that question and so we poured more tea. Neddy opened a pack of cards and we let him win a few hands. Ettie was so full of life that day. Again and again she walked across the room, examining the reflection of herself in the window. She laughed. Though the guvnor tried to remind her that there might be danger ahead, she didn't take any notice, just kept telling him she'd be all right. She and Neddy practised her being mute and him talking for her, what he would say, while Lewis, the guvnor and me watched on. They were a good mother and son, and for a while there, just for an hour or two, it felt the five of us were a family.

Chapter Seventeen

Arrowood was already at Willows' when I got there next morning. He sat by the window reading the *The Star*, a half-eaten bowl of porridge before him. As was his habit, he'd gathered up Rena's *Punch* and *Pall Mall Gazette* and stored them under his leg in case anybody else should try to take them. The only other customers in there were a family—a mother, three children, a couple of grandparents. The children fought; the elders ignored them, wolfing their bread and marmalade and gurgling their tea like it was all they could think about. I loosened my coat and sat down.

"You all right, Norman?" asked Ma Willows, bringing over two mugs of coffee for us. "Heard you had your knee cracked bad."

"It'll be right, Rena. How are things with you?"

"Ordinary. Mr. Arrowood told me about Mrs. B. I'm real

sorry. You need anything, come to me." She squeezed my shoulder with her big, red hand. Her grey hair had been falling out over the last year, and now she wore a scarf over her head. She sighed. "I know how it is from my old man. I know just how it is."

I tried to give her a smile, and she tried to give me one back.

The door opened and a couple of cabbies came in.

She scooted off to the counter.

"Ettie and the boy left this morning," said the guvnor. "There was no point delaying. I've told her to get out at the slightest sign of trouble. Neddy can come for help if things go badly. Oh, and Petleigh's agreed to put some pressure on Root to investigate Mrs. Gillie."

He sipped his coffee and stared out the window. I could see he was uneasy, more uneasy than when he'd hatched the plan the day before. I thought of how excited Ettie was at the idea, how she enjoyed looking at herself dressed as a pauper. Then quickly I thought of those dogs, of how lonely that farmhouse was on the top of the hill, of Walter in his bloody butcher's apron.

"She's to leave a message for us every evening at the church-yard, under the bootscraper in the lychgate. And if she's employed but Neddy isn't, then he's to visit me every day with news."

"What if they won't hire her?"

"Then we think again, Barnett."

I blew on the coffee and had a sip. The guvnor took a great slurp of his, a slop falling onto his jacket front.

"Did Ettie enjoy Petleigh's visit?" I asked him.

"She seems to see something in him, I suppose. He insisted on staying for cards afterwards. It was a very long visit. Lewis took himself off to bed before he left."

"I went to see your builder. Dennis Bryan."

"You what?" he exploded. The two cabbies stopped gabbing and looked over. "That's none of your damned business, Barnett!"

"Ettie asked me to."

"I don't care!" The guvnor rose from the table. "How dare you interfere?"

"He said you hadn't paid him. He said he's asked four times."

"I don't employ you to investigate *me*, damn it!"

"He said your rooms'll be done in two days if you pay him the twenty-five shillings you owe him."

"Shut your mouth!" he roared. He pushed himself out from the table, hurled the newspaper at me, and stormed out of the shop.

I gave him a couple of hours to cool down, then called at Lewis's house.

"Ettie hasn't returned," he said as he opened the door. There was no trace of his earlier temper, and I wondered if he'd been at the laudanum again. I followed him into the parlour, where he sat in the wingback chair by the fire that he'd claimed as his own since moving in six months before. An orange cat I hadn't seen before slept upon the sofa. "It means she was successful. I need you to go tonight after midnight to pick up the note. Disguise yourself. If Godwin hears you've been back it'll only make it more dangerous for her."

I sat on the sofa. The cat looked at me like I didn't know my place, then jumped off. It padded across the rug and leapt onto the guvnor's lap.

"Hello, little fellow," he cooed, stroking its head.

"Where did that come from?"

"He followed me home. The poor creature was hungry."

"I told you not to throw things at me."

"I'm sorry, Norman, but it was only a newspaper."

"I don't care what it was. One of these days I'll lose my temper proper, and I don't want to do that. Sir."

"I won't do it again, I promise. But you shouldn't have interfered. I don't pay you to help Ettie."

This irked me. We both knew that what was between us went past what he paid me for, though it suited him sometimes to ignore it. I didn't need reminding that we came from different worlds, and it bothered me that sometimes he didn't seem able to get over the parts of him that came from his father, his schooling, where his family had sat at church. I knew that when he was a boy he'd had a housekeeper, just as he knew that until ten year old I was a housekeeper's boy.

"Why haven't you paid him?" I asked.

He continued stroking the cat. It sat on his thighs, then lay down, its head on his privates.

"I had another note from Isabel, Norman. You know she wants a divorce so she can marry that wretch in Cambridge. Well, it seems now she wants me to sell my rooms in Coin Street. They're in her name: she inherited them a few years after we were married. With this damned married woman's property law I've no rights at all. I tell you it's that blooming lawyer behind this! The man's a swindler, there's no other word for it! He's in it for the money. Isabel would never see me turfed out of my home if it wasn't for him."

"I'm sorry to hear it, William."

"The minute the rooms are repaired I'll be obliged to put them up for sale. I just can't bring myself to do it."

"Delaying's not going to help, not if she's set on it."

"No, but I've heard the lawyer's not well. It might be cancer."

He stared at me, no expression in his eyes. Lewis's three clocks ticked maddeningly on the mantel.

"I thought he might die."

"What?"

He scratched his raddled conk.

"If he dies she might come back. That's why I'm trying to hold on. Don't tell Ettie. She mustn't know I haven't paid the builder."

"Does Lewis know?"

He nodded.

"D'you think I'm cruel, Norman?"

His voice was quiet. He looked like a child.

"No, William. But you can't keep them waiting like this."

He nodded. "Believe me, I've been feeling uncomfortable the two of us staying here so long. Lewis hasn't said anything, but he's used to being alone. Ettie's very sensitive to his feelings."

The cat leapt off him and started licking itself before the fire.

"I'll pay the builder," he said with a sigh. "Perhaps Isabel won't come chasing me anyway. She might be preoccupied with that hound's illness."

He began to pack his pipe. His stomach gurgled.

"We can't go back to the farm while Ettie's there," he said. "I want the Ockwells to believe we're off the case, at least until she's safely back home. In the meantime, we must increase the pressure on Root to investigate. Petleigh's a start, but Root's more likely to listen if we can find someone of higher station. I think we'll go over to Tasker and Sons, see if we can't be more persuasive with Mr. Tasker than Barclay was. It's a successful firm. I cannot believe Tasker doesn't know people with connections. And we can also have a talk with whoever it was introduced Birdie to her husband."

Chapter Eighteen

———◆———

The bus to Ludgate Circus was packed, but I didn't mind too much standing crammed among the other folk on such a miserable day. It started raining again as we passed over Blackfriars Bridge; the Thames looked cold and choppy as the North-West Passage.

Tasker and Sons was on the second floor of an old timbered building. The door opened into a great room, where men in black overcoats from Moses and Nicholls sat upon high stools, their backs hunched, their collars stiff. After the crowded streets of Ludgate Circus, the office had the heavy calm of an infirmary: pens scraping ledger books was the only sound to be heard. A small fire smoked over the far side, where a few men with bigger desks sat. On seeing us, one of them came over.

"Can I help you?" he asked, peering at us over his eyeglasses. His head was bald, his whiskers thick and grey. His breath was sour.

"We're looking for Mr. Barclay, sir," said the guvnor.

The pens ceased moving: the clerks looked up.

"Mr. Barclay?" repeated the man, his head tilting. "Dunbar Barclay?"

"Yes, it's rather important."

"He's not with us. He left his post some two months ago."

"He found a new position?"

The man moved nearer us and lowered his voice. "He was dismissed by Mr. Tasker senior."

"Dismissed?" whispered the guvnor. "Might I ask why?"

"I'm afraid I cannot say, sir."

"Of course," replied the guvnor. "You don't know why we're enquiring. Let me be open with you: we're investigative agents, hunting for a girl who we fear is being held captive."

"You suspect Mr. Barclay?" asked the man, the quiver of a smile on his tight lips, a shine coming to his wet eyes.

"Any information about him would help, sir. Any information."

The man looked around the room, and at his attention the clerks one by one looked back down at their ledgers and began to write again. He took us to the side of the room.

"Please keep this to yourselves, gentlemen," he whispered. "There was some money missing. It was traced to Mr. Barclay. He was dismissed immediately."

"He was charged?"

The man shook his head. "We didn't want the scandal. There are plenty of other firms eager to take our business."

"D'you know where he works now?"

"We didn't provide a letter of recommendation. He was a bad egg, that one. I don't know if he found another position."

The man leant his head close, rubbing his hands together. "Did you say Mr. Barclay had captured a girl?" he whispered.

"Not exactly. I didn't get your name before, sir. I'm Mr. Arrowood. This is Mr. Barnett, my assistant."

"Mr. Pope," replied the man, dropping his voice. "Assistant Director. And could you keep your voice down? This office thrives on silence."

"Tell me, Mr. Pope, did he have any friends here?"

The man shook his head. "Mr. Barclay wasn't well liked. He had an unfortunate manner. A quick temper. Little tact. This profession suits careful people, sir."

"Of course. One last thing, sir. There's a man who works here who introduced Mr. Barclay's daughter to her husband. D'you happen to know who he is?"

"I'm afraid not," said Pope, straightening. "Now, I must return to my desk. I've endless work to do."

"Could you ask your employees, please, sir? It's rather urgent. As I said we suspect a crime involving a girl."

"A crime of sex?" whispered the assistant director, a glimmer of excitement appearing again in his watery eyes. His fingers fluttered before his nose; he sniffed. "Is that it?"

"Might you ask, Mr. Pope? It would be of great help."

Pope looked sourly at the guvnor.

"I don't want my men disturbed. They've too much work." He put his hand on the guvnor and tried to move him to the door. "I'm asking you to leave, sir."

The guvnor pulled away from Pope's grip and announced to the room: "Attention! I'm looking for the man who introduced Mr. Barclay's daughter to her husband. I believe he works here."

"Ignore him!" ordered Pope. His clerks weren't even pretending to be working now. Some of the younger lads were whispering to each other, having a quiet laugh. The older ones rubbed their cold hands together, tightened their jackets around their necks. "Mr. Brooks, Mr. Wood, please come and help me get these men out."

Two young men rose from their desks, both tall, both with long moustaches.

"Please identify yourself!" shouted the guvnor, his eyes sweeping the great office. "A girl might be in danger! There'll be something for your pocket if you do!"

A side door at the far end of the room was flung open and a man marched out. He wore a brown lounge suit, an emerald green tie; his hair was shiny and grey. Everybody turned.

"What's the meaning of all this noise?" the man demanded.

"No need to trouble yourself, Mr. Tasker, sir," spluttered Pope. "These men were just leaving."

"The noise, Mr. Pope! The infernal noise! How many times do I have to tell you one cannot do insurance work if there is noise?"

"Mr. Tasker," said the guvnor, striding towards him. "We're trying—"

"I know what you're doing, man! D'you think I couldn't hear you shrieking? How dare you shriek in an insurance office? In an insurance office, indeed!" Tasker spun round and faced the rows of clerks. "Back to work!" he cried.

In an instant, all heads dropped, all pens rose, and the scratching began again. Tasker turned back to us.

"I'm the man you seek. Come through to my office." He looked at Pope and hissed: "I'll speak to you later."

We followed Tasker to his room. It was a large office looking onto the busy crossroads below. A deep coal fire warmed the room. A desk the size of a wagon stood at one end, its surface covered in green leather. As we stood on the rug, he picked up the scuttle and dropped more coal upon the fire, then gave it a few thrusts with the poker. He replaced the tool in its stand and straightened the ash pan and bellows. Then he went to a glass-fronted cabinet, removed the stopper of a crystal decanter, and, shutting his eyes, breathed in the fumes of the brandy within. I looked at the guvnor, expecting him to start asking questions, but he was watching Tasker closely. Finally, the man opened his eyes and poured three glasses. After handing them to us, he sat behind the desk and pointed at two high-backed chairs. Only then did he speak.

"I apologize for Mr. Pope," he said. "He has the manners of a navvie."

He looked at me, at my old boots, my jacket repaired in too many places, my battered face.

"Just an expression, old chap," he said with a quick, weak smile. "No offence intended. Now, tell me why you're here."

He was a man of sixty or so, well-groomed and assured. Two gold rings sat on his full, red fingers. A gold watch chain hung from his patterned waistcoat. His grey hair was fine and very pretty. The brandy was the smoothest I'd ever had, the crystal glass the heaviest.

"We're investigative agents," explained the guvnor. He took a sip, sending his eyes rolling in a sudden ecstasy. "Was it you who arranged the introduction between Mr. Barclay's daughter and Walter Ockwell, sir?"

"Is there a problem?"

"The Barclays are afraid she's being mistreated."

"They must be mistaken," replied Tasker. He took a sniff of his glass, then sipped it. "The Ockwells are a good family."

"Have you seen them since the wedding?"

"I'm afraid not," he said, opening a cigar box and bringing it over. When we'd made our selection, and he his, he struck

145

a match and held it for the guvnor and then myself. As he lit mine, he glanced at the bandage around my hand, now ragged and grimy. Only then did he light his own.

"Can you tell us something of Walter's character, sir?" asked the guvnor.

"A hard worker. Perhaps a little slow, but an honest fellow. What have the Barclays told you?"

"They've been rebuffed when they try to visit. Birdie won't return their letters and she hasn't been to see them since the wedding. They say it's most unlike her."

Tasker had a sip of brandy and a puff on his cigar before replying.

"You know," he said at last, stretching back in his chair, "we had to dismiss Mr. Barclay. He's a dishonest man, I'm afraid, sir. I don't know what he's up to, but I'd be careful of trusting what he says."

"He stole from the firm, did he?" asked the guvnor. He drained his glass and put it down carefully upon the side table.

"Small amounts over the last couple of years. We didn't go to the police. Damage to our reputation and so on."

"Why d'you think Mr. Barclay would be misleading us, sir?"

Tasker stared out the window as he pondered the question. I stretched my feet out to the fire, then, seeing the hole in the side of my boot, pulled them back under the chair. The brandy, the fire, the good cigar, were making me relaxed. I could have stayed in that room till spring.

"Perhaps he's getting back at me for dismissing him," he said at last. "Lashing out the only way he can."

"Some will always blame others for what they've caused themselves, I suppose," said the guvnor, sitting forward and frowning. He looked hard at Tasker. "That is, if he's not tell-ing the truth, Mr. Tasker."

Tasker held his eye for a moment, puffing away on his cigar like it was going out. Sheets of smoke drifted from his lips.

"Well, you must decide that for yourself," he said at last. "But I don't think you'll find Walter's to blame for this."

As he spoke, the door swung open and a man walked in.

"Augie!" barked the fellow. "I've been at mother's. Thought we'd go for some luncheon. Have you eaten?"

He wore a green overcoat and suit, a topper, a yellow scarf around his neck. His face was quite a triangle, pointed at the chin and wide at the forehead, where a perfectly straight line of thick, tightly curled hair crossed his skull. His cheeks and chin were smooth like a woman's, his features squashed, his eyes sharp and upturned.

"What luck!" answered Tasker. "I was about to go and get something."

He turned to us.

"This is my brother, Lieutenant Colonel Henry Tasker. He owns one of the farms adjoining the Ockwell land. It's ac-tually he who made the introductions. He knows the family much better than I."

"What's this about, Augie?" asked Henry Tasker.

"These are private agents. Mr. Arrowood and Mr. Barnett. The Barclays have asked them to find out why Birdie won't see them."

"Well, I can tell you that," said the brother. Though his face was squashed up, his voice was open and friendly. "She's decided to break with them. Some sort of a family row."

"They believe Walter Ockwell's preventing her," said the guvnor. "D'you think that might be true?"

Henry Tasker laughed.

"Not him, Mr. Arrowood. He hasn't the gumption for something like that. His sister wouldn't allow it anyway. She's an upright woman."

"My brother's a justice of the peace," said the insurance agent. "He has a sense of these things."

"In Catford?" asked the guvnor.

"And Lewisham," answered Henry Tasker. "I think I'd know if it were true, gentlemen. But it isn't."

"Still, could you ask Sergeant Root to go along and talk to her alone, just to be sure, sir? It would reassure her parents."

"There's no need for that," said the magistrate. "I can assure you there's nothing wrong. And the local police are occupied with several difficult investigations at the moment. There's a gang of thieves plundering the construction sites."

"I did tell you Mr. Barclay's not to be trusted," said the first Tasker as he buttoned his coat. "Now, if that will be all, my brother and I must away to the chophouse."

"Just one more thing," said the guvnor. He quickly described Mrs. Gillie's disappearance and Root's refusal to investigate.

"The police are very busy, Mr. Arrowood," said the magistrate. "And she's a gypsy. She could be anywhere."

"My brother will ask some questions, Mr. Arrowood," said Tasker the first, putting on his topper. "Leave it with him. Now, if there's nothing else?"

We were back on the street in moments, still holding our excellent cigars, the taste of his wondrous brandy in our mouths.

We managed to get a seat on the bus home, but the guvnor was taking so much room with his overgrown behind that I had to sit sideways, my bad leg stuck in the aisle. I tried to shove him up a bit but it was as if he was stuck to the bench.

"Well, well, well, Barnett," he said as we crossed the river. "It seems the Barclays have money troubles. I thought that might be so. Did you notice that cabinet was gone the second time we called? And then the painting of the ship I so admired?"

"Sometimes you sound just like Sherlock Holmes, sir," I said.

The bus had come to a halt on the bridge. He rubbed the damp off the window so he could look out onto the lights of the boats below.

"And sometimes you sound just like an ass, Norman," he replied.

Chapter Nineteen

My brother-in-law Sidney ran a few cabs from a yard in Bermondsey and liked to give us a hand from time to time on our cases: he was the sort of bloke who always needed a bit of adventure to keep him on the level. So later that night it was him that drove me down to Catford in one of his hackneys. A cold rain fell all the way. When we got there the pub was shut up, the streets empty and wet with mud. We pulled up by the churchyard and I hopped out, disguised in a long, black cloak and a broad-brimmed parson's hat we'd loaned from Reverend Hebdon. I found Ettie's note in the lychgate and was back in the cab in less than a minute. I lit my candle to read it.

All well. Lodging at 63 Doggett Road. Sharing room with family. Both taken on.
Begin tomorrow.

There was nothing else.

"Right?" asked Sidney from the box. He was wrapped in a great waterproof cloak, a sou'wester on his head.

"They're fine, mate. Let's go up Doggett Road, just before the station. Check where they're staying."

Sidney turned the cab around and we drove along the side of the green. A big, black horse stood facing us by the site where the bank was being built, a cart tethered behind it. I sank down on the bench least someone should see me, pulling my hat over my eyes, my scarf up across my nose. As we passed, a bloke came out of the half-made building pushing a wheelbarrow piled high with bricks. When he saw us he turned away, covering his face with his arm to hide. It was no use: I knew him from the bush of grizzled hair sprouting out from his cap and the wild beard on his chin. I knew him the way you know a man who's given you a beating. It was Skulky, and he was up to no good.

We rolled on past. Sixty-three Doggett Road was a run-down terraced house on a deep-rutted street, half its windows boarded and its walls stained with soot. There were no lights inside, nor in any other house on the street. We stopped to have a look, then turned back for the long journey home.

I took the letter to the guvnor next morning. He read it and grunted, then had me describe Skulky's behaviour in every detail.

"So he didn't want to be recognized," he said, warming his rumple at the coals. "Was there anything on the wagon?"

"Just a tarp rolled back."

"And he was on his way out." The orange cat strode through from the passage and rubbed its side down the guvnor's ankles. He smiled. "It appears our friend the builder was thieving. I wonder if that's what they were doing the other night?"

"Might explain why they don't like us looking around," I said.

He bent to pick up the cat and held it to his chest, thinking as he stroked it.

"Petleigh's been down to see Root about investigating Mrs. Gillie but the man won't budge. And the Chief Inspector won't allow Petleigh to investigate unless a request is put in from Catford. That imbecile won't do anything unless someone gives him permission."

"Did you lose your temper with him, sir?"

"Well, he's a stubborn fool! Why is it so hard to get them to do their damn job? Why is it that nobody cares about Mrs. Gillie but us? Because she's a gypsy?"

"Because she's poor."

"Because she's poor. Because she's old. Because she's a gypsy. It's all the same, Barnett. Petleigh's at least done one thing: he's secured us an appointment at four today with the Member of Parliament for Catford, Sir Edward Penn. You know the chap, always making speeches about crime and justice. I'm not sure Henry Tasker will do anything about Mrs. Gillie. They were just trying to get rid of us so they could get at their lunchtime claret. But if Sir Edward gets involved, Root's superintendent'll order him to investigate."

"But what if it's Root that told someone about Mrs. Gillie talking to us. What if Root already knows who's behind it?"

"Look, Barnett, we're getting nowhere by ourselves in discovering what happened to Mrs. Gillie. We need to make something happen."

"That something might happen to us."

"I know. But I promised Ida Gillie we'd find out. If whatever's happened to that old woman is our fault, we owe it to her."

We took a bus to Westminster. For once it wasn't too busy, and we managed to get a bench each. The guvnor was deep in thought. As we passed Bethlem, he finally spoke.

"Were you surprised that the man who'd introduced Birdie was the owner of the firm, Barnett?" he asked.

"I thought Mr. Barclay said it was one of the clerks."

"He said it was an *associate* at his firm. I also assumed it was a clerk. Now, why did that mislead us?"

I shrugged, knowing he'd answer himself.

"Because Mr. Barclay's just the type of man who likes to impress others. Remember our first meeting with them? How he mentioned his wife singing with Irene Adler and Kipling's brother living around the corner? If it was a gentleman as high as Mr. Tasker, he'd say it. No, he didn't want us to know."

"Didn't want us talking to Tasker?"

"Exactly, Barnett. But why?"

"Because he didn't want us to know he'd been dismissed."

He shook his head. "Anyone there could have told us that. It must be something else."

The guvnor fell silent again. The bus moved on slow as you like, past Christ Church, then on under the Waterloo railway bridges. The air outside was brown and still: it looked like a fog was coming down again.

The clippie shook a pauper sleeping up front, his head against the window.

"Fare," he said.

The bloke didn't move. The clippie shook him harder.

"Fare!" he said.

"Yes, sir," said the bloke, sitting up. Curled and matted

hair covered his face; a great black boil grew upon his lip. He wore a soldier's greatcoat, torn and dirty. "Help me, will you? I must get to Hammersmith. My only brother's on his death bed and me without a farthing, sir. Please help me, for the love of the dear Lord. I got to get there afore he croaks."

"You can walk," said the clippie, grabbing the bloke under his arms and hauling him up.

"Have a little mercy," pleaded the bloke. We could now see he had a wooden leg. "I can't walk that far. Ain't had a meal for two day. Got no strength in my bones, sir."

I stood up, blocking their way.

"He'll be all right, mate," I said. "You won't even know he's there."

"No one travels without a fare," said the clippie.

The guvnor held out a coin. "There's his fare."

"Thank you, sir," said the pauper, falling back onto the bench. In seconds his eyes were shut again, his head falling back on the window.

"It was odd Tasker didn't mention Walter's criminal past," said the guvnor as he sat back down. "His brother's a magistrate. He'd surely know. And what about his display in the office? How long did he leave us standing there as he fiddled? It was very good brandy, by the way, Norman. Quite the best."

He peered at me like he expected me to be grateful for this information. I looked at him coldly.

He opened his mouth, then, realizing what had happened, he flushed.

"Yes," he said quickly. "A very long time to be silent with strangers. You know what I think, Barnett? I think he was dreaming up a story to tell us."

"Could just be he didn't see us as very important, sir."

He looked at me for a moment, his mouth hanging open. Then he smiled and clapped me on the knee.

"You're right. But why would he cast doubt on Mr. Barclay's story? Why not just say he didn't know? He clearly isn't well-acquainted with the Ockwells. Why would he protect them?"

He fell back to his thoughts.

When we got to Westminster, the pauper opened his eyes and hauled himself up. The guvnor took his arm and helped him off the bus.

"Thank you, sir," said the bloke, patting the guvnor's arm. "You're a proper gent. I won't forget this."

The guvnor took out a farthing and pressed it into the man's hand.

"For the next leg of your journey. I hope you get there in time."

"God bless you, sir," said the man, hobbling away into the fog.

Petleigh was waiting for us outside the Houses of Parliament. The tip of his long nose was pink with the cold, his hands jammed into his pockets. He wore a red and grey scarf tucked inside the collar of his long, black jacket. It was just like the one the guvnor gave me for Christmas.

"Happy New Year, Norman," he said, holding out his gloved hand to me. His eyes fell on my scarf and for a moment he frowned.

"How was your Christmas, Inspector?" I asked, shaking his hand.

"Good, thank you. Very quiet."

"Now, Isaiah," said the guvnor. "Remember this is about Mrs. Gillie. Don't mention the Ockwells. If Sir Edward thinks it's simply a marital dispute, he won't want to involve himself. So, let's get inside out of the cold, shall we?"

The doorman showed us into the central lobby. It was a great, round space, with thin grey statues of kings and queens looking down upon you from ledges in the walls. I'd never seen a ceiling so high before, not even in a church. Thirty or forty people were in there, most of them well-dressed and serious—city men, merchants, land-owners, that type of person. There were a few who weren't so high and mighty sitting alone on the benches at the side. From their slump and the blank looks on their faces, it seemed as they'd been there some time already.

"It's four now," said Petleigh. "He'll be here any minute."

We found a bench under one of the queens and waited.

"I enjoyed our game of cards yesterday, William," said the inspector after a few minutes. He twizzled his waxed moustache and crossed his legs. His boots had a high polish, although they were specked with mud from the street. "I hope Ettie also enjoyed it?"

"My sister will always play cards. She has an unusual passion for winning."

"Well, she certainly trounced me. And you, William."

"She didn't trounce me."

Petleigh smirked.

"Why are you smirking? She didn't beat me."

And so we talked. Half four came.

"Are you sure it was four?" asked the guvnor.

Petleigh took a note from his pocket and gave it to the guvnor. "See for yourself."

The guvnor read the note and passed it back. "I'm hungry."

"He'll be out soon, I'm sure," said Petleigh.

The guvnor reached into his pocket.

"My watch!" he exclaimed, patting his other pockets. He stood and searched the bench and the floor below. "My watch is gone! Do you have it, Barnett?"

"Why would I have it?"

"That was my grandfather's watch! It's gone!"

"Perhaps you left it at home," I said.

"I checked it as we waited for the bus, remember?"

"You must have dropped it."

"It was on a chain, and that's gone too. It was that bloody tramp, Barnett. Damnation! After my helping him out!"

Shaking his head and muttering, he lowered himself on his bench and stared with an angry pout about him.

"Didn't you see him?" he snapped at me.

"Don't go blaming me for this, sir," I said softly.

"My grandfather's watch, for pity's sake. And where the blazes is that damn MP?"

We sat in silence, watching the people wait in the great hall, listening to the guvnor curse and sigh. Every footstep on the tiled floor echoed in the cold air. Now and then, an MP or a peer came out to meet someone. There was frowning, nodding, hand-shaking, then the politician, the lord, the baronet would return to the inner building. Quarter to five came. The guvnor was getting more and more vexed.

"This is an outrage," he said, tapping the stick he'd loaned from Lewis on the floor.

"They're busy men," said Petleigh. "They don't get paid for this, you know."

"They've a duty to represent us, otherwise they shouldn't be here."

"Keep your voice down, William."

"Would it hurt him to at least send a message? We could be here all night!"

At half five, Petleigh gave a note for Sir Edward to one of the clerks, saying it was an urgent police matter. The bloke came back at six.

"Sir Edward says he can't see you today," he said. His voice was flat; his hair was thin. He barely looked at us. "You can try his surgery on Saturday afternoon. The Horse and Groom in Lewisham."

"But we had an appointment!" exclaimed the guvnor.

"I'm sorry, sir. That's what he said. Good day."

The clerk turned back to the House and was gone.

"You'll just have to go on Saturday, William," said Petleigh.

"We can't wait till Saturday! Ettie's there!"

"Ettie's where?"

"On the farm. She's working in the dairy."

Petleigh's eyes widened.

"The Ockwell farm?"

"She insisted. She's trying to talk to Birdie."

"You damn fool, William!" cried the copper, throwing his hands into the air. "Why did you allow it, for God's sake! She's a woman!"

Arrowood looked at him in surprise.

"She's a woman?" he repeated quietly. "What do you mean?"

"You know what I mean. You've sent a woman into a complicated and possibly dangerous situation. If you're right about Mrs. Gillie or Birdie Ockwell, then this is a police matter."

"Which the police refuse to investigate, Petleigh. Listen, nobody sends my sister anywhere. If you wish to become her friend that's the first thing you must understand. And by the way, Ettie's as capable as any officer of the Metropolitan Police, I can assure you of that."

"I'm going down there now to get her," said Petleigh when we were out in Parliament Square. "How do I find the farm?"

"She'll never forgive you if you interfere," said the guvnor. "Believe me, Petleigh. Fighting injustice is important to her. Look at how her mission rescues girls in the courts. She believes the Lord protects her. Anyway, she'll be out in a day or so."

"I don't like this, William," said Petleigh. "I just hope you don't regret it."

"We'll have to catch Sir Edward when he comes out. Will you wait with us, Petleigh? We don't know what he looks like."

The inspector looked up at the face of Big Ben and shook his head. "I must get back to the station. Come and see me tomorrow. I need to know she's safe."

"I need to know she's safe," said the guvnor when he'd gone. "He talks as if they're married."

"I think that's the first time I ever heard you praise her, William."

"It wasn't praise, Norman. It was a warning."

"Sounded like praise to me."

"Well don't tell her. It'll only make her worse."

I laughed.

"I've been aggressive today, Norman. I'm unsettled. I keep worrying about them on that blasted pig farm."

"You will try and be calm with Sir Edward, sir, won't you?"

"Of course I will."

Parliament Square was busy with buses and wagons choking the street all the way round. A few hansom cabs were lined up in the dark opposite Westminster Abbey, the cabbies talking in a huddle on the pavement. We went over and asked if any of them would recognize Sir Edward. No luck. A couple of waiting girls came out on Abingdon Street, but they didn't know him either. After a few minutes, the clerk who'd taken the note appeared, a bowler on his head, a thick woollen overcoat buttoned to his knees. The guvnor asked him if he could describe Sir Edward so we'd recognize him.

The man indicated we follow him. He led us to New Palace Yard.

"That's the members' entrance there," he said. "If he's not dining, he'll be out in five minutes or so. His carriage is the one with the yellow and blue trim."

It wasn't long before men began emerging from the doors and making for the street; at the sight of them, Penn's coachman hopped down from his bench and lit the carriage lamps.

Two men in toppers shook hands at the gate. One of them turned to the landau. As he approached, the guvnor stepped in front of him.

"Excuse me, Sir Edward," he said with a little bow of his head. "We had an appointment today at four with you and Inspector Petleigh. My name's William Arrowood, a private agent. We've been waiting since."

I stood back by the railings, out of the light of the street lamps.

Sir Edward looked at the guvnor coldly. He wore evening dress, a bow tie, a long tail coat. His sparse white hair was oiled down, his eyes thin, two patches of dry, red skin next to his nose. His feathery grey moustache fluttered as he breathed.

"Ah, yes," he said at last. "A police matter. Where's the inspector?"

"He had to go back to the station, sir. Let me explain."

"I'm in rather a hurry, sir," replied the MP, stepping to the side to pass him. "Come to my surgery on Saturday."

The guvnor blocked him.

"I'll be quick, Sir Edward. An old gypsy woman has disappeared from her camp in Catford. She was alone. We know something's happened to her since her coat's still there, her horse was untended for three days, her caravan's unlocked. There's evidence of a violent struggle. It's certain she's been murdered or abducted."

"If it's Catford, then Sergeant Root's the man you want. See him."

"He refuses to help, sir. I've come to ask if you'd use your influence. A criminal's walking free, unpunished, and he might do it again. You always take an interest in matters of crime, sir. You fight for justice and people respect you for it. I used to write for *Lloyd's Weekly* and your reputation was well-known among my fellow newspapermen. We were sure you'd want to help."

Sir Edward straightened up.

"Well, you're right, my good man," he said, looking down his nose at the guvnor. "I have made law and order my first concern as a parliamentarian. Let me make some enquiries. Give your details to my coachman."

"Thank you, Sir Edward. I knew you'd help. It was a great honour to meet you, sir." The guvnor stepped back with a bow, and as he did so a little fart flavoured the night air.

In a show of his breeding, Sir Edward gave only the briefest sign of disgust before climbing into his carriage.

The guvnor was in a better temper as we took the bus back over the river.

"We're getting somewhere at last," he said. "I feel it, Norman. Things are moving."

We stopped for fried fish on the way and reached the house just past eight. As we opened the front door, we could hear

Lewis's voice in the parlour. The guvnor turned to me, his face bright.

"Ettie's back!" he exclaimed. "Thank the Lord!"

Without taking off our coats we hurried along the corridor.

"William!" said Lewis as we entered the parlour, the relief clear in his voice. "You've returned at last."

There, standing with his elbow on the mantel, was Reverend Sprice-Hogg.

Chapter Twenty

The guvnor stopped short, clutching my arm.

"What's happened to her, Bill?" he asked, his face white with panic.

"To who?" asked the curate. His hoarseness was back, and it was a strain to hear him. His face was red, his eyes watery behind his smudgy spectacles. A mug of milk stood on the table next to him. With one hand he stroked his curly white hair, arching his neck like a cat. With the other he held a glass of Lewis's brandy.

"My sister. Where is she?"

The pastor's brow wrinkled in confusion.

"My sister!" barked the guvnor. "Tell me, Bill!"

"I'm sorry, William. I don't know where your sister is."

"The reverend's been here since seven waiting for you,"

said Lewis, a sour look on his blotchy face. As always, he was sweating from being too close to the fire.

"I was just passing and thought I'd call." Sprice-Hogg smiled, his lips wet with the drink. "Mr. Schwarz has made me most welcome." He drained his glass and waggled it at Lewis, who ignored him. "A charming house, these swords and guns everywhere. The only weapon I'm permitted is a cricket bat, but there's a few would testify I'm quite deadly with that." He laughed to himself. "Yes, I was just passing and wondered if there'd been any developments?"

"Nothing to speak of," said the guvnor, pouring a brandy for himself and me. He put Sprice-Hogg out of his misery and filled his glass too. Lewis shook his head.

Sprice-Hogg took a nice swallow, following it down with a sip of milk.

"Yes," he declared as if remembering something important. He peered at Lewis. "Have you noticed how little Jesus attends to his mother in the bible?"

"The bible isn't my book," said Lewis sharpish.

"Ah, of course. But you might be interested to learn that he's severe towards her. Quite different to his kindness to others. And why? Because he foresees the idolatrous nature of the Roman Catholic Church towards Mary. It's a warning to believers, you see."

Not one of us replied. His face fell.

"That reminds me." He put his glass down and drew a paper from his pocket. "Miss Rosanna said you should see this. Mrs. Barclay gave it to her."

The guvnor took the note.

"*Dear Miss Ockwell,*" he read aloud. "*We wish the marriage annulled. I am sure Mr. Tasker can find another wife for Walter, but we miss Birdie terribly and cannot live without her. We will pay you*

*thirty pounds if you agree. Please reply soon. My heart is breaking
for missing her. Yours sincerely, Martha Barclay."*

He looked at me. "That's not what she told us. Listen, Bill,
something I forgot to ask you before. When exactly did you
tell the Barclays about Walter's conviction?"

Sprice-Hogg pondered this for a moment.

"It was when they came to arrange the service. We had
tea and so on."

"They knew before the marriage?"

"Of course."

The guvnor turned to me.

"Didn't they say they'd only learnt of it after the wedding?"

I nodded. "They said they'd been deceived."

The guvnor was staring at me, his mind turning over.

"What the devil are they playing at, Barnett? Almost everything they tell us is a falsity. The only thing that seems
true is that Birdie needs help."

"I must warn you there's great ill-feeling towards you in
the area," said the parson. "The Ockwells are a well-respected
family and people in my parish value their privacy. They
don't like the idea of outsiders poking around into their family lives. After all, which of us doesn't have secrets of which
they're ashamed?" Here he turned to me. "It's being said you
threatened one of our local men in The Plough and Harrow,
Norman. A builder called Edgar Winter."

I laughed. "Him and his brother jumped me in the lavvy,
Reverend. Beat me to the ground."

"Well, that's not what's being said. Pray be careful. There
are some rough elements around that pub. Use the parsonage as a refuge: there's always a welcome for you there." He
gulped his brandy, sipped his milk. A hand went to his chest:
he burped.

"Thank you, Bill," said the guvnor. "Any sign of Mrs. Gillie?"

"I'm afraid not." For a moment he was serious, then a great smile came over his pickled face. "Oh, but it's so good to see you, my dear friends. I've missed your visits. When will you be down again? Tomorrow? We'll have tea."

"I'm not sure." The guvnor finished his brandy and yawned. "But I'm afraid I can be no more company to you tonight. It's been an exhausting day and I must retire."

"So early?" asked the parson, pulling out his watch.

"I've quite a bad head."

Sprice-Hogg looked at Lewis and gave him a smile. He settled back in his chair.

"It's past my bedtime too," said Lewis, getting to his feet.

"Oh, dear!" said the parson, looking at the three clocks upon the mantel.

Lewis made to take his glass, but Sprice-Hogg snatched it from the table and quickly drained it. Then he swallowed down his milk.

When he was gone, Lewis filled up our glasses.

"That's your new friend, is it?" he asked. I'd never seen him so put-out.

"I wouldn't call him that," said the guvnor.

"He was half-cut when he arrived. Had three glasses from me before you returned."

"I'm sorry, Lewis," said the guvnor. "I'd no idea he'd call. You didn't tell him about Ettie, did you?"

"Of course not."

Lewis sat on his chair by the fire, his stringy grey hair stuck to his forehead with the heat. His boots hadn't been cleaned in weeks, and you couldn't hardly make out the colour for the dried mud. His waistcoat was shiny from grime.

"He insisted on asking me how I managed with only one arm. How I cut my meat, how I made tea. Even how I did my doo-doo. Wanted my whole family history as well."

"He's been helping us in the village," protested the guvnor.

"I can't see how. He's a drunk."

I had a smile on my face: I'd never seen Lewis jealous like this before. The guvnor and him had been friends since childhood, but he was acting like they were wed.

"He's a complicated fellow," admitted the guvnor. "But he's the only one in that infernal place who isn't against us."

"You're not going to encourage him, are you?"

"I'm not going to discourage him."

"I'd never trust a man who treats his servant the way he treated Sarah," I said.

"He's a dipsomaniac, Norman. Irritability's part of the condition."

"He doesn't treat us like that. He worships you."

"The only reason he welcomes us so is that we allow him to drink. A parson cannot enjoy his port so enthusiastically with his parishioners, and so for the most part he must do it alone. But solitary drinking's shameful; it brings him face-to-face with what he really is. Social drinking allows him to avoid this. That's why he's always so desperate for us to visit, because we're outsiders, with no connection to his parish. We allow him to drink, and he doesn't care what we think."

The guvnor eased his puffy feet out of Lewis's shoes with a groan. He stretched them out to the fire.

"I saw the builders," he said, looking over at Lewis.

"Oh, yes?" answered Lewis, picking up the guvnor's *Strand Magazine* from the table and pretending to read it.

"We can return to our rooms on Thursday."

Lewis grunted.

The guvnor looked hurt. He had a swallow of his brandy and took up *The Star* from the table.

"Have a look at page four," said Lewis.

The guvnor turned the page. His brow creased.

"Oh, my Lord," he muttered. "No, no, no."

He passed me the paper. Halfway down was the headline:

A SPY IN CATFORD

It is reported that the residents of Catford have for several weeks past been subject to surveillance by a private enquiry agent, William Arrowood, of Lambeth. According to witnesses, the man and his assistant have been acting in a most objectionable manner, prying into the private affairs of a respected local family, asking questions to all they meet and making repeated attempts to gain entry to their house. Mrs. Kitty Wells, an elderly widow, reports having been frightened one evening to find them looking in at her window. Witnesses have seen them following men to their work and attempting to overhear conversations in the tavern, The Plough and Harrow. Sergeant Root of the Catford and Lewisham Police informs us these men have been encouraging him to further harass the family despite no crime having been reported. A good deal of ill-will has built up against these busybodies, who seem determined to provoke the anger of the community.

The guvnor was puffing furiously on his pipe.

"This is Root's doing," he said. "You'd thought the police'd welcome our help, the amount they complain about not having enough men. Well, let's hope they report it when we save Birdie. And apologize."

"I wouldn't count on it," said I. "They never mentioned us for the Fenian case."

"Mentioned Holmes, though. Even though we did most of the work and almost got killed into the bargain."

Lewis filled our glasses. He put down the bottle and scratched his stump, revealing the side of his waistcoat, the seam torn almost all the way down.

"I had a notion, Norman," he said, falling back onto his chair. He brushed back the hair from his eyes. "That since you and I are in the same position, living alone and so on, that perhaps you might... I've become used to company, you see... I mean to say, once William and Ettie have returned to Coin Street you might..."

"Might what?" I asked.

"He's asking if you want to lodge with him," said the guvnor.

Lewis was peering at me. I couldn't think what to say. I hated that room I lived in, with the silhouettes of Mrs. Barnett and me on the wall. That cold room and the cold bed as had lost her warmth long ago. I used it only to sleep when I couldn't stay awake no more, and I left it the minute I washed my face in the morning. But it was all I had left of her. The frozen water in the washstand, the dirty cloth, the grey sheets, the chair she used to sit in. If I left that room I worried I might just leave her for ever.

"Think about it, my friend," said Lewis, seeing the confusion in my face. "The offer is there."

Later that night, Sidney took me down to Catford to collect Ettie's note. I read it in the cab on the way back.

In dairy all day with P. B working at laundry in house. Long hours. Exhausted. No opportunity to converse. Met workers—very pleased with toffee. P speaks little, doesn't make sense, always carries corn dollies, possibly insane. N is well but hungry.

I didn't get back to my bed until gone one, so it was late next morning when I tipped up at Lewis's house. The guvnor took the note the minute he opened the door and turned back to the parlour without speaking. As he read it, I made the tea. He was smoking his pipe when I returned with the tray.

"The parson also said Polly had a nervous disorder, didn't he?" He took two Garibaldis from the box and put them in his mouth, smoking as he chewed. "D'you think it's unusual there are so many people with mental diseases on that farm? Birdie suffers from amentia. Willoughby's a Mongolian. That fellow Digger doesn't talk and has all the signs of amentia as well. And now it seems Polly might be insane."

"Don't forget Walter."

"Is that customary for a farm, d'you know?"

"It'd be ordinary for a London court, that's for sure. Or a workhouse."

"I think a lot of them end up on farms," he said. "I've read nature's good for a disturbed mind. It does seem odd, though, that everyone on the farm except the Ockwells has a weakness of the mind. I'd like to know why there are so many there."

The orange cat leapt onto his lap. He took another gulp of tea and stroked it as his mind worked through something.

"Willoughby said he had a brother John, didn't he?" he said at last. "I think we'll pay him a visit, see what he knows about the place."

"He said his brother was a friend of Godwin's. Won't it get back that we're still on the case?"

"He's a pauper so it's unlikely his brother and Godwin are that close. I think Willoughby's understanding of friends is different to ours. Now, he said he used to live in Kennington, and Mrs. Gillie said he was in the asylum after that. The main asylum for South London's in Caterham, isn't it? They must have an address for brother John."

He stood, pushing the cat to the floor.

"Finish that tea, Barnett. We've work to do."

Chapter Twenty-One

We walked from Caterham Junction station to the asylum. It was cold and windy, the sky grey; the guvnor was limping and moaning about his feet again. The weather was no friend to my injuries either, so I finished off my bottle of Black Drop as we went. Some way outside the town we found the sign—*Caterham Asylum for Safe Lunatics and Imbeciles*. The buildings couldn't be seen from the road on account of a border of fir trees, but once through the gates we saw ahead a fountain and the administrative block, as big as a stately home, a tall spire rising from its middle. On each side, stretching back behind the main building, was a row of plain ward blocks, their windows barred, their walls grey. It seemed a sad and desolate place.

Three women in brown dresses and thick tartan shawls stood at the door of the nearest ward, watching us. One of them shouted, her voice harsh like a gull, shaking her clawed hand as if we'd walked somewhere we shouldn't. I turned away, feeling a shiver go through me.

We climbed the wide, stone steps of the main block and rang the bell. While we waited, a group of four men in brown jackets and britches came out from behind one of the ward buildings, led by a big fellow in a blue suit. They were an odd collection: one a melancholy dwarf with great bulging eyes and a head so big he might topple over, another tall and thin, his hands jerking, his face covered with scabs and scars. Behind him was a handsome fellow with a proud, military bearing. An old man with long, white hair and his hands tied to his belt followed. They trudged along the path until the scabby one caught a sight of us and stopped to stare. The handsome fellow walked straight into him, then he too turned to watch us. The attendant barked at them to get a move on and they started up again, disappearing behind the big house.

The great front door swung open. There stood a large woman in a blue dress and jacket. Her eyes were crossed.

"We'd like to see the superintendant regarding a legal matter, madam," said the guvnor. "I'm Mr. Arrowood, this is Mr. Barnett."

We followed her into a grand wood-panelled entrance hall, a broad, sweeping staircase on one side, a wide fireplace on the other. Above it was a big painting of a country scene. There she asked us to wait.

As we stood, our hands behind our backs, an old, grey-haired woman appeared from under the stairs. She wore the same coarse brown dress and tartan shawl as the women outside.

"You seen Dickie?" she asked. Her voice was warm and gentle. "Either of you seen Dickie?"

"No, ma'am," I answered. "Sorry."

She took my hand. Her own was frozen. Her nails were missing.

"You seen Dickie?" she asked again, pinching the skin at the bottom of my thumb.

"No, ma'am," I said, louder, thinking maybe she was deaf.

She started to pluck the skin of my hand all over, real soft like a little bird was pecking me. I didn't know what she was doing and wanted to pull my hand away, but it seemed to please her.

"You seen Dickie?" she asked again, examining my hand as she worked on it.

"Myrtle!" cried the attendant, returning from the corridor. "You leave that gentleman alone."

The old woman dropped my hand.

"You seen Dickie?" she asked the guvnor.

"No, I haven't, Myrtle," he answered. "But I'll tell him you were looking for him if I do."

"Don't mind her," said the attendant. "Dr. Crenshaw will see you."

As she led us through the passage, she whispered to the guvnor: "Dickie's her brother, sir. Died ten year ago in the Transvaal. She don't ever seem to remember."

"Ah," replied the guvnor. "Very sad."

Dr. Crenshaw was a small man, bald, with a rim beard. He sat behind a long desk wearing a frown like he had a cramp in his guts. In front of him was a pen and ink set with a golden statuette of a lion having a good old roar.

"How can I help you?" he asked. His voice was soft, like it was buried in his throat. He didn't ask us to sit.

His office was also wood-panelled, a painting of a woman in a silky dress above the coal fire. The shelves held a cartload of black ledgers and books, with a whole section given over to medical journals. The windows, protected by rows of thin iron bars, looked onto the front lawn and the drive.

"We're investigative agents, sir," said the guvnor in his most polite voice. Straight away, the superintendent's eyes narrowed. "I'm Mr. Arrowood, this is Mr. Barnett. We're working on a case involving the possible imprisonment of a young woman. We just need some information about a patient of yours."

"Of course you do," said Crenshaw. He fitted a monocle to his eye and peered at us. "Who are you accusing us of imprisoning now?"

"Oh, no, sir. This is nothing to do with your institution."

"Of course it has something to do with my institution. Why else would you be here, Mr. Arrowood?" Crenshaw spoke in a quick, angry stream. "You think I'm a fool, do you? Every week I have people claiming to represent one of our patients. Lawyers, parsons, physicians, men like you, and it's almost always about an inheritance. So get on with it, sir. State your business."

"I assure you this is not about an inheritance, sir. We only need some information about a patient of yours who left some while ago and now works on a farm near Catford. His name's Willoughby Krott. An idiot of the Mongolian type. We need to speak to his brother and hoped you'd be able to provide us with his address."

The superintendent stood up and walked to the door, his boots clicking on the polished floor. It was only when he held the door open I realized just how little he filled his suit.

"Our records are confidential."

"Mr. Crenshaw, sir," began the guvnor. "We believe a crime is being committed on the farm where Mr. Krott works. It's very important we speak to his brother."

"Confidential!" snapped Crenshaw. "Didn't you hear me?"

"You don't und—"

"Get out!" said the man sharply. "I don't know exactly what you're trying to do, but this is a good place. We're the only refuge for the unfortunate people we look after. We're the only people who understand."

"No, sir, we aren't investigating this asylum. We're investigating a farm."

"A farm indeed! D'you think I'm a fool? You're here to gather information like all the rest. Then there'll be a story in the paper, a lawyer, a court case. Get out! Get out or I'll call some of my more persuasive attendants!"

"Please listen, Dr. Cr—"

"Mrs. Grant, show them out!" barked the medical superintendent.

The woman who brought us in was waiting in the corridor. She led us back to the great hallway where old Myrtle stood muttering to herself, her fingers plucking at her shawl.

The guvnor marched over and produced a small chocolate bear wrapped in Christmas foil from his pocket.

"Dickie asked me to give you this, madam," he said, his voice soft.

She looked at him curious. "Dickie asked you?"

"Yes, he did."

She smiled and took the bear. A tear came to her old eye. The guvnor gave her a little bow, then returned to us.

"Do you remember an inmate called Willoughby Krott, madam?" he asked the attendant.

"Willoughby?" replied Mrs. Grant with a soft laugh. "Lovely Willoughby. Oh, we do miss him. How is he?"

"He's living on a farm."

"That's good. He loved his horses. Always at the stables, he was. Is he happy?"

"D'you happen to know where his family live, Mrs. Grant? We're trying to get them a message."

She shook her head. "I don't even know if they're alive. But would you tell him I said hello?"

She pulled open the door to a rush of cold wind. As we stepped onto the stone steps, I felt the guvnor's finger in my pocket, searching for a coin. He pulled out a farthing and pressed it into her hand.

"I'll give you another if you find us an address for Willoughby's brother," he whispered. "Do you think you could do that?"

Mrs. Grant pushed the coin into her jacket. She smiled.

"No," she said, and shut the door.

For the rest of the day, the guvnor voiced his vexation over Crenshaw. If there was one thing he didn't like, it was being prevented doing something by a man behind a desk. It only ever made him more determined, and the more he chafed, the more important it seemed to him to talk to Willoughby's brother. So we returned to Caterham on the last downtrain that night, reaching the gates of the asylum around midnight. The administrative block was in darkness, the fountain dry. We walked on the icy grass aside the gravel drive, taking care not to make any noise. A couple of lights shone from the upper windows of each ward block, but the only sound was the wind in the tall pines. It seemed that all in the asylum were sleeping until we heard a terrible shrieking from one of the dark ward blocks to the left of the big house. I was used to people shouting and screaming, I'd heard it often enough in the places I grew up, but the noise that night was like nothing I'd ever heard before. I stopped in my tracks, paralysed by the tormented cries. They seemed to come from another world, one without words or reason, and they chilled me to the bone. Then came a quick banging, like someone was smashing something hard against the wall, then shouts, normal everyday shouts, over the top of the shrieking. The guvnor took my arm and pulled me behind a bush next to the main house.

"Wait a moment," he whispered. "In case someone comes out."

As we stood in the bushes listening, the guvnor passed me one of his chocolate bears, then unwrapped another and put it in his mush. Usually it was him afraid of things, but he seemed calm and unaffected by the fearful noise. After a few moments, I heard the rustle of paper in his pocket again.

"You know," he murmured, "I always thought Ettie would suit a place like this. Not as a patient, of course, although I've always wondered if she's on the milder borders of some type of mental disease. She's extremely argumentative, you've no doubt noticed, and she gets uncommonly anxious about things which really aren't important."

"Like the builders?"

"It's not just the builders, Norman. You don't know what she's like when we're alone. She's always got something between her teeth. This week it's chalk in the bread. She's been to a different shop every day trying to get Allinsons. And she talks endlessly of my taking up calisthenics. But no, I mean as a job. It would suit her need for commanding people, and her nursing skills, of course. She could live in the staff block."

He couldn't see me smiling, crouched as we were in a dark bush.

"I think I might suggest it," he said.

As the minutes passed, the noises began to fall away, until

finally all was silent. The brick walls of the administrative block rose above us, the icy grass glowed. Peace reigned once more in the asylum.

I got out my betty and tried the lock on the big front door while the guvnor stood crow. Picking locks was a skill I'd learnt from my uncle Norbert when I was apprenticed to him as a locksmith. He'd died before I learnt much, so I could only really do the simpler ones. This one felt like a three-ward tumbler, too difficult for me, and so we crept along the front of the house, checking for loose windows in the offices. They were all shut tight. It was the same down the side. As we got to the rear of the main block, we passed a dark stables between two of the wards. A horse snorted and stamped. We waited there for a few moments, watching in case anyone came out. A bat flew over our heads.

At the back was a yard with big wooden bins that stunk of bones and rotting onion. The little kitchen door there had a simpler back-spring lock and I had it open in a few minutes.

The guvnor lit his candle and we stepped inside. The kitchen was cleaned spotless, the range still warm, the floor of stone. There was nobody sleeping in there, and so we crept across the room, through a door to a corridor. At the end was just the slightest glow of moonlight from a window beyond. Very slow, we crept along the creaking floorboards. Each door we passed was shut. We stopped and listened every few steps. We heard mice behind the walls, a trickle of water somewhere, but no sounds of people.

At the end of the corridor was the great entrance hall, the smell of varnish so strong it was almost choking. We could see a bit better here for the bit of moonlight as came through the windows. Again we paused, listening. All was quiet. We tip-toed past the staircase and into the other corridor. There the guvnor lit his candle and I set to work on the door of Crenshaw's office. I got it straight off and we were in.

"Right," he whispered when the door was shut behind us. "We need to go through the patient records. It'll be one of those ledgers on the shelves."

The room stank of cigar smoke. I lit my own candle and we set to searching. After a few minutes we heard a sound: quick footsteps somewhere in the building. Not outside the door, but somewhere distant. We froze. They seemed to be running. They stopped.

A door shut somewhere upstairs. Then silence.

"Get back to it," whispered the guvnor.

I pulled ledgers off the shelves: *Minutes of the Committee of Visitors*; *Medical Superintendent Reports*; *Financial Statements*; *Payments*; *Wages*; *Contracts*; *Loans*. Nothing to do with patients.

"Found it," hissed the guvnor, pulling out a thick red ledger. *"Register of Male Patients."* He opened it on the desk and found the K section. "Here he is. *Krott, Willoughby.* Let's see. Admitted 1888, age eighteen, occupation *Book Folder*, chargeable to *Lambeth Union*. No discharge date." He turned the page. "This book doesn't record the nearest relative. There must be another register."

We both went back to the shelves and searched with our candles until I found the *Admissions and Discharge Register*. I pulled out the 1888 volume and opened it on the desk. It was arranged by week. We turned page after page until we found him, admitted 29 September, and the address we wanted: *Brother, 11 Waterloo Square, Camberwell.*

The guvnor took out his notebook and copied the address. I put the ledgers back on the shelves.

"I've had a notion," he whispered. "Let's have a look at the *Register of Female Patients.*"

I got the ledger down for him and he found the G section.
"Gotsaul, Polly," he read. "Admitted 1890, age nineteen.
Occupation *Ironer*. Chargeable to *Lambeth Union*. No discharge
recorded either. Get me the 1890 *Admissions and Discharges
Register*. We'll take her relative's address too. They might be
having the same trouble as the Barclays."

We found her entry in March, and the nearest relative: *Sister, 64 Hemans Street, Vauxhall*.

The guvnor noted it in his book, then tapped his fingers
on the table as he studied the right-hand page. "Look at this
list of discharges. Most of them are just recorded as dead." He
turned page after page and sighed. "So many names. It doesn't
say much for the treatment they offer here, does it?" He was silent for a moment, then he whispered, "Look at this, Barnett."

He held his candle over the page and pointed at the entry.
"See who authorized these records."

The name in the ledger was Henry Tasker.

Chapter Twenty-Two

We both stared at the book: the title next to Henry Tasker's name was *Chair, Committee of Visitors*. It was countersigned by the good Mr. Crenshaw.

The guvnor sat back, the candle flickering upon the desk. His breath drifted from his mouth.

"That's Mr. Tasker and Sons' brother, isn't it?" he said. "The one who knows the Ockwells. Bring me the ledger that Willoughby's in."

As he copied the details into his notebook, I brought it over. He found the page and brought the candle close.

"Well, well. Henry Tasker authorized this one also. Farmer, Justice of the Peace, Chair of the Committee of Visitors. He's a busy man." He stood to replace the ledger. "Now, let's get out of this place before they commit us."

It was then we heard footsteps again, but this time they were on our floor. I flew to the table and blew out my candle.

The steps came nearer.

I looked around quick, wondering where we might hide. There was no cupboard and no other doors. Even the curtains were too short to cover us.

Now the footsteps were in the corridor, coming towards the office. The guvnor took my arm and pulled me behind the desk, where we both got to our knees. He blew out his candle. The footsteps were now outside the door.

A key went into the lock and turned.

I held my breath, feeling the guvnor's hot thigh next to mine as we crouched on the rug. The handle squeaked but the door stayed shut. The key turned again. This time it opened.

Someone entered and shut the door behind them. I was trying hard as I could to quiet my breathing, but my heart was pounding away inside. It was so dark I couldn't even see my hands.

We heard a woman's laugh on the other side of the desk.

Then someone else's footsteps in the corridor, approaching, stopping outside the office.

The squeak of the door handle again, then a dim light. I crouched lower behind the desk. The guvnor held his hand over his mouth to hide his breathing. He was bent double on the floor, his legs a-tremble with the effort, his belly threatening to burst through his coat. My knee was giving me hell for putting my weight on it: I grit my teeth and tried to stop shaking.

"Oh, naughty girl," came a man's voice, whiny and playful, loosened with brandy. It was Crenshaw. "How did you get in here?"

"Don't know, sir." The woman tittered, putting on like she was a young thing. They were only a few yards from us.

"Keeping secrets are you, Nelly-Noo? Did you pinch my key?"

"Can't help myself, sir," said the woman like she was scared of him.

"Silly little imbecile."

"Only got half a brain, sir," she said with a giggle.

There was some rustling between them, a gasp, heavy breaths. Just then, the guvnor's stomach let out a little gurgle. I pinched his fat leg hard. He glared at me, his face red, his eyes too bright above his hand. He shook his head.

"Don't know right from wrong, do you, naughty girl?" said Crenshaw.

"No, sir."

"I think it's time for your treatment, don't you?"

"You going to grow my brain again, sir?"

"I'll straighten those eyes for you, Nelly-Noo."

She gasped.

"Take your drawers down, then. I've a special medicine for you."

It was then the guvnor's stomach gurgled so loud it could have woken a whole ward.

"What the hell is that?" cried Crenshaw.

A moment later we saw his face in the lamplight, peering over the desk.

He wasn't the man we'd seen that afternoon. His shirt tails were out from his britches, his grey side-hair stood in wisps from his head, his lips were purple with wine. Behind him stood Mrs. Grant, her jacket unbuttoned, her hair falling over her chest.

Before we had time to do anything, Crenshaw turned and

fled, pulling Mrs. Grant behind him. As we got to our feet, he slammed the office door shut. We heard the key turn in the lock.

"Blazes!" said the guvnor. "We've got to get out of here before he brings help!"

I ran over to the door and got to my knees, my betty in my hand. He lit his candle and held it for me as I tried to work the lock.

"Hurry, Barnett."

It was no use. The key was still in the lock on the other side and wouldn't budge.

We dashed over to the windows and pulled back the thick curtains. A row of thin iron bars protected each one. The guvnor gave me the walking stick he'd loaned from Lewis. I wedged it under one of the bars and jerked hard. The stick snapped.

"Damn it!" he cried, getting wheezy again.

I took an umbrella from behind the door and tried that, but it just bent against the solid bars. Already we could hear shouts outside the house, heavy footsteps running up the drive. I tried wrenching each bar with my hands, searching for a loose one, a weak one, but they all held fast. We heard the rumble of feet in the corridor now, then all at once the key turned and five burly blokes came storming in, all in blue attendants' uniforms. Two of them pounced on the guvnor, one on each arm. The other three went for me, one of them throwing punches while the others tried to wrestle me to the ground. He landed one on my neck and a second on my bad hand as I tried to block him. I got my arm free and whacked him one back, a good one right in his mush, sending the blood streaming out his lip and into his whiskers. It only made them angry, and they had me down on my belly in moments, my arms twisted up my back. There was nothing I could do: they were experts at taking control of a man. While I was down, the one I'd clumped gave me two hefty kicks in my side with his steel-capped boot. It hurt like hell.

They pulled me to my feet. Crenshaw entered the office, smartened up now. His shirt tails were tucked in, his jacket buttoned, his side hair smoothed down.

"What were you looking for?" he asked, his hands behind his back, his little breast thrust out.

"Just what we asked of you earlier," said the guvnor. An attendant held each arm. "The address of Willoughby Krott's brother."

Crenshaw shook his head, his mouth open in a scowl. "What were you really looking for?"

"Only that, sir. I swear it. Now, please instruct your men to let us go."

"Housebreaking," said Crenshaw. "Stealing personal records for the purpose of blackmail is my guess. The magistrate won't look too kindly on that, I can assure you. So, tell me what you were really looking for. I might release you if you do."

"But we've told you, sir," said the guvnor firmly. "Just an address. That's all. Our case has nothing to do with this asylum."

Crenshaw sighed. He turned to the door.

"Seclusion," he said, and disappeared down the corridor.

They marched us out into the night and along a path to one of the ward blocks. I didn't even try to struggle: one of them had my arm wrenched up my back so that every step sent a terrible jolt of pain through me. The one at the front unlocked the door with a heavy set of keys attached to his belt. Inside was dark. It smelt of piss and lye, the wooden floor still wet from cleaning. The bloke I whacked lit an oil lamp and led us down a long, green corridor to the back of the building.

"You can't imprison us," protested the guvnor. "Our people will come looking. They know we're here."

In silence, they bundled us down some stairs to the basement. It reeked of mould and a nearby cesspit as must have been leaking. The tunnel was narrow, the ceiling so low you couldn't stand up straight. The only light was from the bloke's lamp, which lit up the stone floor and the blistered white walls. We stopped at a wooden door studded with iron bolts. The bloke with the key ring unlocked it. When I felt the grip loosen on my arm I tried to twist away, but the one by my side walloped me in the belly, winding me. They threw us in and slammed the door. The key turned in the lock.

It was dark as hell itself in there, not even a glimmer of moonlight from a sliver of window. The guvnor was on the floor next to me. His hand padded around until he found my leg.

"Are you all right, Norman?" he asked.

I was still trying to catch my breath, wanting to puke, my belly aching.

"Breathe slowly," he said.

The men's footsteps in the corridor grew more distant, then there was silence.

"Right," I said at last.

"Have you got your matches?"

"Left them on the desk."

"Oh, Lord. I can't see a damned thing in here."

I found the door with my hands and felt around it like a blind man. There was no latch and no keyhole. The hinges were made of iron. I rammed my shoulder against it, all my bruises and pains screaming out at me in fury; I sat on the floor and kicked it again and again.

"It's not going to shift," I said.

The floor was made of some kind of rubber cloth. The wall was the same. I reached out in the darkness until I caught the guvnor's arm.

"Over here," I said.

On hands and knees, I guided him to the wall, where we sat with our shoulders touching, staring into the blackness. We were both panting, wheezing, coughing.

"I don't like that man Crenshaw," he said at last. "What the hell was he talking about with that lady? Did you hear what he said?"

"We could get a couple of weeks in gaol if he persuades the coppers we were stealing secrets."

"He might not even call them. He won't want us telling anybody what he was doing with Mrs. Grant. Oh, Lord, I should have told Lewis where we were going. Nobody knows we're here."

"He can't keep us. It's a crime."

"I wouldn't be so sure. People disappear in these places. It happens all the time."

"But what about Ettie and Neddy? What if they need help?"

"Be quiet, Barnett! I'm trying to blooming think!"

I let him blooming think. I was blooming thinking myself, thinking what a mess it was. Thinking we could be down there for days and nobody'd know.

The guvnor's belly called out again, an unholy gurgle like a village pump being worked in a dry summer. Then it stopped and a cat cried out from somewhere deep inside him.

"Oh, Lord," he murmured. "There was something wrong

with that soup, Barnett. It was sour as verjuice. I'm sure that meat wasn't mutton."

I didn't reply. His belly fell silent.

"We have to get out when they come for us," he said. "Be ready. We'll find a way."

It didn't reassure me. Those attendants knew how to deal with difficult men, it was their job and they were chosen for it. I'd heard of the treatments they used in some of these places. I'd heard people could be driven mad in an asylum.

He rustled in his pocket and placed something in my hand. One of his chocolate bears. I unwrapped it and put it in my mouth. He had one himself.

"Is that a chocolate?" demanded a voice in the blackness.

"Who's there?" asked the guvnor quickly, gripping my arm. "Where are you?"

I stared into the black, hoping to glimpse some clue as to who it was, but I couldn't see a damn thing in the darkness. The guvnor's grip tightened on my arm. I got to my knees in case the fellow came flying at us.

There was no reply.

"Who's there?" asked the guvnor again.

I waited, my fists tight, ready to lash out if he came close.

"Who's there, damn it?" demanded the guvnor. "Speak up or I'll send my man over to teach you some manners!"

"Montague Arthur Russell," growled the voice at last. He was putting on an uppish accent, and not too well either: there was a hard edge to it I didn't like the sound of.

"Where are you?" asked the guvnor, a quaver of fear in his voice now. I edged a little forward, my fists ahead of me just in case. The bloke was in this cell for a reason: best assume it was a bad one.

"In the corner."

"Are there others?"

"Only us," said the voice. "Toss me one of your chocolates."

The guvnor made a movement. There was a grunt. Then we heard him unwrap it.

"What is it, a bunny?"

The chocolate had made his voice a bit more friendly, and I felt the guvnor relax beside me.

"A bear," he said. "Where are we, Mr. Russell?"

"Seclusion room is its title. Keeping you safe. Keeping others safe."

"Is there a window?" I asked.

"There's a peephole a few inches wide up top here. Looks straight into a bush, so you won't see nothing now it's dark out. You'll see it in a few hour. No way to leave, if that's what you're asking."

"But we must get out," said the guvnor.

"You'll have to wait till they come. There's a bucket in the corner if you need it."

"Why are you here, sir?"

"Caused some mischief on the ward earlier, I'm afraid to say. Bit the attendant with my teeth, so they say. I won't deny it, sir. My spirit was too high, if you like. So here I am. Relaxing. Looking after oneself. And you? Which ward?"

"We're not patients, Mr. Russell," said the guvnor. "We're investigative agents. We were hunting for some information in Mr. Crenshaw's office and they caught us. I assume you are a...a lunatic?"

"So they say, so they say," answered the voice in the dark. "Chaplain believes there might be a demon in me. I cannot believe it. I go the science way: it's one's humours, perhaps. It does go bad with me sometimes, and then the mischief comes, mostly a reaction to cruel treatment by one of the warders. I won't say his name. He's against me. Says I bring him out in a rash. Does everything he can to bring me misery."

"It's natural to chafe at cruel treatment," said the guvnor.

"It does vex me."

"May I ask a personal question, Mr. Russell?"

"You can have a try."

"What was your diagnosis?"

"Oh, only monomania. I had a strong belief. I won't tell you what it was but it was quite wrong, and yet I believed it thoroughly. I'm quite recovered now, been thinking straight for a year at least. They should really have released me some time ago; I don't know why they won't."

"I'm sorry to hear this," said the guvnor. "How very wrong."

"Wrong indeed. I've made a complaint to the Committee of Visitors. A lunatic gives off a smell of henbane. All of them here who still suffer do. I'm sure you smelt it?"

"Ah!" answered the guvnor. "I didn't know what it was."

"That's how you know," said Montague Arthur Russell. "Dr. Burrows himself has said it. How do I smell to you, your lordship?"

The guvnor sniffed the mouldy air.

"Just the usual," he said. "For a man."

"But you don't smell henbane?"

"I don't believe so."

"What about the other gentleman?"

"Nor me," I said.

"On account of me being cured. There's another inmate swallowed hairpins last week. A woman."

Russell didn't sound as if he was dangerous, and so I sat back down against the wall again. My knee'd taken another knock in the scuffle and the side that got kicked was burning. I could find no comfort on the rubber floor.

"Would you like us to contact your family when we're out?" asked the guvnor. "I'm sure they can help."

"You're investigative agents, you say? Like Sherlock Holmes?"

"That's right, Mr. Russell," I replied before the guvnor had a chance to start up on Mr. Holmes again.

There was a soft pop next to me, a vial being uncorked, and the tinkle of liquid.

"What's that, William?" I asked.

"Just a draught of chlorodyne," he said. "My gout's playing up again."

"Give it me," I said. "My side's aching like hell."

"But the attendants might be back. You have to be ready."

"I just want a swallow for the pain."

He passed me the vial. Almost straight off I felt the ease come over me. He felt for my hand and took back the medicine.

"I'll have a little sip, if you don't mind," said Montague Arthur Russell in the darkness. "They don't give you chlorodyne unless you've broken someone's arm."

The guvnor sighed.

"Come over here, then."

The bloke shuffled over until he'd found the guvnor's hand. I heard his swallow.

The guvnor's belly made another long gurgle which filled the room.

"Crikey," said Montague Arthur Russell. "That soup must have been bad."

"I think I might need the bucket," said the guvnor, a strain in his voice.

I cannot describe the horrors of the next five minutes, but when it was over the guvnor found his way back over to me and sat with a little cry. A fresh, much more evil stink than henbane filled the air.

"I don't think it was mutton in that soup, Barnett. I think it was dog."

I could hardly think, let alone speak.

Whether he slept or not I couldn't tell, but there was silence for the rest of the night.

Chapter Twenty-Three

Morning came, and with it a faint glow of light through the peephole at the far end of the cell. It was level with a bed of soil and a thick bush, through which you could make out nothing of the grounds beyond. Montague Arthur Russell lay on the floor wrapped in a thick blanket, so only his head could be seen. He was quite bald, his face battered, his nose red with the cold, a thick beard badly cut. His neck was heavy as a bull, and he snored like the happiest man on earth.

I got to my feet and jumped up and down, rubbing my hands. It was cold as sin in there and my knee was aching like blazes. I'd slept no more than an hour or so on the damp, rubber floor; in my half-dreams I kept seeing Birdie smiling at me, my neighbour who never spoke, Mrs. Gillie with her mouth open and cackling, her horrible tooth, wet and black. Mrs. Barclay's song played over and over in my head.

Soon, the guvnor opened his eyes, his breath coming out in clouds. I helped him to his feet and he also rubbed his hands, walking back and forth from the door to the wall.

"They'll be here to get us soon," he said. "I'm sure of it. We must take the first chance to get away. Are you ready, Norman?"

"I'm ready."

But they didn't come. We began to hear noises from the ward above: doors closing, chairs scraping on the floor, voices. Still no one came. Hours passed in that cold cell.

We were hungry, frozen cold, our mood low.

Russell woke late in the morning. With his blanket clutched around him, he stood, stretching his legs, arching his back. He was a monster of a man, inches taller than me, with hands the size of mangles.

"When do they bring breakfast?" asked the guvnor.

"They let one fast after an incident," said our friend.

"Oh, dear. I must have a cup of tea. I'm very dry after my illness last night. When will they come for you, Mr. Russell?"

"In the afternoon."

"Are you sure?"

"Everything happens the same every day here, sir. Like a clock. But they might perhaps collect you sooner as you ain't patients."

"How many usually come for you?"

"One. With the usual stick. But you gents won't ambush him, if that's what you're thinking. He'll make you stand by the far wall while he opens the door. Always the same. Won't open it least you're there."

The guvnor had a think. As he did so, Montague Arthur Russell emptied himself into the bucket.

"We need your help, sir," said the guvnor. "We're on an

important case, about a girl who's been imprisoned. We must get out of here as soon as we can. This is what I'm thinking: as soon as we hear him coming, you lie on the floor there and cry out for help. I'll pretend I'm strangling you. When the attendant opens the door to save you, Barnett'll overpower him. All you must do is cry out. They won't even know you're helping us."

Montague Arthur Russell performed several knee flexes as he thought.

"Yes," he said at last. "I think I'd enjoy that."

"What if there's more than one?" I asked.

"We'll deal with them together, Norman. I don't want you to fight, Mr. Russell. I don't want you punished for this."

"Nor me, sir," he said.

Hours more passed. We talked for a while, then Russell curled up again inside his blanket and began to snore. We sat, then stood again, then paced, then sat. The light began to fade.

"Not even lunch!" cried the guvnor. He crawled over to Russell and shook him awake. "Are you sure they'll come for you, Mr. Russell?"

Our friend sat up, rubbing his eyes.

"They'll be along for my treatment. Never miss that."

"Your treatment?"

"Cold dousing."

"Good Lord! On a freezing day like this?"

"It's painful, I'll grant you that. I prefer the opium when I'm excitable, or the bromide, but they won't give it one after mischief, sir. Always the cold water."

"We'll contact your relatives when we get out, sir. They'll intervene."

Russell shook his head.

"It was them as put me here, sir. Never visited, not even

once. Never replied to the letters neither. They've abandoned me and that's the truth. Dr. Crenshaw keeps me here because he gets a fee from the workhouse for each lunatic he's got. Nobody listens to the patients, except those as got money. They can hire lawyers and doctors. Folk like me are lost, sir. Lost."

"I'm sorry to hear that, my friend."

"And I'm not the only one in here. A few of us are cured yet still he keeps us."

We heard the clanking of keys above, and steps on the stairs.

"Here he is," said Russell. He crawled over and laid himself out on the floor. "Climb aboard, Mr. Arrowood."

The guvnor got on top. I pushed myself against the wall behind the door. Our friend screamed out and began kicking and bucking, the guvnor's hands around his throat. Footsteps approached on the other side of the door.

"Help!" cried the big man. "Murder!"

The peephole slid open.

"What's going on in there?" barked a gruff voice.

"Murder!" cried Russell, kicking and struggling, while the guvnor did his best to keep his hands around his neck.

"Stop that!" ordered the attendant. A key went in the lock. It turned and the door opened.

The attendant darted in, raising his foot and shoving the guvnor off Russell. I took my chance, bringing both my hands down hard on the back of his head. He fell to the floor, but there was another behind him, his club raised in the air. I didn't have time to get out of the way, and could only raise my arms to soften the blow. But just as the club was about to fall the attendant collapsed onto the floor with a grunt of rage.

I looked down to see Russell's hands around the bloke's ankles, a great smile upon his face. He gave me the wink. Before I had time to think, another big attendant rushed through the door. He whacked Russell's arm with his club, causing him to shriek. As he raised his club again, I caught him good in the jaw, making him stagger across the cell. I was on him even before he fell, grabbing his arm and wrenching it up his back, making him double over, groaning in pain. The guvnor was up now too. He stamped hard on the second bloke's bollocks, then hopped over him to the door. I got my attendant to the floor, then dropped heavy on him, my knee falling hard on his spine. He cried out. Russell was now on his feet, the second attendant's club in his hand.

"Now, now, Montague," said the first, getting to his feet, backing away to the far wall, his arms out before him. "Hand over the club. Don't make this go worse than it needs."

The guvnor was pulling me back into the tunnel. Montague followed, slamming the door behind him. A bunch of keys were hanging from the keyhole: I turned them quick and shoved them in my pocket.

Then came the most furious banging on the other side of the door. Cursing. Threats. The guvnor embraced the big patient, who laughed, his head thrown back.

"Come on, sir," he said. "Let's away."

We dashed along the dark tunnel, up the stairs, along the next corridor to the front door of the ward. We passed a few patients on the way, but no one tried to stop us. I found the key on the bunch. One turn and we were out, in the cold, fresh air, under the darkest cloud so far this winter.

A landau was passing on the track between the administration block and the wards, on its way to the stables.

"That's our ride," I said.

The guvnor and me set off after it, but Montague Arthur Russell didn't move. I turned back. The giant was moving from one foot to the other, his brow creased.

"Come along, mate. You're getting out."

"I think I might stay," he said, a twitch in his eye.

"We'll help you," I said. "But we got to go now. Come on, mate."

"Be brave, my friend," said the guvnor, holding out his hand.

"No," said Russell, wringing his great hands. "I ain't ready. I got nowhere to go. I...I reckon I could maybe do with a bit more treatment after all."

"Are you afraid they'll catch you?" asked the guvnor.

Russell shook his head, backing through the ward door. The guvnor looked at me. We could still hear the shouting of the attendants from the basement, and it wouldn't be long till they were rescued. Montague Arthur Russell gave us another little wink, then closed the door. We heard the key turn in the lock.

The landau was now parked outside the stables. We ran over as the coachman got down and went into a hut. I climbed straight up onto the box; the guvnor scrambled onto the seat.

"Get up!" I cried at the horse, whipping the reins.

The horse started to walk. I steered it round until it was pointing back down the drive, then geed it up again.

"Oi!" cried the coachman, coming out the hut.

"Get up!" I said again, and flicked the reins. The horse kept walking.

The man jumped on the steps.

"This is Dr. Crenshaw's carriage!" he barked. "What d'you think you're doing?"

"Stealing it," I said, lifting my foot to his chest and giving him a good shove. He fell onto the grass by the roadway.

"Get on!" I cried, giving the horse the whip now. Still

it walked. In seconds the coachman was back on the steps, clutching the rail with both hands.

"Jump down, mate," I told him, "or you'll get my fist in your face."

"You ain't taking my horse nowhere without me," he said quick. He was a little bloke, no bigger than a jockey. But he had pluck. "You don't know how to handle it."

Hearing shouting, I turned. Four or five men burst out of the ward we'd come from. One pointed to us and they started to run. I grabbed the coachman by the jacket and hauled him up onto the box with me.

"Make it go faster. *Now.*"

He gave the horse a sharp cut of the whip and it started to trot, then to canter. The men were storming over the lawn. We passed the fountain and gained the road. The horse picked up speed proper now, and we flew away. I looked back. The men stood on the road by the gates, watching us go.

"You take us where we want and we won't hurt you," I said to the coachman.

He nodded, his eyes on the road. I bent down to see the guvnor sitting below.

"We're safe, sir," I said.

"Thanks to Mr. Russell."

"So where we going?" asked the coachman.

"Catford," said the guvnor.

"Oh, no," groaned the coachman, pulling his hat low over his ears. "We only just come back from there."

I patted his knee. "There, there, chuckaboo."

"Don't fucking touch me, mate," he said.

Chapter Twenty-Four

❖————◆————❖

We stopped at a shop in Croydon where the guvnor got us some saveloys and a couple of bottles of tonic wine. We moved off again. After a few long swallows of the tonic wine, I felt more awake. I passed the coachman the bottle. He took a few lugs, then I drank some more, listening to the rhythm of the horse, the turn of the carriage wheels. I forgot about needing my bed. I wanted to get on with the case.

We passed through Thornton Heath and Crystal Palace, where the coachman lit the lamps. It was dark when we reached Catford. A couple of women were hurrying home, heavy baskets hanging from their arms. The lights were on in the pub. The building works were empty.

I hopped down at the church, found the note from yester-day, and passed it to the guvnor.

"She still hasn't spoken to Birdie," he called up to us on the box as we pulled away. "We've a few more errands to run, coachman. There'll be something for your pocket, though, don't you worry. Take us to 11 Waterloo Square, Camberwell."

"Is she safe?" I asked.

"I believe so. Says she thinks Polly has melancholia now. Neddy's being worked hard."

I was relieved. It had been a long night in that cell, and it was longer wondering if Ettie was in any danger. I pulled the cork and had another drink.

"Give us some of that," said the coachman. "Peter's the name, by the way."

He passed me the reins as he had a drink.

"That bloody does something to you, don't it, mate?" he said as he was driving again.

"Wakes you up all right."

"What's it called?"

"Vin Mariani. Best tonic there is."

"I've never had the like before. Feel like I could drive all night." He turned to me quick. "I don't want to, mate. Just got some spirit in me all of a sudden."

Peter turned out to be a good bloke, an ex-soldier who'd fought over in Africa, and he was chatty enough to make the time pass. We'd finished the bottle by the time we reached Camberwell.

It was a block of mansion flats off Lomond Grove, a wealthy place. We were both surprised John Krott would be living there what with how wretched and poor his brother was, but the address was right. His name was on the bell.

The maid checked if he'd see us, then led the three of us into a small study. There, in a wing chair by the fire, was a handsome fellow in a red smoking jacket. His black hair was neatly combed, the sides a little greying. A crystal glass and decanter stood on a table by his arm, a book lay upon his lap. The guvnor did the introductions.

"The coachman can wait outside," said Krott sharply.

"It's rather cold, sir," replied the guvnor.

"He'll survive."

As Peter made to go, I took hold of his arm.

"You're staying here, mate," I said.

Krott's brow creased. Before he could speak, the guvnor said, "We need to ask you about your brother, Mr. Krott. We're private investigative agents, looking into the possible mistreatment of a young woman on the farm where Willoughby works. You're acquainted with Godwin Ockwell, is that right?"

He shook his head. "I've never met him."

"Willoughby said you were friends. He told us he was coming to live with you, and that Godwin was going to arrange it."

Krott laughed, taking a sip from a glass on the table beside him.

"My brother's feeble-minded. You shouldn't listen to him: he's not coming to live here. He's happy on the farm. Nature's good for his type, you know. Nature and steady work."

"Is Godwin his father?" asked the guvnor. "He calls him Dad."

"Don't be ridiculous. Our father died years ago."

Above the small fire was a painting of a country scene, men working in the fields gathering hay, a wagon, the sun. It made you feel good, a picture like that. It couldn't have been further from that frozen pig farm in Catford, with its attack dogs, its slaughter shed, its mountains of stinking dung.

"What do you know of the Ockwell family, Mr. Krott, if I might ask?"

"Why, nothing. I've never met them."

"But how did you arrange for Willoughby to work there?"

"I had nothing to do with it. When the asylum finished his treatment, they arranged for him to make a life on the farm."

"Ah," said the guvnor. "I assumed you must have been involved."

"I don't think you understand the situation with the feeble-minded," said Krott. He lit a long, thin cigar with a golden lighter, quite happy to sit as we stood before him. "One must leave it to the experts. I've always trusted their decisions."

"We met your brother just the other day," said I. "He looks half-starved. Dressed in rags. Seems to do all the work on that farm, him and his mate."

Krott looked at me in surprise, like he didn't think I'd be able to talk.

"I'm sure you exaggerate."

"He wants to live with you," I said.

"Impossible." He directed his speech to the guvnor now. "He's not suited to the city. The noise and crowds confuse him. He'd get into all manner of trouble."

"When's the last time you saw Willoughby, Mr. Krott?" asked the guvnor.

Krott held his cigar by his cheek and sighed. "It only upsets him when I visit."

"But he's your brother."

"He bears the same family name as I, but that's all, I'm afraid. He's a Mongolian type. D'you know of them? A retrogression."

"You've abandoned him?"

"The alienists at Caterham are experts in the treatment of idiocy."

"Don't you care how he's faring on that farm?"

"Listen, Mr. Arrowood. It's very difficult. I've had some

success in my life, thanks to the good Lord and my own efforts over the years. I own four chandlers. You clearly don't have a person like him in your family. I've two daughters, both looking to be wed in the next few years, and both perfectly capable of marrying well. But which man of worth will have them if they see Willoughby? They'll think there's a taint in the line, and I can assure you there isn't. My daughters are as bright as buttons. Should they be brought low because of him?"

Krott glared at him. When no answer came, he continued: "He's caused us a good deal of trouble already. We used to live in Kennington. We had to leave our home to set up here where nobody knows us."

"You don't care to know if he suffers?" exclaimed the guvnor, raising his voice.

"They don't feel as acutely as we do," said the chandler, waving away the guvnor's question. "Their senses are quite dulled. Did you know their brain hardly functions in cold temperatures? The best place for him is the asylum or just where he is: a farm where they can control him. Imagine if he had children?"

The guvnor stared at him in silence. Krott rolled his eyes and brought the cigar to his fine lips.

"Have you heard Galton speak, Mr. Arrowood?" he asked. "I suppose not. The fact is, if we want a better future for our children and grandchildren, we must focus our care on the better members of our race. What good would it do to risk my daughters' chances of a good marriage for the sake of a regression? Surely you don't disagree with human improvement?"

"I've never been able to decide about Galton's ideas," said the guvnor. "But now I see them personified in you I realize how odious they are."

Krott stood.

"I'd like you to leave," he demanded. "And take your rab-ble with you."

I nudged Peter. "That's us, mate," I said.

"Charming," declared the little fellow.

"Get out!" barked Krott.

We turned to leave. The owner of four chandlers walked behind us to the front door. The maid stood further back in the corridor, watching.

"Willoughby's a better example of the race than you are, sir," I said as we stepped out of the apartment.

"That's a rather ignorant comment," said Krott, and slammed the door on us.

It wasn't far from Camberwell to Vauxhall. The guvnor was keen to talk to Polly's sister to find out if she'd also been pre-vented seeing her. If she had, we'd know for certain the Bar-clays were right. Each of us had lost a bit of the energy we had before, and so we stopped at a shop to pick up another bottle of Vin Mariani before we arrived. When we were feeling a little perkier, we called at number sixty-four. It was a run-down terrace, the glimmer of candlelight in every sooty window, the chimneys throwing out thick streams of smoke. A red-faced, round-bellied woman opened the door. She was the owner, she said, since three years past, but she'd never heard of any Gotsaul. All the other families in the house came after her.

Peter helped us try the other houses up and down the road, but we couldn't find anybody who'd heard of Polly or her sister. There was a little pub opposite. Inside, where a fire was blazing, five or six gloomy-looking navvies stood around smoking pipes, pint pots in their hands. They nodded at us as we went in, then went back to their talking. Their britches and boots were thick, ragged and muddy; their faces were burnt and veined with the cold. The whole place smelt of smoke and man-stink.

The guvnor ordered us each a mug of porter, asking the landlord if he knew a Polly Gotsaul. He shook his head.

"Don't get many ladies in here, sir," he said, nodding at a little old crow sat alone in a corner. "Except old Mrs. Fleg, there. She just about lives here."

I went over. She wore a wide-brimmed hat as would have been very fashionable on a society lady about forty years past, a black veil covering her face. Her brown coat was buttoned up to her neck; a pipe lay upon the bench beside her.

"Hello, mum," I said. "You know a Polly Gotsaul?"

"I know her," she said. Her voice was so thin I could hardly hear it. Her hands lay on the table next to her empty mug, her knuckles swollen, her fingers twisted. She turned her head towards the guvnor, who sat with Peter at the next bench.

"That's Mr. Arrowood, mum," I said. "He's my guvnor. We're detective agents, working on a case. We're trying to find her kin."

"Buy me a drain of plane, mister."

I got the gin and sat on a greasy stool opposite. When she lifted her veil to drink it, I saw that her eyes were milky. She was blind.

A cockle-seller came into the pub, and I got her a pot of eel jelly. She held it up to her chin, using her fingers to spoon it into her mouth. When she'd finished, she put the pot on the table and took another sup of gin.

"Lived over the road with her sister, Molly. Twins, they were. Never apart. I knew them from babies. Knew their old ma. And her brother too."

"She got any kin left?" I asked.

"None of the old people left round here no more. Cholera

came through here like a wind. I'll be dead soon and just as well, I'd say. Looking forward to a nice, cool bed in the dirt and don't you try telling me I ain't."

"D'you know the man Polly married?" asked the guvnor.

"Got married, did she? That's good. Hope he's treats her right. She had more than enough hardship when she was here."

"Can you tell us about her?" I asked.

"Parents died when she was fourteen or fifteen. Molly got in with a nasty fellow, made her take to the streets. With child in no time, she was. Poor soul passed over the other side giving birth. Reckon she would have lived if it was only one, but twins was too much for her. Twins ran in the family, see?"

The old woman lifted a rag from her lap and coughed into it. When she brought it away from her face, strings of bloody phlegm hung from the threads of her veil. She checked it with her twisted fingers, then wiped it away with the filthy rag. She finished her gin.

"Another?" she asked.

I got her another.

"Polly raised those babbies for three or four year. Earned a crust on the street. She loved them little creatures, loved them with all her heart. A girl and a boy, but the little boy took a fever and give it to his sister. She passed over real quick and the boy a few days after. Polly was hurt real bad from it; her nerves went. Wouldn't talk to nobody, wouldn't eat. Landlady threw her out. I said I'd take her in, happy to have the company at my age, but she wouldn't speak to you, see? Poor girl. She was always quiet, but that finished her. Heard they put her in the asylum after that. But she's married now, you say? She doing all right?"

"I think she still suffers, mum."

The old woman shook her head.

"Got to be better on the other side." She lifted her mug. "I'm looking forward to it. Just hope it ain't too warm."

I glanced over at the guvnor. His jowels were droopy, his mouth open, his eyes vacant. He shook his head in pity. Peter shifted on his bench.

We were silent for some time, each deep in our thoughts.

Finally, the guvnor rose.

"Thank you, Mrs. Fleg. You've been so very helpful. I wish you well."

When he reached to take her hand she flinched. But she allowed it. He squeezed those bony fingers and stroked her wrist, then placed a shilling in her palm.

"God bless you, sir," she whispered as we left the pub.

Chapter Twenty-Five

We stood by the landau finishing off the Vin Mariani. There were no lights in the street.

"Thank you, Peter," said the guvnor. "You can drop us at home, then we're finished. It's been a pleasure meeting you."

"I had quite a jolly, sir," said Peter.

He strapped a nosebag to the horse and stroked its neck as it crunched away. It looked a young thing, all black and shiny. A handsome fellow.

"Home time, mate," he said to it. "Twice in a day's a bit too much for you, ain't it, lad?"

"Tell me, who was your master visiting this morning?" asked the guvnor.

"We was at Mr. Tasker's farm first, out near Catford, then we came up here. Master had to call on someone in the Poor Law Union."

The guvnor's eyes met mine.

"D'you know who, Peter?"

The driver finished the bottle and tucked the empty in the landau.

"Couldn't tell you, sir. The Union gentlemen are often down in Caterham for one thing and another, though. It's them as send us most of our lunatics."

He unhooked the nosebag and let the horse drink from a bucket.

"Does Dr. Crenshaw often visit Tasker's farm?"

"Never has before, far as I know. Mr. Tasker's Chair of the Committee of Visitors. They usually come to Caterham."

The guvnor nodded, stroking his whiskers. He paced up to the streetlamp, turned and paced back, working over something in his mind.

"Tell me," he said at last. "Had you planned the trip this morning?"

Peter shook his head.

"Didn't know nothing about it, Mr. Arrowood. Maid came over first thing this morning and woke me up."

"Does he usually order his carriage at the last minute?"

"Not him, sir, he's a very well-planned man. I always know the day before if he needs me. Mrs. Crenshaw's a different story. Always the last minute for her."

"One more thing: how did Dr. Crenshaw seem to you this morning? His emotion."

"He had no emotion, sir."

"People don't have no emotion, Peter. Think again. Anything you noticed."

"Well, he didn't. He'd usually be chafing at the road, sir, complaining about every little bump. He was quiet."

We climbed back onto the landau.

"You get some rest, Norman," said the guvnor as I got down on Borough High Street.

"You're not going to the Hog, are you, William?" I asked. "You need to rest as much as me."

"Of course not," he said. "What do you think I am?"

The fog had come down again by next morning, and folk coughed and choked as they walked to work, wrapped in scarves and gloves and layers of coats and jackets. Paces Walk was a short street ending against the wall of a board school. It was a poorer street than Saville Place, a few of the buildings being doss-houses. I called on every door up and down that road but nobody I spoke to recalled the Barclays. Even the coalman who'd served that street for thirty years couldn't remember them.

Nobody answered at Lewis's house when I first knocked. I called through the letterbox and checked the window, then hammered on the door again. Eventually the door creaked open and there he was, in all his glory, his face crossed and creased as a road map, his eyes raddled with blood, his lips cracked and purple. He wore the same clothes as yesterday, creased and muddy; the collar of his shirt was grey.

He turned back into the house without a word and fell onto the sofa in the parlour. He cried out in pain, then let out a slow, trembling groan.

I lit the fire and made some tea. I poured a bowl of hot water and brought it through.

"Laudanum," he moaned.

I righted him, smelling his awful stink, propping his fat belly against the arm of the sofa. Then I unlaced his shoes and pulled. They were stuck fast. I wiggled and pulled, twisted and wrenched, as he breathed his awful gin-whelk gas over my head. Inch by inch, those shoes managed to escape his bloated feet, until finally they slid away. I peeled the wet socks off next, seeing the red corns, the dead white skin come away with the sodden wool, the twisted yellow toenails edged all the way round with black putty.

"Ah!" he cried as I shoved his monstrous hooves in the hot water.

"Be quiet."

I gave him a dose, then wet his sheet of brown paper and laid it over his oily head. He closed his eyes.

I picked up the *The Strand Magazine*, poured myself a cup of tea, and sat by the fire to read the Holmes story. After ten minutes or so, I looked up to find him staring at me.

"Feeling yourself now, sir?" I asked.

He nodded. I poured him some tea.

"You told me you weren't going to the Hog."

"It was that damn Mariani wine," he said. "I couldn't settle."

"I went to Paces Walk this morning. The Barclays never lived there, far as I can see."

"I thought not."

"You thought not? You didn't say."

"It was when I asked her where they'd lived before—there was the slightest frown, a fraction of a second, no more. You'd have missed it if you weren't looking carefully. But I was watching and I hope you were too, Barnett: once a person has played me false I assume they'll do it again. Did you see where her eyes fell at that moment?"

I shook my head.

"To the mantel. There was an envelope there. I had a look as we left: the address was Paces Walk. Are you sure I didn't say?"

I shook my head. He leant over the steaming bowl, his

mouth open wide, like he was about to vomit. A thunderous burp emerged, then a groan. He sat up again and rubbed his temples. He sipped his tea. Then he continued, his eyes shut tight:

"It's always the things people don't want us to know that are the most important parts of the story. I can believe their other falsities were made to impress us that they've been wronged and that they have the money to pay us until the case is concluded, but not too much that we'd overcharge. Quite understandable, I suppose, if one's insecure of one's position in the world and has little faith in others. But why mislead us about where they lived previously? That's something we need to understand."

He took on more tea.

"And there's something else that puzzles me. Why would Godwin marry a woman from the lunatic asylum? A woman who used to be a streetwalker? It's unlikely he knew her before. Wouldn't he choose someone more reliable? Those farmers are practical people. It's always about the land for them."

"Maybe he paid for her services as a whore. Became attached to her. It wouldn't be the first time."

"Perhaps, although remember he already had a lover in Lisa. And what a strange coincidence that both Walter and Godwin married women with mental disorders. It's as if they're running a private asylum on that farm."

He looked at me suddenly, the brown paper falling off his head.

"Is that what they're doing, Barnett?"

"Doesn't explain why they married them. They could have just lodged them."

"Of course." He rubbed his temples and sighed. "That picture Birdie pressed to the window, it made me feel so alone, Norman. As if a great ocean opened inside me. Did you feel it?"

"I felt she needed help."

He took another draught of laudanum and shut his eyes for some time.

Finally, he spoke again: "Even though the Barclays are employing us we must remember our job here is to discover what happened to Mrs. Gillie and to help Birdie. Our duty is to them. Until they're honest with us, we cannot assume the Barclays have Birdie's interests at heart."

He sent me to collect the money while he waited around the corner. Mrs. Barclay opened the door. A white headscarf covered her shiny black hair, making her face seem browner than before; her long nose was dry and red around the noseholes. She told me Mr. Barclay was at work.

"We've put another agent inside the house, ma'am," I said as I stood on the doorstep. "A woman. They've taken her on as a dairymaid. She's talking to Birdie as we speak."

"That's good," she said, relaxing into the smile as so warmed me that first time. "If she can get Birdie's trust she might be able to persuade her to come home."

"It's just the expenses, Mrs. Barclay," I said. "You see, we must pay the lady, and the boy she has with her pretending to be her son. He's the one brings us messages. We agreed to pay them twenty shillings for three days' work, and I need to collect another three days' payment for us. Total of eighty shillings. Plus another five to cover train fares."

She sighed. "I see. Well, let me see if I have it."

She brought me inside to wait in the parlour while she climbed the stairs. Minutes passed, and the loud metal ticking of the Neptune clock on their mantel started to get on my nerves. I moved over to the doorway and listened. I could hear voices upstairs.

A few minutes later came the guvnor's knock on the front door. I let him in.

"She's upstairs seeing about the money," I told him. "Been up there five minutes or more, arguing with him."

"Good," he answered, lowering himself onto the couch. The crumb in his whiskers told me he'd been in the pudding shop.

We heard her steps upon the stairs and then she appeared, a purse in her hand. She greeted the guvnor, holding out the money to him. Pretending not to notice, he pulled his watch out and studied it.

"I'll take that," I told her.

Only when I'd folded the notes into my pocket did he look up.

"Could you ask your husband to come down?" he asked, removing his bowler.

"He's at work, Mr. Arrowood."

"He's upstairs, ma'am," he insisted gently. The same sweet smile he always had after a pudding was on his face. "I've just seen him at the window."

She strode out of the room and climbed the stairs. After a few minutes they came down. Mr. Barclay was wearing his waistcoat buttoned over a long nightshirt, a nightcap on his head. His broad shoulders drooped, his mouth hung open as if he had the flu.

"You didn't need to put on a costume, sir," said the guvnor.

"I'd just returned to bed." Mr. Barclay coughed. "I'm very ill."

"If you say so, sir."

Mr. Barclay remained in the doorway of the dark parlour,

his wife at his side. They made a queer pair: him broad in the shoulder, pink in the face, his moustache black as tar and some part of him always on the move, while she was thin, still, her dark features and long face.

"Thank you for your patience, sir. You've been most understanding. Now, I need some help. I was wondering something about Birdie..." The guvnor paused and began to knock the second walking stick he'd loaned from Lewis upon the leg of the sofa, just out of time with the loud tick of the clock upon the mantel. "About whether you'd ever considered asylum treatment for her? I had a relative with a mental disorder, you see, sir. The asylum proved very effective for him." He continued talking as if the tapping wasn't happening, but it was maddening, like having a poker wiggled inside your head. Mrs. Barclay watched him with a frown. She glanced at her husband, whose eye flitched at each tap. "Very effective. I must say I've nothing but admiration for the experts in psychological medicine. They've made such advances in our understanding of the mind."

"We've never considered it," replied Mr. Barclay with a scowl. He rubbed his fuzzy nose-tip as the maddening tapping continued. I kept my eyes on his wife: she glanced at her husband again, her throat clenched in a swallow. "No, no. She's our daughter. Quite a few friends at church did advise us to, and my mother before she died. She wouldn't even allow us to bring Birdie when we visited. But no, and, you know, it was difficult keeping her, what with my job and Martha out teaching singing, very difficult keeping an eye on her. She set light to her skirts twice, you know."

"Three times," said Mrs. Barclay.

"Three times, yes. Could have been fatal."

The guvnor smiled, his great knuckle head tilted in sympathy. He said nothing. The tapping continued. Mr. Barclay pulled his watch from his waistcoat pocket and consulted it.

"But I'm afraid I must ask you to leave, gentlemen. The doctor's due any minute. Was there something else you wanted? Besides more money."

"I think that's all, Mr. Barclay," said the guvnor, getting to his feet.

"Why did you call me down? I'm ill, you know."

"In case you had any questions for us, sir. Or anything you wanted to tell us."

"We want it finished this weekend, Mr. Arrowood," Mr. Barclay's voice quickened. "It's been going on too long. You won't get another penny from us until Birdie's off that farm."

"Our job was to arrange a meeting," said the guvnor. "That was all."

"Well it's changed!" cried Mr. Barclay. "You've had all our money off us. You've bled us dry. I want her off that farm!"

"Don't raise your voice, Dunbar," said Mrs. Barclay.

I could see the guvnor tense beside me. He didn't like being shouted at, and not by one as had played him false. A flush came to his cheeks. I took his arm and made a move to the door.

"It's all about money with you two!" cried the senior clerk, throwing his hands in the air and dislodging his nightcap. It was like he was having a fit. "You won't put your coat on least we pay you. Good Christ, I wish to blazes we'd gone to someone with a better reputation! What the hell have you been doing this last week?"

"Dunbar! Be quiet!"

"Well, what do we really know about these two, Martha? For all we know they might be swindlers!"

"How dare you!" barked the guvnor. "Everybody knows

our reputation in South London. If we've taken a long time, it's on your account. You've played us false from the start! And we have an agent on the farm collecting information right now!"

I opened the front door and pulled him outside. Mr. and Mrs. Barclay stood in the doorway.

"No more payments until Birdie's out of there," barked Mr. Barclay. "D'you hear me?"

The guvnor turned back. His voice was suddenly calm.

"Why didn't you tell us you lost your job, sir?"

"What?" spluttered Mr. Barclay. "Are you investigating me? Is that what I'm paying you for?"

"D'you have money troubles, sir?" asked the guvnor, a smile like a baby angel on his face.

"That's not your concern!" cried Mr. Barclay. His whole head was flushed with blood, his eyes flitching furiously. He was scratching the white hair around his bald scalp, one side of his face raised like he was fitting. "I'm paying you to investigate the Ockwell family, not us! Do you understand?"

"Yes, sir," replied the guvnor, bending with his humblest bow.

The door slammed shut in our faces.

"What now?" I asked him as we stood on the pavement.

He thought for a moment, looking up at the house with a curious smile to his face.

"Now we investigate the Barclays properly, Barnett," he said at last.

Chapter Twenty-Six

We waited in the doorway of the King Lud pub, on the corner opposite Tasker and Sons. It was just before twelve o'clock. As we arrived, some of the clerks came out for their lunch. They were back within the half hour, and another line of them came down. Ludgate Circus was busy, with crowded open-topped buses heading to Oxford Circus and Liverpool Street, to Blackfriars Bridge and Kings Cross, coming up against the cabs and carriages and wagons. A bent woman sat against the wall of the bank, a basket of boiled eggs in her lap. Men in suits, women with shawls and baskets, street hawkers with pies and muffins and potatoes, all crossed the roads and dodged each other on the paving. The owners of two coffee stalls across the road from each other battled over how loud they could shout their wares, having a good old laugh as they did. And then our man Pope came out, a tall black bowler on his bald head, a long overcoat, thick gloves on his hands. He was about to cross when he glanced us. A sour look came over his face. He turned and went the other way down Fleet Street.

I set off across the road and soon caught him, landing a hand on his shoulder. He turned.

"What do you want?" he asked. His eyes were watery with the bitter wind. He coughed.

"Quick question, Mr. Pope," I said.

The guvnor had reached us now.

"We need a favour, sir," he said. "Could you give us Mr. Barclay's address, please? The place he used to live, not the new one."

"D'you think I remember the addresses of all those clerks?" Pope's gloved hand was by his face, the fingers fluttering as we'd seen before.

"Would you get it from your records, sir? We'd be very grateful."

"No, I could not. Good day."

As he turned I landed my hand on his shoulder again, firmer this time. I gripped his arm.

"Oh!" he gasped, a little of his spit falling onto his thick grey whiskers. "You're hurting me. Leave me go!"

"This is important, Mr. Pope," said the guvnor. "We're trying to rescue a young lady, as we told you."

"I'm late for lunch!" he hissed. "And why should I help you? You won't even tell me what he's done!"

The guvnor leant forward, his voice low. "We'll tell you if you get us that address."

Pope's muscles went loose.

"Yes?" he asked. I felt him twitch. "You'll tell me what he's done?"

I dropped his arm and patted him on the shoulder.

"All the details," murmured Arrowood. "All his loathsome actions with that young lady. How he held her captive. How he used her." The guvnor shuddered violently and gasped. "The parsnips."

"The parsnips?"

The guvnor nodded, his lips clenched tight.

Pope glanced up at the office windows. A sharp tongue flicked out his gob. He coughed.

"Parsnips?" he asked again.

The guvnor raised his eyebrows.

"And this will help with your case?"

"You'll be doing London a great favour, sir. I assure you."

He looked at us each in turn as he thought. He breathed through his raw nose, then nodded.

"Wait here."

He was back in five minutes with a scrap of paper.

"There," he said. "Now tell me. What's he done?"

"Oh, nothing," said the guvnor, pushing the paper down in his pocket.

"The sex crime," replied Pope, his fingers fluttering by his lips. "What did he do with that girl?"

"He hasn't done anything with a girl, sir."

"But what about the parsnips?"

"I was thinking how much I enjoyed the parsnips I had last night."

"But you said he'd done something to a girl!"

"I'm afraid that was a blind, my friend. Mr. Barclay couldn't misuse a grape."

Here the guvnor stuck his finger upright in the air, then gave a little whistle as he let it droop. He smiled.

"Damn you!" cried Pope.

The guvnor gave the assistant director a little curtsy, then smiled.

"Come, Barnett," he said. "We must find this house."

The bus took us down the Clapham Road to Stockwell. Elden Road was just before the Smallpox Hospital, a poorer place than Saville Terrace but not a slum. The door of number thirty-two was opened by a squashed-looking woman whose head was wrapped in a red woollen scarf. A grey apron was tied over her dress.

"Good day, madam," said the guvnor. "We've some business with Mr. and Mrs. Barclay."

"They don't live here no more, sir. Moved up Waterloo way a month or two past."

She had a good deal of flesh on her, and her clothes looked like they were straining their stitches. A girl of six or so ran up behind her, a ball of wool in her hand.

"Are you the landlady?" asked the guvnor.

"Rent collector," she said. "Look after the building for the landlord."

"We're private enquiry agents, madam. Could we ask you a few questions?"

"What's it about?"

"About their daughter, Birdie."

She led us into her rooms by the front door. The little kitchen was warmed by a compact black range.

"Kettle's just boiled, sirs," she said, stroking her belly. "Fancy a drop of tea?"

We sat on the only two chairs as she made it. The girl with the ball of wool knelt on a cushion on the floor, staring at us. One of her legs was in a brace.

"Such a nice girl, Birdie," said the woman as she poured the tea and gave us each a mug. "She in trouble?"

That tea was a blessing on such a cold day. I cupped my hands around the chipped brown mug, getting the most of its warmth.

"The Barclays are worried she might be, madam," said the guvnor. "Did you know her well?"

"They lived on the floor above. Had three rooms all to theirselves. Birdie used to play on the stairs when she was little. I give her a cup of tea when her parents was out, bit of cake. Lovely girl, she was. Bit slow, but she had a good heart, did poor Birdie. Used to look out for Maggie when she was a nipper."

"Are you Maggie?" asked the guvnor, bending down to the girl on the cushion.

"Yes, mister." The girl pointed at her brace. "Me leg's bent. That's why I got to wear this."

"Well, it looks very fine to me, Maggie. Tell me, do you remember Birdie?"

"She was my friend." The girl's hair was tied tight into two tails at the back of her head. She held one between her fingers, twisting it this way and that. "Wasn't she, ma?"

"Followed her about like a Tantony pig, didn't you, darling?"

"I give her a feather too. It was her favourite."

The woman laughed. "You did, darling. A lovely black raven feather."

The guvnor took a rusk from the plate the woman held out to him.

"Birdie's been prevented from talking to us by her husband," he said. "We saw her through a window and she held

224

up a picture for us to see, of the Brighton Pavilion. Have you any notion what that might mean?"

The woman thought for a while. "She did used to carry magazines around with her. Used to look at the pictures again and again. She lived in those magazines more than she did here, I sometimes thought. Good little worker, though. Just wasn't so clever when you talked to her is all. But she's married now, is she?"

"Yes. A farmer called Walter Ockwell."

"Well, they didn't tell me that. Thought she was living with some relatives."

"They went to see the elephants," said Maggie.

"Did they?" asked the guvnor, his eyes wide. "My, my, Maggie. What elephants did they see?"

"In Crystal Palace, sir."

"Birdie must have liked that, did she?"

"She was crying."

"Oh, dear. Was she afraid?"

"She wanted to see the elephants. They didn't take her."

"That was summer before last," said the woman. "They was always off on jollies and they'd let you know they was. Up at the Canterbury Music Hall, the South London Palace, that sort of place. They'd make sure you knew. Up to Whiteley's as well they used to go, looking at the bits and bobs. Bon Marché. Derry and Toms. Martha used to tell me about it all, the chairs, little china things and so on. Parasols, shawls. Wanted to buy a piano, quite desperate for one, she was. And they was always out at Lyons' having a bit of a lunch, just the two of them. I suppose that's the Spanish in her. Never took Birdie with them. My heart broke for her, poor thing. She was a lonely little lady, all right. And Mr. Barclay, he never gave us a hand with any small thing. And oh, did they work her hard: made her do all the housework, take the laundry down to the washhouse, darn the clothes, beat the rugs out. He was always shouting at her. We'd hear it through the ceiling. And them always out on a jaunt somewhere."

"Was Birdie happy, mum?" I asked.

"What's happy got to do with it?"

"Did she love her parents?" asked the guvnor.

"That I cannot tell you, sir. All I can say is I love my little Maggie and she loves me." She held out her arms to her daughter and picked her up. "That's right, ain't it, darling?"

Maggie nodded and lay her head on her ma's neck. She put the braid she was twisting in her mouth and sucked on it.

"Anyways, we ain't seen her for a year or so."

"I believe the wedding was six months ago," said the guvnor. "July."

"Oh. Thought it was January or February she left," said the woman, a puzzled look on her face. She shook her head.

"That was what we were told," said the guvnor.

Maggie gazed at him, her thin arms around her ma's neck. A look of peace was on her little face.

"Anyways, she's wed now," said the rent collector. "That's what she always wanted."

"Did you meet Walter Ockwell?"

"He never came here as I know."

"I see. Well, that's very helpful, ma'am. Very helpful. Tell me, d'you know why they left their rooms here?"

"Must have come into some money, that's what Mrs. Brent, she at the top, believes. Bought theirselves a whole house over by Waterloo."

"Did Mrs. Barclay have wealthy pupils?"

"She did a few girls over in Clapham, but not many. Only worked an hour or two a day, I'd say."

The guvnor stood.

"Well thank you, madam." He took Maggie's finger and squeezed it. "And a pleasure to meet you, my little lady."

The guvnor had another singing lesson that afternoon, so we arranged that I'd come with Sidney to pick him up at ten that evening. I went back to my room in The Borough for a rest. There was no sound in the house that afternoon, and I climbed the dusty stairs feeling like my limbs were cast of lead. The cold was making my hand ache, and the blow on the neck I'd got in Caterham pained me every time I turned my head. It wasn't just that: my whole body was stiff from the beatings I'd had on this case.

The room was silent. Mrs. B's trunk rested by the wall, her mug on the shelf. I pulled my boots off and got under the blankets. For some time I stared at the ceiling, stained brown and yellow from the smoke of my old sweetheart's pipe. Cobwebs drooped from the corners. I shivered. A chair scraped the floorboards next door.

I pulled the shawl from the floor and brought it to my nose, breathing in the smell of lavender as was getting fainter by the day. It felt like the last of her, and it came to me that when there was no scent there'd be nothing left of her in the room. Folk said I'd maybe feel a presence, but all I felt was the January cold freezing my nose and creeping inside every joint in my body. I could see more clear than ever now how my old girl had given me comfort against the raw wind and the beatings and the days tramping the hard streets. But there was no comfort left for me here.

There and then I came to a decision, that when the scent was gone from her shawl I'd leave this room for ever and take up Lewis's offer to lodge with him. But just as soon as I'd made the decision, I felt the room whisper to me again, begging me not to leave it, and it sounded like my old Mrs. B whispering.

I wrapped the shawl around my head, against the grey light from the window, against the room's whispers, and slept, waking to hear the bells of St. George the Martyr strike seven. The room was dark. The family upstairs were arguing. The elder lad shouted, slamming the door, his boots heavy on the stairs. His ma screamed after him.

I got out of bed, wrapped myself up in my scarf, my hat, my gloves, pulled on my muddy boots. Hard as it was to come home to nothing but stale air and silence, it was harder still to leave now that there was nobody to notice me going.

I touched her coat hung on the back of the door and stood for a moment listening for her whisper.

Chapter Twenty-Seven

I had a plate of cabbage and potato in the cookshop, then walked over to Bermondsey to see Sidney. After a couple of pints, we picked up a four-wheeler from the stables and trundled over to collect the guvnor. When we were on the road again, he pulled a bottle of Mariani wine from his coat and we passed it between us. He started up singing just before Lewisham.

We reached Catford around eleven. Not a soul was around, and, except for the pub, no lights were on in the buildings around Rushey Green. I hopped down at the church and put my hand under the bench in the lychgate. There was nothing there but a few wet leaves. I knelt on the hard flags and ran my hand up and down the cold floor. Nothing.

Just then I heard a noise in the graveyard. I got up quick, peering into the blackness. Feet running. Then I saw him, flying down the church path. It was Neddy.

"Hello, lad," I said, bending to give him a hug.

"Get in, my dear," ordered the guvnor from the cab. "Quick. Before someone sees you."

The lad climbed inside. I followed.

"What are you doing here?" asked the guvnor.

"Miss Arrowood told me to come," he said. "Said I'd to give you this."

He held out his hand and dropped something in the guvnor's glove. Arrowood brought his candle near and peered at it.

At first it just looked like a little bit of a mucky stick.

He turned it over, then looked up at me, the horror on his face lit by the flick of the flame.

The base split into two awful prongs that twisted across each other, dark and scaled, uneven. The muck was muck all right, but mixed with bloody, stringy roots. It had haunted me in my dreams since that first day we met her, and now here it was again.

It was Mrs. Gillie's black tooth.

"Where did you get this?" asked the guvnor. He took off his muffler and wrapped it round the boy's neck, pulling his torn cap further down over his ears.

"Willoughby found it, sir."

"Where?"

"The dung pit in the barn. He was showing me where to do my business. Turned it over with a shovel."

"D'you know what it is?"

"No, sir. But Willoughby was right upset by it. He made me put it in my pocket. Kept saying 'police.' Miss Arrowood told me to bring it to you. Oh, and this."

Neddy handed him a note. The guvnor read it and passed it to me.

230

You told me of Mrs. Gillie's tooth. If this is it, take Neddy home. I'll say he's ill. No chance to speak with B yet. Doing laundry with her tomorrow. Hope to find out something then. Home tomorrow night if all goes well.

As I read, a lice dropped from Neddy's head and fell on the paper.

"That wasn't me," said the lad, brushing it off real quick.

The guvnor patted his shoulder.

"Get on the box, my darling. Show Sidney the way to your lodgings. When you get there, tell Miss Arrowood to pack her things and come down. We'll wait at the end of the street."

We pulled over at the corner of Doggett Road and Neddy hopped out. He was back in five minutes with Ettie. She greeted Sidney, then, giving me a quick nod, climbed on the step.

"Where's your bag?" demanded the guvnor.

Her head and most of her face were wrapped in a thick and ragged shawl. She smelt of hard labour.

"I'm not coming, William."

"You damn well are coming! It's too dangerous."

"I'm staying one more day," she said firmly. "This might be the only chance we have to get to the bottom of what's going on."

"This is no job for a woman."

"You watch your tongue!" she hissed. "I journeyed four days in the Afghan desert to bring back two nurses. I've sawn a man's leg off. No job for a woman, indeed! You wouldn't say that about Caroline Cousture, so don't say it about me."

"You'll return home with us and we'll alert the police to-morrow."

"And they'll ignore you again. No, Brother. I'm staying."

"Norman, tell her," he said, turning to me.

Ettie looked at me. In the candlelight I could see her thin lips clenched, her eyes tired and hard as stone.

"What if they suspect you?" I asked.

"Why should they? They haven't suspected me yet. It seems I'm good at acting, and the harder they work me the better I get."

I said nothing.

She climbed out the carriage, shaking off the guvnor's hand.

"Ettie! Be reasonable."

"Come back tomorrow night," she said, and marched off round the corner.

The guvnor banged Lewis's stick down hard on the floor, cursing under his breath. He uncorked the bottle and took a long glug.

"She's impossible!" he said. "Neddy tell me, how's Miss Ettie performing? Do they believe she's dumb?"

"She's done real good, sir. Never spoke once. I got to do all the talking."

"That's good. Now, you go back with her. At the least sign of trouble I want you to get out of there. Come straight to us on the train. You have that money I gave you?"

"Yes, sir."

"If we don't hear from you, meet us at the church tomorrow night," said the guvnor. "Same time. Don't ask any questions. Just do your work."

Neddy was already out of the carriage when he replied:

"I'll look after her, sir."

"She doesn't need looking after. Keep yourself safe. And remember, run if there's any trouble up at the farm. Don't go looking for clues. Promise me?"

"Yes, sir."

The guvnor felt about inside his coat and pulled out a greasy packet.

"Here. A bit of ham."

Neddy reached up and took it.

"Thanks, Mr. Arrowood. They don't hardly feed us, sir. Just a bit of cabbage soup at midday and a cold potato at dusk today. Miss Arrowood's gone real quiet too."

"I'll treat you at the pudding shop when you get back. Whatever you want, lad. You make sure she has some of that ham too."

The guvnor uncorked the Mariani wine on the way back to town. I shook my head when he passed it to me: the cold was in my bones and my injuries were paining me. I needed a proper sleep more than a glug of tonic wine that night.

"Best lay off that bottle, sir," I said. "You'll be up all night."

"I'll be fine," he said sharply, and took another loud swallow.

"You won't be right tomorrow."

He pulled the blanket tighter on his knees, and off my own. I pulled it back.

"Don't be selfish, Barnett," he snapped.

A few minutes later he became thoughtful again.

"She's dead," he whispered, his eyes fixed on the dark road outside. "There can be no doubt. Someone on that farm killed her." He took another swallow. "D'you think it might have been Digger?"

"Could be."

"He knew where she was. He knew she was telling us secrets about the family, and he fills that heap with Willoughby. He has a bitter face, hasn't he? There's anger there, no doubt about it. Who knows what's going on in that mind of his."

He fell silent. The carriage hit a hole in the road, sending us both into the air with a grunt. The bottle fell from his hand. He cursed, scrabbling around wildly to rescue it.

"Or perhaps the family ordered him to do it," he continued when he'd found it. "Perhaps they're afraid of us finding out something. Root might have informed them she was talking to us. I don't trust him: someone cleared away those broken flowers after we asked him to investigate."

"If he's in with them it'd explain why he won't investigate Birdie either."

"It would. But let's not jump to conclusions too quickly. There's another reason why he might not be helping us: he's a low-born, uneducated man in a position with a degree of authority over his betters. It's an uncomfortable place to be, I should think: he must be seen to be masterful yet he's no doubt looked down on by those of higher station. How many times have we seen the police's insecurity before their betters, Barnett? Our presence suggests he's missed something. If he's not in with the family, he's certainly threatened by our interfering with his parish. And, of course, he might just be lazy."

I'd usually enjoy listening to him talk like this, but tonight I felt nothing but wretchedness over Mrs. Gillie and worry over leaving Ettie in Catford now we knew for sure there was evil on that farm. The guvnor uncapped his pipe, stuffed it with tobacco, and got a blaze going. We were now out of the houses and travelling through fields, on our way to Lewisham. The clouds had cleared, the stars were out, the moon was big and bright.

"Want me to drive for a bit, mate?" I asked Sidney through the hatch.

"No, matey," he answered. "I got them going real nice now."

There wasn't much as gave Sidney more pleasure than when

a horse was going smoothly through the night: he always said that when they were running just right he could feel horse energy fill his body and wash through his soul, and it wasn't like nothing else on this earth.

"We'll take the evidence to Petleigh tomorrow," said the guvnor. The more he drank the more fidgety he was getting. "And we'll go to that wretched MP's surgery and try to hurry things along."

"Best you leave off that bottle then, sir. You'll be up all night."

"Will you please stop lecturing me, Barnett! You sound like my sister."

I didn't take offence. I knew he was as worried as I about leaving them there alone. I knew that was why he was sucking on the bottle like his mother's breast. I lit a smoke and let him get on with it. As we approached New Cross he began to sing:

"We've been together now for forty years, and it don't seem a day too much.

"There ain't a lady living in the land, as I'd swap for my dear old Dutch.

"Oh, she's a dear good old gal, and da da da dada."

Though it was supposed to be a happy song, he sang it with anger, his fists clenched on his lap. He kept shifting on the bench.

"She's doo um…

"Ah, what a wife to me she's been, and what a pal.

"We've—"

A pounding came from Sidney's boots up above, which brought the recital to an end.

"Sorry, Mr. Arrowood, sir," cried my brother-in-law from the box. "It's the horses. They're getting spooked."

"Not from me," said the guvnor.

"Begging your pardon, sir, but I think it might be your song."

"They want a different song?"

"I mean your singing, sir."

"My singing teacher says I've a voice like silk," he snapped.

"It's the silky ones they don't like."

The guvnor was silent.

"Same with all horses," Sidney said after a while.

"Ah," replied the guvnor, sounding a little hurt. "Well."

He started up humming instead.

Losing interest in that, he began shifting in his seat again, complaining of the cold.

"You should take up Lewis's offer, Norman," he said suddenly. "It must be lonely in that room now that Mrs. Barnett's gone."

"Maybe."

"Ettie and I are worried about you. Your soul seems… missing…"

He was trying to say something, but it seemed to me he didn't know what it was. And I didn't want to hear it anyway.

I held up my hand to stop him.

He tightened his lips and sighed, giving me one of those sorrowful looks. Silence for a while. Then he said: "I think he'll die."

"Lewis?"

"Isabel's lawyer, from the cancer in his stomach. Not many survive, do they?" He was talking quick now, panting. Tonic wine and fear was never a good mix, and he'd had a big dose of both. "Then she must decide. There won't be much for her there, I suppose. She won't even be a widow. She may have no choice but to come back to London."

"She'd want to be sure you've changed, William," I said.

"Of course I've changed. Ettie's rearranged me."

"She'd look at you more favourable if you were back in your rooms."

"We'll be moving this week. I'm thinking of getting new teeth, anyway. After this case." He leant across and gripped my arm. "Love is everything, Norman. You know that. You and Mrs. Barnett, what an example that was. Through thick and thin. One thing Isabel can't deny is my love. If I can find some way of making her remember how she once loved me then...well, it's nature. The infernal chemistry."

He went on in that fashion for some time, then fell silent, wringing his hands and jiggling his legs as the carriage jumped and lurched along the road. It was a relief when we dropped him at the Hog, and I knew Sidney felt the same.

He let me down in Borough High Street. Poor old Sidney was wrapped in two thick blankets, with scarves tied under his hat and around his face so just his eyes showed. In the yard of St. George the Martyr, every bench along the path was occupied by bodies, grey in the bright moonlight, their shapes like piles of rags ready for the shoddy factory. Sidney saw me looking at them.

"Ain't right, is it, Norman? They need to build more workhouses." He hacked up a big gob and spat into the road. "You need me again tomorrow night?"

"We can get a cab, Sid," I said. "Honest, you've done enough."

"Think I better come along. I got a bad feeling about this."

We looked at each other in the frozen street.

"Me too, mate," I said.

Chapter Twenty-Eight

❖━━━━━━◆━━━━━━❖

There was no reply at the house next morning, so I walked down to Bankside where Lewis's weapons shop was squeezed between two warehouses. Inside it was dark and piled high with things he'd bought on the cheap from the roughs and thieves who came in to trade with him. All about were boxes of bullets and gunpowder; barrels of swords and clubs and walking sticks; sheaths and ammunition holders hanging in bunches from the beams; rifles lined up in glass cabinets.

Lewis's head appeared from behind the desk.

"Norman," he mumbled, blinking from sleep. One side of his face was bright red. He cleared his lungs, spitting it out into a twisted pewter mug.

"Did William come home last night?" I asked.

He shook his head. "He must have stayed at the Hog. Here, have you seen the paper?"

He bent behind the desk and produced the *The Star*, a coffee stain as big as a hand on its front page. He watched as I read.

PEEPING EYES AT THE ASYLUM

Private enquiry agent William Arrowood of Lambeth and his strongman have been up to their mischief again. Last week we reported their intrusion into the private affairs of families in Catford. Now they have appeared at Caterham asylum. The medical superintendent, Dr. Crenshaw, caught these fiends housebreaking and inspecting the asylum files, searching for personal information on patients and their families. Blackmail is thought to be the motive. They later made their escape by stealing a brougham, kidnapping the coachman into the bargain. An ivory pipe rack was missing from Dr. Crenshaw's office. Arrowood is no Sherlock Holmes. We can find no reports of a single crime he has solved. This creature was involved in the Fenian arms case last year and was so much out of his depth that Holmes had to be brought in at the last minute to retrieve the arms. Are his claims to be a detective a cover for theft and blackmail? The evidence is growing. *The Star* says enough is enough!

"I'd like to see his face when he reads that," said Lewis with a smile. "How's the case?"

"One of the labourers found Mrs. Gillie's tooth in the dung heap up on the farm. We're sure she's been murdered now."

"You know who did it?"

"Someone on the farm, that's all we know. We got to get Ettie and Neddy back tonight. It's too dangerous."

He nodded. "Then you might need this." He waddled over to a cabinet and unlocked it. From inside he pulled out a battered pistol, then collected a box of bullets from a pile on the table. He loaded the gun and dropped it in my coat pocket.

"You be careful, Norman," he said. "Bring them back safe."

I walked on down to the Hog. In there were a couple of lightermen I'd seen a few times before, already a bit far gone for the morning. A sailor with a knife in his belt and a gummy eye stood at the counter holding a mackerel in his hand.

"She's bloody fresh and all, my darling," he growled at the barmaid, who sat upon a low stool behind the counter. He was Italian or French or something. "In today and all."

"Your guvnor ain't here, Norman," she said, ignoring him. "Left last night."

"You know where he is?"

She took her pipe from her mouth. "Ask Betts."

"Eh, mate," said the sailor, holding out his little fishy to me. He gripped the battered counter to stop himself unbalancing. "You like the baby, no?"

"No, mate."

The sailor took hold of my arm, waggling the fish in my face. His breath was thicker than beer.

"Eh, mate. You give two penny and all."

I grabbed his throat and squeezed. His face went red, his eyes bulged.

"Fuck off. Understand?"

I pushed him away, then went behind the counter and down the dark corridor to Betts's narrow door. I knocked and knocked and finally it opened up, letting out an awful gust of stink. Betts was in her nightcap, her face lined and pale, a thick nightgown under her woollen jacket. Her eyes were puffy slits.

"Sorry for waking you, Betts. He didn't come home last night."

"He didn't go home, Norman," she answered, her voice rough from the pipes and the gin.

"Did he say where he was going?"

"Just reared up in the bed like a horse. Said he'd had a notion. Believe it was Caterham, he said."

"Oh, Christ, no."

"Oh, Christ, yes."

Betts burped, then covered her mouth with her hand.

"Do excuse me, sir," she said in a posh voice.

"How'd he get there?"

"He just stuck his feet in his boots and left. Didn't say no more'n that."

"Cheers, Betts," I said, turning back down the corridor.

I felt a pull on my sleeve.

"Only he forgot to pay me again, Norman."

I looked at her in silence.

She smiled, showing me a full half-set of yellow teeth.

"My sister ain't well. Got to bring her nippers some food later."

I fished in my waistcoat for her usual half a crown.

I hurried to the police station. What the hell was he thinking? After what we'd done, that asylum was nothing but danger. Those attendants'd be bloody glad to see us again, that was certain. And with Ettie and Neddy still on the farm needing our help too. He was a damn fool sometimes, a damn, bloody fool.

PC Reid was at the desk, a rash of weeping pimples broken out across his young face. A bit of bread and dripping lay on the newspaper in front of him.

"Inspector Petleigh ain't here," he said in his booming voice.

"How long's he going to be?"

He shrugged, wiping the dripping from his blond moustache and licking it off his hand.

"I'll wait," I said.

"I see Mr. Arrowood's been up to his tricks," he said, lifting the paper for me. It was *The Star*.

"They're going to look bloody stupid when they find out we're after a murderer."

For an hour or so I watched the people come and go. A tailor who'd had a load of kicksies nicked; a landlady whose rooms had been set fire to; a cabbie whose horse had been stabbed. All of them angry; none of them really thinking the coppers would be able to help. That was the way it was. Too many crimes and not enough coppers. Just as I was dozing off, Petleigh came in, neat and immaculate as usual, wearing that same red and grey scarf. When he saw me he rolled his eyes.

"Come upstairs, Norman," he said. "Though I'm not sure I want to hear what you have to say."

When we reached his small, cold office, I told him about Mrs. Gillie's tooth. He sat behind his desk, his hands, still in their calfskin gloves, in a praying pose before his face. He stared at me as I spoke.

"But it's just a tooth," he said when I'd finished. "It could be anybody's."

"You've never seen a tooth like it, Inspector. It was split in two at the gum and then one twisted round the other, and black as the devil's hole. It was a horror. The labourer knew it was hers too. It was the only one in her mouth, right at the front. Like a demon's tooth."

"Show me."

"William has it."

"And where is he?"

He read my face before I had a chance to answer.

"Oh, no. What's happened?"

"I think he's being held in the Caterham asylum."

"What the bloody hell's he doing there?"

I told him about our visit, about being caught looking at the ledgers, about our escape.

"For Christ sake!" he said, slamming his fist onto the desk. "I sometimes think you two are the biggest fools in London. I could arrest you, you know?"

"Something's going on at the farm, Inspector. Something's wrong. We're just trying to find out. Listen, can you come down there with me and get them to release him?"

"I haven't got time to go all the way to Caterham." His nose twitched; he dropped his voice. "But you may tell them I demand they release him. Use my name."

He fiddled in his pocket for his snuffbox. A cold draught came from his little window, its cracks stuffed with newspaper.

"I suppose you want me to talk to Sergeant Root about the tooth as well?" he asked. "Damn it, this isn't even in my area."

He had himself a toot, then drew out a handkerchief ironed into a neat square. He wiped his nose.

"Thanks, Inspector. But can you wait till Ettie and Neddy are out of danger? We're picking them up tonight."

"You don't trust Root?"

"Things we tell him always seem to get back to the family."

He nodded, rising to his feet. I could see he didn't like it.

"You're taking me away from the crimes we have here in Southwark, Norman."

"A crime's a crime, isn't it, Inspector?"

"My Chief Inspector's only interested in the crimes here."

"But you'll help?"

He looked at me, stroking his moustache with his finger in its calfskin sleeve. His thin nose-holes flared.

"Yes," he said at last. "But William had better be grateful."

Chapter Twenty-Nine

It was just after two when I pushed open the great wooden doors and entered the hall. Mrs. Grant sat at a desk at the far end, her hands clasped before her.

"Dr. Crenshaw's not here," she said, rising from her chair.

I ignored her, opening the door of the side passage.

"Come out of there!" she cried, hurrying towards me, her heels clicking on the polished floor. "He's not here!"

I marched down the corridor and entered his office. Crenshaw was sat behind his long desk, a cigar in his hand. A well-to-do couple sat on the other side.

"I tried to stop him, sir," said Mrs. Grant, coming in behind me.

The couple looked at each other, likely wondering if I was a lunatic. Superior people, I could see. High-born, well-laundered.

"Bring him out, Crenshaw," I said. "Now."

"I'm having a meeting," said the medical superintendent when he'd got over his suprise. He waved me away. "Now get out before I call my attendants."

"I've just been to see Inspector Petleigh of Southwark Police. He demands you release him."

Crenshaw turned to the couple and made the sort of smile as said "The man's an idiot." Yet it seemed to me just then that everything in the room made him look small: his over-sized desk, the leather chair whose back rose above his head, the golden lion on the desk as roared in a way he never could with his soft voice.

"If you'll just give me a minute, Mr. and Mrs. Lovell," he said with a little bow of his head and a smirk on his face. "I believe there's been a misunderstanding."

He turned back to me.

"If it's your master, you mean, he's not here, and you can tell the inspector the same. Now, are you going to leave quietly?"

"Bring him out and I'll be on my way, Doctor."

"Mrs. Grant, get the attendants."

"You don't want to do that, Mrs. Grant," I said, real quick. "Least you want the world to know of Dr. Crenshaw's special treatment for straightening a lady's eyes."

"He's not here, I tell you," said Crenshaw, stubbing his cigar hard into the ashtray. "Now, leave. You'll only make things worse if you persist."

"Mr. Arrowood was with *Lloyd's Weekly* before he became an enquiry agent," I said. "He's got a lot of friends who'd be very interested in a story about Caterham asylum. And even more a story about a superior man with his britches about his boots."

Crenshaw turned to the couple again.

"It's the nature of the thing, I'm afraid," he said with a weak laugh. "The line between truth and fantasy, you know. If you'll just excuse me, I'll deal with this chap outside."

He strode past me into the corridor. I followed him out to the great, empty hall, Mrs. Grant hurrying behind.

"See if you can find Mr. Arrowood hiding anywhere and bring him over here, Mrs. Grant," he whispered. "Be quick so we can be rid of this filthy ape."

She hurried out the front doors.

He came close and looked up at me. His eyes were hard, though his voice never could get more than soft. "If I catch either of you back here you'll never be seen again. I guarantee it."

"'Course you do, Doctor."

"And if you make any trouble for me or this institution I'll have you hunted and split in two down the middle. I know men who'll do it, believe me."

"Oh, I know," I said, dusting a bit of soot from the top of his bald crown.

He jerked his head away.

"This is the end of your enquiries into this asylum, d'you hear?"

I took hold of the lappets of his suit and jerked him close, then lifted till his feet were off the ground. He struggled and twisted but it was no bother to me. I put my lips next to his ear, breathing in his Eau de Cologne.

"I hear you real good, chuckaboo," I whispered. "But the case isn't closed till Mr. Arrowood says it is."

At that I dropped him.

I went outside and waited by the fountain. A few minutes later, the guvnor rounded the corner from the wards, a burly attendant on each arm, Mrs. Grant walking behind. He was hobbling, the flaps of his overcoat wet with mud, one eye so bruised and swelled it had closed up. His britches were torn at the knee.

"Thank the Lord you're here, Barnett," he gasped.

The men threw him to the ground.

I helped him up and marched him straight down the drive without saying a word. He groaned and limped.

"I've lost my gloves," he mumbled. "And my hat."

I said nothing.

"And Lewis's walking stick. Go back and fetch them, Norman, will you?"

"You're a damn fool, William."

He went silent. We reached the gates and turned onto the road.

"That's no way to talk to your employer, Norman."

I hurried along the road back to the station, him trotting behind, wheezing and groaning. We didn't speak again until we were on the uptrain, crowded with folk going into town for the Saturday shopping. He was an ugly sight: the bruise around his eye was like an artist's rag: purple and blue, red and gold, puffed out like a dumpling. His jowels were drooping, his nose round and red like a boil. There was grit in his greasy hair, soot on his forehead. The mud on his astrakhan coat matched that on his torn yellow britches.

I sat opposite, glaring at him while the men read their papers, the women chatted. A governess with three restless nippers sat in the middle of the bench.

"I'm sorry, Barnett," he said as we neared Purley Junction. "I should have told you, but last night it seemed so easy. I can't explain it. Something got into me."

"Mariani wine got into you. Didn't you think about Ettie and Neddy? They're still on that farm. In danger!"

His eye fell to the carriage floor. He pursed his lips.

"It was foolish," he said.

"What if I couldn't find you? What if there's trouble to-night?"

"Don't go on, Norman. I made a mistake. But I'm tired and hungry and stiff with cold. I've suffered enough."

I folded my arms and turned my face to the window, watching the frozen trees go past, shining and twinkling in the sun. A few minutes passed.

"I discovered something interesting in Crenshaw's files," he said, sitting forward and lowering his voice.

"How did you get in his office?"

"A stone on a small pane of glass."

I shook my head. "They heard you, didn't they?"

"But not before I found what I was looking for, Norman. Listen. I knew there was something queer going on between the Ockwells and that asylum." Now he whispered, his left eye staring me out. "Digger was also there, and that other worker, the one Mrs. Gillie told us of. Tracey Childs. I had a quick look at his case file before they caught me. He also has amentia. Convictions for petty theft, absconding from school. In the workhouse before the asylum. No next of kin, and only thirteen years old when committed."

"So they're all from Caterham. It doesn't mean anything. Working on a farm's better than staying in an asylum, I'd say."

"Is it?" he asked. "And what about Polly? Does an asylum also marry off its patients?"

"I don't like Crenshaw any more than you do, but it seems to me that place is doing what it's there for, to treat them and get them back into the world."

He nodded slowly.

"Then tell me this. Why is it none of them are recorded as discharged?"

"I don't know. A mistake. It's only bookkeeping."

"Well, hundreds of other patients *are* recorded as discharged. The most recent was last week. And those ledgers are important, Barnett. The Lunacy Commission use them when they make their inspections. Asylums are required to keep that information: how else can anyone check who is and isn't there?"

"I think you're trying to make something out of nothing, sir."

He sat back and gazed at me for a few moments.

"We'll see," he said at last. "Anyway, I found something else."

I watched him as he arched his eyebrow and pulled out his pipe. He smiled.

"Birdie Ockwell was admitted last February."

Chapter Thirty

He lit his pipe, getting a terrific blaze on the shag, his lips popping again and again on the stem. Smoke belched out of his mouth and swirled round his battered face. A bloke in a check suit took that as his cue and lit up his own, and then another took out a cigar. Soon the air was white and the children coughing.

"Same as the others," he went on. "Her admission's recorded but not her discharge."

"What made you go back?"

"The Ockwells are preventing us seeing Birdie, that's clear, but I've always felt they're being sincere when they tell us her parents mistreated her. I just haven't seen any signs of deception when they say it. So I wanted to go deeper with the Barclays. That's why I spoke so approvingly of asylum treatment, why I told them of my relative. It was a ruse to get at their true attitude to Birdie. I let them know that if they'd considered putting her away it would have met with my approval. But d'you remember what Mr. Barclay did?"

I shook my head.

"He denied it, then gave four reasons why it would have been a good idea: his own mother rejected Birdie, their friends at church urged them, they were both out at work and couldn't watch her, and—"

"And Birdie set her dress on fire."

He nodded. "Three times. It was almost as if, while denying it with one part of his mind, another part was seeking to justify it. Then immediately he looked at his watch and told us he had an appointment. In that way, he cut off further questions. Now, it could have been true that he had an appointment, but what made me suspicious was that Neptune clock not a foot from his face on the mantel, yet instead of looking at it he pulls out his watch. Remember I was tapping with my stick when he did it? I've told you before that it's easy to reveal yourself in a falsity if there are other distractions. The mind can only work on so much at the same time."

I nodded. It was a trick I'd seen him use before, sometimes to good effect, sometimes to none.

"Anyway, when he gave himself away with his watch, I assumed only that he'd *considered* putting her away. After all, that was what I asked. But then last night I remembered the rent collector. It just came to me. She thought Birdie'd left a year ago, when in fact it was only four or five months before that she was married. A rent collector would know who's living in the building, I think. When I told her it was July she raised her eyes as people do when they try to remember. She was confused. Then she frowned, indicating she remembered it differently. She didn't want to contradict me, that would be impolite, but her face betrayed her. So where was Birdie during those months? That's when it came to me: perhaps our Mr. Barclay hadn't just *considered* putting her away. Perhaps he'd actually done it. Perhaps he'd put away his own daughter."

"You don't approve? You said your relative's treatment was effective."

"It was effective. It killed him."

I watched him puffing away, expecting him to explain. He didn't; his head drooped. His eyelid was low over his good eye, his skin, specked with grit and smudged with soot, was dull and lifeless. He looked like he hadn't slept for days.

"Who was he?" I asked at last.

"It's a long story, Norman; I'll tell you another time." He took a deep breath, trying to rouse himself. "Right now we need to think through the case. It explains why the Barclays have been deceiving us about where they lived. They didn't want us to believe they'd had her committed, else we'd question why they want her back now. We'd question all they've told us. So, what else? It seems the asylum has an arrangement with the farm. The country air's doubtless very good for a lunatic. All laudable enough. But this is what I'm puzzling over: why did Crenshaw run off to consult Tasker when he imprisoned us?"

"He'd found us breaking into the office. Tasker's the chair of the board."

"Yes, but if we agree he didn't go to the police because he was afraid we'd let out the secret of his affair with Mrs. Grant, why then did he go to Tasker? He wouldn't want to explain that to the Chair of the Visitors, would he? Tasker's the last person he'd want to admit it to."

"They may be closer than you think. Or he may have invented a story about us."

He nodded.

"Yes, you're right of course. But there's something wrong with that asylum, I'm sure of it."

"You're getting distracted, William. This is nothing to do with the case. There's a killer on that farm and we need to make sure Ettie and Neddy are safe. That's the most important thing right now."

"We'll get them tonight, Norman. Rest assured we'll bring them home. But first we must make sure the police search that dung pit. We must away to Lewisham before the MP's surgery closes."

It was only then I remembered *The Star* I'd taken from Lewis that morning. I pulled it out of my coat and passed it to him.

"Page three," I said. "You're not going to like it."

He read it in silence, his eye moving across the page. His temples pulsed; his lips pressed together so tight they went white.

Then, with a howl of fury, he threw down the carriage window and hurled the newspaper out of the speeding train. It exploded into pieces in the grey afternoon and was gone.

"Out of his depth!" he cried. "We solved that damn case, Barnett! Holmes did almost nothing! Good Christ, I'd like to know who's behind these reports."

A roar of cold air swept through the carriage.

"Shut the window, you fool!" commanded a broad fellow in brown. His wife, right in the blast, clutched her bonnet to her head, her hair dancing wild in the wind.

"Hurry and pull it up!" demanded an officer by the other window.

The guvnor grunted and spluttered but couldn't get it back up.

"Get a move on!" grumbled an old woman, her eyes shut against the icy blast. "We'll freeze to death."

I had a go, but much as I tried I couldn't raise it an inch. The officer had a shunt, then the bloke in brown. It wouldn't move.

The guvnor looked around at the angry faces, the weeping noses, the pinchy eyes. "It's stuck fast," he mumbled, his hands in his pockets. He shook his head. "I'm so very sorry. And on such a cold day."

The brown-clad man also shook his head, his eyes raised to the roof. The others, pulling up their collars, hunkering down inside their coats, glared at Arrowood as the icy gale ripped through the carriage. Each and every one of them looked like the most miserable person in the world.

The guvnor went directly to the post office at London Bridge and sent a letter to Sherlock Holmes. He requested most politely that Holmes write to *The Star* to correct them, confirming we'd helped unravel the Fenian arms thefts of the year before and add any further endorsement he saw fit.

"Let's hope he does the right thing, this time," he said as we left the telegraph office. "Now, where's the Lewisham train?"

He fell asleep the minute we boarded and snored all the way. We reached the Horse and Groom just before four and sat waiting our turn in the public bar, each with a mug of mild and a bit of bread and butter. The guvnor was silent, in half a daze still from his sleep. Near five, the clerk led us upstairs to the private dining room where Sir Edward met his constituents once every month. The MP sat at the far side of the table, his back to the coal fire. A pot of tea rested at his elbow, a ledger open in front of him.

"Please sit," said his clerk, indicating two chairs at the other end of the table. "Mr. Arrowood and Mr. Barnett, Sir Edward," he announced.

Only then did the MP look up.

"Are these the last, MacNaught?" he asked.

"Yes, sir."

"Get my carriage ready."

The clerk backed out the door.

"State your business, gentlemen," said Sir Edward, finally looking at us. He shut his ledger and pushed the teacup away from him. "I've five minutes for you."

"We came to see you at the House on Tuesday," said the guvnor. "About Mrs. Gillie, the missing woman. You asked us to come here today."

"Ah, yes." The MP opened a small pot of balm and began applying it to the red patches of skin around his nose. "You aren't constituents, are you?"

"No, sir. But the woman went missing in Catford. You said you'd look into it."

"And I have. Sergeant Root assures me there's no crime been committed, Mr. Arrowood. But he thanks you for your interest."

Sir Edward rose from his chair and took his coat from the stand.

"Root won't investigate because the woman's a gypsy," said the guvnor quickly. "Her horse is there, her winter coat, her boots, and there are signs of a struggle, signs that were tidied away the next day. Someone would only do that to hide a crime, Sir Edward. Her cat's head was stoved in with a tool of some kind."

"It doesn't mean a crime's been committed, Mr. Arrowood. Gypsies wander, you know that. We cannot launch a search every time one goes missing."

"There's more," said the guvnor. "We think we know where the body's buried, and we've been given clear evidence she's dead."

"Well? What is the evidence?"

"We can't tell you that today, Sir Edward. It's too dangerous for the informant. But we can bring it tomorrow."

The MP patted his white hair down onto his scalp and put his topper on. He buttoned his coat, then looked at Arrowood coldly.

"You have evidence that you won't show me," he said. "Come, come, Mr. Arrowood, d'you think that'll convince me? Sergeant Root assures me there's no evidence of a crime. And let me tell you something else: my constituents in Catford have had enough of you prying into their private business. Decent people spied on, gossiped about, pursued! You see, I know who you are. You're no more a detective than I'm a tanner, sir. You're a fraud. You've been exposed in *The Star*, don't you know? You've never solved a case in your life!"

"I've solved many a case! I've worked with Sherlock Holmes!"

"I doubt Sherlock Holmes needs help from the likes of you."

"Oh, dear, dear," said the guvnor, the disappointment dripping from his voice like vitriol. "Not another Holmes worshipper."

"Holmes is a national hero, you insolent rogue. He saved the country from war when he retrieved that naval treaty. And he's just rescued the heir of one of the most important families in England."

"The Holdernesse case?" said the guvnor, waving his hand away. "A stroke of luck, Sir Edward. A stroke of luck."

"Luck! Don't be absurd. The man's a genius."

"A genius?" barked the guvnor. "Didn't you read about the bicycle tyres?"

"The what?"

"The bicycle tyres!"

Sir Edward turned to the door. "Our interview is over, Arrowood."

"Wait!" demanded the guvnor, stepping quick between the MP and his door. His eye was bulging, his lips wet. "The whole damn thing rested on those bicycle tracks. Holmes, by some miracle, knows the tracks of forty-two bicycle tyres, or so he claims. But that's not the point." His words rushed out, his finger rose in the air. "It said in the paper he read the direction of the bicycle because the heavier indentation is left by the rear tyre, and the track of the heavier tyre often crossed the lighter. That's what he told them. But what he failed to realize is that this is only the case if the rider is sitting back on the seat and not putting pressure on the bars. When riding fast, a rider will either stand on the pedals or put pressure on the handlebars, resulting in the opposite pattern. Even a blind man would know it. And the riders would without doubt have been sprinting across that moor."

"Holmes found the boy, you idiot!" exclaimed the MP.

"Despite reading the clues incorrectly! It was luck, Sir Edward! Blind luck!"

Penn saw his chance, pushed past the guvnor, and hurried down the stairs. Arrowood went after him. As Penn stepped into the crowded pub, the guvnor caught him by the arm and pulled him back.

"There's a murderer at large!" he cried.

"Get your hands off me!" demanded Penn.

"You'll be to blame if he strikes again, sir!"

The clerk jumped up from a bench by the door and ran over.

"Let me help you, sir," he said, moving his body between the guvnor and Sir Edward. "Please let go, Mr. Arrowood. It's not permitted to pull the MP."

"There!" cried the guvnor, thrusting Mrs. Gillie's black

tooth at the politician. "That's the evidence! Her tooth. Found in the dung pit of the Ockwell farm. The whole place must be searched, and if you won't help I'll make sure *Lloyd's Weekly* covers the story. I used to work there. I'll make it clear how you refused to do anything."

Penn swallowed. He raised a monocle to his eye and peered at the tooth.

"How do you know that's her tooth?"

"Three people have identified it. I know you doubt me, but don't doubt them. Anyone in Catford will tell you it's her tooth. It was her only tooth. Right in the middle of her mouth. Two people couldn't have a tooth like that."

"How did you find it?"

"Someone in the village found it. We believe they're in danger, so we cannot give you the name just yet. Please, Sir Edward. There's a murderer out there. He must be brought to justice."

Penn looked long at his clerk.

"I'll only instruct Root to carry out a search for the body if you give him the name," he said at last.

The guvnor nodded.

"We'll be there at nine tomorrow morning. But he must search that dung pit immediately we tell him in case word gets out and evidence is moved. And you must bring in a team from London to assist him. Root's not up to a murder. Ask for Inspector Petleigh. Southwark Police."

"Don't tell me what to do, Mr. Arrowood."

Penn pulled on his gloves and tightened his scarf. He raised his ebony walking stick, moved Arrowood from his path with it, and hurried out to his carriage.

Chapter Thirty-One

We reached Catford about midnight. It was below freezing, the moonlight coming and going as clouds passed before it on their way south. No lights shone from any window around the green, the pub was dark, the police station closed. The pump stood like an icy sentry among the grass hard with frost. As Sidney pulled the four-wheeler up outside the church, Neddy came running down the path. We helped him into the carriage.

He didn't speak at first, his teeth chattering so from the cold. I took the blanket from our knees and wrapped him in it. The guvnor began to rub his back.

"You're frozen, lad."

"Didn't know when you'd come, sir." He was talking in jerks, like he couldn't catch his breath. The guvnor lit the candle: the lad's nose was red, his lips almost blue. "I been there a while."

"Where's my sister, son?"

"Still on the farm, sir. They wouldn't let her come back. Got a load of laundry in from one of the big houses today. Miss Ockwell said she wouldn't be finished till late, and they'd have to be up before dawn tomorrow." He was talking fast, his words coming in quick breaths. The guvnor rubbed his back as he spoke. "I tried to stay with her, Mr. Arrowood, but she shoved me out the door. She couldn't speak 'cos they was all there, Miss Ockwell and both the men, sir. They was right angry."

"Angry about what?"

"Mr. Godwin said Sergeant Root was paying them a call. Said you'd put him up to it, you're a liar, you're still interfering. I tried to listen in but I couldn't hear what else. Something to do with Birdie, but I don't know what."

"D'you think they suspect Ettie?"

"Don't know, sir."

"Did they mention the barn or the dung pit? Did they start digging in there?"

"Not as I heard. Just that the Sergeant was coming to call."

The guvnor looked over at me in the dark carriage. "Let's hope Root's only told them about the visit. He'd have to be a fool to warn them about the search, but as he is a fool I wouldn't put it past him. The last thing we need is for the killer to panic while Ettie's still there. He's killed once. He'll do it again if he thinks he's at risk."

"To the farm, Sidney," I called up to the box. "Fast as you can, mate."

"Wait!" said the guvnor quickly. "Let me think."

"We must go now while the family are abed," I said. "It's too dangerous. What if they've already caught her talking to Birdie?"

"Hold your fire, Barnett."

"Whoever it is has killed once and they'll do it again."

"You don't know it was one of the Ockwells. It could have been Digger."

"Root's told the family about the tooth," I said, just now realizing what could have happened. "That's why they've kept her back! They must suspect her."

"Barnett, calm yourself!" said the guvnor with some heat. "You don't know what he's told them. Neddy, where d'you think Ettie'll be?"

"Reckon she'll be in the laundry. They don't let us in the house."

"Is there any way to get there without waking the dogs?"

"Don't reckon so, sir."

The guvnor sighed. As we let him work on a plan, one of the horses snorted and shifted its feet. The church bell marked the quarter hour. I had a terrible fear rising in me, and each second that passed made it worse. My leg was jigging away, my heart racing. What if the murderer knew someone had passed on the tooth? What if they suspected Ettie on account of her being the newest?

The guvnor pulled the lad tight to him.

"We've got to get her now!" I burst out, pulling Lewis's pistol from my pocket. "Forget those bloody dogs. We'll force our way in there."

"Quiet!" he snapped.

"She's in danger!"

"I know she's in danger!" he cried, raising his arm and swiping at me. "What's got into you, Barnett? We need a plan. Keep your mouth shut while I think."

"We'll get her, Norman," came Sidney's voice from above. "Be calm."

The moon went behind a cloud and the carriage darkened. I was wild with panic thinking about Ettie up there alone, but knew I must control myself. I wasn't thinking straight anymore. At last the guvnor spoke again.

"Wait here," he said, opening the door and climbing down.

We watched as he waddled to the parsonage gate, squeaked it open, and hurried up the path. He hammered at the door, then stood back. No lights came on. He hammered again. The dim glow of a candle came to an upper window, and we could just make out the parson's face behind the misted glass. It opened and the head, clad in a sleeping cap, poked out. They exchanged a few words, then the head retreated. The window shut and turned black. A few moments later the door opened and the guvnor went inside.

He was back in the carriage minutes later. He passed me a greasy package.

"Bones for the dogs, Barnett. Sidney, take us to Blackshaw's Alley. Just past the pub on the left."

"No," I said. "We need to go direct to the farm."

"Listen," said the guvnor, trying to slow me down. "D'you remember how that builder Edgar was playing with those dogs when we visited the second time? He's our only chance of getting in there without them causing a riot. I fear he might need some persuasion, but don't pull that pistol again; we don't want to shoot the fellow."

Sidney stopped at the entrance to the alley and passed the truncheon to me from under the box. The guvnor led me down the track to a house in a tight-packed row of run-down buildings. There were no streetlamps, and the ground was pitted and rucked, the mud frozen solid. Not a sound came from within. I rapped hard at the door. We waited a few moments.

I rapped again and didn't stop until we heard a woman's voice on the other side.

"Oi!" she moaned. "Keep your hair on!"

The door pulled open. She held a tallow candle. Her face was pale, drawn tight, her eyes half-closed.

I pushed past her, the guvnor following.

"Where's Edgar Winter?"

"Basement room," she said. "But you keep your voices down."

The guvnor lit his candle and we went down the stairs. At the bottom was a door. I pushed it open and we went in.

"Who's that?" came Edgar's voice in the dark. We could hear him moving about, getting up from his bed. A child's voice said, "Pa?"

Another one started up whimpering.

The guvnor stepped forward with his candle, and there was Edgar, coming towards us with a pick handle raised in front of him.

"Get out," he hissed.

He wore all his day clothes except his boots. The bed behind him held three kiddies, their dirty faces wide-eyed with fear. At our feet was another mattress with another three kids there, buried under a pile of coats. A little girl began to cry. An older girl next to her hugged her close.

"We ain't going to hurt anyone, mate," I said, tapping the truncheon on my open hand. "We just need your help for an hour."

"Get behind me!" he barked at the kids. The three on the floor got up and scurried to the bed. A baby began to bawl. The oldest girl got out of the bed and went over to a box at the back of the room. She picked up a bundle of rags and began to rock it. It was only then I noticed the woman lying on a thin mattress in the furthest, darkest corner. She was piled high with sacks and blankets, just her grey, pinched face showing. Her eyes were shut, and from her mouth came the slow, rattling breath of the dying.

"Your family'll be safe if you do what we ask, Mr. Winter," said the guvnor.

"Get out of my bloody room!" roared Edgar, jumping forward and swinging his pick handle at me. I raised my truncheon to block it, but it slid down my weapon, cracking my knuckles. It stung like a bugger, but before he could take another swing I pogged him hard in the belly.

He doubled over, clutching himself, the pick handle falling to his side. I fell on top of him. Quickly, I slid the truncheon into the wild beard and under his chin, and, as he gasped for breath from the jab, I pulled his head back until he was looking at the ceiling.

He was gasping, his breath rasping, water streaming out his eyes and running down the side of his bald head.

"Now listen, my friend," said the guvnor. "You're going to come with us and make sure the dogs on Ockwell's farm don't bark while we rescue someone who's there. If you refuse, or if the dogs wake up the farm, then we'll tell Sergeant Root it's you and your brother who've been stealing the building materials from the construction sites around here. We've three witnesses, and no doubt a little visit to wherever your yard is will confirm it. Now, do you agree?"

Edgar's face had turned crimson; his whole body was shaking as he gasped for breath.

He nodded.

I pulled the truncheon away from his throat and he fell to the floor. Three of the kiddies were crying now. The baby was wailing. I pulled him to his feet.

"Get your boots on."

"Now, children, there's no need to cry," said the guvnor softly. "We'll bring your father back in an hour. I promise."

He stepped further into the room and moved his candle around, peering at the little faces in the bed, at the baby wrapped in rags, at the girl holding him.

"Is that your mother over there, my dear?" he asked her.

She nodded.

"I'm so sorry."

Edgar now had his boots on. He took his heavy coat off the bed, its pockets gone, its lining hanging in tatters, then found his greasy cap, his neckcloth.

"You look after all these children yourself, Edgar?" asked the guvnor.

"Fuck off," he answered. "Now, let's get this over with."

Chapter Thirty-Two

We reached the outer gates of the farm ten minutes later. Edgar went off first. After five minutes, we climbed down. The night was clear and crisp, the field pigs in their huts. A breeze rustled the treetops. When we reached the farmyard, we could see Edgar hunched by one of the barns, murmuring to the dogs as they chewed the bones.

The mastiff looked over as we crossed the yard, his ears pricked up, but Edgar soothed him and he got back to chewing on his bones. The farmhouse windows were all dark. We crept over to the barn where Willoughby had escaped the dogs that first time we visited, and made our way along the wall to the dairy at the end. At the corner there was about twenty yards of open ground to reach the side of the house. The laundry door was at the back.

We checked the windows again, then hurried over to the

corner of the house. From there we followed the wall, ducking under a bay window, along a bit, then under another window.

The rear of the house faced a paddock. The guvnor was getting wheezy, so we had a bit of a rest till he fetched his breath. A fox, loping along the back of the barns, stopped to watch us.

A few more yards along and we found the laundry door. I got to work straight away, wiggling the betty, trying to work its system, but the lock was fitted out with escutcheons I wasn't used to. I couldn't do it.

"What is it?" whispered the guvnor as I pulled out the betty.

I pointed at the window next to the door. He nodded.

I wrapped my scarf around my hand and was about to put it through the glass when there was a creak from one of the windows upstairs.

We froze. The back of the house had no shrubbery or ivy growing next to it: there was nowhere to hide.

We pressed ourselves to the brick, listening.

"Hurry, Barnett," he whispered when no more sounds came.

I put my hand through the window quick as I could. There was a tinkle of glass as it fell onto the floor on the other side, then I found the latch. It was locked, screwed into the wood. I got out my little jemmy, passed it through the hole, and worked the end under the latch arm. A couple of sharp tugs and it cracked open, splintering the wood. I opened the window and hoisted myself inside.

The air smelt of damp wool and ammonia, and there was a thin warmth from the coals. First thing I did was feel the door for a key. There was none: the only way out again was through the window. I stood there quiet, letting my eyes adjust to the darkness within. I listened hard. If they were awake upstairs, they'd surely have heard that window. I needed to move fast.

The sound of deep breathing was coming from somewhere in the room. In the gloom, my eyes took in the outlines of great boiling pots, a couple of mangles, a clothes press. Baskets of linen and stacks of clothes. Drying racks hung from the ceilings, dripping with linen.

Quiet as I could, I moved past the boiling pots until I was facing the door to the house. I crept on, round the last of the great pots. A few coals glowed in the grate of a small fire, throwing a little orange light onto the floor. And there lay a person wrapped from head to toe in a blanket. A soft snore came from inside.

I quickly checked the rest of the room, but there was nobody else there. Kneeling, I lifted a corner of the blanket to see a pale white face inside.

It was Ettie, letting out a low whistle with every outbreath.

"Ettie," I whispered, touching her shoulder.

She didn't budge.

I took both her shoulders and raised her to a sit. Her eyes opened, then shut. Her head rolled on her shoulders.

"Wake up, Ettie," I said, loud as I dared. I gave her a better shake.

"What?" she murmured, her eyes opening at last.

I hoisted her to her feet.

"Andrew?" she slurred. "Andrew?"

"Norman," I said, getting my arms round her waist and dragging her across to the back door. "We got to get you out. Police are searching the place in the morning."

"Norman." Her voice was weak. She slumped again. I pulled her upright. She flinched when I touched her hand, bound though it was in a rag.

The guvnor's face was at the window.

"I'm going to lift her out," I whispered to him. "You take her legs. I think she's drugged."

"I'll manage," mumbled Ettie.

I hoisted her up and after a few goes got her legs through the window. The guvnor took hold of her boots and pulled.

"Ooh," she murmured as her arse jagged on the latch.

I put my shoulder to her rumple and hoiked it over the sill. From there she slid through quickly, falling on top of the guvnor on the other side.

"Oof!" he moaned, hitting the floor.

As I climbed out myself, I heard the squeak of a door somewhere in the house. Then steps on the floorboards.

"Someone's coming," I said, jumping out.

The guvnor was already on his feet with Ettie's arm over his shoulder.

"I can walk," she said. She was limping now, but seemed stronger.

I took her other arm and we hurried across to the dairy, me looking back at the house every few steps. A little flare of light appeared behind one of the front windows. The flicker of a candle flame played on the glass.

We pushed back into the ivy that grew thick on the dairy wall. That side was dark, sheltered from the moonlight. My hand went over Ettie's mouth. I felt her lips cold, her breath hot.

"Ssh," I whispered.

Her eyes twisted towards me. She'd got her focus back now. She nodded.

A figure appeared in the upper window, the candle behind them. The window rose.

We crouched in the ivy, barely even breathing. We didn't even dare turn our heads.

For some time the figure stood there. Then the window slid shut and the person was gone. The house was in darkness again.

"This way," whispered Ettie, leading us behind the dairy and out of sight of the house. We ran along the length of the stock shed, keeping tight to the wall. At the end was a narrow wooden door.

"In here," she said.

"We've got to go to the carriage," hissed the guvnor. "They've heard us."

"In here," she said again, disappearing inside.

We had no choice but to follow. It was dark and close in there, a fug of dung and horses. I could just make out her form ahead, feeling along the wall as she moved.

"We've got to leave, Ettie," said the guvnor. "They heard us. They'll be out any moment."

"I'm not leaving without the lads."

"The lads? We can't take them!"

"We're taking them," she whispered.

Just then we heard the front door of the farmhouse groan open. The hounds began to bark; next we heard them run across the yard.

"Dogs!" shouted Godwin.

A horse was moving close to me in the dark. I felt out and found a low wooden fence between me and it.

Now two sets of footsteps were moving across the yard, getting closer.

"What the bloody hell's got into them?" It was Godwin's voice.

"Probably just a fox." Walter.

My eyes were getting used to the dark. We were in a small walled-off section of the barn. Three horses stood in a little pigpen beside us, crammed so close their flanks touched each other. On the other wall, horse equipment. A stack of straw sat in the corner, and next to that a half-door leading into the main part of the barn.

The guvnor was peering into the farmyard through a crack in the wall.

"They're coming over," he whispered.

"Behind the horses," I said.

I took Ettie's arm and pulled her into the pen. The guvnor followed, pushing us right up against the animals, who shifted on their feet and snorted.

It was tight in there. There was only really room for one horse let alone three. I ducked under their heads, pulling Ettie with me to the other side of the stall where we squeezed into a corner. A big black horse stood inches from my nose. Its leg twitched. It blew smoke out its nose.

The guvnor couldn't squeeze past the first horse, so he crawled under it and sat against the low wall, right below its belly. His lungs made a low whistle each time he breathed out.

The footsteps got louder as the brothers approached, the patter of dogs' feet with them. Dim light came and went through the holes and slats of the shed as their lamp swung past. They were right outside now. Their boots crunched on the frozen ground and stopped a few yards further on. The sound of the latch lifting. The barn door scraped on the ground as it swung open.

We could now hear the brothers moving on the other side of the wall dividing the shed from the barn. The weak lamplight came through the half-door. The black horse next to me snorted again; his mane twitched; he bent his head round to have a look at us. He was a big, sad bugger, his legs wearing stockings of mud and shit.

There was a sudden sharp thump next door.

A voice cried out in pain.

"What have you two been up to?" asked Godwin.

"We sleeping, Dad," said a voice. It was Willoughby.

"Something woke the dogs."

"We been sleeping."

"Digger, you shit," said Godwin. "You've been nosing around again."

"Digger been here too. Been sleeping."

"Like you? Then how d'you know he wasn't nosing?"

"He… We been sleeping, Dad."

"Stand up," said Godwin softly.

There was a creak of wood and more movement.

"Open your coats. Turn out the pockets."

A few moments passed.

"Digger, I swear it," said Godwin. His voice was low, mean. "If I find you've got into the pantry it'll be the bit for you."

"Could have been a fox, Godwin," said Walter in his slow voice.

It was quiet for a few moments. Then a little whistle and one of them made a sudden yelp. The boards creaked again.

"You know I love you, don't you, Willoughby?" Godwin's voice was soft now. "I don't know what we'd do without you. Both of you."

"Best workers."

"That's it. Best we've ever had. We're a big family, don't forget it. You're as important as anyone."

"And John," said Willoughby. "And my nieces."

"And them too. And we've got to watch each other. You watch Digger. Digger watches you. That's right, isn't it?"

"Watches you."

The white shire horse next to the guvnor let out a thunderous roar of gas from its backside. It edged over, rubbing its flank on the low wooden wall. The guvnor twitched under its belly, trapped against the planks.

"You happy, Willoughby?" asked Godwin.

"Happy, Dad."

"You're happy with us?"

"Happy."

As they talked, I could see the white horse's thick cock start to extend out from its groin, slow and sure like a dock-yard crane.

In the dim light, the guvnor stared at it in horror, his eyes wide. He was hemmed in where he sat, unable to rise for the horse's belly, and feared to crawl least he be heard. The thing inched its way closer.

Then, when it was about a foot long, it stopped.

All of a sudden, a torrent of steaming piss shot out of it. The guvnor clamped his hand over his mouth, straining to get his head out of the way, but he was trapped. The great, hot gush exploded over his face, his coat, his britches.

"Sounds like Count Lavender," said Godwin with a laugh, his voice warm now. "Ought to get him a chamber pot, eh, Willoughby?"

"Get a chamber pot," laughed Willoughby, though it seemed to me he was forcing it. "Get him a chamber pot!"

And then the gush stopped.

The guvnor crouched there under the horse, soaked through, his face wild with fury, his hand clamped over his mouth. He glared at me.

Footsteps next door, and the light faded.

"Up early tomorrow, lads," said Godwin as the barn door scraped shut. "Need twelve baconers for slaughter."

We listened to the brothers march back across the yard,

the dogs trotting along behind them. The door of the farmhouse banged shut.

We were in darkness again.

Only then did the guvnor let out a groan.

We waited a few more minutes, then we rose and squeezed
out of the stall. The guvnor's teeth were already chattering.

"We must go," he whispered, the spirit in him gone.

Ettie ignored him, pushing open the half-door to the barn.
She pulled a candle from her rags and lit it.

"Willoughby," she whispered.

"Miss Ettie?"

"Get up. We're taking you somewhere safe."

As she walked forward, the candle began to light up the
space. The first thing we saw was the dung pit taking up half
the floor. It was fenced on three sides, the dung piled high as
a horse. Streams of brown liquid oozed from it, covering the
rest of the dirt floor completely, turning it to mud. As I followed her in, the stench of that pig shit almost knocked me
off my feet. It was worse than anything I'd smelt even back
when I lived in the court, and so heavy and thick I felt it sting
my eyes.

Willoughby and Digger were sat on two wooden boards,
held just above the lake of stinking, brown mud by a low row
of logs. They had no mattress, their only comfort being layers of newspaper under them. Each was wrapped in the same
torn and muddy sacking as the horses.

"Good God," murmured the guvnor.

"Mr. Arrowood!" exclaimed Willoughby when he finally
saw us in Ettie's dim candle light. "Mr. Barnett! Got our
friends here, Digger. Look. And Miss Ettie!"

"Hello, Willoughby," said the guvnor, his voice low with horror at how they lived. "And Digger."

Digger stared at him, his eyes hard. He glanced at the barn door.

"Listen, lads," said Ettie. "We're going to take you away from here. To somewhere better."

Digger shook his head violently, waving us away with his hand.

"Got to work tomorrow, Miss Ettie," said Willoughby. "All family, we are. Got to finish the drain."

"But you must come, Willoughby," she went on. "We'll find you somewhere nice to live, with a proper bed and proper food. They don't treat you right here."

"Got to work hard. Dad says. He get me back with John."

Ettie turned to me. I knew what she wanted: I took hold of Willoughby and lifted him up.

"Murder!" he screamed, twisting and turning. "Murder! Help!"

"Shut up," I said as he wiggled and jerked in my arms. He was so light: through the sacks he was wrapped in I could feel his bones. There wasn't a scrap of meat on his body.

"Murder!" he cried.

Digger leapt to his feet, bound over to a ladder stood by the dung pit, and scurried up to a ledge ten or twelve feet above.

The dogs started barking again.

"Get him, William," demanded Ettie.

"We've no time," he answered, taking hold of her arm and pulling her towards the stable door. "We must go, Ettie. Quick!"

I hauled Willoughby over my shoulder, still shouting and twisting, and followed them through the stable and out to the field at the back. With the dogs barking in our ears, we ran down to the drive where Sidney was waiting. Neddy threw open the door and helped me get Willoughby inside. I jammed him in the corner, my body stopping him from getting out.

"Murder!" he cried one more time, but the struggle was going out of him.

Ettie and the guvnor climbed in behind and Sidney whipped up the horses. I stuck my head out the window and looked back towards the yard as we moved away: the dogs were barking up a storm at the gate. Just as we turned onto the road, Godwin and Walter ran up next to them, pointing at our carriage.

Then we were gone.

Chapter Thirty-Three

We fled through the night, only slowing to a trot once we reached Lewisham Road. Willoughby was silent, his breaths coming in fits and starts. Ettie was doing her best to soothe him, but he was frightened.

The guvnor sat opposite me, complaining about Count Lavender. The smell coming off him was frightful, and he was getting cold in his wet clothes. Neddy took a blanket and wrapped it round him, tucking it into the guvnor's collar and under his thighs. Then he turned his attention to Willoughby.

"You're safe, mate, I'm telling you straight," said the boy. "You trust me, don't you? I'm your mate, ain't I?"

Willoughby nodded.

"These gents are my friends, Willoughby. We're going to help you, understand?"

"Help you," said Willoughby, his voice flat and slow, his face bewildered.

"Ettie," said the guvnor. "Are you going to explain why we've kidnapped him?"

"Because they're slaves, William," said Ettie sharply. "They sleep in that awful barn with not even a mattress. They never leave the farm: all they do is work and sleep. I doubt they get paid. They're given just enough to eat to keep them working, but they're always hungry. They drink from the horse trough."

"I seen them eating the pig slops," said Neddy.

As the carriage wobbled and bounced along the road, Willoughby bowed his head, his arms hugging himself across his chest. I felt sick just remembering how his body felt when I lifted him. His arms were thin as tapers; it was like hoiking a bundle of rags.

The guvnor leant over to Willoughby and gripped his shoulder.

"Is this true, my dear?" he asked in a soft voice.

Willoughby didn't look up.

"Are you afraid, Willoughby?"

"Best workers," he said, looking up now, his jaw jutting forward as he spoke. His tongue came out his mouth and scraped over his scabby lips. "We are. Family."

He shut his eyes and began to rock, as slow and gentle as a mother rocking a baby.

"Why did you come for me?" asked Ettie. "I was just beginning to understand the place. I needed a few more days."

"We had to get you out tonight, Ettie. It was too dangerous. The police are searching the barn for Mrs. Gillie's body tomorrow. Root knows Willoughby gave the tooth to somebody. He'll let it out and the murderer'll suspect you or Neddy. Did they drug you?"

"No, I'm just exhausted. I worked from six this morning until midnight. They'd seven hampers of laundry from one of the big houses to do. I was already weak from being in the dairy for the last few days, but that was too much. But I spoke to Birdie today. She helped me in the laundry for a little while. We were alone."

"What did you discover?"

"She doesn't want to see her parents. Whether it's really what she wants or they've trained her I don't know, but she said it clearly enough."

"Did you ask about the picture?"

"Her cousin Annabel lives in Brighton. She doesn't understand why Annabel hasn't answered her letters."

"Birdie can write?"

"Walter helps her."

"Well, well. I wonder if they ever get posted. What did she say about him?"

"Only good things. Walter's strong. Walter's handsome. *Dear old Poomps*, she calls him."

"What else? Any signs of fear?"

"Not of Walter. Her face lights up when he comes into the room. It's Rosanna she's afraid of."

"Did you ask if he prevents her seeing her parents?"

"Rosanna took her off to the dairy before we could speak more."

The guvnor shivered. The smell seemed to come off him in waves.

"You fall in the trough, Mr. Arrowood?" asked Neddy, tucking the blanket into the guvnor's collar where it had come loose.

"Yes, my dear. Thank you for this. I am rather cold."

"What's up with your hand, Ettie?" I asked, pointing at the rags wrapped around it.

"Rosanna pushed it in the sterilizing fluid when I was in the dairy. She said it was the only way of toughening it up."

"Does it hurt?"

"I'm fine, Norman, but I own I screamed at the time. It was boiling. You know, I think she enjoyed it. I'm sure she's done the same to Birdie: her hand was wrapped too. Rosanna treats the two wives as servants: I saw her strike Polly across the face for dropping a plate."

"What are Polly's duties?" asked the guvnor.

"She tends to the mother, up and down those stairs all day. When she isn't doing that she cleans and cooks. The poor girl's worked endlessly, just as Birdie is."

"How did she seem?"

"Melancholy. She barely speaks, and I believe she pulls out her hair. She wears a scarf over her head, but it doesn't hide it all."

"Birdie had a patch of hair torn out," said I. "I saw it at the station that time. Rosanna said it was the mangle."

"Could Rosanna have done it?" asked the guvnor.

"I don't know," answered Ettie. "She's a hard mistress and they're both in fear of her. But I think Polly has some illness of the mind. She carries three little corn dollies in her apron pocket. I saw her sitting in the hallway feeding them Dalby's Calmative."

"Three corn dollies," he said real slow, having a think about it as we rolled and jolted along the road. "Mrs. Gillie said three dead children. Perhaps she was telling us something about Polly. Perhaps she wanted us to help her. Did you hear anything about children, Ettie?"

She shook her head.

"Polly's dead infant is one," he said. "But who are the other two?" The carriage hit a pothole and lurched, throwing the guvnor forward onto me. I pushed him off quick. "Polly's sister had twins," he went on. "Polly was left to look after them when she died. Mrs. Fleg said it was their deaths that led to her committal in the asylum. Is that the three? Her own child and her sister's twins? The three dollies must represent those three dead infants. She feeds them infant soother. She cannot stop caring for them. Perhaps Polly's not insane, Sister. Perhaps she's grieving."

"Perhaps she's both, William."

We rolled on for a while, busy with our thoughts.

"By the way," he said, "we're moving back to our rooms tomorrow. The builders are finished."

Ettie turned her head to me, her eyes smiling in thanks. I nodded.

Willoughby was silent, looking out the window at the dark buildings. Neddy'd fallen asleep, his head against Ettie's shoulder. I rolled a cigarette to keep myself awake and we rode on, past New Cross Station and onto the Old Kent Road, past Deptford Hospital and the gas works, over the canal. A few early wagons on their way to the markets were on the road, but nothing else at that time of the morning. When we reached Bricklayers' Arms, the guvnor's head had dropped to his chest. I took the pipe from his hand and laid it on the bench.

"Thanks for rescuing me, Norman," whispered Ettie.

"You saved me once, remember?"

She nodded. Though she smelt real bad, I was glad to be sat next to her as the carriage jerked and bumped along the road.

"I was worried about you," I said.

I felt her finger creep along the bench and link with mine. In the dark, a tired little smile came to my lips as her fingers, hard and cold, slotted between my own. I closed my hand softly on hers and, after a minute or two, heard her quiet snore.

When we reached the Elephant and Castle, they put Willoughby to sleep in Lewis's bedroom. He was silent, neither happy nor unhappy. Tired more than anything. The guvnor decided I'd sleep in the parlour with Neddy, the door open least Willoughby should decide to make an escape in the night. Lewis brought down a pile of blankets. Though there was little comfort and the couch too small for my long legs, I fell asleep the moment my head touched the cushion, a strange contentment in my heart.

Chapter Thirty-Four

We were at Southwark Police Station at eight the next morning. I wasn't feeling too clever after only four hours' sleep and the guvnor looked even worse. He'd grown a crust on his lip and his eye was still closed up by his swollen, purple cheek. He'd changed into his Sunday best, but it didn't look nor smell like he'd had a wash.

Petleigh wasn't there, but a shilling to the new PC got us his address in Walworth. The landlady let us in and directed us up the stairs, where he had the whole second floor. There the door was opened by a woman of middle age who seemed about to leave for church. She wore her hair pinned up inside a straw hat and held a pair of leather gloves which she wrung in her hands, nervy from seeing the guvnor's battered face.

"Is Inspector Petleigh in, madam?" he asked. "It's a work matter."

"We're just leaving for church," she said, regaining her bravery. Her nose wrinkled as she caught the eau de cheval that still freshened the guvnor's air. "Could you come back later?"

"Who is it, darling?" came Petleigh's voice from within.

"For you," she said. She looked at me again and decided against inviting us in.

The moment Petleigh appeared his face went quite pale.

"Arrowood? What are you doing here?"

"There's to be a search for Mrs. Gillie's body this morning," said the guvnor, his face like thunder. "Did you speak to your superior?"

"I'll only be a minute," said Petleigh to the woman. He stepped past her onto the landing and shut the door behind him. He wore a smart black suit, a striped tie.

"You didn't introduce us to the lady, Petleigh."

"Who gave you my address?" Petleigh's hands gripped the doorknob behind his back. The guvnor held his eye; he didn't reply.

"I'm to assist Sergeant Root," said Petleigh at last. "They've requested a detective. I don't know how you did it, but you've got your way."

"We saw the MP yesterday," answered the guvnor. "We showed him the tooth."

"I've heard nothing about a search. Have they a warrant?"

"I assume so."

"Is Ettie—"

"Safe!" barked the guvnor.

Petleigh stood against the door, shifting his feet. He swallowed as he looked from the guvnor to me.

"Well, what are you waiting for, man!" cried the guvnor. "Get your blooming coat!"

We took a cab to the station in silence. Petleigh and the guvnor wouldn't even look at each other. At London Bridge we found the downtrain; it wasn't until Ladywell that the guvnor finally spoke:

"So you're married, Petleigh."

The copper's eyes twinged. He looked out at the foggy morning jerking past the window. He cleared his throat.

"I am," he said, his voice carrying none of its usual shrill bite. "Although not happily."

"Children?" With each word the guvnor's voice was rising.

"No. Look, Will—"

"You've played false with my sister," interrupted the guvnor. The other passengers turned their eyes to us. "And with me. What the hell were you doing? Would you have asked for her hand? Was that your plan?"

"I...I don't know. Ettie's a most wonderful woman." Petleigh was looking straight at the guvnor, his head unmoving. He spoke quiet, trying to pretend there weren't five strangers listening to every word. "I was considering a divorce."

"Oh! Considering a divorce! *Considering* a divorce. How noble! What a gallant you are, Inspector."

"Be quiet now, William," said Petleigh.

"Don't tell me to be quiet, you cur! Does your wife know about my sister?"

"Leave it, sir," I said.

"Leave it?" he demanded.

"At least till tomorrow. Remember what he's got to do today."

The guvnor opened his mouth, about to round on me, then thought better of it. He pressed his lips in a thunderous frown, gave Petleigh a last furious glare, then turned his face to the window.

★ ★ ★

They needed someone who'd seen Mrs. Gillie quite recent to identify the body, but Root was angry as hell about it all and out and out refused to let the guvnor come along. He wasn't too pleased about me coming either but Petleigh persuaded him, and so they sent PC Young to wake the gravedigger, who collected us in his wagon and took us up to the farm. Rosanna answered the door.

"A body in the dung pit?" she exclaimed when Root showed her the warrant. She was fiddling with the silver cross that hung from her neck as she spoke, a vexed frown on her face. "What rubbish. Who said there was a body?"

"We've had information, ma'am," answered Root, his face and chins colouring.

She took a great breath and looked up at me like she'd be happy to kill me. Behind us the dogs growled and spat on their ropes.

"From him and his master, I suppose? And you're taking their word over ours? They who made out there was a will and told us Birdie was due an inheritance? Sergeant Root, you should be ashamed."

"The orders come direct from Sir Edward, ma'am. I don't like it any more'n you."

"I want him off our land," she said, crossing her arms.

"He's only here to identify the body," said Root.

"There isn't one! I've told you that. And who are you, if I may ask?"

"Inspector Petleigh, Southwark Police. I've taken over the case as Superintendent Jones is ill."

"What a waste of time. Whose body is it supposed to be?"

"We cannot tell you that yet, ma'am," said Petleigh. "We

need to make a start now, if you'll just show us where the body is."

"Where the body is?" she cried, her voice hard and screeching, her eyes wide. "I told you there's no body, you damn fool! This is persecution."

"I meant to say the dung pit, ma'am."

"You've come down from the city to do this?" Her thick eyebrows were hooked, her eyes like blue fire. "Him and the fat one are just making trouble for us, you do know that, I suppose? It's been in the papers. Paid by my sister-in-law's parents to make up lies about us."

"We have a warrant to search the barn," said Petleigh.

"Well, you'll just have to wait until Godwin's back. He runs the farm."

"I'm afraid we cannot wait," said Petleigh. "But first I need to speak to Birdie, Miss Ockwell. Could you call her?"

"She's not here. She's out visiting. I don't know where."

"Might I come in and have a look around to satisfy myself?"

"No. Now, do what you have to do and get off our land."

She slammed the door so hard it rattled the windows.

Petleigh tucked his trousers into his stockings and we walked around the outside of the yard, keeping out of reach of the two dogs who were barking up a storm, straining at their ropes to get a bite of us. The wide barn doors were open, the stink of pigshit almost bad enough to make a man pass out. The gravedigger lit a lantern while we picked our way across the great pool of dungwater to the pit. It was about twenty foot wide, with wooden walls on three sides, another twenty foot deep, the dung piled up tall as a man.

PC Young and the gravedigger took up their shovels and got digging, moving each load of dung to the other side in a barrow. I lit up a smoke and sat on a crate, while Petleigh stood watching, his handkerchief clasped over his precious nose. Root stood at the edge of the dung pit, his helmet rising high on his long head, poking deep into the shit with a pole. The dogs slowly quieted themselves but stood watching outside the barn doors, waiting in case we should trick them.

Five minutes passed.

Petleigh drew out a cigar.

Ten minutes.

Fifteen.

I rolled another smoke. In front of me were the planks that Digger and Willoughby slept on, held just above the pool of slurry by a few logs resting on the dirt floor. Around one wall were stacked ricks of hay, but all those workers had for comfort on their beds was newspaper and a bit of old sacking. Tools hung on another wall, a feed-caking machine in a corner.

"Here," said Root, pointing to a spot about halfway along the far wall of the pit. He poked with his stick again about a foot further on, and then again another foot on. "There's something in here."

I came over to get a better look. Young and the gravedigger started digging by the wall, flinging the dung behind them now instead of loading the barrow, getting closer and closer to where Root's pole was planted.

"I got something," said PC Young.

It was a thick woollen sock, filthy brown and wet from the dung. There was a foot inside.

They dug and scraped until we could make out a leg with long, dirty undertrousers, then another foot. The dung was uneven, dark brown with grey veins, oozing liquid that was black like treacle, bits of bones and feathers in there, straw and seeds. They kept working till we saw her skirts, three different types stuck together, sodden, black with muck.

"You want me to pull her out, Sarge?" asked the young copper, panting a bit from the work.

"Just uncover her," said Root, his eyes fixed on the legs.

They dug out her arms, clad in a thick, coarse jumper, wet and brown, then her body. At last they got to her face.

With the corner of his shovel, the gravedigger moved the dirt off Mrs. Gillie's forehead, her nose, her cheeks. The deep lines on her face were filled with it, etched like a thick, black net had been sunk into her old skin. I shuddered. Her eyes were open wide but their glint was gone, hidden under a paste of pig dung. The gravedigger took out a rag and gently cleaned her face, her chin, her lips. Her nose-holes were plugged with muck.

"What's that?" asked Petleigh.

Sticking out from between her lips was a clump of twigs and leaves.

The gravedigger made to draw them out but Petleigh stopped him.

"Let me," he said, pulling on a pair of canvas gloves.

He stepped with care onto the soft, wet dung, and leant over Mrs. Gillie's body. Slowly, he removed the posy of sticks from her mouth. He took a cloth from his pocket, wrapped the stuff in it, and handed it to Root. "Be careful with that," he said. He looked at the gravedigger. "Give me some light."

When the lamp was brought over, Petleigh stuck his fingers inside Mrs. Gillie's mouth and pulled out a few more twigs and leaves. Then, with his other hand, he brought out a lump of moss. He gave them all to Root.

Now he came over to the other side of the body and put his fingers into her mouth again, further this time. He grimaced, holding my eyes as he fished about in there. Her face seemed so small, so unhappy, his hand so brutish. He shook his head.

"I can't get them."

He took off the canvas glove. Now he held her chin while he put his soft pink fingers between her lips and into her mouth, down until his knuckles touched her wet brown lips. He shuddered, then angled his hand better, his mouth a tight circle. Finally, he drew out a few jagged red pieces of a wooden flower.

They were dark with blood. Little bits of black meat stuck to the wood, on the broken petals, the splintered stems. A gob fell on Petleigh's shoes. He grimaced, handing the pieces to Root.

"Pushed down her throat," he said. "There's more lodged in there, but we'll have to leave the rest to the police surgeon."

Only then did I see that on her filthy neck, jutting out from a puncture in the side, was a single blue stem.

PC Young, who'd been so keen and willing when he was digging, was pale, his shoulders drooping. He sat on the crate, his elbows rested on his knees.

Petleigh turned to me. "Is it Mrs. Gillie?"

"Yes, Inspector," said I. "Is that how she died?"

Petleigh nodded. "It's likely. It looks like they forced these things down her throat until she choked. Look at the bruising around her mouth. I think they've blocked her nose with mud as well." He stepped back. "Get the body on the wagon, please, gentlemen. Then search the rest of the pit for any clues—fabric, paper, anything." He looked at me. "Wait for us at the police station, Norman. We need to talk to the family."

I walked all the way back to town. When I told the guvnor what we'd found, he bit his lip, clasped his head in his hands. For a long time he didn't speak; he knew it was his fault—he shouldn't have told Root about the dead children. It was only because he'd got riled up that he did, but he should have learnt by now. People talked to us. People got killed.

It being a Sunday morning, the pub was shut, and by the time the coppers came back three or four hours later, we were frozen and miserable. In the back of the wagon, among the gravedigger's shovels and picks, Mrs. Gillie's body was covered in an old tarp. The guvnor gripped the side of the wagon, his eyes fixed on the form beneath. He touched it.

"I'm sorry," he whispered.

"Out the way, sir," said the gravedigger. With PC Young he lifted the body down and carried it into the station. Root followed them in, saying: "Put the kettle on, Young. I'm parched."

"What kind of fiend would do that to an old woman, Petleigh?" asked the guvnor.

"I've never seen the like before," said Petleigh. He opened his snuffbox and took a toot. "There were no clues in the pit. We dug right down to the cobbles."

"Did you speak to Birdie?" asked the guvnor.

"Rosanna swore Birdie and Polly weren't there. We had to accept it: we don't have a warrant for the house. Godwin and Walter returned so we were able to interview the three of them. They all denied knowing anything about it, but it seems one of their workers disappeared last night. Willoughby Krott, his name is. Seems as if someone might have tipped him off. The other worker, Thomas Digger, can't speak, but he's got violence written all over his face, that one. A nasty case, I'm telling you."

The guvnor grunted and rolled his eyes at me.

"If we can find this Krott, I believe we'll have our murderer," Petleigh went on. "I'll put officers on the trams and the railway and send a message to the other police stations in the area. It shouldn't be too hard to track him: he's feeble-minded, one of the Mongolian types. Hard to hide a face like that."

He drew a cigar from his pocket and planted it in his mouth.

"You'll have him caught and convicted in hours, I'm sure, Inspector," said the guvnor. "A man of your genius."

Petleigh caught his mocking tone.

"What's wrong with you, William? Did you want it to be one of the Ockwell family? That would help your case, I suppose."

"Petleigh, you imbecile," said the guvnor, shaking his great boar's head. "Willoughby Krott didn't kill Mrs. Gillie. It was him who found the tooth! He's staying at Lewis's. We took him against his will last night to keep him safe. Ettie insisted."

Petleigh stroked his waxed moustache. His eyes narrowed.

"Once again, you withhold vital information," he said. "Making me look an ass. I'm trying to help you, you know?"

"You're only helping so I'll continue to allow you to woo my sister."

"I don't need your permission."

At that the guvnor's head drew back. His lips quivered in disbelief.

"It's got to be one of them up there, Inspector," I said real quick. "Willoughby was tight with Mrs. Gillie. He was that upset when he found the tooth. He wanted someone to know."

"Who d'you suspect?" asked the copper.

"Walter, perhaps," said the guvnor. "He's a history of violence. Or Digger. Godwin's a suspect too. He took a shot at us the other day. Struck Norman with a club."

"Did the old girl have anything of value?"

"I don't know. I suppose it could have been a robbery, but it happened directly after I informed Root that she'd told us about those three dead children. You need to ask Root who he told."

"I've already done that. He swears he told nobody."

"I don't believe that. He's unreliable. He was so drunk in the pub the other night he fell over, in front of the whole village. Listen, Petleigh, how about letting me question the Ockwells? I think I might be able to—"

"They've already been questioned!" Petleigh snapped. "You should go home now, William, and make sure you don't lose Willoughby. I'll speak with him later today or tomorrow. I also need to inform the family." He sighed. "Though I don't know how I'll find them. They could be anywhere."

"I have her granddaughter's address. She came to see us when Mrs. Gillie disappeared." The guvnor opened his notebook, copied it out onto a blank page, and handed it to the inspector. "Mind you tell her about this before it gets into the papers. You'd better get onto it straight away."

"I know my job, William."

"Of course you do, Petleigh."

When we reached the house, Lewis and Neddy were sat in the parlour playing draughts. Neddy'd been washed. His hat was on, his boots laced, his coat done up.

"He's waiting for his money," said Lewis.

"Ah, yes, of course," said the guvnor. "You've done a good job, my dear. I'm very proud of you."

Neddy smiled, his face going a little red. He only ever wanted to make the guvnor happy.

Arrowood stuck his fat fingers in his purse, pulled out a few coins, and pressed them into Neddy's little hand. The boy's face fell.

"You said six," I said.

"Six?" asked the guvnor. "I thought it was four."

"It was six, sir," said Neddy.

"I was sure it was four." His voice was low and soft, like he wasn't really interested in winning this one. It wasn't like him at all.

"It was six, William," said Lewis, shaking his head. He grabbed the purse from the guvnor and emptied another couple of bob into the lad's hand.

"Thanks, Mr. Arrowood!" exclaimed Neddy. He ran out onto the street and was gone in a flash.

"Ettie's in bed," said Lewis. "Willoughby also. I gave him some eggs when he woke but he brought it up immediately. He's been farting like a bishop. His clothes were crawling with mites so I got the tub out and drew a bath for him."

"Thank you, Lewis."

"He managed to keep down some thin porridge later on. I think we should stick with that for a while. But come. You must see something."

He led us to the back kitchen, where a pile of rags lay on the linoleum. Lewis lowered himself onto a stool and pulled out sheaves of yellowing newspaper and handfuls of leaves.

"He wore these under his smock, to keep him warm. The leaves were packed between the papers."

He threw them down, picking up a few filthy and torn dress sleeves.

"His ankles were wrapped in these. He had no stockings. His feet were bound in these sacks." He showed us torn shreds of sacking, tarred, stringy. He pointed at the pile. "He wore those pieces of wood on his soles, padded out with straw and more paper. His feet are beyond repair. His toes are bent out of shape, some of them broken, I think. The skin everywhere's open, infected."

He stood, kicking out at the pile.

"Prepare yourself. There's something else."

He took us up the narrow stairs and into his bedroom, where Willoughby slept. Without his hat we saw that our friend's head was shaved like a prisoner, the stubble growing in patches among a spread of dark scabs and hardened white scars. His Mongolian face, now that the grime was gone, was quite covered in freckles, his thick tongue resting between his lips. He looked in such peace as I'd never seen in my life.

With care, Lewis pulled back the blankets and unbuttoned Willoughby's grey nightshirt. Finally, he opened it out.

The guvnor gasped, stepping back and stumbling against the washstand.

I reached for the doorframe to steady myself.

His sides were striped by dozens of painful lacerations, the flesh split open like swollen crimson mouths. There was no skin on his belly, instead a glistening sheen of yellow and pink where filthy scabs sat like islands in puddles of infected jelly. One of his tits was gone, in its place just a rough brown hollow, while the other hung off on a rope of meat. His arms were a horror of burns and wheals, a mush of meat and pus, raw and bright and crawling with mites. There wasn't an inch free from someone's fury. And what was left of his skin sagged like a bruised and bloody cloak off his bones. His belly was sunk, the button standing up like a pipe, his ribs rising as fences on his chest. It was as if all the torments of Hell had been visited on his one miserable body.

Willoughby opened his eyes. He sat up quick, pulling his nightshirt tight over him.

"No!" he said.

"Willoughby," said Lewis, sitting on the bed next to him and taking his hand. "Don't worry. You're safe."

Willoughby's chest was heaving. He looked at us, confused.

"It's only me. It's Lewis. We're not going to hurt you. We're going to help you."

"We'll never hurt you, my dear," said the guvnor. "I promise you that."

"It's the same on his back," said Lewis, fighting hard to control his quivering voice. "It must have been going on for years."

"Who did this to you, darling?" asked the guvnor in a whisper.

But Willoughby only turned his face to the wall and pulled the blanket over his head. Four of his fingernails were gone, replaced by an ugly black mess.

"Last night in the barn when Godwin and Walter came, we heard someone being hit," said the guvnor. "Was it you, Willoughby?"

There was no reply.

"Who hurt you, Willoughby?"

Just a sigh.

Lewis patted his leg.

"You get some sleep, my dear. We'll have a nice cup of tea when you feel like it."

Chapter Thirty-Five

I made the tea and joined them in the parlour, where Lewis put more coal on the fire.

"Is he in pain?" asked the guvnor, gripping one hand with the other. "I've heard they don't feel pain as we do."

"The hot water pained him, William." Lewis sat in his armchair and sipped his tea. When he returned his cup to the side table, I could see his eyes were moist with tears. "He's been beaten for years. A grown man."

He pulled out his handkerchief and blew his nose.

The guvnor watched his old friend, his eyes tender. He'd told me once that Lewis's old man, a goldsmith, would thrash him with a switch for every little thing he did wrong. Lewis was set to learn the family trade but was a boy born with no delicacy, and a little mistake in goldsmithing could be a costly one. Once, when Lewis ruined the brooch of a rich family, his father flew into a rage worse than usual. He thrashed Lewis on the arm with a poker, over and over, going on even as the skin came off and the bone shattered. Lewis was ten. His arm never healed: it took a few weeks before it went black. Then his father tied him down while the doctor sawed it off. It was only when Lewis was fifteen years old the thrashings stopped, and only because that was when his old man was found in his bed one morning with a jeweller's knife stuck right through his eye and into his brain.

We sat drinking our tea, watching the haze burn off the coals. Lewis wiped his eyes; he lit a pipe. When finally he spoke again, the emotion made his voice quiver.

"You must find who did this, William."

"He didn't tell you who it was?"

Lewis shook his head. "He wouldn't say. You must bring them to justice, promise me."

"We will," said the guvnor. "One way or another."

"I'll pay you," said Lewis. "As a case. Twenty shillings a day."

"You won't pay me. I want it as much as you."

Lewis looked at me.

"I'll pay you, Norman. Normal rates."

"I won't take it, Lewis."

He began to blink, then rose quickly and waddled to the window, where he stood with his back to us. His shoulders rose and fell, rose and fell.

"We must keep Willoughby until we know what to do with him," said the guvnor. "One of us shall remain here at all times. I doubt he'll try to escape: he's no money and I'm sure he'd get lost. But he has a singular attachment to that family and could do anything."

"We can't keep him here for ever," I said.

"There'll be time to think about the future later, Norman. Now I want you to go to Petleigh. Find out what news from the police surgeon."

It was raining again and the mud in the streets had turned to slop. Petleigh stepped out of the police station just as I arrived, gesturing me into his carriage.

"Did he tell Ettie about my wife?" he asked when we were out of the rain.

"She's been asleep."

He nodded. A steady procession of horses and wagons plodded past, one after the other.

"He misunderstands me, Norman. I am planning a divorce, have been for some time. I wanted to tell her myself."

"Perhaps you should have done it before you started courting her, Inspector."

He took a flask from his pocket, had a swallow, and passed it to me. Whiskey. Next out came his snuffbox. He had a toot and passed that to me too.

"I've been a bloody fool."

"What did the police surgeon say?" I asked, not wanting to talk about Ettie with him.

"She died of suffocation. Her windpipe was completely blocked. He found more pieces of those wooden flowers in it, and leaves and moss and so on, some in the lungs, the stomach. The fiend had stuffed her nose with mud as well. Held her down by the neck as he did it." He shut his eyes. "What a way to die. We've searched the campsite but found nothing to help us. Root and his man are enquiring about the neighbourhood in case anybody saw anything or knew of animosity, but unless something turns up it's going to be difficult to find the culprit."

"What's your theory, Inspector?"

"Well, we've ruled out a gypsy killing due to the location of the body. I think we can rule out the three women on the farm: they're all too small. Mrs. Gillie was about six foot; Rosanna's the tallest and she's only five two or so. It'd take a much bigger person to kill her the way they did, and it would have been a job moving the body up that hill. That leaves six in the frame. Godwin, Walter, Digger and Willoughby. I know it isn't you two, but Root and that blasted MP want you questioned. Sir Edward's not on your team, I hope you know that. There's evidence against you: you were the last to see her, you reported her missing, you had the tooth."

"But no motive."

"Nobody has a motive, that's the problem."

"We think the Ockwells didn't want us talking to her."

"But why?"

I told him about Willoughby, about how he and Digger lived, about the hideous scars all over his body. Just to describe it made me feel sick.

Petleigh took out his flask again and passed it to me.

"You think Mrs. Gillie knew?"

"Maybe. The lads used to visit her."

"Why didn't she tell you?"

"Reckon she didn't know if she could trust us."

He nodded. "What about those three dead children. Any idea what she meant?"

"Polly carries three dolls about with her which we think might be her dead infant and her sister's two children. Why Mrs. Gillie'd be telling us that we don't know."

"Well, I'll be over to interview Willoughby later. Maybe he can explain. Don't let him go anywhere."

"I doubt he'll tell you anything. He's pretty scared. Listen,

Inspector, don't tell anyone he's at Lewis's, eh? Let Mr. Arrowood try and get through to him. You know he's good at that."

"I wasn't going to. Sir Edward's directing Root, and Root won't hear anything against the Ockwells. I've no doubt he'll have Willoughby removed if he hears where he is."

We shook hands and I stepped down to the muddy street. The carriage moved away in the lashing rain.

The guvnor was in a fury when I reached the house. He strode up and down before the fire, puffing furiously on a cigar, his face pinched. An almost empty bottle of Mariani wine stood by his chair; a letter from Sherlock Holmes was on the side table.

"Read it yourself!" he cried when I asked what it said.

I sat on the couch and straightened out the mashed-up paper.

221B Baker Street, London
17 January

Dear Mr. Arrowood,

I am afraid I can neither confirm nor deny the newspaper reports to which you refer. I believe I have heard mention of your name, but have no knowledge of your involvement in the case in point, although I did, as they report, track down the stolen weapons and retrieve them with the help of Inspector Petleigh. I am afraid I do not know your other cases, and cannot, therefore, provide you a letter of recommendation.

I wish you luck in your future endeavours,

Yours truly,
S. Holmes

The guvnor tore the note from my hand and hurled it into the fire. He turned back to me. His head seemed to be throbbing. The blacks of his eyes were small as pinpricks, the whites tangled with pink threads. His lips were chewed to shreds.

"A letter of recommendation!" he cried. "I didn't ask for a blooming letter of recommendation, the arrogant swine!"

He glared at me, the poison in his look enough to finish off a regiment of the Black Watch. I turned to the window; it was as much as I could do not to break out laughing.

"I'll throttle Petleigh when I see him!" he went on. "He didn't even mention our names to Holmes. And we worked that case for weeks! The worthless hound! Probably took all the credit himself. I don't believe for a minute that charlatan knows nothing of our work. And why do the newspapers never report our damn cases? Is there only room for one detective in their imaginations?"

As he spoke, he kicked out wildly at the pile of psychology books as stood by his chair, sending them flying in the air. The sharp corner of a William James volume hit the back of my knee.

I spun round in a fury, taking his chin in my hand and hoiking it upwards. He stumbled back, falling onto the couch, me on top of him.

"Stop!" he cried as he landed.

"How many times must I tell you?" I said, my blood near boiling over. "I won't be treated like that by nobody, least of all you. When you pay a man you must respect him!"

My hand was over his mouth, squeezing his cheeks together as hard as I could. I wanted so bad to throttle him.

"I'm sorry, Norman," he mumbled, his eyes bulging, his lips squeezed into the ugliest kiss I'd ever seen. "Let me up."

I got to my knees, pushing my rage back inside, shutting

it down. I knew we both had work to do. Much as I wanted to smash him in the face with my fist, I wanted more to find who it was who'd tormented Willoughby for so many years.

The guvnor sat up, brushing off his britches. "It was stupid of me," he said. "I'm so sorry."

"You're acting like half an idiot. It's that bloody tonic."

"I know. This case is turning me wild." He shook his head. "We must see it through, my friend. For Willoughby. For Birdie. For Mrs. Gillie. We need to find some justice in all this evil."

I looked in his eye and saw inside him what was inside me. We were both close to breaking now. But we had to work.

It was evening. Lisa, Godwin's lover, lived in a room on the top floor of a house in Doggett Road, just four down from where Ettie was lodging. I waited at the door until the guvnor, wheezing and bent double, climbed the stairs. There was singing from inside: a hymn. Adults' and children's voices.

The singing stopped when I knocked; a man answered the door. He was old, his beard grey, his eyes yellow. He held a clay pipe in his hand.

"Evening," he croaked.

"Is Lisa there?" asked the guvnor.

Inside the gloomy attic room stood a couple of about middle age, a baby in the woman's arms. A smell of chamberpots and stew filled my snitch. Two children sat upon the bed, and there, stirring a pot over a small cooker at the back of the room, was Lisa.

She looked pale, her face drawn, her hair tied up in a scarf. Her dress and jacket were of coarse, brown shoddy. She looked little like the woman we'd met in the pub before.

"You remember us, Lisa?" asked the guvnor. "Mr. Arro-wood. This is Mr. Barnett."

"I thought you said you was off the case."

"And so we are. But you've heard they found a body up on the farm, I suppose. We're just trying to help. To make amends for the problems we caused."

"Here," said the other woman. "You gents have a sit. Children, off that bed."

She went to the stove to tend the pot while the children brought over their only two chairs for us. The old man and the husband took the family bed. Lisa pulled up a stool. The floor was brown linoleum, old and cracked, and standing against the wall were three straw mattresses.

"Now, Lisa," said the guvnor. "D'you know anything about Mrs. Gillie's murder? Anything you've heard? Anyone who might have fallen out with her?"

"It was Digger," she said straight off. She nodded, her hands clasped in her lap. "And Willoughby. That's why he ran off."

"Are you sure?"

"It's got to be them. That Digger never talks, just looks at you with those eyes like he wants to kill you."

"But why would they murder her?"

"From the asylum, ain't they?"

"What about Walter? Could it have been him?"

She laughed.

"He's a lamb, that one. He'd never hurt an old woman."

"But he's been in prison for violence," said the guvnor. "A man lost his eye."

"That wasn't his fault," she said with a shake of her head. "His pa packed him off to market to sell pigs. He shouldn't never have sent him on his own. Walter was always a bit slow, see. Told him not to come home least he got a certain price.

Well, Walter did get the price but he stopped for a few drinks after. A friend of mine was in the pub, she saw it all. These fellows in there were ribbing him, saying he was bird-witted, about the pigs having quicker minds than him. Bullies, they were. After Walter'd had a few drinks he must have forgot he'd left the money in the wagon. He thought he'd been robbed and as they'd been ribbing him all night he thought it must be them. He was only fighting them to get his pa's money back."

"But they didn't have it."

"I know. But that's the only reason he fought them. He's no more violent than a stuffed bear."

"Are you sure?"

"I swear it, sir. I've known him from way back."

"Tell me, Lisa, did you ever meet Tracey?"

"He worked up there on the farm a few year, but I never spoke to him, no."

"Why are there so many from the asylum?"

"That's Mr. Tasker who sorts it out. He's something to do with the asylum. They treat them somehow, and when they're better they find them places to work."

"And the two wives?"

She sighed, looking down at her hands.

"Don't ask," she said. "I don't approve of that. But what's this got to do with the murder?"

"You said it was Digger and Willoughby. I'm just trying to understand how they all came to be there."

"Farm has debts, has done for a few year. It's the imports, see? Couldn't afford house girls or dairymaids so they got those girls. Thought they could work them proper hard, sir. Harder than you'd work a normal wife. They're easier to control too, don't talk back. And I think the family get a few bob a month for their upkeep."

"Who decided to get the wives from the asylum?"

"Maybe old Mrs. Ockwell. They all look up to her. Or Rosanna. I don't think it's right, though. Godwin never wanted it. He wishes he hadn't agreed to it now."

"Did you ever meet his parents?"

She sighed and shook her head. "That's another story, that is. Godwin's pa never let up on him. On at him for every little thing he done wrong. Every little mistake he made. They gave up on Walter, didn't expect nothing from him, but Godwin was supposed to be the clever one. He was to take over the farm, but nothing was good enough for old Mr. Ockwell. Wounded poor Godwin to this day, it has, all that riding he took. Reckon that's what done him for the apoplexy."

"His mother?"

"She'd just sit there and watch with that face of hers. It didn't help that the grain prices fell the way they did just as Godwin took it over. His pa seemed to believe it was all his fault when it wasn't."

"Were you courting him before he married Polly?"

She sighed again. Nodded.

"I been waiting a long time for that man."

"He treats Lisa bad," the mother piped up. "It ain't right how he treats her."

"Has Godwin ever struck you, Lisa?" asked the guvnor.

She blinked like she was surprised to hear his question.

"He loves me," she said.

"Tell him, Lisa," said the old fellow.

She turned to him, a look on her face like he'd betrayed her.

"Tell him else I will," said the old man.

"He loves me, and that's all," she said, crossing her arms.

"Broke her arm last year," said the old fellow. "Couldn't work for three month on account of that."

"You shut your head," she said, scowling at him. "That weren't his fault."

"He does treat you bad, Lisa, dear," said the woman.

"You don't understand him. He aims to divorce her, or she'll die she's that ill all the time. Then we'll be together. He'd be a rich man if he hadn't been tricked with that engine and then Polly wouldn't even be in the picture. He'd have been happier marrying me. Made for each other we were."

"Would you be happy being their housemaid?" I asked.

"Least she wasn't with child when they wed," said Lisa, ignoring my question. "Least he had the sense not to do that. That's what I can't understand about that family. Choosing a wife from the asylum's bad enough, but one who's with child's just foolishness. There must be a thousand poor girls who'd be happy to marry a farmer."

The guvnor looked at me in silence, his brow creased in confusion.

"With child?" he asked. "But who?"

"Birdie," said Lisa. "Birdie was with child when she got wed."

Chapter Thirty-Six

We were at the Barclays' house at eight the next morning. "I hope you've recovered from your dysentery, Mr. Barclay," said the guvnor the minute we were sat in the parlour. The one eye he could use in that swelled and battered face was cold; he hadn't washed in a week and it was apparent. He could hardly sit still.

"It wasn't dysentery, sir," replied Mr. Barclay, his elbow upon the mantel. He looked sheepish. "It was just a—"

"Birdie was with child when she married," interrupted the guvnor. "It was stillborn."

Mrs. Barclay went to stand behind her husband. He blinked, his cheek twitching. He ran his hand over his bald head.

"Ah," he said at last. "So you know that."

"You've deceived us from the start," said the guvnor. "When we take a case we go on a journey into people's souls, and that, Mr. Barclay, is often a dangerous and cruel journey. More so than you can imagine from the comfort of your little house here. We freeze, we miss our sleep, we anger people. Mr. Barnett was clubbed on the floor of a pub for your sake. I was assaulted about the face with fists. Look at this eye!" He pointed to his face, pausing for a moment.

"Mr. Arro—"

"We abuse and betray ourselves, we wear ourselves to the bone on your account, and we expect your honesty and integrity in return. Well, it seems you're not that sort of people."

"Mr. Arro—"

"Birdie has no desire to return to you," said the guvnor, holding his hand up to stop him from speaking. "Our agent spoke to her at length, on her own, with no duress. I'm satisfied with the outcome. It's exactly what you deserve."

"No, sir!" cried Mr. Barclay. "You cannot give up!"

"Give up? Why, the case is concluded, sir. She doesn't wish to return to you. That's it."

"But her mind's weak, damn it! She doesn't know what's best for her."

"She knows what she wants. And she doesn't want you two. I cannot blame her."

"Wait, Mr. Arrowood," said Mrs. Barclay. She left her husband's side, sitting down on the piano stool, close to the guvnor. She was calm, her long Spanish face as sombre as the black dress she wore. "We've played you false, I admit it. We felt we had to do it to convince you to help. Everyone else we went to refused to take the case. They said it was just a family dispute. We were desperate."

"You approached other agents before us?"

"Yes," she said.

He didn't speak, and I knew he was trying to decide whether to ask who they'd gone to.

"Please don't abandon us," she said. "We beg you, please help us. Help us and we'll reward you handsomely."

The guvnor's eyes fell on the space behind her where the pianoforte used to be. He thought on.

"Have you pawned it?" he asked at last.

"We've no money," said Dunbar Barclay. He seemed bigger stood there above us, as if his shame had grown him. "Nothing."

The guvnor nodded, his face sad. The bite in his voice was gone: it was gentle now.

"I knew it. It's hard on a family when a man loses his position, and after so many years of loyal service. I see it too often."

"Twenty-two years with never a complaint against him," said Mrs. Barclay. "He made some errors in the accounts, we admit it, but he didn't deserve to be thrown onto the streets without even a letter of recommendation."

"Men like Mr. Tasker tolerate nothing but their own weaknesses," said the guvnor.

"Thank you, sir," said Mr. Barclay. "Thank you for saying it. I don't like to speak against my betters, but I do feel let down. It's proving hard to find a similar position. They all want a younger chap."

"I can see how difficult your situation's become, sir, and I hate to see it. May I ask something delicate?"

Mr. Barclay nodded.

"Is your house at risk?"

"It is."

"I thought so. Mortgage or renting?"

"Mortgage." His pink face fell in a weak frown. His wretched nose twitched. "We cannot make the payments."

"Oh, no, no. My dear fellow, I'm so sorry. I recently lost my own rooms through fire. It's quite terrible to lose one's home." The guvnor stood and stepped over to Mr. Barclay, laying his hand on his shoulder in comfort. Mr. Barclay flinched: he was not a man easy with being touched. "It must be a great worry."

"Yes, sir, it is," replied Mr. Barclay, stepping away from the guvnor's reckless sympathy.

"You offered Miss Ockwell thirty pounds for Birdie," said Arrowood, turning to Mrs. Barclay now. "We've seen the note. I must assume that means it'll help your situation to have her back somehow." He sat down next to her and looked her kindly in the eye. He was doing what he does best, playing with them, and I was enjoying the watch. "We can help you, but only if you tell us the whole story. We're good at what we do: look at what we've discovered about you and Birdie and that farm. I tell you we can help you, but we must know everything, good and bad. I don't expect the truth to be entirely wholesome, but which of us can claim to be pure? Life in this city is hard. One stroke of bad luck can send a hard-working person into the workhouse. We do what we can to survive, and the Lord strike me down if that's not the truth. I'm saying we can help you. We *want* to help you. So tell me, Mrs. Barclay, the truth now. Why d'you need her back?"

She looked at her husband, her hands gripping each other tight upon her lap. Mr. Barclay frowned, his leg jiggling. He nodded.

"I had one brother," she said, her voice at first very low and quiet. She stroked the ends of the long black hair as fell on her shoulder. "Gaspar. A year ago he became ill with cancer. He declined rapidly; it was quite awful to watch. The doctor said he wouldn't survive, so we prepared ourself for his passing. Since he had no family of his own we thought I'd be the beneficiary in his will. He'd become quite successful dealing in tea. He was comfortably off."

"I see," purred the guvnor. "Yes, of course. That's why you bought this house. All the new furniture."

"We must seem selfish," she murmured, her eyes cast down.

"Martha always wanted her own house," said Mr. Barclay. "A place to develop her talents. She couldn't practise her singing in Elden Road. The woman below was forever telling her to be quiet, pretending it disturbed the other tenants. Poppycock! I know for certain the people upstairs delighted in her singing. Yes, they did. But it made it difficult for Martha to practise. She's a God-given talent, sir, and will be famous one day, there's no doubt about it. Lord Ulverstone said she had the voice of a siren. But it's a competitive business. To go to the next level requires dedication and, I'm afraid, a little selfishness. She could never do it in rented rooms where every little noise is listened to. Mr. Arrowood, we were quite desperate."

I watched Mrs. Barclay as he spoke. Her face was troubled, as if it was only hearing it described that made her realize what kind of people they were. Mr. Barclay continued.

"We hoped something good would come from the tragedy of Gaspar's cancer."

"My brother died two months ago," said Mrs. Barclay.

"And left his whole estate to Birdie," added Mr. Barclay, his pitch rising in excitement. "Mrs. Barclay was heartbroken. She loved her brother so. She doted on him. He came for Christmas every year. Every year!" he cried in a sudden sharp squawk. "She thought he loved her as deep as she loved him. But he was nothing but a selfish man in the end."

"Please, Dunbar. Don't say that."

"It's the truth." He slapped his hand down onto the mantel. "Selfish, damned hound!"

"I'm so sorry," whispered the guvnor. He removed his handkerchief from his pocket and dabbed at his eye as if he was crying. He sniffed and gasped. His voice trembled. "How cruel."

"Are you all right, Mr. Arrowood?" asked Mrs. Barclay. "Can I get you a cup of tea?"

"I'll be fine," he replied, wiping his eye again. "Just give me a moment."

We sat listening to the great clock of Neptune. Mr. Barclay shifted on his feet again and again. He went to the window and peered out, then returned immediately to the mantel. He collected the newspaper from the table then put it down again.

"I'm sorry," said the guvnor when he'd recovered from his attack of the sorrows. "My heart breaks for you, madam. It truly does. That your own brother could do that to you."

"It was a mortal shock, I admit it," she said.

"Unless we get Birdie back, the Ockwells will persuade her to invest the money in the farm," said Mr. Barclay. "We'll lose the house; we'll get nothing. This is why we need the marriage annulled."

"Call us selfish, but we believe it our right."

"Of course you do," said the guvnor. "Of course you do. Now tell me, may I ask you something? Just one last thing?"

"Anything," declared Mr. Barclay.

"Why did you send Birdie to the asylum?"

"She was becoming impossible," he answered. "Demanding to go on outings as if we had all the money in the world. Saying she wanted to live with her cousin. Wanted to get married. She was unhappy with her life. They often are, you know, on account of being born without the full set of faculties. They want to be like us, you see. Our doctor suggested a short period of treatment by an alienist would help. A year or two at most. As you said yourself, Mr. Arrowood, expert care can improve mental disorders."

"We always said she should return," added Mrs. Barclay. "You must believe us on that."

The guvnor nodded. He turned to Mr. Barclay.

"Who fathered her child?"

"There was a baker she was fond of. She used to do the shopping when Martha was unwell. It happened in the back room of the shop. My wife found the evidence on her bloomers and she confessed. He denied it; his parents were behind him."

"He violated her?"

"She was keen on him. She thought it meant they'd be married. But we didn't know she was with child when she entered Caterham. It was only later she showed. That's when Dr. Crenshaw came to see us with Henry Tasker, Mr. Tasker's brother."

"He's the one helped us get Birdie into the asylum in the first place," added Mrs. Barclay. "He's Chair of the Committee of Visitors there."

"They said marriage to Walter was the best solution for the child," continued Mr. Barclay. "A stable family, away from prying eyes. Away from the real father."

"And you agreed?"

"She always wanted to be wed. It seemed perfect."

The guvnor thought about this for some time. The Barclays watched him.

"One last thing," he said finally. "She's on the asylum records as a pauper lunatic. But you weren't paupers; you were still in employment, sir. How did that arise?"

"Henry Tasker made us an appointment with Mr. Waller Proctor, the Relieving Officer at the Poor Law Union," said Mr. Barclay. "He's very friendly with Dr. Crenshaw and Mr.

Tasker's brother. The three of them sang with the Streatham Choral Society. Martha was with them briefly. It was Mr. Proctor suggested it. He said if she was down as a pauper she'd get in quicker and we'd not have to pay for her as a private patient."

"Then who pays for pauper lunatics?" I asked.

"The Poor Law Union do."

"And Proctor offered to do this?" asked the guvnor.

"For twenty pounds," said Mr. Barclay. "It's him that signs the form."

"You mean he asked for a bribe?" I asked.

"He made it sound quite regular; he said many families do it."

"But you know paupers aren't treated as well as private patients?" said the guvnor, his face darkening. "Their food's poor. Their clothes are shared. They sleep in large dormitories and it's not properly heated. Private patients have their own parlour, with a fire. Thick mattresses. Amusement."

"Mr. Waller Proctor said she'd be treated just as well," Mr. Barclay insisted. "We only did what he suggested."

The guvnor stood. "Thank you," he said. "You've both been very honest."

"No, thank you, sir, for being so understanding," said Mr. Barclay. "So how are you going to bring her back?"

"I'm not going to bring her back," said the guvnor, buttoning his coat.

"But you just said you'd help us," said Mr. Barclay.

"I am helping you. Helping you be better parents."

The guvnor popped his hat on his head and strode out the parlour.

"Come, Barnett. We've work to do."

Mr. Barclay followed behind to the front door.

"Mr. Arrowood!" he pleaded. "We'll give you a share of the estate!"

We gained the street and began to walk back towards Waterloo.

"Fifty pounds!" he called after us. "How's that? Fifty pounds? Or sixty!"

After twenty yards, the guvnor turned to Mr. Barclay, who still stood in the doorway, his face wild.

"I forgot to tell you," he said. "There's been a murder at the farm."

And with that, we walked away.

Chapter Thirty-Seven

We went to Willows' for coffee and beef sandwiches. There were no other punters in there so the guvnor did his usual, collecting the newspapers and stuffing them under his thighs least anyone else should want one. He scanned *The Star* as he ate, looking for news of the murder. It was on page four, a small article, saying only that the body of a woman was found buried on a farm in Catford. Foul play was suspected. Root and Petleigh were in there, but not us.

He shook his heavy head, then picked up *The Times*, adjusting his spectacles and bringing the paper up close to his face. He turned the pages.

"Oh, dear," he said after a few moments.

He threw the paper onto the table.

"Read it."

Lord Hahn, the bloke who wrote the Beagley explorer stories, had made a speech in the House of Lords the day before demanding an investigation into the activities of private enquiry agents. The guvnor's name was in that one, all right. They'd started up a petition to have us stopped, and a few toffs had already signed it: Mary Martha Wood, the founder of the Ladies Kennel Club; the fourth Earl of Pevensey; Langford Pike, the society gossip; Thomas Orme Smith, the slum landlord who owned Cutlers Court; his business partner Samuel Chance.

The guvnor had moved on to *The Daily News*. "Chief suspect Willoughby Krott in this one," he said. "Ex-asylum inmate, disappeared at the same time. They've got a witness, saw a crippled man walking through fields towards Lewisham the day before the body was found. Looking around as if he was being followed."

He drained his coffee, gathered up the crumbs on the table and put them in his mouth. He stood.

"I cannot bear any more of this, Barnett," he said.

Back at Lewis's, Ettie told us that Petleigh'd already been to interview Willoughby.

"He wouldn't say who's been hurting him," she said. "And Isaiah got nothing out of him about Mrs. Gillie either."

The guvnor nodded. We were in the parlour, the fire not yet lit. Lewis was in his chair; Willoughby was back in bed.

"I'm afraid he said he wanted to return to the farm," she added.

"I feel like shaking him," said Lewis. "He just can't seem to admit he's been mistreated."

"He's not being stubborn, my friend," said the guvnor, lowering himself into his seat with a grunt. "Willoughby's been hurt by someone again and again over the last few years. He cannot fight back, so the only power he has is to try to avoid the next attack that might come. But that means his mind's focused only on the next assault, the one that might come today or tomorrow. He doesn't know if we can really protect him, but he does know one thing: if he gives us the name and is taken back, he'll be beaten for sure. That's why he won't say. He can't see further than that."

Ettie bit her lip. Her eyes were troubled, and I could see that what her brother said meant something more personal to her.

"But there's more," he went on. "In a situation like he's been forced to endure, the mind starts to find reasons for not escaping. That's why an effective captor will tell you he loves you, he values you, he depends on you. He plays on your need for respect and affection, and the more you're brutalized, the more you crave those things. Love from a bully can be more intoxicating than love from a kind heart."

He looked at his sister, who picked at a loose thread on the couch.

"Isaiah told him he must stay here," she said.

"Well, that's something, I suppose."

"He told me about his wife, William."

"Ah," said the guvnor. He pushed himself to his feet, went to the couch, and touched her hair, a little sadness in his eyes. He took her hand. "He didn't deserve you, Sister. Are you disappointed?"

Ettie shrugged and patted his hand.

"Thank you, William."

They looked at each other for some time, Lewis and I watching them. We knew how the one loved the other, of course, but it seemed they often forgot it themselves.

Finally, she stood. "Let's have some tea."

I rose to help her in the kitchen.

"Are you going to lodge with Lewis?" she asked as I looked out the wafers.

"I'm thinking about it."

"You should, Norman. I don't think being alone's so good for you. And Lewis needs the company."

I turned to watch her filling the teapot. Her brown hair was tied up on her head, a few strands falling onto her strong, white neck. Her unbound fist rested on the dresser. Without thinking, I put my hand on top of it. Her fingers twitched, but she didn't turn to me, nor make any sign that she'd noticed, and I kept it there as she poured the rest of the hot water. When she was finished, she put the kettle down and looked at me, her stone-grey eyes calm but for the smallest glisten. Then, without a word, she pulled her hand away, put the kettle on the tray, and left me in the kitchen.

For a moment there was no sound in the world. Then I was crushed with shame. What was I thinking? In that one movement I'd destroyed the slow and cautious understanding we'd spent so long building. I stood there, staring into the black night outside the kitchen window, certain now I was right about Ettie. I'd been a fool. And with the shame came Mrs. B, heavy in my heart. I'd let her down already.

I went outside into the little courtyard, clenching and unclenching my idiot fists, breathing the night air long and slow and looking through the darkness at the hazy row of houses behind. When I'd gotten hold of myself, I took a sad piss in the outhouse, then carried the tea tray through to the parlour. Ettie was staring into the coal fire, listening to the guvnor telling them about our visit to the Barclays.

"They had her committed as a Poor Law patient when they could easily have afforded to pay private patient fees," he said in disgust. "Barclay was still working at the time."

"They don't care about her at all," said Ettie.

"Do private patients really get treated so much better?" I asked, trying to find my voice again.

"They do," he said. "Private rooms, better food, more activities, more visitors. It's nothing like the general wards, but also the strangest thing to see. A parlour that wouldn't look out of place in a gentlemen's club, with books upon the shelves, a rug, a blazing fire. And then you notice a few of the gentlemen are chained to their chairs."

His voice was weary, his fingers fiddling the cat. His good eye was fixed on the pile of psychology books on the floor.

"Our father was in an asylum for several years, Norman," said Ettie at last. "Emotional monomania."

I shook my head.

"They call it moral insanity now," murmured the guvnor, pulling out his pipe and starting to pack it.

"He had his reason, but little control of his feelings," Ettie went on. "Pride and envy, they were his demons. Eventually he lost control to them. They made him wild. He did things he shouldn't have done."

She sipped her tea and glanced at the guvnor. A gust blew on the street, rattling the windows. Lewis hauled himself to his feet and made to light the fire.

"That's where he died, Norman," said the guvnor. "I was seventeen. Ettie fifteen. We know a little about it, you see. You're marked when someone in your family was in an asylum. That's what I don't understand about Walter marrying Birdie. There must be thousands of poor women in London looking for a secure husband with a home. Why choose to marry an asylum inmate carrying another man's child?"

"Perhaps he fell in love with her," said Ettie.

She held my eye for a moment, the faint smile on her lips

seeming to mock me. I looked down, feeling the colour rise to my cheeks. Then my shame gave way to a bitter anger: it seemed it was all right for Ettie to touch me, but not for me to touch her. I'd been right all along: it was a bit of comfort she wanted that night in the carriage, that was all. I was too low-born for a woman like her and I should have remembered it. With Mrs. B gone, I was becoming something like a fool.

We sat in silence for some minutes. I watched Ettie as she turned her eyes back to the fire, her brow knitted in thought. Then I noticed something uncertain in her face, and I wondered.

Chapter Thirty-Eight

There was nothing more to do until the police investigation was over, and so we waited. Each day the voices against us in the papers grew louder. More signed Lord Hahn's petition against private enquiry agents: Reverend Hudson Harris, the writer-parson who signed every petition there was; Baron FitzHugh; seven members of the Wandering Minstrels; Mrs. Dorothy de Clifford, the anti-slavery campaigner; a handful of pig farmers.

The guvnor complained of bad sleep and drank jugs of ale for breakfast. His temper grew more foul. He hired a bloke with a wagon to move their possessions back to his rooms behind the pudding shop on Coin Street. Ettie bought a rug and two beds and had them delivered. She was out of the house every day working for her mission in one of the Shoreditch slums, giving out castor oil and carbolic soap, leaving early and returning late. She was vexed with her brother; she was distant with me. We kept a vigil over Willoughby. He slept long and deep, often crying out in words we couldn't understand. I stayed over in the parlour in case he should try to leave in the night, though he never did. He was always hungry, but would vomit when he had a bit of meat or cheese. He managed soup and porridge better, and he guzzled down tea like a builder. His wind was constant and violent. But though he was weak and frail, he was quick to smile at the slightest kindness, his laugh sometimes bubbling from his chest like he had no problems in his life. Every day he asked to go back to the farm.

The guvnor had a doctor in, who guessed at some of the marks on Willoughby's body. The burns were from hot irons and cigars; the bruises from a shovel or a chain; the incisions from a whip. The bite marks on his arms and legs were probably from the dogs. We rubbed him with Whelpton's and dosed him with Pepper's Tonic. We asked him again and again about his injuries, but each time his lips closed and he looked away, falling deep into himself as he so often did over those days we waited for news of the police investigation.

"When you get a horse, Lewis?" Willoughby asked as we took a walk one day.

"I can't afford a horse, my friend."

"Can't afford it?" repeated Willoughby, his hands in his pockets as he limped down the street on his chilblained feet. "I got Count Lavender. He's my friend. And Tilly. You know where she is?"

"She's on a farm," I told him. "She's being looked after."

"John wants me back, Norman. My brother. You know him? Get his house ready first. Dad get me back at John's. He do it. Got to finish my work first."

"But you're happy to stay with me for a while, Willoughby, aren't you?" asked Lewis. "Like Inspector Petleigh said."

"Happy," said Willoughby.

We walked up Walworth Road, where we saw a newspaper seller outside Elephant and Castle station. The guvnor opened his purse, winced, then put it away again. He patted his pockets.

"Lewis," he said. "You couldn't lend me something for a few days, could you? Just until the case is over? Perhaps only twenty shillings?"

Lewis got out his purse and handed over the money in silence.

The guvnor bought a paper and we turned down Newington Butts to head back to the house, walking along past the Tabernacle and the graveyard of St. Gabriel's. As we turned into Steedman Street, a little mongrel dog came bolting around the corner, almost colliding with Willoughby's legs.

Willoughby screamed, seizing Lewis's arms and jumping behind him.

"No!" he cried, stumbling into the path of a carriage and causing the horse to rear up. "Get away! Lewis! Get away!"

The coachman cursed, pulling hard on the reins to bring the horse down, while Willoughby kept dragging Lewis across to the other side of the road. His eyes were fixed on the dog, not even seeing the wild horse and the angry coachman.

The mongrel turned and trotted away. Willoughby watched it until it was gone, his hands gripping Lewis tight.

"There, there, my dear," said the guvnor. "The dog's gone. You're safe."

"Safe," whispered Willoughby. His freckled face was quite white. He wouldn't let go of Lewis's arm until we were inside the house and the door bolted.

★ ★ ★

Later that day, Petleigh called.

"We've nothing to go on," he said, standing on the front step. "We've scoured the area, but there are no witnesses, no clues. The chair of the magistrates has ordered an inquiry to see if there's enough evidence to bring charges against anyone. I've already told him there isn't, but what would a detective inspector know, eh? These blasted inquiries never come to anything: it'll just be the magistrates asking the same questions we've already asked. Anyway, they want to see you and Willoughby there. Eleven o'clock Monday at the Mission Hall in Catford." Petleigh clapped his hands together and shifted from foot to foot. "Let me in, William, before I get a chill."

"Willoughby's not really a suspect, is he?" asked the guvnor, not moving from the doorway. "They know we kidnapped him."

"At the moment everybody's a suspect. Even you."

"Will the inquiry look into his mistreatment? The person who did that to him's likely the same as killed Mrs. Gillie."

"We can't be sure of that," said Petleigh. "There are six people on that farm and others Willoughby had contact with over the years. The builders and Mrs. Gillie for three. Unless he tells us who it was there's nothing we can do. But it's not up to me. It's up to the chair, Reverend Sprice-Hogg."

"Sprice-Hogg, eh?" The guvnor chewed his lip. "Well, well, I hope he can remain sober. I assume you questioned the Ockwells about Willoughby's scars?"

"I was only instructed to investigate the murder. I'll be handing it all over to Root after the inquiry."

"But you know Root won't do it!"

"Willoughby's safe now, William. Look at it that way."

He glanced past us into the house.

"How's Ettie?" he asked.

The guvnor closed the door in his face, then turned back to me.

"They'll never solve this by themselves, Norman," he said with a snort. "Everybody's lips are shut tight. We must make something happen at that inquiry. We must find a way of opening them."

I nodded.

"We mustn't fail." He scratched at his whiskers and looked towards the stairs, where Willoughby slept above us. "Because sure as anything he's going to tell them he wants to go back."

Chapter Thirty-Nine

Mission Hall was already full when we arrived on Monday morning. The first row of pews were for the witnesses and there we took our places aside Petleigh and Root, Willoughby sitting between me and the guvnor. We wore our Sunday best and the guvnor'd put something in his patchy hair as turned it a deep, oily black. He'd read somewhere that an idiot will think better if you warm his brain, and so he'd wrapped Willoughby's head in hot towels over breakfast and bound his skull for the journey with scarves tied under the hat Lewis found for him. We could only hope that once Willoughby saw how serious it all was he'd see sense and say who'd hurt him so.

Every seat in the hall besides those at the front was taken. The second row was filled with newspapermen. Behind that the pews held spectators, with more in the balcony. A crowd stood at the back and along the walls and more filled the aisles. With a payment here and there, the poorer folk in the seats near the front gave way to the young ladies in satin bonnets, the concerned local dignitaries, the excited bachelors in tight, grey suits and colourful waistcoats. Coachmen and servants brought in blankets, arranging them around their masters and mistresses. The three old blokes from the pub were sat in the balcony; the Winter brothers stood against the wall. We'd sent a wire to Mrs. Gillie's granddaughter, Ida, but she was nowhere to be seen.

Godwin and Rosanna appeared just before the magistrates. As soon as they spied Willoughby, they made to come over. Our friend saw them and stood, his hands raised in the air: "Dad!" he called. "Miss Rosanna!"

The Ockwells waved back, moving through the press of people in the aisle, heading towards us. They were dressed smart, both in thick overcoats, the one tall and lean, the other small and fierce.

"Got to drain lower field, Dad!" Willoughby called out, his face flushed. He didn't notice that all around us were watching him. "Get back to work now. You come get me?"

I rose and pushed through the people towards the Ockwells.

"We've missed you, Willoughby, lad," said Godwin over the heads of the crowd. "Come sit with us. Over there at the front."

"How's Count Lavender getting on? He miss me too?"

I stopped in front of Godwin, took him tight by the arms, and pushed him backward down the aisle.

"Take your hands off me," he hissed. Rosanna was behind him. With nowhere else to go in the jam of people, she was forced back too, the both of them stumbling and tripping as I kept pushing and walking. Godwin struggled and cursed, but couldn't find a strong foothold to stop me; the crowd was so tight nobody could really see what was going on.

I brought my lips up close to his ear and whispered: "He's never going back with you lot. Come near him again and I'll set a demon on you."

I gave him my knee in his bollocks. He groaned, his legs buckling; I hoiked him up quick and shoved him away. Rosanna caught his arm and pulled him towards the other side of the hall, her eyes hard on me all the way.

As I sat, Sprice-Hogg came through a side door with two other men and they took their places at the table. I recognized one of them straight away from the green suit he wore, the same green suit he wore the day we met him at Ludgate Circus. It was Henry Tasker, the brother of Mr. Barclay's ex-employer. The man who'd introduced Birdie to Walter Ockwell.

The guvnor glanced at me and shook his head. I don't know why I was surprised, really. They were all linked together, everyone we came across in this bloody case. But I knew it couldn't be good for us. Tasker must have heard of our breaking into Caterham from Crenshaw: he was the first person the medical superintendent visited after we'd been captured. Likely the Ockwells had done a bit of complaining to him as well. Tasker'd be against us, there was no doubt of that.

The doors were closed and the parson whacked a mallet upon the table. He cleared his throat.

"Ladies and gentlemen. This inquiry is to establish whether there's enough evidence to bring charges in respect to the murder of the gypsy, Mrs. Edna Gillie. I'm Reverend Sprice-Hogg of St. Laurence's, chair of the magistrates and governor of St. Dunstan's."

Sprice-Hogg looked the same country parson as always with his red face and thick, white curls, his white moustache and little round eyeglasses, but gone was his desperation, his clinging need, his sozzled chortle. Instead his voice boomed and his red hand gripped the mallet. He was master of this crowd. He turned to the man next to him.

"This is Mr. Rhodes, Justice of the Peace, master butcher and owner of Rhodes and Sons of Lewisham."

"And Forest Hill," said Rhodes, his voice like gravel. He was a man of too much cheek and too little lip, his mutton-chops sparse and thin, one eye small and the other big. "Soon to be another in Brockley. Best meat in the region. Prices most reasonable."

Sprice-Hogg nodded. "And the third member of our panel is Lieutenant Colonel Tasker, Justice of the Peace, owner of Doggett's farm, also Chair of the Committee of Visitors at Caterham Asylum."

Tasker was the most finely dressed among them: a red waist-coat sprayed with pictures of the hunt beneath his suit, a crisp white shirt. His sharp eyes swept over the crowd. When they fell on the guvnor they halted for a moment, a quick blaze coming to them. He took out a notebook and wrote something in it. In reply, the guvnor took out his own notebook and did the same.

Sprice-Hogg called the coroner first, who said that Mrs. Gillie died of suffocation caused by the wooden flowers, twigs, leaves, and mud that were stuffed down her throat and shoved up her nose while she was still alive. The bruising around her mouth and neck indicated they kept forcing it down until her windpipe was blocked: a good amount of the material was in her stomach. She'd been hit once in the face with a club of some kind. There was no evidence she'd been tied.

"She fought," he said. "Her nails were broken. There were bruises on her forearms."

"Any idea where she was killed?" asked Sprice-Hogg.

"Impossible to say. The body was very filthy with pig manure."

Magistrates Tasker and Rhodes had no questions, so Petleigh took the chair. He looked every inch the detective from London, his creases sharp, his collars and cuffs free of grime. He addressed the hall rather than the magistrates as he explained that they'd questioned everyone around the farm, made enquiries in Catford and searched the fields, but had found no clues, nor any obvious motive.

"I assume the body was hid in the dung pit inside the barn because the ground's frozen and difficult to dig," said Petleigh. "The murderer might have been meaning to move it once the thaw came. We believe she was killed around the caravan. Her coat and boots were still there and a box of wooden flowers was discovered upturned with several of the flowers broken and trampled into the ground. This was later tidied away by persons unknown. No traces of blood, however."

"Bootprints?" asked Sprice-Hogg.

"The ground's been frozen for weeks. It's only recently thawed."

"Anything else? Buttons? Torn cloth? Letters?"

"Her cat's head had been beaten to pulp," said Petleigh. "No animal could have done it. The crows had been at it so there wasn't much left by the time we arrived. No other clues. We searched all around, the barn as well. We dug the dung pit right to the bottom."

"This sounds like a case for Sherlock Holmes," said Rhodes.

I felt the guvnor's great mound of flesh stiffen beside me. "An old gypsy?" he muttered, just loud enough for those around us to hear. He turned to me. "He'd never be interested."

"Tell us how the body was discovered, Inspector," asked Sprice-Hogg.

"Her tooth was found at the dung pit by one of the labourers, Mr. Willoughby Krott. Mr. Arrowood brought it to us."

Tasker looked up from his notebook, a frown upon his face. Again his eyes fell on the guvnor. A little twitch of his sharp nose, then he went back to his notes.

"That was when I was brought onto the case. We found her body buried there."

"And who had the opportunity to carry out this murder?"

"Anyone who works in the fields and the farm buildings. That would be Godwin and Walter Ockwell and the two labourers, Mr. Digger and Mr. Krott."

The noise in the hall rose as folk in the crowd started to talk.

"What about the women?" asked Sprice-Hogg.

"They don't work in the fields. And Mrs. Gillie's considerably taller than the three Ockwell women. It would be difficult for them to hold her down all the time it took to kill her that way."

"Then which of the men had the clearest opportunity, would you say, Inspector?" asked Sprice-Hogg.

"Probably the workers. They slept in the barn and managed the dung pit. They'd stop at her camp sometimes for food when they were working in the fields. But I believe Mrs. Gillie was their friend."

"They're both former inmates of the Caterham Asylum, aren't they?" asked Sprice-Hogg.

"I believe so."

"You've questioned them?"

"Mr. Digger cannot talk, sir. He has some damage to his mind."

"Is he here?" asked the parson.

"No, sir. He cannot talk."

"Make sure he's here tomorrow. Now, what about Mr. Krott? I understand he disappeared the day before the body was discovered."

"He's the one!" cried someone from the back. "That's why he ran off!"

"Silence!" cried Sprice-Hogg, banging a mallet upon the table in fury. "We'll conduct this inquiry in private if we must!"

"He didn't run away," said Petleigh, looking over at us. "Mr. Arrowood and his assistant captured him."

People started up murmuring again. The reporters watched us, chewing their pencils, checking with each other they'd heard it right. The guvnor sighed, took out his pipe, and lit it. He stared at his shoes.

"Why did they do that, Inspector?" asked Sprice-Hogg.

"I believe Mr. Arrowood had honest reasons, Reverend. Mr. Krott's conditions were very poor. They suspected he wasn't being paid."

"Nonsense!" cried Godwin. "We save his wages for him. He's happy with us. Ask him yourself!"

"Please, Mr. Ockwell," said Sprice-Hogg. "You'll get your turn to speak."

"Let's concentrate on the murder of the old gypsy, shall we, as that's what we're here for?" said Tasker. His voice was warm and friendly but his triangular face was pinched. He was suffering a stye in the corner of one eye, an angry red thing that made him blink. "Now, did you question Mr. Krott, Inspector? Could he have done it?"

"I wasn't able to gain any information from questioning him, except that he seems most upset about it. He describes Mrs. Gillie as his friend."

"Friends often kill each other," growled Rhodes the master butcher.

Willoughby sat next to me with his arms crossed, rocking back and forth, his nose red and damp, his eyes shut tight. I couldn't tell if he was listening.

"Did anybody else have the opportunity, Inspector?"

"Edgar and Skulky Winters, local builders. They've been up there working on the well."

Anyone who knew them turned. The brothers leant against the wall, shaking their heads. Skulky in his red neckcloth, Edgar in his cap with a knob of wool.

"What about motive, Inspector? Any thoughts on that?"

"We believe she might have had gold or jewellery. Gypsies often do. There was nothing of value when we searched the camp, so the most obvious motive is theft."

"Any other possible motives?"

"Mr. Arrowood has another idea related to the case he's working on, but it's best if he tells you himself."

"We'll examine him later." Sprice-Hogg turned to the magistrates. "Any questions, gentlemen?"

"I assume you searched the builders' houses for jewellery, Inspector?" asked Tasker, an odd smile on his face.

"Not yet, sir."

"Rather late now, isn't it? You should have done it before this inquiry."

"Yes, sir," answered Petleigh. "We did search the barn. There were no valuables there."

"You're a detective inspector, aren't you?"

"Yes, sir."

Tasker snorted, shaking his head. He took up his pencil and wrote in his book. He blinked.

"Now, Inspector," said Sprice-Hogg, "I want you to take us to the camp so we may see the scene. And Mr. Ockwell, Miss Ockwell, if you don't mind coming, we'll need to look at the barn."

Chapter Forty

⸻ ❖ ⸻

The talking started up like a roar. Boys came among the reporters, fetching food and drink from the pub and the chandlers. Coachmen brought in hampers for those in the best seats, and soon they had crisp white linen on their knees, eating roast chicken, slices of ham, drinking red wine from crystal glasses. The young swells wandered among them, paying compliments to the young ladies, shaking hands with the dignitaries. The guvnor sent me for bread and cheese.

"Now, Willoughby, Mr. Godwin and Miss Rosanna aren't supposed to talk to you, d'you understand?" he said as we ate. "It's forbidden."

"Forbidden?"

"That's right, my friend. And you must stop calling him Dad. It'll confuse the magistrates."

"Is John coming?"

"I don't think so."

When the food was eaten we sat there, smoking, fidgeting. Willoughby even took half a pipe, though it made him cough. He knew the inquiry was about Mrs. Gillie's murder, but I wasn't sure how much of it all he really understood.

After two hours they returned and Sergeant Root was called to the front. He sat on the chair before them, his police uniform buttoned up tight to the collar, his flabby neck bulging over the top. He placed his helmet on his knee and looked over the audience.

"When did you first learn of Mrs. Gillie's disappearance, Sergeant?" asked Sprice-Hogg. There was a shading of wine to his lips, and his voice had relaxed some from the morning.

"Mr. Arrowood alerted me she was missing on Saturday, tenth of this month," answered Root. "I investigated the camp and noted there'd been signs of a struggle, with the upturned box and such. I suspected foul play."

"Rubbish," mumbled the guvnor. Sprice-Hogg glared at him.

"Me and PC Young did a search of the area," Root went on. "There was no trace of her. Most likely idea then was a row between the tinkers. They do like a fight, you know. I was preparing to apply to you for a warrant to search the barn, sir, when I had a moment. We've been busy with the livestock mutilations."

"Poppycock!" cried the guvnor. "You refused to do anything!"

"Mr. Arrowood!" barked Sprice-Hogg. "You'll be waiting outside if you don't control yourself. Now go on, Sergeant."

"Well, Sir Edward Penn had got involved by then and Inspector Petleigh was brought down. We managed to get a warrant and searched the barn."

"Did you recognize the tooth when Mr. Arrowood brought it in, Sergeant?"

"Mr. Arrowood never showed me the tooth. I don't know

why. He took it to Sir Edward Penn, our Member of Parliament."

Sprice-Hogg nodded, his eyes narrow like he was thinking real hard. He leant back in his chair and stretched out his legs, clasping his hands behind his curly white hair.

"Who do you think murdered the woman, Sergeant?"

Root stroked his droopy chops and appeared to think. "I can't see as Mr. Godwin or Mr. Walter would have done it. Maybe the labourers, Krott and Digger. Or the other worker who left. Tracey Childs. He might have come back to rob her. Any of them could have done it on account of their mental diseases, and they sleep by the dung pit too. But there's Mr. Arrowood and Mr. Barnett as well. They had good reason."

A hush fell over the crowd.

"How so?" asked Sprice-Hogg, sitting up again.

"Well, sir. They was the last to see her, far as I can tell. They'd been visiting her out there alone and they were the ones who reported her missing. It was Mr. Arrowood who had the tooth in his possession."

"What would be their motive for killing her, Sergeant Root?" asked Rhodes. "Theft?"

"Could be, sir. Them tinkers always have a bit of gold hidden away. Or they could be trying to put the blame on the Ockwell family, trying to make trouble for them. They was hired by Birdie Ockwell's parents to get Birdie off of them."

"You think we'd kill an old woman for that?" barked the guvnor. "We're detectives, not assassins, you imbecile!"

Sprice-Hogg whacked his mallet down on the table again and again. "No, no, no!" he said with each blow. "This won't do, Mr. Arrowood! It won't do! Go and stand outside until you're called."

"It's a pack of lies!"

"PC Young, please escort the gentleman outside."

As the boy copper came over, the guvnor got to his feet.

"I'll go, lad. No need to escort me." He glared at Root, at Sprice-Hogg, then, shaking his head, lumbered through the crowd to the door.

"Please explain what you're saying again, Sergeant," said Sprice-Hogg.

"Mr. Arrowood and his assistant was employed by the Barclay family to make trouble for the Ockwells. We've had complaints about them since they first came here. They've been poking around the farm, asking in the pub, trying to get their noses into the private affairs of the family. The Ockwells are good, decent people, as you know, sir. Been on the farm for generations, and these two turn up and get onto them like dogs on a fox. When they can't find anything they decide to make trouble. Maybe they stole her gold or something, killed her for it, then put the body on the farm so we'd think it was somebody in the family. I don't know for sure but it's got to be possible, that's all I'm saying. They was the first to report her missing, before anyone else noticed."

The butcher nodded, Tasker wrote in his pad.

"But murder, Sergeant?" asked Sprice-Hogg. "Risk of hanging? Would they really go so far for their work?"

"You can hire killers in London for a couple of pounds, sir, and that's the truth."

"And where's Mr. Arrowood from, Sergeant?" asked Tasker without looking from his pad.

"London, sir."

The noise from the crowd rose again.

"In your opinion, Sergeant," said Tasker, examining the sleeve of his green jacket for dust. "Is there anything else against Mr. Arrowood?"

"There's his assistant, Mr. Barnett." Root hesitated, adjusting his long legs in front of him. I felt a quiver of rage tickle my belly as I waited for what he would say. And also a quiver of fear. But surely this stupid copper hadn't found out anything about me.

"When you've been doing police work as long as I have, you can tell from his look when a man has criminals in his line," he went on. "I was cautious of him from the first moment I saw him. I get a sixth sense over it, always do, but you can see clear as day he's all the signs Mr. Lombroso shows you in his book: bulging forehead, long ears, patches in his beard."

My hand went to my chin.

"That's not just me, that's science says it," Root went on, his face big and honest. "You can see it in the eyes, set too far apart. Makes you go cross-eyed just to look at him, that's what my PC said."

I felt the whole crowd watching the back of my head, the side of my face. The magistrates were peering at me. Even Willoughby turned to have a look.

"With respect, Sergeant," said Petleigh, "those ideas are quite debunked these days."

"That might be your opinion, Inspector," said Tasker, looking up from his pad towards the high, vaulted ceiling, "but I can tell you many prominent alienists would disagree. There's good evidence for it."

"No, sir," said Petleigh. "There isn't. My police would never suspect a man because of his face."

"When we wish you to speak we'll ask you a question, Inspector," said Tasker, returning to his notes.

Sprice-Hogg spoke: "If it was the private agents, why would they do it the way they did? Pushing all that material down her throat seems a very odd way to kill a person, doesn't it? Wouldn't they do something easier?"

"I can't tell you about that, sir," said Root. "The mind of a killer's murky, I should say. There's no telling what they'll do when killing takes hold of them."

"Seems more like the work of a lunatic," said Rhodes.

Since none of them had any more questions for Root, Sprice-Hogg called Godwin Ockwell to the chair.

I turned to have a look at the people come to enjoy the inquiry. So many different folk, young and old, women and men, the poor, the rich, the in-between. And there at the back, hidden behind a tall bloke in a thick woolen coat, stood the guvnor. He winked at me, then pulled his bowler lower over his mush.

"Your family own the farm, Mr. Ockwell, is that correct?" asked Sprice-Hogg.

Godwin's whiskers were clipped, his chin long and solid. He wore a brown overcoat, a little ragged but clean and pressed. His lazy arm was cupped upon his lap.

"Our mother owns the farm, Reverend," he said. "She's an invalid. The three of us manage it: Rosanna, Walter and I."

"And when was the last time you saw Mrs. Gillie?"

"I spied her through the trees about a month ago when I was working the lower field but we didn't speak. She took against us after my father died. I don't know why."

"D'you know anyone who might want to kill her?" asked Sprice-Hogg.

"I thought at first it could be gypsies, sir, settling a score, as they do. They've their own justice, as you know. Or it could be thieves."

"That wouldn't explain how her body ended up in the barn."

"No, Reverend."

"I must ask you direct, Mr. Ockwell. Did you murder Mrs. Gillie?"

"No, sir," said Godwin. He looked around at the crowd, shaking his head. "I know you must ask it but I did not murder Mrs. Gillie. I had no reason to. Sergeant Root'll tell you I was never one of the suspects."

"Thank you, Mr. Ockwell. Now tell me about Thomas Digger, your labourer. He's from the asylum, I understand. Is he a violent man?"

"He was an orphan, in the workhouse before the asylum so I don't know what stock he's from. But I can say he sometimes becomes angry in his work."

"Angry? In what way?"

"With the pigs. Sometimes they're difficult to reason with. I've seen him thrash them when they resist."

"He attacks the pigs?" cried Rhodes the butcher, a look of horror on his face.

"With a shovel. He loses his temper."

"And Willoughby Krott, your other worker," said Sprice-Hogg. "Is he also violent?"

"I've never seen him in a fury, no." He turned and gave our new friend a wink and a smile. A great grin broke out over Willoughby's face, like that smile from Godwin was the richest present a man could ever have; he rocked forward and back, rubbing his palms together in delight.

"But Willoughby'll do whatever you tell him," continued Ockwell, turning back to the magistrates. "He won't question, he'll do as he's told."

As they spoke, the guvnor appeared at the end of our row. Quietly, he crept past Petleigh and slipped into his seat.

"Will he do what Mr. Digger tells him?" asked Sprice-Hogg.

"If Digger shows him, then he'll do it. Digger's a clever fellow for a lunatic. It's often him teaches Willoughby on the farm, if I'm not there."

Willoughby had his eyes fixed on Godwin, but his face was now blank: I wasn't sure he was listening. He rubbed his eyes and coughed, not realizing what they were suggesting. His tongue came out and rolled over his lips.

"Did you notice anything unusual around Friday the ninth of this month?"

Godwin looked up at the beams, his jaw stuck out as he thought.

"Digger was melancholic that weekend, sir. Ashamed, perhaps, from his face. A bit slower about his work."

"Any signs of disruption around the dung pit?"

"I wouldn't know. Digger and Willoughby are responsible for managing the pit. They take in the dung from the fattening boxes and store it there. Bring it out for the fields when it's needed: I just leave them to it. They know what they're doing."

"So they're the only ones whose work involves the dung pit. What about the other worker, Tracey Childs?"

"It couldn't be him, sir. He left four months ago, before Mrs. Gillie was killed. Decided to try his hand in America. He'd saved enough for the steamer from his time with us. I do encourage them to save."

"You got him from Caterham Asylum as well?" asked Rhodes.

"Yes, sir," answered Godwin. "We get a few from there, once they've been treated. Mr. Tasker arranges it for some of the farms around here."

Tasker nodded, a serious pout on his face. He wiped his eye.

"Well, now, here's an idea," said Rhodes. "Maybe he didn't go. Maybe he found out Mrs. Gillie had gold or jewellery and came back to rob her. Maybe he plotted it out with the other two workers."

"No, sir. I arranged the ticket as he wasn't so good with that sort of thing. I took him to the dock myself."

At that moment a peppermint struck Godwin, bounced off his shoulder and fell to the floor. He looked up towards the beams, then out in our direction, wondering where it came from. The magistrates did the same.

"Out, Mr. Arrowood," said Sprice-Hogg, noticing the guvnor back in his seat again.

The guvnor rose without a word of complaint and pushed his way through the crowd to the doors.

"I watched him on the deck as it sailed off," Godwin went on. "I had a tear in my eye, I don't mind telling you. Tracey was one of the family just as Willoughby and Digger are."

"Well, that rules out Mr. Childs, at least," said Sprice-Hogg. "Now, Mr. Ockwell, let's get back to Thomas Digger. D'you think it's possible he might have killed Mrs. Gillie? With or without help from Mr. Krott?"

"More than possible," said Rhodes the butcher. "They had the opportunity. Krott had the tooth in his possession. We know Digger gets into rages. And the way she was killed, surely only a lunatic would do it like that? You know them better than anyone, Mr. Ockwell. Do you think it's possible?"

There wasn't a sound as each person in that hall watched Godwin. He sighed. He bit his lip. He shook his head.

"I don't like to say it," he said, his eyes falling to the floor. "But yes. It's possible."

Chapter Forty-One

We marched to the station in the fading winter light, ignoring all those who tried to speak to us. Petleigh caught up with us on the platform, and we made the journey in silence, standing all the way on the crowded uptrain packed out with with journalists and spectators from the Mission Hall. Willoughby stood solid between us in Lewis's bowler hat and coat, his eyes empty. Other passengers stared: they couldn't take their eyes off him, his wide face and cracked lips, his Mongolian eyes, his mouth as hung open the whole journey. I knew they were thrilling that maybe there, stood before them, was the murderer, the one who held Mrs. Gillie's neck as he shoved sticks and mud down her throat. I pushed myself in front, opening my coat so as to hide him.

"Barnett, take Willoughby and wait for me at the bus stop," said the guvnor as we gained the gates at London Bridge. "I need a word with Petleigh."

They joined us a few minutes later, Petleigh hailing a hansom while we walked to the Elephant and Castle. The guvnor was lost somewhere in his mind, a haunted look in his eyes. Every now and then his lips began to move; his fingers traced out steps in the cold air.

Willoughby'd been coughing again on the way back and went straight upstairs to bed when we reached Lewis's house. He was asleep in seconds, still in his coat, the bowler crushed under his head. I pulled off his boots and covered him with a few blankets.

There was more order in the parlour now, more air: the guvnor's boxes and books were gone back to their rooms in Coin Street, the portrait of himself that he thought resembled Moses leaving a grimy space on the wall. I told Ettie and Lewis all I could remember as the guvnor sat deep in thought, the orange cat upon his britches, his feet stretched out to the fire. He ate ginger nut after ginger nut. He gave that cat a hell of a stroking.

"They really do suspect you, then," said Ettie when I'd finished. She sat perched upon the edge of the couch, her back straight. A little frill went all the way round her neck.

"Root does," said the guvnor, finally joining in. "But it's Digger and Willoughby they seem to be going after. So far nobody's suggesting it was one of the Ockwells."

"There's no chance they'll send Willoughby back to the farm, is there?" she asked.

"They'll try, and unless we can prevent him he'll say he wants to go back when they ask him. He just won't say who hurt him."

"We have to do something," said Lewis. "We have to stop them."

The guvnor nodded as he uncapped his pipe and filled it

346

with his friend's tobacco. When it was lit, he looked over at me.

"Listen, Norman," he said. "I have a plan."

Mission Hall was already full when we arrived next morning, a crowd waiting outside hoping to get in. The old couple from the pub were hawking sheep's trotters from a bucket and doing a good business too. A couple of filthy girls, no more than ten or twelve year old, stood behind a crate of oysters. Shells were scattered along the street. The guvnor pushed his way to the door, where the clerk let him in. He was out again five minutes later.

"There's a door to the kitchen at the front left side," he said to me. "Bring him there. Willoughby, you come with me."

They went inside.

Petleigh arrived a few minutes later.

"Did you wire him?" I asked.

He nodded.

"I hope this works, Norman. I can't get the sight of those scars out of my mind." He squeezed the bridge of his nose with his fingers and shook his head. He pulled out his flask and had a swallow.

I went over the plan with him again. As I talked, a newly painted brougham pulled over on the other side of the road and John Krott stepped down. He looked at the crowd in irritation, then turned to say a few words to the coachman.

"There he is, Inspector."

Petleigh went over to meet him. They shook hands, then went into the building. It was clear Krott was none too pleased to be there.

I went in just after them, following as they pushed their way to the front. When they reached the kitchen door, Petleigh opened it and said: "Wait in there, Mr. Krott. I need a word with the magistrates."

"Tell them to see me first," said Krott. "I've many things to do today."

There was always something about a handsome fellow giving orders I found hard to resist, and Krott was even more handsome that day in his cashmere overcoat and silk topper: he was surely a man you could fall in love with with only a pint of gin inside you. I followed him into the kitchen, closing the door behind us. He turned, but there was no sign he recognized me.

"Damn nuisance," he said, shaking his pretty head.

"Damn nuisance," I said. The little greying hair over his ears gave him a look of wisdom that was hard to disagree with.

The kitchen was damp and cold. A wooden table stood in the middle, a range cooker by the wall. The guvnor sat on a chair, his hands atop Lewis's reserve walking stick, the one side of his face still puffed out and bruised.

"Good morning, sir," he said, peering at Krott through his eyeglasses. "We met in your apartment, if you recall. Mr. Arrowood. The monster behind you is Mr. Barnett."

"Ah, yes." Krott looked down on the guvnor like he had a flood of bile in his throat. He glanced back at me and nodded. "I remember. So they've summoned you as well."

"Damn nuisance," said the guvnor. "You've heard about the murder, I suppose?"

"Of course. I've never even been to that farm, though. Waste of damn time."

"Waste of damn time," agreed the guvnor. "He's staying with us at the moment."

"Who's staying with you?"

"Willoughby, of course. Didn't you know?"

"Why isn't he on the farm?"

"That'll become clear in the inquiry, sir. But I really must know when you can take him back to live with you."

Krott laughed.

"He's not coming to live with me! I made that very clear to you last time."

"But Godwin told Willoughby you'd take him back when you had room."

"I've never said that." He stood erect and superior, a cherrywood walking stick in his hand. His chest was out, his chin high. Magnificent.

"Willoughby believes if he works hard then the Ockwells will arrange it all."

"Oh, it's just a ruse to get him working no doubt. I don't want him anywhere near my home."

"Mr. Waller Proctor believes it was part of the agreement."

"Waller Proctor? What are you talking about, man? I didn't promise him anything."

"Oh, dear, dear. I'm afraid Mr. Proctor asked me to tell you that if you're reneging on your agreement, he'll need another twenty-pound payment."

"You're working for him, are you?" Krott's voice rose. "Well, that explains it. Tell him he can damn well whistle for it. The agreement was a single fee and I certainly promised nothing about taking Willoughby back."

"You believed the payment was just to put him on the pauper list? To avoid private patient fees? Nothing else was agreed?"

"Of course not." Krott looked at the guvnor like he was a fool. "Him coming to live with us was never even discussed. It sounds as if Proctor's just trying to chisel more money out of me. I won't pay, d'you hear?"

Arrowood stood and walked over to the door to the hall. There he paused, tapping his stick on the floor. He spoke loudly now. "But Mr. Krott, sir, whether you discussed it with Mr. Proctor or not, wouldn't you enjoy having your brother Willoughby at home with you? He's such a nice fellow."

"No, I would not."

"He's your flesh and blood, damn it!" cried Arrowood, suddenly in a fury. "Have you no heart?"

"He's a regression!" barked Krott. "I wish my parents had left him in the passage when he was born. My flesh and blood, indeed. I've more in common with an Irishman than that overgrown child, for God's sake."

"He's a kind soul and a hard worker, sir. We like him very much."

"What do I care if you like him? He'll never live with me, I promise you that, and don't for a minute start judging me for it. People'll think there's a taint in my daughters' blood if they know their uncle's a natural. It'll ruin their chances."

"You're an odious creature, sir," said the guvnor. "You don't deserve him."

"I know I don't deserve him!"

"That's not how I meant it. Now get out."

I opened the door. Petleigh stood outside, waiting.

"You can go, sir," said the inspector. "We don't need you anymore."

"What!" cried Krott. "You've brought me all the way here and now you don't need me?"

"Sorry, sir. You've been very helpful. We'll be in contact should we need you again."

"Damn you all!" hissed Krott, his face quite red. He caught his topper just as it began to fall. "And damn this damn inquiry! And damn bloody Catford!"

He strode past Petleigh and pushed his way through the crowd.

The guvnor crossed the room to the pantry door and opened it. Willoughby stood there with his hands in a clasp, his eyes cast down like his spirit was broken.

"I'm sorry you had to hear that, my friend," said the guvnor, taking his hand and bringing him out. "Mr. Godwin's been deceiving you. He was never going to let you off the farm."

"Farm," said Willoughby, his face wretched with sadness.

The guvnor looked back at us and shook his head. Petleigh came over.

"Willoughby, I'm a police officer; you know that, don't you?"

Willoughby nodded.

"The Ockwells have been lying to you. They just want to keep you there working for them. Now, you heard what your brother said. He doesn't want you. You'll never live with him, but Mr. Arrowood here's going to find you somewhere safe to live. Somewhere good where you'll really be happy."

Willoughby sniffed, shutting his eyes. The guvnor put his arm over his shoulder. He straightened his bowler for him.

"You've got to tell the magistrates who hurt you," said Petleigh. "D'you understand?"

For a long time, Willoughby made no response.

The guvnor bit his lip. Petleigh caught my eye, shook his head.

Then, at last, Willoughby nodded.

All the seats in the hall were taken, the crowd standing thick along the walls and at the back. Upstairs in the balcony sat the Winter brothers, the old fellow that shared a room with Lisa, the three blokes from the pub. Stood next to the door wrapped in a thick shawl was Ida Gillie, and the Ockwells had brought Walter and Digger, both of them brushed and polished up.

Petleigh'd arranged with Sprice-Hogg that Willoughby be questioned first, so when the magistrates were on their seats and the parson had got a bit of quiet in the place, he said, "Mr. Krott. Please come to the chair."

Willoughby sat in the pew next to me, staring at the magistrates' feet under the table. He gave no sign he'd heard.

"Come on, mate," I murmured, taking his arm and leading him to the chair. There I whispered in his ear: "Now, you just answer their questions and don't say anything else. Tell them who hurt you, but whatever you do, you mustn't tell them you want to go back to the farm. Understand?"

He nodded and swallowed. What he'd heard from his brother had shaken him, and I could see he was afraid of talking in front of such a big crowd.

I went back to the pew and sat next to the guvnor.

"How long have you worked at the farm, Mr. Krott?" asked Sprice-Hogg.

Willoughby gave a great sigh, his shoulders rising and falling.

"Yeah do," he said. His voice was flat. "Work at the farm."

"No, listen. How long? How many years?"

"I been…" He looked over at the Ockwells, his face empty. "About… How long I been, Miss Rosanna?"

"Four years," she answered.

"Get back to work," mumbled Willoughby, his wide face tilted down at the floor again. The bowler he'd loaned from Lewis was a couple of sizes too big, and it shaded his eyes. "Drain lower field."

"No, Willoughby," hissed the guvnor. "Remember what John said."

"Mr. Arrowood!" barked Sprice-Hogg. "Once more and you're out again!"

Willoughby leant forward at the waist, crossing one leg over the other. He started to rock.

"Mr. Krott," said Sprice-Hogg. "Willoughby. Look this way."

Willoughby glanced up as he rocked.

"Did you know Mrs. Gillie?"

He nodded. "My friend."

"Yes. You know we're trying to find out who killed her, don't you?"

Willoughby's eyes fell to the floor again.

"Killed her," he said very quietly.

At this, there was a murmuring in the crowd.

"D'you know who killed her, Willoughby?" asked Sprice-Hogg.

"Killed her," said Willoughby again, his bottom lip thrust out. Still he looked at the floor.

"Listen, boy," said Rhodes the butcher loudly. "Listen careful. *DO YOU KNOW WHO KILLED HER?*"

"Mr. Rhodes!" exclaimed Sprice-Hogg. "He's not deaf."

"Answer us, boy!" demanded Rhodes. "Do...you...know... who...killed...her?"

"Killed her," said Willoughby.

"You killed her?" demanded Rhodes.

"No, don't."

"He's repeating what you say," said Sprice-Hogg. "Listen, Willoughby, you must answer properly. Did you see anyone bury her in the dung heap?"

Willoughby shook his head, his fists clenched tight.

"Did Digger kill her?"

"No. Digger don't."

"Did Mr. Arrowood or Mr. Barnett kill her?"

"Kill her."

Now there were gasps. Someone cried, "No," from the balcony.

"They killed her?"

"No, don't."

"What about Mr. Walter or Mr. Godwin?"

Willoughby looked up at Sprice-Hogg. A change seemed to come over him, like he'd forgotten what this was all about. "You know my brother, John?" he asked.

"I'm not asking about John. Did Mr. Walter or Mr. Godwin kill Mrs. Gillie?"

"Got work to do. Get back to farm. Dad say. He's my friend. Best workers, we are."

"This is gibberish," said Rhodes.

"Did you kill her, Willoughby?" asked Sprice-Hogg again.

"No, don't."

Sprice-Hogg smiled and his voice became gentle. "Then why did you run away from the farm?"

"Mr. Barnett took me. Got me with Lewis, now."

"Did you want to go?"

"He's my friend."

"Damned nonsense," said Rhodes. "The boy's feeble-minded. Thinks everyone's his friend."

"I must agree, Reverend," said Tasker. "His thoughts are clearly disordered. He's contradicting himself. It's quite impossible to determine which parts of his answers we can take seriously."

"He wants to get back to work, Reverend," said Rosanna Ockwell from across the hall. "That was clear enough. You heard him. We'll take you back today, Willoughby."

"Get back to work, Miss Rosanna," said Willoughby, turning to look at her.

"No, Reverend, I beg you," said the guvnor, getting to his feet. "Don't let them take him back."

"He wants to go back, Mr. Arrowood," said Sprice-Hogg. "He's just told us."

"No, please. You cannot allow it. He was imprisoned. They've mistreated him. He was almost starved."

"Are you going to allow him to say these things, Reverend?" cried Miss Ockwell. "Willoughby, tell them. You do want to come home, don't you?"

Willoughby wrapped his arms around his chest. His eyes were shut now, his head bowed low. He nodded.

"Thank you, Willoughby," said Sprice-Hogg. "You may return with the Ockwells today."

The guvnor strode over and whispered into Willoughby's ear. As he did it, he began to unbutton our friend's coat.

Willoughby sat watching the guvnor's fingers work away, his mouth open.

"What are you doing?" demanded Sprice-Hogg.

"Leave him alone!" cried Godwin, rising from his seat. "Stop interfering with him, you fiend! Sergeant, do something!"

The guvnor ripped open Willoughby's waistcoat, then unbuttoned his shirt and pulled it over his shoulders.

"Mr. Arrowood!" demanded Sprice-Hogg. "Leave the man alone!"

"No, Mr. Arrowood," said Willoughby. He raised his hands to stop him, but the guvnor kept on.

Godwin pushed out from his pew and ran over. "Let him go!" he cried, seizing the guvnor by the neck and wrenching him away from Willoughby.

I jumped to my feet, got hold of Godwin and threw him to the floor.

The crowd cried out in outrage.

"Root, stop him!" shouted Sprice-Hogg.

But before the copper was out of his seat, the guvnor pulled Willoughby to his feet and tore open his vest.

Chapter Forty-Two

The hall fell silent as each soul took in the horrors of Willoughby's body. Sprice-Hogg's face paled. The butcher's gaze travelled this way and that, unable to comprehend what he was seeing. Tasker looked for a moment, blinked, then shut his eyes. All around the hall, folk were open-mouthed, staring, blinking. Others held their heads in their hands in despair. A child began to cry.

"That's why he must never go back to the farm," said the guvnor at last.

Willoughby was trembling, his eyes screwed up tight. The guvnor covered him, buttoned his shirt, his waistcoat, his jacket, sat him down again, then knelt, pulling him into a hug.

"I'm sorry, my friend," he whispered. "But they had to see. Nobody must hurt you again."

"Who did this to him?" asked Sprice-Hogg.

"Ask him," answered the guvnor.

"Willoughby, open your eyes and look at me," ordered Sprice-Hogg. "I need you to tell me who hurt you."

Willoughby looked at the parson. His lips parted. But he said nothing.

"Go on, my dear," said Arrowood, standing but keeping his hands on Willoughby's shoulders. "There's no need to be afraid. We'll keep you safe."

Willoughby shut his eyes again. He wrapped his arms around himself. He rocked.

Sprice-Hogg waited for several more moments, then said: "Willoughby, listen. We must know who did this to you. We're the magistrates, and you must do as we say. So, please tell us...who did this to you?"

The great hall, crammed to suffocation, was silent except for a single, ragged pigeon flapping in the beams. Rhodes the butcher watched Willoughby. Tasker held his pencil, his gaze on the notebook before him. I looked over at Rosanna and Walter. Godwin was back by their side, their eyes all fixed on Willoughby. Petleigh leant forward, willing our friend to speak.

"Willoughby, please tell us," said Sprice-Hogg when no answer came. "Who did this to you?"

"Come on, lad!" urged Rhodes. "Tell us!"

Willoughby shook his head.

"All right, Mr. Krott," said Sprice-Hogg at last. "You may sit down."

The guvnor was next. He sat his over-served shanks on the witness chair and looked out at the crowd. He might have had his Sunday best on and his hair dyed tar-black but his battered eye, sealed shut in his puffy purple cheek, made

358

him look like the worst vamper in London. I wouldn't have trusted a word he said.

"You're a private investigative agent, Mr. Arrowood," said Sprice-Hogg.

"Yes, Reverend. I work with my assistant, Mr. Barnett. We help people to right the wrongs they've suffered when the police are unable to help."

"We know what you do," said Tasker, his pinched face even pinchier than before. He sat back, hooking his thumbs in his fine red waistcoat. "You find evidence of infidelity and such. You spy on people and expose their private affairs to the world."

"There are many types of case, sir. We investigate theft, missing persons, other crimes. Similar to Sherlock Holmes, although we have a different app—"

"Similar to Sherlock Holmes?" interrupted Tasker. He was looking into the audience, a smile on his face. He laughed. "Well, well. So the police come to you when they cannot solve a case?"

"Well, not exac—"

"No, I didn't think so. But I'm sure the government approaches you on matters of national security?"

"No, that's not what—"

"No, of course they don't. Similar to Sherlock Holmes indeed! You've a very high view of yourself, Mr. Arrowood, if I might say."

The Ockwells had a good laugh at that, along with just about everyone else. Digger sat with them, washed, his beard trimmed, wearing an old Norfolk jacket. His eyes were on Willoughby, who was back next to me, his head bowed, his fists clenched. A low hum was coming from his throat.

"*The Star* says you've never solved a case," declared Tasker, pretending to consult his notebook.

"*The Star* says many things," the guvnor came back at him. "They've accused four different men of being the Ripper. Last year they informed us there are a people in the Far East with wings."

"Tell us what your interest in Ockwell Farm is, please, Mr. Arrowood," said Sprice-Hogg.

"Birdie Ockwell's parents hired us, Reverend. They hadn't seen nor heard from her since her wedding six months ago and were worried. They asked us to check she was safe and well."

"And how did you come to meet Mrs. Gillie?"

The guvnor told them about the time we'd had tea with her, and how we'd found her missing the next day. Sprice-Hogg then asked how we came by the tooth.

"Mr. Krott found it in the dung pit as he was digging."

"Why did he give it to you and not his masters?" asked Rhodes.

The guvnor looked over at me. I knew this was the bit he didn't want to say, but he had no choice.

"He didn't give it to me. I had two of my irregulars take up positions on the farm. They posed as a mute woman and her son."

"You put spies in our house!" cried Godwin, jumping to his feet. "You fiend!"

There was uproar in the hall. Angry faces were everywhere, heads shaking, fingers pointing. Rhodes the butcher stared at the guvnor in disgust. Tasker fixed his sharp eyes on the balcony, tapping his pencil against his teeth, scratching at his tightly-curled bonce with his other hand. The guvnor crossed his arms and looked calmly around. Sprice-Hogg thrashed the table with his mallet till peace returned.

"He gave it to the boy," said the guvnor.

"Why?" asked Sprice-Hogg. "Why didn't he give it to the Ockwells?"

"He was frightened of somebody on the farm. I can only suppose he knew someone should see it, but he didn't know who. The boy was an outsider. He might have thought it safer."

"Why did you capture Mr. Krott?"

"The workers were held as slaves. Given insufficient food, cruelly treated. Unable to leave the farm."

"Lies!" cried Godwin, on his feet again. "They could leave whenever they wanted!"

"You saw Mr. Krott's body," said the guvnor, his voice rising. "The doctor tells us he's been burnt, whipped, beaten, bitten. Branded by hot irons. For the last three years at least."

"Are you accusing one of the Ockwell family, sir?" asked the butcher.

"His tormentor's someone on the farm, that's certain." The guvnor was in his stride now, his voice booming around the hall. "I understand this inquiry's about bringing charges for Mrs. Gillie's murder, but these events are connected. They must be. Please, sirs, we must discover who did this. They must be brought to justice!"

A few people clapped, but most were silent. Rosanna Ockwell shook her head, her eyes narrow. She hissed a few words into Godwin's ear.

"Who d'you think killed Mrs. Gillie, Mr. Arrowood?" asked Sprice-Hogg.

"It's likely to have been the same person as hurt Mr. Krott. A person connected to the farm and with a tendency for violence. Which means that Mr. Krott didn't kill her."

"And rules you out of the frame, Mr. Arrowood," noted Tasker. He crossed his arms. "Very neat."

"I didn't kill Mrs. Gillie, sir. I don't know who did, but it happened just after she told us about three dead children on the farm. She refused to tell us what she meant by it, and we've been unable to find out. I reported this to Sergeant Root, and I believe the murderer might have learnt of it somehow. It's possible she was killed to silence her."

"To silence her about what?" asked Tasker. "These three dead children who nobody knows anything about?"

"I'm not sure. It's something to do with the farm, though, and the family. She also told me she suspected the Ockwell men were responsible for the death of her husband several years ago. He was attacked on the lane that runs to the farm."

"Slander!" shouted Godwin, on his feet again. "You can't let him do this, Reverend! We had nothing to do with it. He's only trying to blacken our name."

"Sergeant Root," said Sprice-Hogg. "Is there any truth to this?"

Root got to his feet. "Mr. Gillie died after a fight at the Spring Fair. We never did find out who he'd been fighting with. Mrs. Gillie accused them, but there was nothing in it. Mr. Godwn and Mr. Walter were already home. Their parents swore it."

"Might we limit our inquiry to the death of Mrs. Gillie, Reverend?" asked Tasker. "We can't drag up old crimes every time someone mentions them."

"Sergeant, what do you know of three dead children?" asked Sprice-Hogg.

"Only one child died on the farm, Reverend, and that was Mr. Godwin's newborn," said Root. "I've made enquiries.

There's nothing in what the gypsy said. Just telling tales, far as I can make out. It wouldn't be the first time neither."

There were no more questions for the guvnor and so Sprice-Hogg called Rosanna Ockwell to the front. She strode to the witness chair, her eyes hard and challenging, her thin lips pinched in determination. She wore a green satin skirt, a neat jacket buttoned to her neck, a hat with a part-veil.

"Who do you think might have killed Mrs. Gillie, Miss Ockwell?" asked Sprice-Hogg.

"Well, I first suspected those private agents." She spoke slow, her white-gloved hands resting tidily in her lap. "It seemed too much of a coincidence that they appeared at the same time it happened. But I suppose it could have been Digger or Willoughby. I hate to say it as we've welcomed them into our family for all these years, but..." Her voice started to crack, like the emotion was getting the better of her. "I...I heard Digger had fallen out with the old woman over some food he'd taken."

"How did you hear this?"

"I overheard Mrs. Gillie complaining of it in the chandlers. Digger does become overwrought at times, as my brother explained."

"Mr. Arrowood says you keep the workers as slaves and treat them cruelly. Is this true?"

"That's a scandalous thing to say, Reverend. We save their wages for them, they prefer it that way. They're free to leave at any time but choose to stay with us. You've just heard Willoughby say it. Why would he wish to return if it were true? And, you know, we also provide board and lodging."

"You provide a plank of wood and a turnip!" cried the guvnor, twitching beside me like a pot on the boil.

"Quiet!" demanded Sprice-Hogg. "And what about Mr. Krott's injuries, madam. What caused them?"

She looked around, first at Digger sat next to Godwin, and then at Willoughby.

"I think it must have been Tracey. Or perhaps Digger, but I suspect Tracey."

"What about your brothers, Miss Ockwell?" asked Sprice-Hogg, his voice suddenly quite gentle. He peered at her through his little round eyeglasses. "Walter has a conviction for violence, has he not?"

"If you knew the affection my brothers have for our workers, you wouldn't suggest that, sir," said Rosanna firmly. "We treat them as our family, with love and care. I was as shocked as anyone at what we saw yesterday, and last night we prayed for poor Willoughby's suffering. We had no idea, really no idea: he never complained. The only consolation is that Willoughby's type don't feel pain as we do."

"One last question, Miss Ockwell," said Sprice-Hogg. "What did Mrs. Gillie mean when she spoke of three dead children on your farm?"

"My brother Godwin lost an infant, and Walter's wife Birdie had a stillborn. The only other I can think of is our brother, who died before we were born, but I can't imagine she meant that. I think Mrs. Gillie must have been drinking, perhaps? Or she'd heard some gossip and misunderstood it. It doesn't make any sense, Reverend."

Walter was called next. He seemed nervous as he lumbered over to the seat, looking out around the crowd, swallowing. He took off his hat: his blond hair combed down tight on his head and his white eyelashes made him seem a meek giant.

The guvnor scribbled something in his book, tore out the paper, and passed it to Petleigh.

"I'm going to ask you the same questions, Mr. Ockwell," said Sprice-Hogg gently. "D'you understand?"

"Yes, Reverend," answered Walter, sitting side-on in the chair like he wasn't sure which way to face.

"Did you kill Mrs. Gillie?" asked Sprice-Hogg.

"It wasn't me, I promise." His voice was loud, his words slow.

"Who d'you think did it?"

"I don't know anything about it. I just don't. I do hope you find them, though, Reverend. It's really terrible."

"What about Mr. Krott's injuries? D'you know who did them?"

"No, sir," he said, real quiet now. His hands clenched into fists in his lap. He glanced back at his family.

"Are you sure about that? You must tell the truth, Mr. Ockwell."

Walter nodded. All this time, Willoughby sat beside me, his eyes shut, his body tight and upright. But I knew from the little twitches of his ears, the little breaths. I knew he was listening.

"Did you hurt him, sir?" asked the butcher.

"No."

"Was it you, sir?" repeated the butcher.

Walter turned to look at his sister, a deep, worried frown on his face.

"It's all right, Walter," she said. "Just answer his questions."

"I didn't hurt him, Mr. Rhodes."

"I think you did, Mr. Ockwell," said the butcher, his voice low and threatening. "Just like you hurt those men in the pub."

"No!" boomed Walter, fear in his eyes. "I never hurt him. Don't say that!"

"I must say it," the butcher insisted. "Because it is true, isn't it?"

"It's not true! I never hurt him. It's not true!"

"You've been up before us a few year ago, Mr. Ockwell, for breaking a man's arm and taking out another's eye. You told us that time you didn't do it, but you had done it, hadn't you? You served time in gaol. That's correct, isn't it?"

"I thought they'd stolen the pig money!" Walter seemed desperate now, looking around for help. "They were ragging me all day, Mr. Rhodes. Called me bird-witted and everything else."

"You lost your temper, didn't you, Mr. Ockwell?" declared the butcher.

"Only that once!" replied Walter. "I thought they'd robbed me."

"And you lost your temper again with Mrs. Gillie!"

"No, I never did!"

"And with Willoughby Krott!"

Walter was becoming frantic.

"No, I didn't!" He turned to his sister. "He can't say that. It isn't true. Tell him, Rosanna!"

"Leave him be," demanded Rosanna. "He didn't do it."

"I didn't ask you, madam," said the butcher.

"I didn't do it," said Walter.

Silence for a few moments. The magistrates looked at each other.

"Mr. Ockwell's given a clear answer," said Sprice-Hogg at last. "Now, Mr. Tasker, do you have any questions?"

Tasker shook his head.

"I have one if I may, Reverend," said Petleigh. The guvnor's note was folded in his hand. "Mr. Walter, did Tracey talk a lot about going to Australia before he left?"

"Yes, Inspector, he did," said Walter. "He was always talking about Australia."

"Thank you, sir," said Petleigh.

Sprice-Hogg called Digger to the front next. He didn't look too comfortable in the old Norfolk jacket they'd given him, and you could tell by his shuffle his boots were too big. He was washed. His hair cut. He looked like he'd been skinned somehow.

"Mr. Digger," said Sprice-Hogg. He was speaking slowly, pronouncing each word carefully. "I want you to try to answer my questions. Do you understand?"

Digger looked at him with his thin, cold eyes. He shifted in the chair.

"He can't answer, Reverend," said Sergeant Root. "We tried to question him. He's a mute."

"Just nod for yes."

Digger did nothing. I nudged the guvnor: Willoughby's eyes were open now; he was watching real careful. "Mr. Digger, please try and answer this question," continued Sprice-Hogg. "Do you know who killed Mrs. Gillie? Just nod or shake your head."

Digger breathed slowly. He coughed.

"Was it you, sir?"

Sprice-Hogg waited a few moments, then asked:

"Did you cause those injuries to Willoughby Krott?"

Digger looked over at Willoughby, a little smile on his face like he was playing out a plan somehow. I'd never seen him smile before, and it seemed to change him. Willoughby smiled back, his tight body loosening just a bit. There was something passing between the two of them.

Suddenly, my blood ran cold.

I looked over at the guvnor, who'd noticed it too. He stared at Willoughby, at Digger, his mouth open in horror.

The two labourers held each other's eyes.

Digger rose from the chair.

"We're not finished yet, sir," said Sprice-Hogg. "Sit down, please."

Digger ignored him. He started to unbutton his Norfolk jacket, then his loose white benjamin. The hall was silent, all eyes watching him as he peeled off his scarf, pulled his long shirt from his britches. Then, in a sudden rage, Digger ripped open his vest.

His wretched body was the same as Willoughby's.

Chapter Forty-Three

Digger faced the crowd, his hands clasped behind his back. The ribs stuck out like flints, the bones of his shoulders and elbows there for all to see, and where his skin should be was only a tangle of horror, striped with gaping, bloody wounds, stained with bruises and oozing with infection. I had to look up to escape it, towards Digger's severe face, and only then did I understand that what was in his eyes all this time wasn't anger, but torment. He breathed in and out slowly. He turned to show his back. It was a mass of wheals, a bloody pulp of putrid meat from his belt right up to his neck.

All was still in the hall; the air itself seemed to moan.

"Mr. Digger," said Sprice-Hogg, his voice choking. There were tears in his eyes. "Mr. Digger... If the person who did this is here, please help us by pointing."

Digger glared at him, at all the powerful men at the table.

"Point!" pleaded Sprice-Hogg. "Please, Mr. Digger, point."

Digger kept on glaring. Then he began to pull on his vest, his shirt.

"Is the person here, man?" demanded the butcher. "Just nod or shake your head!"

Digger took up his jacket from the floor and came towards us. Willoughby shifted closer to me, making a space. Digger sat next to him.

Sprice-Hogg banged his mallet.

"Break for two hours," he said.

The noise in the hall was like a great waterfall of babbling, arguing voices. People rushed and pushed to get the best places in the pub, to get to the ale, the gin: their hearts had been truly tested.

"Godwin never took Tracey to the boat," said the guvnor to Petleigh as we stood watching the crowd clear out. "It's a lie."

"This had something to do with that question, I suppose?" asked Petleigh.

Arrowood nodded. "Remember yesterday, when Godwin said Tracey went to America? Well, sometimes the best clues can be found if you keep your eyes on the person who isn't talking. I don't suppose you were watching Rosanna at the time, were you?"

"Get on with it, William."

"When he said it, her mouth opened and her eyebrows rose a fraction. Universal marks of surprise, so says Darwin. Then something passed over her face, the expression people have when they no longer see what they're looking at. It continued as he described taking Tracey to the docks and waving him off. That was why I threw the peppermint."

"I knew that was you."

"I was testing how distracted she was. You noticed how

everybody in that hall turned in our direction to see who'd thrown it? Well, Rosanna didn't. Didn't move her eyes away from her brother. And why? Because what Godwin was saying about Tracey took her by surprise. I asked Willoughby last night if Tracey had ever mentioned going to America. He also said no. That's why I gave you that question for Walter about Australia. Godwin said that Tracey was always talking about going to America. If that was the case, Walter would know it, slow-minded or not. But if Walter had only heard about it for the first time yesterday, well, then he might just doubt his memory about whether it was America or Australia. A man like that is always misunderstanding, I should think, and a question from an inspector carries authority. He'd assume it was him who misremembered, not you."

"You're saying Rosanna and Walter didn't know about Tracey going to America?" asked Petleigh. "But how?"

"Because it didn't happen, Petleigh! Do I have to spell everything out for you? The question is why would Godwin say it?"

Just then, someone in the crowd caught the guvnor's eye. "Harold!" he cried, raising his hand.

The bloke was about the same age as the guvnor but tall as me, a trim, brown beard matching his brown bowler. He had the sort of creased face as told you he'd seen a lot of life, good and bad.

"William," said the bloke, pushing through to us. "How good to see you."

"It's been too long, my friend," said the guvnor, clasping his hand.

"That's quite a shiner you've got there," said Harold. "Can you see?"

"Just out of the good one. And you don't look any better. You've aged."

"Sounds like you've been up to your tricks again."

"How are things at *Lloyd's*?"

"I don't work there anymore. He finally got rid of me too."

"Where are you now?"

The bloke hesitated. He frowned.

"*The Star*," he said at last.

"You? My Lord, I never thought I'd see the day. So you must know who wrote those pieces on us?"

"It was the editor's idea," said the reporter. "His wife has some connection to Catford. I didn't want to do it, William. I swear I didn't. But I must do as I'm told. If I lose this job I don't think I'll get another one. Not at my age."

The guvnor blinked. The smile fell from his face.

"It was you?"

"I'm sorry, William. I had no choice."

"But we're friends, Harold. We started out together, learnt our trade together."

"I had no choice. The editor's an odious creature and the proprietor's on his back. But you've done something good here, I think. I'm going to try to get that into my report."

"Try? But we discovered this! The police would have done nothing if we hadn't forced their hand!"

"I'm not the editor, William. There's so many against you."

The guvnor looked at his old friend, hurt written over his face. The bloke bit his lip.

"Listen, Harold," said the guvnor at last. "I'll tell you how you can make amends. I've got a story for you. A big scandal involving an asylum and the Lambeth Poor Law Union. Nobody knows about it but us. I'll give it to you on condition your paper stops hounding us and you give us our due in your report on this case. You ask your editor. It's a great scandal. Bigger than the socialist woman who didn't want to marry. Bigger even than Mrs. Weldon. It's yours if you get that promise." He took my arm and pulled me closer. "Harold, this is my assistant, Mr. Barnett." He gave me the wink.

"We'll need ten pounds as well, sir," I told him. "To get the evidence for you."

"Ten pounds! I'll need to know what it's about for that much, Mr. Barnett."

"Talk to your editor today and meet us tomorrow," I said. "We'll tell you more then and if you don't want the story, that's fine, we'll take it elsewhere. But you'll want it."

He thought for a moment.

"Bigger than Mrs. Weldon, you say?"

"Bigger and better," said the guvnor. "Greedy men lining their pockets with money meant for the poor. Just the type of story you used to like, Harold."

The reporter frowned. Finally, he nodded. "I'll ask him."

He patted the guvnor's behind and moved off to the door.

"We've got to do something, sir," I said when he'd gone. "They're going to take Willoughby back unless we can prove who hurt him."

The guvnor nodded, staring into my eyes. His fists were clenched tight around his walking stick. He had a wild look to him. He paced over to the empty magistrate's table and looked up to the ceiling, muttering to himself.

"No!" he said, shaking his head.

He looked over at Willoughby and Digger who sat in silence next to each other. His purple lips went loose, his eye began to shine. He shook his head again, blinking back the tears. Then his face turned to anger, his mouth pinched, his brow dropped. He cracked his stick against the stone floor and paced across the front of the hall, muttering again now. Behind us, servants were bringing in hampers for some of the toffs who'd stayed seated. They were talking furiously, laughing, exclaiming. I was close to losing my rag, to turning and smashing up their bloody picnics, stamping on their glasses and terrines.

The guvnor spun round.

"I have an idea," he said, a pained look on his face. "Not a good one, but it's all I can think of. It'll be difficult. You mustn't go soft on me now, Norman. Promise, whatever happens, you won't go soft."

I nodded.

"Mr. Arrowood?" said a young woman coming down the centre aisle. She was tall, with dark, confident eyes, a bonnet, a matching blue jacket. She held out her hand. "I'm Annabel Ainsworth. Birdie's my cousin."

It was then I realized where I'd seen her before. She was the young lady in the photograph we'd had from the Barclays, the one Birdie was looking towards as they stood in the park.

"I'm very pleased to meet you, miss," he answered, unable to draw a smile on his face. "This is my assistant, Mr. Barnett."

She nodded at me.

"I was hoping to see Birdie here," she said.

"I expect she's at the farm. Did you ask the Ockwells?"

"They prevented me seeing her the last time I visited. Do you know if she's coming?"

"I doubt it. But we're on our way to the farm now, Miss Ainsworth. Would you like to share a cab?"

She smiled. "That would be perfect. I've just seen them go into the pub, so if we leave now we'll avoid them."

"Will you get one of the four-wheelers outside, miss? We'll

meet you in five minutes. There's something Mr. Barnett and I must do first."

We left Willoughby with Petleigh. He sat on the pew, Digger next to him, both in silence. They held hands. Despite all as had happened that day, I'd never seen our friend so content; even Digger had lost the sharpness to his face. The guvnor was struck by it too. He paused, a worried look on his face, and the fear I'd felt over the smile they shared returned; there was something wrong about their contentment. Something very wrong.

"What's the plan?" I asked as I followed the guvnor across the green.

"I'll explain it all on the way," he said. "But first we must persuade Edgar to deal with the dogs again."

"This should help him make his mind up," I said, pulling Lewis's pistol from my coat pocket.

The guvnor nodded. "Good. But let me try first."

The pub was jammed, a crowd at the bar jostling to get served. The landlady was out of temper, her face red, the cowboy hat gone. Her son was pouring pints for her. A new serving girl, brought in for the inquiry I supposed, was carrying a tray upstairs where the richer punters would be eating. People stood in every space, arguing about the case. The Ockwells sat in a far corner, hunched close to each other. Edgar was just inside the door.

"Not you two again," he groaned when we approached. He drained his pint quick, spilling some on his moleskin.

"I need your help for half an hour," said the guvnor. "I'll give you two shillings."

"Four."

"Three, then. Come along. I'll explain on the way."

We found the cab Miss Ainsworth had hired and set off for the farm.

"We need to bring the mastiff back to Mission Hall," the guvnor explained to Edgar. "I'm going to try something. If it works, we'll find out who hurt Digger and Willoughby."

"And how're you going to do that, exactly?" said Edgar.

"You'll find out in good time."

"I ain't doing it least you tell me."

"You must do this, or else Root'll find out about those building materials, Edgar. Worth a year in gaol, I'd say."

"Maybe more," I added. "So don't get curly with us, mate."

Edgar cursed under his breath. The guvnor turned to Miss Ainsworth.

"When's the last time you saw Birdie, miss?"

"Oh, perhaps a year ago. I've tried to see her many times since, but Aunt Martha kept putting me off, and then I heard she'd wed. They didn't invite me, nor mother." Miss Ainsworth had a clear and direct way of speaking that made you want to listen. She seemed mature beyond her years. "We couldn't understand it, and Birdie hasn't replied to any of my letters. When I read of the inquiry, I recognized the farm."

"Were you close to Birdie?" asked the guvnor.

"I love her as a sister. We grew up together, but my family moved to Brighton when I was ten. That's why I don't understand it. Birdie would never cut me out like this."

"I don't think it's her that's done it, miss," I said.

"She was going to come and live with mother and I in Brighton. We'd always talked of it: we've so much room now my brothers are gone, and she wanted to get away from Uncle Dunbar and Aunt Martha. They didn't treat her well, I'm afraid."

"That's it, Barnett," said the guvnor. "That's what she was

trying to communicate to us! I knew that picture meant something."

As we rode out to the farm, the guvnor explained to Miss Ainsworth what had been happening over the last few weeks. She listened to it all, her keen eyes wide, taking it all in.

When we stopped at the first gate, the dogs were already barking. Edgar hopped out. When he'd quieted them, we got down and approached the house. It was a bleak day, the wind whipping across the hill, the light grey and low. There was no answer at the door, no face in the window upstairs. As we approached the dairy, we heard the churn.

Miss Ainsworth hurried ahead of us. She threw open the door and there, in a stained and tattered apron, stood Birdie. She looked up from her work and stopped, her little face breaking into the brightest of smiles, a smile more warming even than her mother's. She ran over. The two cousins hugged.

"Oh, Birdie," said Miss Ainsworth.

"My Annie," said Birdie. "My dear Annie."

She began to weep, the tears filling her round, brown eyes, then Miss Ainsworth did so too. They clung to each other.

"I got wed," said Birdie, her face buried on her cousin's shoulder.

"I know."

"I'm nuts on him, Annie."

We watched them as they talked breathlessly, as they broke their embrace and embraced again, looking each other in the face, taking each other's hands. They guvnor was smiling as much as they. He patted me on the shoulder, biting back a tear of his own.

"I'm afraid we must return to Mission Hall, miss," he said at last.

"You go," she answered. "I'll walk."

"It's a long way. And cold."

"I must talk with my cousin."

"We haven't met, Miss Birdie," he said, turning to her. "I'm Mr. Arrowood. You met Mr. Barnett at the station."

"I saw you through the window," said Birdie. Her voice was slow, as if she had to think of each word. Her little face was so white and smooth beneath her red headscarf. "I showed you the picture."

"Yes, and I'm sorry we didn't understand. I must ask you directly, ma'am. Do you want to go and live with your parents? Tell me plain."

"No, sir."

"So you want to remain here?"

"I want to live with Annie."

"But, Birdie, my dear cousin," said Annabel, stroking Birdie's arm. "You live here, with your husband. This is your life now."

"Poomps wants to live with you too," answered Birdie. Her words rose and fell slow like the lap of the Thames on a calm day. "He don't like it here. They bully him. We agreed it."

"Why didn't you tell me that at the station when I asked you?" I said.

Her mouth opened and closed; her little tongue licked her lips. She looked down, a desperate unhappiness suddenly crossing her eyes.

"Rosanna," was all she said.

"You were afraid of Rosanna?" asked the guvnor.

She nodded. "She beats us."

Annabel pulled her tight again. She raised her hand to stroke Birdie's hair but Birdie gasped, pulling away.

"She's got a wound on her head," I said.

Annabel undid Birdie's headscarf and pulled it off, while

Birdie stood, eyes down, her hands pressed together across her apron. Annabel breathed in sharp. The scar on the back of Birdie's head was bigger than I remembered, an angry pink, a festering yellow, the raw flesh wet and putrid. Around it, the hair had been cut away.

"What happened to you?" she asked.

"Rosanna put it in the mangle," said Birdie, her eyes filling with tears again. "I did a blue streak on Walter's shirt. She took my hair."

"You poor thing," said Annabel. "Now listen, Birdie. You're coming with me. Both of you. You're coming to stay with me."

"And Polly?"

"Who's Polly?"

"She's Godwin's wife," I said.

"If she wants," said Annabel. "I'm going to arrange it. You must trust me, cousin. Will you do that?"

Birdie smiled again, though her eyes continued to weep. She tried to control herself but her breathing was jerky.

"Help me, Annie," she said.

Chapter Forty-Four

Edgar held the bull mastiff on the floor as we trundled along the lane in the bumpy four-wheeler. It was calm; the black skin on its face drooped below its jaw; its eyes were hooded. When it wasn't trying to kill you, that dog looked like sorrow itself.

"Shh, Toby," said Edgar over and over, running his hand along its flank. When he stopped, the dog would turn and lick his britches. "Shh," he'd say again.

As we reached the green, the guvnor told us the plan.

"No, sir," I said. "You can't do it."

"Have you got another idea?"

"I'm not helping you."

"Listen," he said, his voice hard, his eyes weary and troubled. "If we don't do something, they'll take both of them back to that infernal farm to be beaten, to be burnt, to be starved.

They can't help themselves—it's been going on too long for that, and I've tried everything I can think of. We've shown Willoughby his brother won't take him back. We've all asked him again and again. What else can we do?"

"There must be something."

"For pity's sake, can't you see I haven't any more ideas! D'you think I'm a magician? I don't like it any more than you but damn it, Barnett, I don't know what else to do!"

I found Willoughby still sat next to Digger, Petleigh stood behind talking to one of the toffs. I took his hand and led him through the kitchen and out into the side passage. It was a dirt path maybe six foot wide, a high wall on one side, the Mission Hall on the other. By the back corner of the building, a few old bins stood.

Almost as soon as we appeared, the guvnor entered from the street. Edgar came behind him, his hand around the dog's collar.

Willoughby grabbed for the kitchen door when he saw them.

"Sorry, mate," I whispered, stopping him.

He fought me, his fists swinging, horror across his face.

"Get back in, Norman!" he moaned, straining to get to the door. "Get back!"

The dog, seeing Willoughby's fear, lurched towards him. Edgar held the collar tight. It was now a few yards away, a low, threatening rumble from its throat, its lips pulling back to show its wide jaw, its yellow teeth. Saliva hung in long, swaying drips. Willoughby's panic seemed to make it angry. It barked and lurched again.

Willoughby grabbed my arm, pulling me in front of him while Edgar wrestled the dog back.

"Help me, Norman," he wailed, staring in horror at the dog from around my side. "Help me!"

He pinched my arm, using me as a shield. With his other hand he scrabbled at the door handle.

"No!" he cried, trying to climb on my back. "Get inside!"

The guvnor stepped over, took Willoughby by the shoulders, and pulled him towards the dog. The beast strained and snapped, its eyes like the devil's.

"They let him hurt you, Willoughby, didn't they?" said the guvnor.

The mastiff jumped. Willoughby screamed.

"Toby!" hissed Edgar, just managing to hold on. "Get down, boy!"

The guvnor pushed Willoughby a step closer.

"If you go back they'll hurt you again, Willoughby," he said. "You cannot go back."

"Too close!" cried Edgar, only just managing to hold back the dog. It jerked and tossed, a solid mass of angry muscle, yelping in fury, its feet scrabbling to get some hold on the dirt.

Willoughby kicked out at it. The dog snapped, catching his foot in its teeth. Willoughby screamed as it thrashed its head back and forth, jerking Willoughby's whole body with each twist and turn. The guvnor tried to pull Willoughby away but the dog's teeth were clamped on his ankle now. With each jerk of the dog's head, Willoughby's cries got more awful.

I sprang forward and gave the dog the hardest kick in its head I could. It fell on its side, stunned just long enough for me to prise its dripping, bloody jaw off Willoughby's leg.

"Get the lad back inside, you prick!" cried Edgar, falling with the dog.

But the guvnor pushed Willoughby forward again.

"Your brother doesn't want you back," he said. Willoughby, out of his wits with terror, kicked and twisted, moaned and cried. Edgar was lying over the dog now, pinning it down while it struggled to get back to its feet.

"Godwin deceived you," said the guvnor. "He doesn't love you, Willoughby. He only wants to work you. This is how he keeps you, because you're afraid."

Willoughby swung his arms out, landing his fist on the side of my face, but the guvnor still held him fast. I'd never seen such fear in my life before. Tears ran down his cheeks. He was whimpering, twisting, crying out:

"Murder! Murder!"

The guvnor pushed him once more towards the dog.

"Let him go!" I yelled.

For the first time I hated Arrowood. I hated all his bloody schemes. I hated to know that he could make a man suffer so.

The dog was on its feet again now, straining to get at Willoughby, its skin gathered on its snout, its teeth wet and yellow. An awful noise came from its throat, like a demon fighting to get out. Edgar, lying on the floor with his arms stretched out over his head, gripped its collar as it thrashed to get free.

Then, with no warning, the guvnor released Willoughby, pulled Lewis's pistol from my coat pocket, and shot the dog. It howled, falling onto its side.

"What the hell are you doing?" screamed Edgar, the dog whining and squirming in pain on the dirt path.

The guvnor stepped over, held the pistol to its head, and shot it dead.

He turned to Willoughby, who stared open-mouthed at the mastiff, his body convulsing. His nose was streaming with snot, his eyes red, his face wet.

"We're going to keep you safe, my friend," said the guvnor, his hands on Willoughby's shoulders. "I promise you that. You don't have to go back to the farm, or the asylum, or the work-house. We'll keep you safe now. Nobody will hurt you again."

Willoughby trembled violently. His breath was quick. The guvnor looked into his face.

"But you must tell us who hurt you."

Willoughby's eyes were fixed in horror on the body of the dog, the blood seeping out of the great red gash in its side and the mess of brain and bone where the crown of its head was blown off. He puked onto the dirt floor.

"Who was it?" asked the guvnor again. "Who hurt you?"

"Dad did," he whispered, then heaved over his boots.

"And did Walter also hurt you?"

Willoughby shook his head. His eyes were shut now. "Godwin."

"Thank you, my dear. We'll keep you safe, I promise."

"And Digger," said Willoughby.

The guvnor looked back at me, a frown on his face.

"Digger hurt you?" he whispered.

"Keep Digger safe."

"Yes, of course. We'll keep Digger safe too."

Arrowood took out his hankie and tried to wipe the tears and puke from our friend's face, but Willoughby twisted away.

"One more thing," he said. "Did you and Digger kill Mrs. Gillie?"

Willoughby shook his head.

The guvnor looked at him in silence, his eyebrows raised as if Willoughby was about to tell him more. Finally, he opened the kitchen door.

"Pay Mr. Winter, Norman," he said, and led our friend back into the hall.

The room was full, the magistrates just taking their seats after lunch. The guvnor talked to Sprice-Hogg. Digger was now back sitting with the Ockwells, the same angry look as always upon his face. While I took my seat next to Willoughby on the front pew, the parson banged his mallet.

"I call Mr. Krott back to the chair," he announced.

"What?" said Tasker, looking up. He raised his hand to his eye and wiped away the goo as was collecting around the angry red stye. "Not again, Reverend, please. He only repeats what you say to him. We must finish the inquiry today."

"Yes, he's had his chance," added the butcher. "He won't say."

"Mr. Krott, please come up," said Sprice-Hogg.

When the guvnor tried to take Willoughby's arm, our friend shook it off, and so I helped him to the chair instead. I stood by him for the questions, my hand on his trembling shoulder.

"Willoughby," said Sprice-Hogg softly, "will you tell us who caused those injuries on your body?"

Willoughby seemed to think for a moment. He looked around the silent hall, at all the staring faces. Then he bent forward. His eyes, still marked with tears, closed.

"Tell him, mate," I said. "Then we'll take you home."

"He's not saying," said Tasker.

"Quiet!" barked Sprice-Hogg, his white brows hooked in fury. He glared at Tasker. Then, softly: "Give us the name, Willoughby. Who hurt you?"

Willoughby swallowed.

"Dad," he said. "He do it."

"Dad?" asked Sprice-Hogg.

"Godwin Ockwell," said the guvnor. "He calls him Dad."

"Was it Mr. Godwin?" asked Sprice-Hogg.

Willoughby nodded, his eyes still shut. "Godwin do it."

It seemed like everbody in the hall started to speak at once. Godwin was on his feet, shouting something as was drowned out by the noise of the crowd. Tasker threw his pencil down, shaking his head. Sprice-Hogg pounded again and again on the table.

"He doesn't know what he's saying!" cried Godwin. "He's feeble-minded. He doesn't understand."

Willoughby turned to him.

"You do it," he said.

"No, Reverend!" cried Godwin. "This is a farce! He shouldn't even be called as a witness. He's the mind of an infant."

"Sit down, sir, or I'll have you arrested!" ordered Sprice-Hogg.

"It was Tracey Childs, sir," protested Godwin, his eyes frantic. He clutched his weak hand. "I was trying to protect him. That's why I made sure he got on that boat. Tracey was from the asylum, just as these two. A dangerous lunatic. I made sure he got on that boat. It was him that hurt them. I swear it before God."

"No," said Willoughby, twisting in the chair to look at him.

"I think I can help here, Reverend," said Tasker. "Childs did have some violent episodes in the asylum. The medical superintendent believed him cured, but they can easily lapse. There's no way of predicting."

"He did lapse," said Godwin. "But I made sure he was no danger. I protected my two workers. May the Lord be my witness, it was I that saved them."

Now the butcher spoke: "Mr. Tasker, you're the expert. What's your opinion of Mr. Krott's evidence? Seems clearer than before, but can it be trusted?"

Tasker pressed his fingers together over his lips and made a thinking face. He spoke slowly: "Idiots and imbeciles have a very uncertain understanding of events. It's the nature of the mental weakness. Their memory of people and sequences is poor and as a result they may appear convinced of something which is nothing more than a fantasy. They may also deliver the answer they think you want to hear without quite grasping what it means. In my professional opinion it would be dangerous to take the word of a mental defective over a hard-working man from a good family, at least not without a good deal of corroborating evidence."

"Well," said Rhodes. "We saw before that Mr. Krott doesn't know what he's saying. And if Childs has a history of it, then of course. He has an unstable mind, the doctor's confirmed it. Mr. Ockwell has no history of violence, has he?"

Sprice-Hogg shook his head.

"How did you discover it was Mr. Childs?" Rhodes asked Godwin.

"I came into the barn one night. Late. I caught him at it. By the look of the scars, he must have been at it for years."

"But why didn't you tell us this yesterday, Mr. Ockwell?"

"I should have had him arrested rather than put him on the boat, I know it." As Godwin spoke, Rosanna watched him closely. He was talking real careful, trying to hide the slur in his voice, and a sweat had broke over his face with the effort. "I thought he'd be better with a fresh start. He thought he was keeping them in line, thought he was doing it for me. His intellect is limited, sir, but I had faith he'd learn from his mistake. I know I should have gone to the police at the time. I didn't even tell my brother or sister about it. But you're right, Reverend, I should have come clean yesterday when I had the chance. I must apologize for that. It was wrong, but I only wanted to protect him."

"Can we return to the murder now, Reverend?" demanded

Tasker, pressing a silk handkerchief to the corner of his eye. "There's nothing we can do about Childs now."

"No!" cried the guvnor. "You can't let him get away with that! The victim's named him!"

"Be quiet, Mr. Arrowood!" ordered Sprice-Hogg. "You may step down, Mr. Krott."

"You must listen to him, sir!" protested the guvnor.

"PC Young, please take Mr. Arrowood outside."

Just then, another voice came from the other side, a singular, blurry voice that was more a stuttered groan than words.

"Eee dd…d…ddded," it seemed to say.

Everybody turned, looking where the voice came from.

Digger stood up, his eyes cold and angry.

"In a dd…d…doon-pi," he said, labouring over each sound.

"Again," said Sprice-Hogg, his face clenched, his hand to his ear. "He's what?"

"In d…doon-pet."

"In what?"

"Trrr…ay…ay…" His face was screwed up tight, his hands gripping each other as he tried to get the words out. "O…o…wii…kiiyed."

"Killed? Who killed?"

"G… K… Go… Ko'wi… G…go'wiii'…" He was breathing hard with the effort, long gaps between each bit, each sound causing him pain. "Triyss…ss…sca'e."

"No!" cried Godwin beside him.

"D…dd…d…doon…piii…pyee…"

"Dung pit?" asked Sprice-Hogg. "Are you saying there's another body there?"

Digger nodded.

Gasps filled the air.

"Why didn't you answer our questions before, Mr. Digger?" asked Sprice-Hogg.

Digger shook his head, his eyes on the floor.

"How d'you know there's another body there?"

Digger pointed to his own chest. "Sa...aaaw."

"What?"

"Sss...aw...li...li...l...a'e...go...godg...gogwii'i..."

"Don't listen to him!" cried Godwin, waving his good hand in the air in fury while the lame arm swung wretchedly by his side. "He's feeble-minded. A lunatic! They've searched the dung pit. There's no other body there!"

Petleigh rose to his feet. "It's the truth, Reverend. There was no other body in the dung pit. We searched it thoroughly for clues, I can assure you."

"But are you absolutely sure you didn't miss anything in there, Petleigh?" asked Sprice-Hogg.

"Yes, sir. That's right, isn't it, Sergeant?"

"Dug right down to the cobbles, sir," said Root.

"I see. Well." Sprice-Hogg seemed to be lost. He looked at his magistrates hopefully. "Well."

"My God!" murmured the guvnor, his eyes widening. He leant across Petleigh to speak to me. "That's it, damn it! It's Tracey, Barnett. Tracey Childs." He clutched my jacket, his eyes burning, the words coming thick and fast. "Mrs. Gillie said there were three dead children. I thought it was Polly's baby and her sister's twins. The three corn dollies. But why would Mrs. Gillie tell us that? It's been troubling me all this time. If that was all it was, why didn't she just say it outright? But it was Tracey Childs! Childs, Norman! Three dead children: Polly's baby, Birdie's stillborn, and Tracey Childs. She was telling us about Tracey's murder. That's what she wanted us to discover!"

"Why didn't she just tell us straight?" I whispered.

"She was afraid of him." He sat up, looking at Petleigh. "She said she wouldn't say any more in case something happened to her. That poor old woman stuck there all winter on her own because her horse was lame and her people were gone. Anything we told Root got around that place in no time. She must have thought she was telling us just enough to get us asking questions, but not enough for Godwin to think she knew about the murder. But she was wrong, poor woman. He must have heard she'd talked to us and decided to silence her. It was him, Petleigh. It was him!"

"But how did she know?" whispered the inspector.

"Perhaps it happened in a field and she saw it. Or perhaps Willoughby told her."

"But there wasn't any other body in the dung pit, William."

The guvnor frowned. He stared at his doughy knees. His fists clenched as they did when his mind was deep in on itself. His great hooter turned a violent purple with the effort in his brain.

Tasker was talking now, his voice confident and friendly again:

"Well, there's more than enough proof that these two men's testimony can't be trusted. Mr. Digger can hardly speak, let alone form thoughts. I believe what you see here is part confusion, part delusional monomania. Any alienist would confirm it. It's wrong to allow this to go on, Reverend. It's not fair on the family, nor is it fair on Mr. Digger."

The guvnor shook his head.

"Something's wrong," he muttered to himself. "Something's wrong. Something's wrong."

Sprice-Hogg looked across at the other magistrates. "D'you

think we need to hear from Godwin Ockwell again, gentlemen?"

"Dug right down," muttered the guvnor to himself, his face screwed up like a sheep's arse. "But what is it? Dug down..."

Rhodes shook his head.

"I think we've got the full story," said Tasker, crossing his arms over his green suit.

"Wait," said the guvnor, jumping up. He turned to Root. "Did you say you dug to the cobbles?"

"Right down to the bottom, yes we did," said the copper.

"But the barn floor's made of dirt."

"I don't know about that," said Root. "But the base of the pit is cobbled."

"You need to lift the cobbles," said the guvnor.

"Dear God, no!" exclaimed Godwin. His bowler was tilted to its side now; a bit of drool was collecting on the droopy side of his mouth. "This is persecution! The barn's already been searched! Those cobbles have been there for years. They have, haven't they, Rosanna?"

Rosanna looked up at her brother. It took a moment before she spoke.

"They have, sirs," said she. "My father put them in."

"Mr. Arrowood, please keep your mouth shut unless you're asked to speak," said Tasker, throwing a quick look our way. He adjusted his tie. "We're not here to pursue your employer's vendetta, whatever that may be."

"Thank you, sir," said Godwin, breathing hard. He looked round the crowd like he was just the right sort of fellow. "We're not on trial here, are we, Reverend?"

"It ain't true," came a voice from across the hall.

It was Edgar, standing in the kitchen doorway. He held a bit of string tied to the mastiff's collar.

"I delivered a load of cobbles to them not four month back."

Noise broke out all around. Cries and accusations. Sprice-Hogg pounded his mallet. Godwin shook his head, protesting, though he couldn't be heard above the crowd. Men stood in the aisles trying to yell their points at the magistrates. The reporters scribbled furiously.

When he'd finally got a bit of quiet back to the place, Sprice-Hogg ordered Petleigh and PC Young to go direct to the farm and dig up those cobbles.

The crowd slowly cleared from the hall, all talking, looking over at Willoughby and Digger. Godwin stared at us, then turned and followed his brother and sister.

Chapter Forty-Five

We took Digger and Willoughby back to Lewis's house, where they ate some soup then went upstairs to sleep. Willoughby hadn't forgiven the guvnor: he didn't speak nor even look at him all the way back, even when the guvnor tried to talk to him, and on the train he made sure I was stood between them. Arrowood was trying to be cheerful, but I knew it upset him.

It was late when Ettie arrived from the mission; she was tired, worried about what had happened to a young girl who'd come in, angry about the landlord they were fighting. I sometimes forgot that while we battled all day in our work, she did so herself in hers. It took her two cups of tea, a sniff of brandy, and a loosening of her corset afore she calmed. Only then did the guvnor fill her in on what had happened at the inquiry. She listened carefully but didn't ask her usual questions. Tonight she was too tired.

"Sprice-Hogg came good, then, did he?" asked Lewis.

"I sent him a note last week praising his book on the bells of Kent and Surrey," said the guvnor. "I suspect that helped. But he's certainly a different fellow when there's no bottle upon the table."

"Well, William," said Ettie, getting to her feet. "It's time to go home: our first night back in Coin Street. Lewis, you've been so kind. I can't thank you enough for what you've done."

"I'll miss having you here," said Lewis. "And thank you for fixing that window."

I could see Lewis meant it. He'd be lonely once they were gone. I'd thought a lot about his offer to lodge me over the last few days and wanted to say yes, but if there was something of Mrs. B still lingering in our room I didn't want to desert her. Or maybe, I wondered, maybe I just didn't want to get past her death.

"I'll fetch you a cab, Ettie," said the guvnor. "Norman and I have one more job to do tonight."

A few hours later we were outside the Lambeth workhouse on Renfrew Road. It was a place I knew too well: my ma and me had been in and out of that place years ago, after she'd lost her housekeeping job. That was a long, cruel winter, full of cold and hunger, and I'd promised her then I'd do anything I could to never see her in the workhouse again. We'd got out, all right, and I didn't much like being back. It was a place thick with bad memories.

The Poor Law Union offices were in the administration block, a great brick building as separated the men's and women's accommodation. A weak glow of light flickered upstairs in the porter's lodge, but all the other windows were black. We crept round to the back, where we found the door to the dining hall: I had my betty out and was inside in minutes, the lock as poor as those the building served. It smelled of boiled bones and damp and we heard vermin all about, getting at the crumbs jammed in the crevices and cracks of the long room. The smell carried things I hadn't thought of for years: the watery soup floating with chewy grease; the woman with the red eye who tried to steal my bread; the old bloke who touched me under the table as he whistled.

We hurried over the tacky floor, the rats scattering before us, and into a corridor where the guvnor lit his candle. There we paused, checking for noises. We heard the clank of heating pipes but nothing more. The smell was now of wax and bleach, the walls washed with grey. We passed the chapel, the boardroom, and then found the relief offices. Again we stood listening. The vermin; the pipes; the bells of St. Gabriel's rang the half hour. We found a door signed Treasurer, another Chief Medical Officer, then the one we wanted: Relieving Officer.

The guvnor held his candle to the lock. A few minutes of jiggling to find the catch and we were in. Shelves lined three of the walls, filled with ledger after ledger. A wide desk stood in the middle of the room, a smaller one in a corner. The other wall was whitewashed, scuffed, the paint blistered. I lit my own candle and we set to work.

After a few minutes, the guvnor pulled out a few ledgers and put them on the desk. He picked his hooter as he turned the pages. He farted.

"Right," he said, snapping the book shut. "These are the payments, but the names aren't listed. We need the records of pauper lunatics."

He put the pile of books into his carpetbag, then turned back to the shelves.

"You think it might have been Digger and Willoughby that killed her, don't you, sir?" I whispered.

"They're hiding something, Barnett," he said. "I'm sure of it. But now we need to search."

Five minutes passed. A bit of shouting started up in one of the accommodation blocks, men's voices. It went on for a few minutes, then it was quiet. We took down ledger after ledger. Then I found it, a thick black book marked *Register of Lunatics*, and next to it *Register of Imbeciles*.

The guvnor opened the lunatic register on the desk, flipping through until he found the pages marked *Persons Chargeable to the Parish of Lambeth in Caterham Asylum*.

After a minute or two, he shut the ledger, put it in the carpetbag, and opened the *Register of Imbeciles*, quickly finding the pages for Caterham.

"Willoughby Krott, 1889."

His breath drifted in the flickering candlelight and disappeared into the dark. I moved from foot to foot on the wooden floor, my hands under my arms. He found Tracey and Birdie, then dropped the ledger in his bag. Next he pulled out the book marked *Financial Statements, 1894-5*, had a quick look, and that went in the bag too.

Another few minutes and we'd found all we wanted. We left the office, crept down to the dining hall and out into the night.

It was after two in the morning by the time I unlocked my door, the first time in days I'd been back. I took off my coat, my hat, my boots, and got straight into bed. Though I'd just about had my fill of other people, a deep and painful loneliness overcame me as soon as I felt the weight of the cold blankets on my body. I pulled her shawl over and held it to my nose. The scent of lavender was gone, and I knew that what-ever remained of her was finally dissolved into the air. Every corner, every crevice and crack was empty. A biting draught crept under the door and through the holes in the window-frame, getting inside me, running through my blood. I drifted in and out of sleep, never getting comfortable. In the darkest hours before dawn, I decided it was time to leave. Tomorrow I'd tell Lewis I'd take up his offer of lodgings. I couldn't live like this anymore.

Chapter Forty-Six

⬥ ————————— ⬥

Next morning, I met the guvnor in Coin Street, at his old rooms behind the pudding shop. All around were his possessions in boxes and piles. I sat with him as he went over the ledgers, writing notes on loose leaves of paper. His gout was playing up, and he grumbled and complained, and stood and sat, demanding hot water for his feet, then cold. He took Varalettes and laudanum, and every time he heard a noise in the pudding shop he stopped, thinking it was news of the search. It was like being caged with an angry hen.

A wire from Petleigh arrived just as he'd finished going through the Poor Law Union records. "They're still breaking the cobbles," he told me. "He'll call at Lewis's after six."

"Why not here?"

"Idiot's forgotten we've moved back. It doesn't matter: Ettie has another case to pick up and I wanted to talk to Digger and Willoughby again."

"What are we going to do with them?" I asked.

He said nothing as he packed the ledgers and notes into his carpetbag. Though it had been six months since the fire, you could still smell the smoke in his little parlour, mixed up with the smell of puddings baking in the front of the building. The orange cat appeared and leapt upon the couch as if it had lived there all its life.

"Tell me, Norman," he said at last. "Did you feel anything when they sat together in the inquiry?"

"I felt they had a secret," I said.

"Yes. But why? Why did you feel that?"

"It was the way they looked at each other when Digger opened his shirt. It gave me the shivers."

He sighed. "I felt it too. But then when they sat together it all changed. There was a sense of peace. They mean a lot to each other, those two: I wonder if that's one reason Willoughby wanted to go back to that hell."

There was something tender in the guvnor's expression as he spoke, a look I'd become used to.

"Have you heard from Isabel?" I asked, thinking that was what was on his mind.

"Her lawyer died two days ago," he answered, prising open a tin of cream crackers. "Poor fellow. So young."

"Weren't you hoping for this?"

"You know, while he was ill I could safely hope. But now it's happened I find I'm afraid." He took a bite of two crackers, staring at the vase his wife left behind when she fled. "I'm afraid that now she's free she still might not return. Then I'll have no hope left."

"Let her grieve, William. It can take a long time."

He smiled. "She's married to me, yet she grieves for another man."

He shook his head hard, as if trying to get rid of his thoughts.

"I'm ashamed I wished him dead, Norman," he said at last. "I don't know what got into me."

We met Harold in Willows' at two. Outside was cold and wet; inside was noisy and warm.

"Have you got the money?" I asked before we started.

"You'll have it if the story's worth it," the newspaperman answered. There were flecks of soot in his neat brown beard. "So tell me about this fraud."

"Four people on that farm are ex-inmates of the Caterham asylum," said the guvnor. "Willoughby Krott, Thomas Digger, Polly Gotsaul, she's Godwin's wife, and Birdie Barclay, Walter's wife. Tracey Childs makes five. The magistrate Henry Tasker arranged for them to come to the farm. He's Chair of the Committee of Visitors at the asylum. At first I thought they might be running a private asylum there, but I checked with the Lunacy Commission and it isn't registered."

Harold nodded, lighting a cigarette.

"All five are certified as pauper lunatics through the Lambeth Poor Law Union. Here's their *Register of Lunatics*."

The guvnor pulled it from the bag and found the page. He pointed.

"*Gotsaul, Polly*. Admitted 1890. Look at the discharge column. It's empty." He turned to the pages for male lunatics. "And here. *Digger, Thomas*. Admitted 1889. Nothing in the discharge column. This other book's the *Register of Imbeciles*. You'll find the same for Willoughby Krott, Tracey Childs and Birdie Barclay. All with an admission date to the asylum but no discharge date. Now, for each pauper sent to Caterham, the Union pays four and six a week for their upkeep. We've managed to obtain the record of payments to Caterham asylum from the Lambeth Poor Law Union over the last few years." The guvnor lifted the carpetbag to show him the ledgers.

"Where did you get them?" asked Harold, putting on his spectacles and looking through the bag.

The guvnor tapped his liverish nose. He pulled out a black ledger.

"This book lists the actual payments for each pauper lunatic and imbecile to Caterham for over the last fifteen years. Let me show you who they paid for in November and December just past."

He opened the book and put it on the table. He pointed his finger, wrinkled and grimy, at a name near the top.

"Polly Gotsaul. She's been living on the farm for at least three years, yet here she is in the book. The Union's paying the asylum as if she's still a patient."

The guvnor went through the pages, showing him the names: Childs, Digger, Barclay, Krott.

"All five of them living on the farm while the Union's paying Caterham for their upkeep."

"An error, William," said Harold, pulling his watch out of his pocket. "Look, I have to get to Catford to see if they've found that body. Is this it?"

"We've also seen the records in Caterham asylum. Not one of those five is recorded as discharged. Officially they're all still inmates of the asylum."

"Spell it out, William, please," said Harold, stubbing his cigarette in the can. "I need to go."

"There's a conspiracy between at least three people. Dr. Crenshaw, Medical Superintendent of the asylum, Waller Proctor, the Relieving Officer of the Poor Law Union, and Henry Tasker. Proctor sends pauper lunatics to Caterham and is responsible for providing a list to the treasurer each month for payments. It's also he that confirms those patients are at the asylum. The next step is at Caterham. Crenshaw identifies pauper lunatics there with no family or whose family wish to be rid of them, and, if he's able, moves them out. Tasker's the arranger. He's in a perfect situation to do this, he's Chair of the Committee of Visitors and therefore responsible for confirming patient lists and numbers. He's also a farmer with contacts in that community. The farms are desperate for workers. There's a severe shortage. Wages are just too low."

"Well, well," murmured Harold, a smile slowly growing on his face.

"Crenshaw doesn't record them as discharged from the asylum and so the payments from the Union continue. Each month the asylum receives money for patients that aren't there. With a little crafty accounting, the excess disappears somewhere between the ledgers. A good bookkeeper would be able to spot how it's done. That would leave the money for the missing inmates to be shared between the three of them."

Harold lit another cigarette.

"How d'you know it was Proctor?"

"He suggested to Willoughby's brother and Birdie's parents that he could classify Willoughby and Birdie as pauper lunatics if they paid him a bribe of twenty pounds. Neither family was poor enough to qualify, but it meant they'd not have to pay private patient fees to the asylum. That in itself is crooked: it drains money that could be used to assist real paupers. But it also increases the number of so-called paupers in Caterham who could then be farmed out. I suspect he offered this arrangement to the families of those he thought easy to marry off or most able to work. But, as we've seen with Digger and Willoughby, because these workers aren't protected by anyone, they're ripe for exploitation."

"How d'you know the other two are involved?"

"Crenshaw receives the payments. Tasker and Crenshaw are both responsible for signing off patients when they enter and leave. But this is what convinced me of the conspiracy: Crenshaw caught us in the asylum offices examining the records a few nights ago, yet he didn't report it to the police. His coachman told us that early the next morning, Crenshaw took an unplanned trip, something he never does. First he called at Tasker's farm, and then at the Lambeth Poor Law Union."

Harold nodded. "How much money's involved?"

"Five people in one year makes fifty-eight pounds ten," said the guvnor. "Over three years nearly a hundred and eighty pounds, but I'm sure some of them have been there longer. It's hundreds of pounds, anyway. A good sum. And if Tasker's doing it for one farm, what's the chance he's doing it for others? It's quite a story, Harold. People love a scandal in an asylum, but this one involves fraud on a grand scale, a magistrate, the Poor Law Union. Think of the outrage!"

Harold laughed. He sat back on the bench, crossing his arms. He laughed again.

"I'll give you these ledgers on condition you don't reveal your source. What we've done in getting them could land us in trouble. I've written all the details you need here." The guvnor handed him a battered yellow envelope. "You hand over the ledgers to the Lunacy Commission this afternoon and publish the story tomorrow. Then go to the police just to make sure the Commissioners do their work."

"Agreed."

"Your editor promises to cease denouncing us?"

"He does."

"Then there's just the matter of the money," I said.

Chapter Forty-Seven

"We found a body," said Petleigh as he entered the parlour that evening. It was close to seven. He was frozen through, his lips blue, mud spattered over his precious boots and up his perfect britches. He nodded at Ettie, a sudden crease in his brow: she looked right through him. "There was an old dung pit underneath the cobbles, just as you thought, William. It took most of the day to raise it. It's a young man, Tracey Childs we assume, quite decomposed. The police surgeon thinks his windpipe was crushed. Godwin was picked up boarding a steamer at Dover this afternoon. We've charged him with the murder."

"Thank you," said the guvnor.

Ettie took Lewis's spare pipe from the mantel, put a speck of tobacco in it, and set it alight. The guvnor watched on, astonished.

"What are you doing, Sister? You don't smoke."

"I used to," she said, letting puffs of smoke out the side of her mouth. "I need a calmative."

"Are Willoughby and Digger still here?" asked Petleigh.

"Resting upstairs," said Lewis.

"Will Godwin be charged with false imprisonment?" asked the guvnor.

"No. They were free to leave. God knows why they didn't."

"They were brutalized, Petleigh. Look what he did to Tracey. I assume you'll charge him with mistreatment at least?"

"That would rely on their testimony, which any good lawyer'll demolish. He'll hang for the murder of Tracey, though. Him telling us he'd seen the boy sail off on the steamer seals it, I think. We'll check the shipping company books tomorrow: I expect there'll be no record of a ticket sold for Tracey Childs. Godwin also bought the cobbles at just the time he disappeared."

"What about Walter?"

"There's no suggestion he was involved. He seems as shocked as anyone."

"Rosanna?"

"No evidence."

"She didn't know about the murders," said the guvnor. "It was clear from her reaction at the inquiry."

"She's a brute," said Ettie. "She enjoyed pushing my hand in the sterilizing fluid. Birdie was terrified of her, and God only know what she's done to Polly. I wish you could arrest her, Inspector, she's quite as guilty of mistreatment as Godwin. Violence must be in their family line."

"The Chief Inspector's decided we can't pursue mistreatment charges," said Petleigh. "I'm sorry, Ettie. It's just too difficult to secure a conviction."

"I knew you'd say that," said Ettie, revealing a bitterness

to Rosanna I hadn't seen before. "She walks around as if she's God's greatest servant, but really she's a tiger in a cage. D'you know about her past, Inspector?"

Petleigh tilted his head.

"She had two chances of escaping that farm, marriage and medical training, and she lost them both. Not through her own fault, through bloody bad luck. But she hasn't the goodness or the courage to turn the other cheek and allow Providence to strike her again. Instead she takes out all her disappointment on those two women because they cannot fight back. We must make sure they get away."

"We will, Sister," said the guvnor. "Miss Ainsworth won't be put off this time."

Still standing, Petleigh took a brandy from Lewis and lit his cigar. When he'd got a good blaze on it, he spoke: "Well, they'll be safe now, and at least Godwin'll get his punishment. It took some doing, but we got there in the end."

"*We* got there?" spluttered the guvnor.

Petleigh swallowed his brandy and stepped closer to the fire.

"Give Inspector Petleigh his due, William," said Ettie coldly. "He's done a good deal on this case."

"But—"

I put my hand on his arm, stopping him once again. We needed Petleigh then and we'd need him in future. Even if he hadn't solved the case, he'd helped us.

"Of course he has," said the guvnor at last. "We all have. Ettie and Neddy too."

The gas lamps flickered as a gust of wind outside rattled the windows. Ettie put the pipe in the ashtray and her hand over her mouth.

"Lewis," she said, "may I have another brandy?"

He brought over the decanter.

"Edgar told us how you got Willoughby to talk," said Petleigh. "That was quite a trick, William."

"There was no trick," said the guvnor. "Now, how about another drink, Inspector?"

"Well, it worked," said Petleigh.

"That's enough, Petleigh," snapped the guvnor.

"What did you do?" asked Ettie, her eyes narrow with suspicion.

"Nothing."

"William. What did you do?"

"Nothing. Now, who'd like another brandy?"

"How dare you hide things from me!" exclaimed Ettie. "I risked my life for this case. You tell me, Inspector."

The guvnor rose from his chair with a groan and went to the outhouse. By the time he returned, Petleigh'd described what happened in the side passage of Mission Hall the day before.

"That was unforgivable," she said. "He must have been terrified."

"It was all I could think of," said the guvnor sharply. "I couldn't reason with him, and God knows I tried. Words weren't enough, you saw that yourself. I had to get through to him some other way, some way he would feel it in his heart. I had to take him into the fear and show him we'd protect him. And if we'd protect him from the dog, I hoped he'd understand we'd protect him from Godwin."

"You planned to kill that innocent creature." She drained her mug and put it on the side table. "It's odious, Brother."

"I didn't plan it. All I meant to do was frighten Willoughby, but when I saw his terror I felt such rage. Rage as I'd never felt before. I lost control." He gulped at his drink, his hand trembling. His voice went low. "There's something ill with me, Sister. There always has been. When I see fear, when I see suffering, I feel anger. And I confess, when I shot that dog I felt relief just as Willoughby did. But I didn't plan to do it, Ettie. Something inside me made the decision."

"You mean you don't know what it was?" asked Ettie. "Then let me tell you, shall I? It was your desire to punish Godwin. And it was the instinct for violence inside you."

"That's too simple, Ettie."

"Admit it, Brother. It might be buried, you may choose to ignore it, but the craving for violence *is* inside you. I've known you for too long for you to deny it. I'll wager you had a thrill when you pulled the trigger."

The guvnor looked at her coldly.

"There was more to it than that," he said at last. "But it worked. Killing the dog was a symbol of breaking his chains. Willoughby finally understood, perhaps not through his intellect, but through his emotions. And sometimes, Ettie, there's no choice but to commit a smaller sin to avenge a larger."

"You could have tried something else."

"I didn't know what else to do."

I watched them argue, still wondering how he had it in him to be so cruel. The terror we put poor Willoughby through was no better than torture, and I'd never know if there was another way.

"You act like you're a god," she said. "When you're just a selfish little man."

Though she was angry with the guvnor, her eyes glanced at Petleigh as she spoke, and I knew what she said was really meant for him. Petleigh knew it too, for he coloured up and looked away.

The guvnor pursed his lips and sighed.

"I know, dear Sister." He shook his head, his eyes glassy like he was dizzy. "I know what I am."

★ ★ ★

Almost the moment Petleigh left, Willoughby and Digger came down the stairs.

"They find Tracey?" Willoughby asked me as they stepped into the parlour. His eyes were tight, nervy. He didn't look at the guvnor. "They got him?"

"Yes, they found him, Willoughby," said the guvnor. "Godwin's been arrested for murder."

"He been arrested?" asked Willoughby, still looking at me.

"Yes," I said. "He's in gaol."

Digger breathed out long and slow, a tremble to his shoulders. He gripped Willoughby's arm. Willoughby's eyes fell to the rug as if he was sad. They didn't seem to know what to do.

"Sit," said the guvnor.

They didn't move.

"Come," said Ettie. "We need to talk about this."

She guided them to the couch by the fire. The guvnor poured them each a mug of brandy and handed it to them.

"How do you feel?" asked the guvnor.

Neither of them spoke.

"Willoughby, how do you feel?" he asked again.

They both drank.

The guvnor sighed, and I could see he needed Willoughby to forgive him before he could forgive himself. He opened another bottle from a box on the floor and filled our glasses. Our friends drank again. Willoughby coughed.

"Ain't had brandy for a while, have you, mate?" I asked.

"I like it," he said. His face started to soften. The guvnor poured them both more.

"Are you sure you should be giving them so much?" asked Ettie. "They're not used to it."

The guvnor ignored her.

"Drink up, gentlemen. You deserve a bit of goodness after all you've been through. Enjoy it."

Willoughby took a big slurp.

"Digger, please drink," said the guvnor. "I want to see you enjoy it."

Digger had a sip. He coughed, and now his scowl softened a little too.

"Have more," said the guvnor.

They drank again. He poured another big lug into each cup.

"William, they'll get drunk," protested Ettie. With the brandy she'd had, and with Petleigh departed, a rosy glow had returned to her cheeks, and the tiredness around her eyes had quite gone. Since she'd taken my hand in the carriage that night, I felt something frightening wash through me just seeing her, something that touched only the better parts of me. But then her grey eyes lingered on my face, and the shame I felt when she pulled her hand from mine returned.

"Why didn't you talk before, Digger?" asked the guvnor.

"Dd...d...dow...d...o..." stuttered Digger. It was painful to watch him try to speak. He was working so hard, his jaw clenched, his hands in a fist. But it was impossible to make out any of the words.

"I'm sorry," said the guvnor. "I can see how difficult you find it. I shouldn't have asked you."

"He don't like it," said Willoughby. "Tease him. People do. Copy."

The guvnor smiled at Willoughby, happy he was talking to him again. Digger took another drink. He coughed again.

"Why didn't you ever leave, Willoughby?" asked Ettie.

"Said he find me." He pointed to his face with its Mongolian eyes, its tongue too thick for his mouth. "Got this, see. He find me. Dad do."

"What about you, Digger? You could have run away."

Willoughby was about to answer for him when Digger took his arm.

"F...ff...ray..." He was straining to make his voice clear, taking big breaths, his face turning scarlet with the effort. "F...fro...f...fren...uh...ss."

"Friends," said Willoughby. "That's us."

He put his arm over Digger's shoulder.

Digger drained his cup. The guvnor stepped over and poured them more brandy. As he sat, Ettie snatched the bottle from his hand and poured herself another.

Lewis opened his cigar case. Digger and Ettie shook their heads, but Willoughby was happy to take one. He was moving lazy now from the brandy, like he was half-dreaming. An odd smile sat on his freckled face. When the cigars were lit, the guvnor leant forward and took Willoughby's hand.

"I'm not proud at what I did, my dear friend," he said. "Will you forgive me? I saw no other way to save you."

Willoughby swallowed, the cigar already gone out in his hand. He scratched the thin, blond hair on his chin.

"Bad man, Mr. William," he said, his words soft from the booze. He sat back in the chair, his head against the antimacassar, looking at the yellowed ceiling. He seemed at peace. "Got us safe now."

Digger rose. He clutched the arm of the chair as if he might fall, then staggered out the door. We heard the heavy boots that Lewis had borrowed him plod up the stairs.

"Willoughby's been helping me around the house," said Lewis.

"Have," said Willoughby, a smile returning to his broad and beautiful face. The row of black stumps in his mouth only seemed to add to his beauty. The guvnor gave him another light of his cigar. "I like it. Do the fire, do sweeping."

"Mary Ann hasn't come then, Lewis?" I asked.

Lewis shook his head. "Not since I was stupid enough to ask for her hand."

"Did you send for her?"

"Neddy took a note. No reply."

"Oh, dear," said the guvnor. "It seems we'll have to get Petleigh to dig up that dung pit again, Norman."

We laughed, even Willoughby though I wasn't sure he caught the joke. The guvnor took his hand and squeezed it. He leant close to him, looking him in the eye, laughing.

"You're a fast one, my friend." He patted Willoughby on the shoulder. "You've done well. Very well."

"Happy," said Willoughby. He took a puff on his cigar and coughed; he put the mug to his lips, but it was empty.

"You must have been afraid you'd be caught," said the guvnor. "But you're safe now. Both of you. We won't tell anyone. You have my word. Your secret's safe with us."

"Safe now," said Willoughby. His tongue came out from between his cracked lips and rounded his mouth.

"You must have been scared those dogs would bark. Digger was trying to tell me before but I couldn't catch what he was saying. Did he say a barrow?"

"Barrow," said Willoughby, nodding. His head swayed a bit as the brandy took effect proper. The smile had gone, and sadness made his thin eyes sparkle. "It was dark. Get up the hill. Digger said."

"Godwin must have been wild. He didn't suspect you?"

"Got us out looking. Couldn't find her." His voice rose now. *"Couldn't find her, Dad!"*

"He got you out looking!" cried the guvnor in delight. "And he didn't know it was you!"

"He was cross."

"Whose plan was it, my dear?" asked the guvnor, holding a match out for Willoughby again. "Was it you?"

"Digger said."

"Was it your plan, Willoughby?"

He shook his head. "Digger plan. He tell me."

"You must have been very sad when you found her body."

"Sad." He swallowed, and his eyes shut for a moment. "She's dead. My friend. Dad do it."

"You've been so brave, Willoughby. So very brave. But who were you going to give the tooth to?"

"Edgar," said Willoughby with a shrug. "Or butcher cart. Digger say someone come. Or you, Mr. William."

"Well, it was lucky Neddy was there. Here, let me take that cigar from you before the ash falls." He put Willoughby's cigar in the ashtray. "Tell me, how did you know it was Godwin who killed Tracey?"

"Put him in dung pit. He thought we sleeping. We watching. He dig it."

"Why did he do it?"

"Run away. Tracey." Willoughby's lips trembled. "Too hard. All work. He had enough. A boy. A boy, Mr. William. Seventeen year. My friend. Dad find him."

He wiped his eyes, and we sat in silence for a few moments. Eventually, he got up and staggered off to the outhouse.

"Well?" demanded Ettie. "Are you going to tell us what that was about?"

"There was a moment in the inquiry when they looked at each other and something passed between them," said the guvnor. "A secret. I felt a sudden horror, as did Norman. We both worried it was really them who killed her. I've been going over the details ever since, trying to fathom what it could be. We knew her body was buried in the pit. We knew the killer returned to the site and cleared up the broken flowers. Why? To avoid there being evidence of a scuffle, so that the police would assume she'd just abandoned her camp. Yes, that would fit. But if the killer had been so careful to carry the body up that damned hill to hide in the barn, then why didn't they also hide the broken flowers and the cat at the same time? It's not impossible they'd overlook one, but surely not both. And then it occurred to me. What if the person who buried the body wasn't the person who killed her? What if the murder was done in a fit of fury, the killer fleeing the scene? And what if, later, when the killer had got their senses back, they returned to the camp to hide the body, only to find it gone. What if Willoughby and Digger discovered the dead body? After all, it was they who visited her most often. What if they carried it up to the dung pit?"

"But why?" asked Ettie.

"To bring Godwin to justice. It was Digger's plan—he's sharper than he seems from his speech. He must have thought if they could lead the police to her body in the dung heap, then they'd also find Tracey's. Their only problem would be how to alert the police without giving themselves away. Showing the tooth to the Winter brothers was one way, but it would have been risky. That was when they had their only stroke of luck. You and Neddy arrived, Sister."

"There's no such thing as luck, Brother. It was the good Lord."

"Are you sure they didn't kill her?" I asked. "Willoughby might just be hiding it."

"What do you want to believe, Norman?"

"That it was Godwin."

"So believe it."

"Truth doesn't go that way, William," I said.

"That's exactly how it goes. Which of us knows another perfectly? Eventually, we must decide who we trust."

"So, let me get this clear," said Lewis slowly. "You felt Willoughby and Digger might have murdered Mrs. Gillie. That was the horror you felt, but you decided to ignore your emotions and look at it logically?"

"In a nutshell."

"Like Sherlock Holmes might do?" asked Lewis.

Ettie laughed.

"Just like Holmes!" she exclaimed.

When the guvnor realized he'd been trapped, he scowled.

"It was my emotions that alerted me that some further thinking was needed. It's not the same."

"Oh please, Bro—"

"It's not the same and I'm not going to discuss it further," he barked.

Ettie and Lewis smiled at each other, and we sat in silence until Willoughby returned. He stood in the doorway, watching us.

"Sidney needs a bloke to work in his stables," I said. "I thought maybe you'd like it, Willoughby. Looking after his horses."

"Oh yes, Norman." He rubbed his calloused hands together, a look of glee on his face. "I love stables, I do."

It made you glad helping the fellow, I can tell you. I felt a great smile breaking out in my heart.

"Mrs. Button's agreed for Digger to lodge with her next door," said Lewis.

"Ah, excellent," said the guvnor. "We'll need to find him work, though."

"Willoughby's staying here, Norman," said Lewis. "I forgot to tell you. He's going to take the spare room, help me out around the house."

"Oh," I said. "Good."

I tried to hide my disappointment, but he must have caught it.

"Oh, Norman, I'm sorry," he said. "I assumed because you didn't say anything you'd decided not to—"

"No, Lewis, it's me who should say sorry. I was going to tell you I'd decided to stay in The Borough. What with the case and so on, I just forgot."

Lewis relaxed. "Good. Good."

I took a puff of my cigar, and tried to hold the smile on my face. It was only right. Willoughby needed it more than me.

"You'll be happy here, Willoughby," I said, aware of Ettie watching me.

"Happy here," he said. "I like it."

His eyelids were falling. He yawned.

"You need some sleep," said Ettie.

"Go see Digger," he said. "He's sleeping now. Dreaming about Miss Birdie."

We wished him goodnight and he climbed the stairs.

"They're so close, those two," said the guvnor.

"They've been through a war together," I said.

Lewis put his cigar out in the can. "What I still don't understand," he said, "is that even when Willoughby was safe here, when he had the police and magistrates listening to him, he still wouldn't say who hurt him."

"Bondage isn't just a matter of violence," said the guvnor. "Sometimes love's involved. And sometimes it's easier if someone else frees you."

"Is that from one of your books?" he asked.

He shook his great, gnarly head.

"No," he said, glancing at Ettie. "From father."

Ettie's eyes blazed as she stood.

"It's late, William. We must get home."

Chapter Forty-Eight

The next day I took a downtrain to Catford and walked out to the grove of bare trees where Mrs. Gillie's caravan still stood. The sun was shining, the sky a painful blue in the freezing wind. I tidied away her cooking things and stacked them by her bed, then took her will from the black jar to send to Ida Gillie. I padlocked the door and turned to have a final look before leaving. The caravan was bright and pretty in the brown and grey of the January trees. As I gazed at it, I thought I heard her cackle somewhere in the trees. A sudden fury arose in me, and I picked up a stone from her firepit and hurled it with all my might at the caravan. It bounced off the slatted wood and fell onto the frozen ground. Then there was silence.

Harold was as good as his word: *The Star* carried the story of the conspiracy on its second page. He sent a note to the guvnor in the afternoon saying the Lunacy Commission had agreed to investigate payments from the Lambeth Poor Law Union to Caterham Asylum, and that he'd submitted all the details to the police. It felt like finally the case was closed.

"It's only a shame he couldn't give our names," said the guvnor, taking a bowl of mutton soup from Rena. We were in Willows', early afternoon. He'd bought five newspapers and they sat in a pile next to him. "Still, we'll get credit for Godwin's arrest. Better cases now, Norman, you can be sure of that. More money, regular work. And that blooming Holmes'll see there's a rival in London."

He took a few slurps of soup.

"Delicious, Rena!" he called to her. He was in a better mood than he'd been in for weeks.

I smiled. He was delaying reading the court reports, like a child delays the best part of the meal. He'd been ignored too long, but now he'd get the recognition he deserved. His eyes were bright with excitement, his face shining with pride.

"Well?" I said with a chuckle. "Aren't you going to see what they say?"

He turned the pages of *The Star* to find the column on the Mission Hall Inquiry. I picked up the *The Illustrated Police News* and quickly found its report. It described "one of the witnesses" revealing Willoughby's scars. It described Willoughby blaming Godwin. There was an illustration of Digger pulling up his shirt and showing his wounds, but no mention of Arrowood. I took up *The Daily Chronicle*. In the reporter's summary, the guvnor featured once, as a witness.

I looked up to see his great, fleshy face downturned, his eyes running over the article in *The Star*, ever more concerned. His mouth was open like he was going to be sick.

"That bloody dog! He doesn't say what we did, Barnett!"

"Most of what we did was somewhere else, sir," I said.

In a fury, he screwed up the paper.

It was the same in *The Telegraph* and *The Standard*. By the time he reached for *The Daily Chronicle*, he was almost weeping. I took his hand to stop him, shaking my head.

"Same story," I said.

He looked at me, dazed. His eyes were blinking fast.

"What. Nothing?"

"Let's get a proper drink, sir," I said, helping him up before he had a proper fit.

Over the next few months, the Lunacy Commission found one hundred and eighty-seven pauper lunatics registered as living in Caterham but living on farms in Surrey, Kent and Hampshire. The fraud went back eleven years and involved the theft of over £24,000 of Poor Law Union money. A small fortune. Waller Proctor was the first to be charged. He turned Queen's evidence, giving up Crenshaw and Tasker. It wasn't only labourers and dairymaids—there were a dozen other asylum wives married off to poor farmers too. Turns out it isn't hard to persuade a family with money troubles to take a feeble-minded wife with the promise of a small monthly fee and a maid for life.

In April, Godwin was convicted of murder in the Old Bailey. By then, the Ockwell farm was sold and Rosanna had emigrated to Canada, where she had a cousin. We heard later they'd set up a home for distressed women. Birdie and Walter went to live in Brighton with Annabel Ainsworth. Within a few months the Barclays had chiselled more than half Birdie's inheritance money out of her to pay for their house, but it didn't matter. Birdie was happy now.

Ettie even found a place for Polly in the refuge, where her

corn dollies continued to go everywhere with her. There she worked with the other women, who accepted her silence. She helped some of them look after their own little babies, and slowly, over time, she began to weep less often.

Godwin Ockwell was hung in Newgate Prison on 11 August. It should have been a solemn day for us but by then we were on a different case, and in a world of horror even worse than the Ockwell farm.

★ ★ ★ ★ ★

Historical Notes and Sources

Diagnostic terms

Throughout history, many of the terms used to describe mental health conditions and cognitive disabilities have passed into common use as insults. In this book, I've used the official and colloquial terms of the late Victorian period. Official labels included 'idiot' and 'imbecile' (for people with learning, developmental and intellectual disabilities), and 'insane' and 'lunatic' for those with mental health conditions.

'Idiots' and 'imbeciles' were either distinguished by age of onset ('idiots' were thought to have the condition from birth while 'imbeciles' acquired their disability at some point in their lives) or by degree of disability ('idiots' having more severe forms of impairment than 'imbeciles'). Intellectual disabilities (leaning disabilities in the UK) were also referred to as 'amentia.' What we now call Down's syndrome had recently been identified by John Langdon Down of the Earlswood Asylum. Down noted similarities between the facial features of people with this condition and people from the Mongolian regions of the world, and named it the 'Mongolian type of idiocy.' He believed that 'feeble-minded' people were often a 'retrogression' from the race of their parents to another race, and claimed he could also identify 'idiots and imbeciles' in Earlswood of the Ethiopian (who he called 'white negroes'), Malay and indigenous American varieties, all born to white European parents. The term 'Down's syndrome' only began to be used in the 1960s.

'Monomania' was a term commonly used by experts in the second half of the nineteenth century to describe a type of 'insanity' where the person's mental functions and/or behaviour was affected in one area only, with no effect in other areas. This sets it apart from dementia and amentia, for example, where it was thought the mind in general was affected. Versions of monomania still remain in current terminology, for example in pyromania (fire-starting), kleptomania (stealing), nymphomania (sexual addiction) and dipsomania (alcoholism). According to Esquirol, 'intellectual monomania' affected beliefs (delusions), convictions and opinions relating to one topic in particular (e.g. the royal family; religion; being watched by the police). 'Affective/emotional' or 'instinctive monomania' was when the person was considered unable to control one emotion or instinct (e.g. nymphomania; suicidal urges; intense fear of death; chronic jealousy; anger; pride). Depending on the diagnostic scheme used, 'emotional monomania' was also called 'moral insanity' because it affected the person's moral sense and their behaviour.

Mental health diagnosis was hotly debated during this period, and there were differences of opinion among experts as to terminology and diagnostic schemes. Diagnostic systems in Britain were developing, informed by ideas from Europe and North America. As a result, experts might well use different words and disagree over diagnoses, particularly in court cases. The socialist, feminist woman in Clapham Junction that Arrowood mentions in Chapter Four is based on Edith Lanchester, who was diagnosed in 1895 with monomania regarding marriage. This case is described by Sarah Wise in her excellent book *Inconvenient People*. I've added the detail about menstruation, which would have been consistent with many experts' understandings of women's vulnerability to mental health conditions at the time.

Asylums

In the late Victorian period, counties in England were required to use public money to build and run asylums for people with mental health conditions who couldn't afford private care. As well as in public asylums, pauper lunatics could be found in workhouses, prisons and in the community. 'Pauper lunatics' were those whose family could not afford private care (this was the majority of the population) and who were certified by the local authorities as unable to work due to their condition. Their care was funded by the Relieving Officers of the local Poor Law Union, whose offices were often in workhouses. Each pauper patient in an asylum cost the Poor Law Union three times as much as they would have cost in the workhouse. Private patients were cared for in private or public asylums, or as single patients in houses. The 1890 Lunacy Act in England required a magistrate to issue an order for admittance to an asylum. Paupers required statements from one doctor and a Poor Law official. Private patients required statements from two doctors.

Asylums were supposed to be inspected and regulated by the Lunacy Commission, which employed lawyers and doctors as Commissioners. In addition, each asylum had its own Committee of Visitors for oversight. These were usually wealthy men, whose job it was to inspect and approve asylum reports and examine complaints. Throughout the nineteenth century, the asylum system, treatment approaches, and legislation were developing and changing. There were great scandals about poor and inhumane treatment, inmates being kept unnecessarily and against their will for the payments that came with them, and people being committed by family members and others who stood to gain financially. As Sarah Wise describes in her book, there were many court cases and hearings in which expert 'alienists' offered differing opinions as to whether a person was insane or simply eccentric, and some of these trials were covered enthusiastically by newspapers.

Vin Mariani

This popular tonic wine sold in the 1890s was a mixture of Bordeaux wine and cocaine.

Sources

Many thanks to the British Library Newspaper Collection and the London Metropolitan Archive for invaluable access to historical documents. I've also relied on a number of books. Below are some of the main ones.

Roy Brigden, *Victorian Farms*, The Crowood Press, 1986.

John C. Bucknill & Daniel Hack Tuke, *A Manual of Psychological Medicine*, Lindsay & Blakiston, 1874.

Kathryn Burtinshaw & John Burt, *Lunatics, Imbeciles and Idiots. A History of Insanity in Nineteenth Century Britain and Ireland.* Pen & Sword History, 2017.

John Langdon Down, Observations on an Ethnic Classification of Idiots, London Hospital Reports, 3, 259-262, 1866.

Jean-Étienne Esquirol, *Mental Maladies: A Treatise on Insanity*, Lea and Blanchard, 1845.

Judith Flanders, *The Invention of Murder: How the Victorians Revelled in Death and Detection and Created Modern Crime*, HarperPress, 2011.

Jack London, *The People of the Abyss*, Hesperus Press, 1903.

Francis Galton, *Essays in Eugenics*, Ostara Publications, 1909.

Ruth Goodman, *How to Be a Victorian*, Penguin, 2013.

Henry Maudsley, *The Pathology of Mind: A Study of its Distempers, Deformities and Disorders*, Julian Friedmann Publishers, 1895.

Kate Summerscale, *The Suspicions of Mr. Whicher or the Murder at Road Hill House*, Bloomsbury, 2008.

Mark Stevens, *Life in the Victorian Asylum: The World of Nineteenth Century Mental Health Care*, Pen & Sword History, 2014.

Barry Turner, *The Victorian Parson*, Amberley, 2015.

David Wright, *Downs: The History of a Disability*, Oxford University Press, 2011.

L. L. Whyte, *The Unconscious Before Freud*, Julian Friedmann Publishers, 1979.

Sarah Wise, *Inconvenient People: Lunacy, Liberty and the Mad-Doctors in Victorian England*, Vintage, 2013.